About the Authors

Yahrah St. John is the author of forty-four published books and won an award from *RT Book Reviews* for *A Chance with You*. She earned a Bachelor of Arts degree in English from Northwestern University. A member of Romance Writers of America, St. John is an avid reader, enjoys cooking, travelling and adventure sports, but her true passion is writing. Visit: yahrahstjohn.com

Melanie Milburne read her first Mills & Boon at age seventeen in between studying for her final exams. After completing a Master's Degree in Education, she decided to write a novel and thus her career as a romance author was born. Melanie is an ambassador for the Australian Childhood Foundation, is a keen dog lover and trainer, and enjoys long walks in the Tasmanian bush. In 2015 Melanie won the HOLT Medallion, a prestigious award honouring outstanding literary talent.

Cathy Williams is a great believer in the power of perseverance as she had never written anything before her writing career. From the starting point of zero, she has now fulfilled her ambition to pursue this most enjoyable of careers. She would encourage any would-be writer to have faith and go for it! She derives inspiration from the tropical island of Trinidad and from the peaceful countryside of middle England. Cathy lives in Warwickshire her family.

Sins and Seduction

Sins and Seduction:
A Deal in Passion

YAHRAH ST. JOHN

MELANIE MILBURNE

CATHY WILLIAMS

MILLS & BOON

First Published in Great Britain 2023
by Mills & Boon, an imprint of HarperCollins*Publishers* Ltd,
1 London Bridge Street, London, SE1 9GF

www.harpercollins.co.uk

HarperCollins*Publishers*
Macken House, 39/40 Mayor Street Upper,
Dublin 1, D01 C9W8, Ireland

ISBN: 978-0-263-31914-9

Printed and Bound in the UK using 100% Renewable Electricity
at CPI Group (UK) Ltd, Croydon, CR0 4YY

HIS MARRIAGE DEMAND

YAHRAH ST. JOHN

To my best friend and sister, Dimitra Astwood, who
passed away while I wrote this, but will live on
in my heart.

Prologue

Fallon's hands trembled with anger as she placed the phone receiver in its cradle. Rising from her chair, she strode across her stylishly appointed corner office and stared out the window overlooking downtown Austin. Although she understood why her older brother, Ayden, wasn't returning her calls, she was still annoyed he'd gone to Jamaica while she was in such a desperate state.

Stewart Technologies was on the brink of bankruptcy. As CEO, Fallon had done her best to keep the company afloat, working sixty-and eighty-hour work weeks, but she was bailing water from a sinking ship. The last few weeks she'd been unsuccessful in her attempts to secure a bank loan.

She'd gone to Ayden, the black sheep in the Stewart family, for assistance nearly a month ago. Ayden had rejected her assertion that he help the "family business." The more Fallon thought about it, why should Ayden rescue the company started by a father who would never claim him as his son? Ayden owed no allegiance to her or any other Stewart for that matter.

Was it any wonder he'd ignored her calls?

Although she'd acquired personal wealth of her own through sound investments, Fallon wasn't in a position to bail out the company. Her baby brother, Dane, certainly wasn't about to, either. He, like Ayden, wanted nothing to do with Stewart Technologies. Dane was happiest in front of a camera being someone else, and it served him well. He was an A-list actor and got paid millions of dollars. Fallon doubted he'd put up his hard-won earnings to save a company he'd never wanted any part of in the first place.

What was she going to do?

"Perhaps you should let it fail," Shana said when they met up for drinks at their favorite martini bar across town an hour later. Shana Wilson was one of Fallon's favorite cousins on her mother's side. Nora hated them spending time together because she tried to disassociate herself from her back-country roots. But Fallon didn't care. Shana was loud and opinionated but down-to-earth.

Fallon stared at Shana incredulously. After all the hard work she'd put into Stewart Technologies, interning in the summer while home from Texas A&M University, learning the business from the ground up and climbing the ladder to finally sit in the CEO chair, she was supposed to give it all up? "Have you lost your mind?"

Shana chuckled. "Don't have a coronary. It was just a suggestion. I hate seeing you stressed out."

An audible sigh escaped Fallon's lips. "I'm sorry, Shana. I know I haven't been a joy to hang with lately."

Shana had come dressed for the evening. She was wearing a glittery sleeveless top, miniskirt, strappy heels and large gold-hoop earrings. Her curly weave hung in ringlets to her shoulders. Shana was on the prowl for more than a martini and usually Fallon didn't mind playing wing woman, but she was in a sour mood.

"No, you haven't been," Shana said, sipping her drink, "but that's why I asked you to come out tonight. All you do is work and go home to that mausoleum. You are too uptight." Shana looked around the room at the host of men milling around. "Maybe if you met a man and got some good loving, you'd loosen up a bit. I bet I know who could loosen you up while supplying you with the cash influx you need."

Fallon sat forward in her seat. Although she loved her cousin, she doubted Shana, who worked as a hair stylist at a trendy salon, knew much about finance. "Oh, yeah? And who might that be?"

"Gage Campbell ring a bell?"

Fallon's heart plummeted at the sound of his name. "G-Gage?"

"Yeah, you remember him? The guy you had the hots for, for over a decade?"

How could Fallon forget? She'd thrown herself at him and inadvertently set in motion a course of events even she, at her tender age of sixteen, couldn't have predicted. "Of course I remember. What about him?"

"Word in the salon is he's back in town," Shana responded. "A couple of clients have come in talking about dating him. He owns a successful mutual fund business and has become quite the catch. Not to mention, he's still as sexy as when we first saw him when we were eight years old."

Fallon would never forget that day. She'd been prancing around on her pony when Gage and his mother Grace toured the estate with Nora. Fallon had been showing off and the pony had become agitated and thrown her. If it hadn't been for Gage's quick reaction and his catching her before she landed, Fallon would surely have broken something. When he'd looked at her with his dazzling brandy-colored eyes, Fallon had fallen head-over-heels in love with the twelve-year-old boy.

Fallon blinked and realized her cousin was still talking. "According to his current lady loves, he knows his way around the bedroom, if you catch my drift."

There was no mistaking Shana's meaning and Fallon blushed.

"Oh, lord." Shana rolled her eyes upward. "We really do need to get you out if a little girl talk makes you blush. Perhaps Gage could help with Stewart Technologies? I hear he's quite the financial wizard."

"That might be so, but Gage would never lift a hand to help me," Fallon replied. Why would he? She'd ruined his life and she only had herself to blame.

One

Two weeks later

"Stewart Technologies is in dire straits," Fallon told her parents over Sunday dinner.

Thinking about the past and what she'd done to Gage Campbell had weighed heavily on her mind ever since she'd had drinks with Shana a couple of weeks ago.

Fallon had never been able to forget the hateful stare Gage had given her moments before her father had closed the cottage door all those years ago. She'd never learned what had happened to Gage and his mother after they'd left Stewart Manor. She hadn't wanted to know because she'd been the cause of his mother losing her livelihood and the guilt had eaten her up. She'd felt so bad that she hadn't balked when her parents had sent her to a finishing school her final year of high school to avoid her spending time with the "wrong crowd."

"Must you be so dramatic?" Nora Stewart said, glancing at her daughter from the opposite end of the table. Even though it was just the three of them at dinner, her mother had insisted on eating in the formal dining room when Fallon would rather be in the kitchen.

Her mother was the epitome of sophistication, wearing cream slacks and a matching cardigan set. Her smooth chestnut-brown hair was stylishly cut in a chin-length bob while her makeup was perfection. Nora was well-preserved thanks to personal trainers and weekly visits to the salon and spa for massages and facials. Since marrying Henry Stewart and becoming pregnant with Fallon, Nora hadn't worked. *Why should she when she was lady of the manor?*

"I'm not being dramatic," Fallon responded. "We're bleeding money and it has to stop."

"And whose fault is that?" Henry inquired. "You've been CEO for two years now."

When she'd turned thirty Fallon thought she'd finally achieved the height of her career only to find out it had been built on quicksand. Stewart Technologies was leveraged to the hilt all because of her father's poor judgment and her mother's notorious spending habits. Every few years she was constantly redecorating Stewart manor to keep up with the latest fads and, as for fashion, there wasn't a bag, shoe or piece of clothing in her mother's closet that didn't have a designer label.

"Not mine," Fallon said hotly. "Stewart Technologies was in trouble well before I became CEO."

"You're the leader now and it's up to you to fix things. It's what you said you wanted, Fallon," her father replied. "It's time you show what you're made of instead of running to me."

Fallon bristled at that. She'd come to level with her parents, but clearly they were beyond reason. They wanted to stick their heads in the sand and refuse to accept the inevitable: that they were running out of funds and wouldn't be able to live in the style to which they were accustomed. "I have shown my commitment to the company over the last decade. But since it's clear I don't have your support, I'll take my leave." She rose from her seat and made for the door.

"Sit down, Fallon." Her father trained his hazel-gray eyes on her, causing Fallon to pause and retrace her steps.

"If you're going to talk business—" Nora used her napkin to lightly tap the sides of her mouth "—I'm going to make myself scarce because it's such a bore."

Fallon sucked in a deep breath and reminded herself to count to ten, which was more than enough time for her mother to depart. She loved Nora, but she found her exhausting.

"Yes, Father?" Fallon turned and, for the first time, truly looked at her father. She saw more salt and pepper in his normally black hair and a few more lines were etched across his features, showing life wasn't as easy as her mother portrayed.

"I'm sorry if I was harsh before," Henry said. "I know you've been doing your best."

"Which isn't good enough," Fallon stated. "Don't you get it? We could lose everything."

"Surely it's not as dire as you predict?" Henry countered.

"It is. I've exhausted all options," Fallon said. "I even asked Ayden for the money."

Her father's eyes widened. "Why on earth would you do such a thing? He isn't a member of this family. How much did you tell him of our circumstances? What did he say?"

Fallon waited for her father to finish peppering her with questions before answering. Did he wonder if Ayden had told her about his infidelity with her mother? "I was desperate. But I didn't get to explain because he told me he isn't interested in bailing out *our* company because he's not a part of this family." She didn't share that Ayden had had a change of heart and had come to her days ago.

Henry sighed. "It's just as well. We don't need him. You can figure this out, Fallon. There's a reason I let you become CEO."

"*Let me?*" Fallon repeated. "I worked hard to get where I am. I don't recall Dane or even Ayden getting in line to step in your shoes."

"Listen here, young lady—" he began.

"Don't bother chastising me, Father," Fallon interrupted. "I'm the only child you have who cares one iota about Stewart Technologies, so I suggest you stop fighting me and get Mother to understand we are just a few steps away from going broke."

Fallon shot to her feet and, without another word, left the room, her stunned father sitting with his mouth open at her insolence. She walked quickly to the door and headed for her cottage. Her haven. Her safe place.

The cool night air hit her immediately when she exited. The leaves that had begun falling a few weeks ago crunched under her heels, signaling fall was in full swing. Once inside the cottage, Fallon turned on the lights and sagged against the door. Why was it she felt safe here? The one place that had once caused such misery to others.

Her mother had long since renovated the cottage after the Campbells left. It now had an open concept with a stainless-steel kitchen, sitting area, master suite with en suite bath as well as guest bedroom and powder room. It was all Fallon needed while allowing her to be close to her horse, Lady.

Kicking off her boots, Fallon plopped onto her plush leather sofa, leaned back and thought about the weekend. Once again, she'd scoured the books looking for ways to make cuts and keep the company afloat, but it was pointless. They were going under. And tonight was a complete bust. Her parents refused to accept their new reality: they were broke. The only bright spot had been on Friday evening when Ayden had shown up at her office. He'd looked drawn and tired, and there were lines under his eyes, but he'd wanted to talk. She'd been hard on him because he'd treated her like the enemy for years. She and Dane had been the chosen ones, the children Henry Stewart claimed while leaving Ayden to languish in poverty with his mother.

Fallon understood she'd had the life denied him: the houses, cars, travel, fancy clothes and schools. He'd listened when she'd explained it hadn't been easy for her, either, with a disinterested, self-absorbed mother and a demanding father who'd pushed her to excel. She was angry that Ayden blamed her when she'd only been a child. However, Ayden had told her he was sorry for ignoring her calls and for turning down her requests for a loan. He wanted to start over, to try to be a family, a brother to her and Dane.

Fallon had been overjoyed. Then Ayden had held her hand and shockingly offered to give *her*—not the company—a personal loan. Fallon knew the sacrifice it had taken for him to make the offer. But, after everything he'd been through, her pride wouldn't allow her to accept his money, knowing how their father treated him. He hadn't supported Ayden as a child. Not to mention she'd had more advantages than Ayden had ever had. She couldn't take his hard-earned money, money he might need one day for his future. He'd nodded and let her keep her pride. And they'd agreed to take baby steps and work on their sibling relationship. Fallon couldn't wait to tell Dane. She hoped he would be as happy as she was to forge a bond with their big brother.

"Welcome back to Austin, old friend," Theo Robinson said to Gage Campbell when they met up for lunch at the country club. They were sitting outside on the terrace by the fire pit, drinking brandy and reminiscing about the good old days.

"It's good to be back," Gage said. And it was. It had been well over a decade since he'd lived in Texas. After finishing college at the University of Texas at Austin, he'd gone on to New York and then overseas to make his fortune. Now that he was a successful man in his own right, he'd come back to his hometown to settle down and take care of his mother. Though he doubted Grace Campbell felt she needed taking care of. Although she'd retired a few years ago, his mother was active and traveled the world with her circle of friends. She deserved it after all the hard work she'd endured to ensure he'd had a future.

"What're your plans now that you're here?" Theo inquired.

Gage sat back in his seat and regarded his friend. "Settle in, find a nice home and a good woman and have some babies."

"Oh, really?" Theo raised an eyebrow. "Since when? I thought you were a die-hard bachelor."

"I was. Hell, I still am," Gage replied. "I'm still indulging until I find Mrs. Campbell."

"Look out, women of Austin!" Theo laughed and drank his brandy.

"There's only one woman who should ever fear me," Gage said, a serious tone to his voice.

"Let me guess. Fallon Stewart? I would think after all this time and your success, you would have forgotten the mistakes made by a young, naïve girl."

"She wasn't so naïve if she had the audacity to show up to my house half naked," Gage responded. He'd never forgotten how stunned he'd been after having a few beers at the bar only to come home to find Fallon in his bed.

"She was sixteen with a crush on you," Theo said. "She

was feeling herself, but then her parents caught her. She got scared and lied about what happened."

"Her lies cost my mother her job. And without references from the Stewarts, Mama couldn't find work. It took her months to recover, especially since the Stewarts were paying her minimum wage to work day and night."

"Well, she recovered and so have you. I mean look at you." Theo motioned to him. "You're the wizard of Wall Street. I'd say you've done well."

"No thanks to the Stewarts."

Theo sighed. "Then you'll probably be glad to hear this. The rumor is that Stewart Technologies is leveraged to the max. No bank will loan them money and they've run out of options."

"Serves Henry right," Gage responded. "Though I have to wonder what happened. I thought he had a good head on his shoulders. I even looked up to him once upon a time, admired him when he took me under his wing."

"Henry Stewart isn't running the show."

A knot formed in Gage's stomach. He didn't need Theo to say his next words; he already knew. "Fallon's in charge."

"She's been looking for a handout from anyone she can and has come up empty."

"Is that so?" Gage rubbed his jaw. Fallon Stewart had been taken down a peg and was essentially on the street begging for scraps. Now, if that wasn't karma, he didn't know what was.

"Could be a good time to go in with a consortium and pick up the pieces," Theo stated. "Think about it."

The two men parted right after lunch, but Gage didn't return home to his penthouse at the Austonian in downtown Austin until late evening. It was a temporary oasis with all the modern conveniences a bachelor required. There was a large television with a surround-sound system, an enormous master suite with a king-size bed and a luxurious master bath with room for more than one occupant in the hot tub and massive steam shower.

He went to the wet bar, opened the snifter of brandy and poured himself a glass. He swirled the alcohol around and took a generous, satisfying sip. Sliding the pocket door to his balcony aside, he opened the living room to the over-size terrace with its panoramic views. Austin's city lights twinkled in the distance, but Gage didn't see them. All he saw was a beautiful teenager, wearing the sexiest teddy he'd ever laid eyes on, in his bed. Gage gritted his teeth and forced himself to remember that night. He hadn't just been angry when he'd found Fallon in his bed. He'd been intrigued.

Fallon had been everything he wasn't. Spoiled. Rich. Entitled. She'd had more money than she'd known what to do with, ponies and cars, while he'd worked two jobs. He hadn't wanted to want her, but he had. He'd seen the coy looks Fallon had given him when she'd thought he wasn't looking, but she'd been sixteen. Jailbait. Gage had been de-termined to steer clear, but she'd poked the bear and Gage had hauled her against him and kissed her.

If her parents had found them any later, the result might have been him being led off in handcuffs. Instead he and his mother had been shown the door. But now things had changed. He held all the cards and Fallon was on the bot-tom. He was no longer at the mercy of the Stewarts and whatever scraps they doled out to him. Gage relished how the tables had turned.

Fallon arrived at the Stewart Technologies' offices the next morning feeling out of sorts. She hadn't slept well the night before. She'd been thinking about her lack of a love life. It had been ages since she'd been on a proper date, let alone had a steady boyfriend.

She tried to focus on the day ahead. There were several meetings scheduled, including a negotiation to sell off one of the company's long-held nanotech patents. Fallon didn't want to do it—it was one of her father's significant achievements—but she was running out of options. The cash influx would stave off the bank and ensure thousands of employees kept their jobs.

The morning flew by quickly with Fallon only stopping long enough to eat a quick salad her assistant, Chelsea, had fetched from the deli downstairs.

Fallon was poring over financials when a knock sounded on the door. "Not now, Chelsea, I'm in the middle of something," she said without looking up.

"You don't have time for an old friend?"

Fallon's heart slowed at first and she closed her eyes, leaning back in her leather executive chair. *Surely, it couldn't be.* Perhaps she was imagining things, conjuring up the past. Because she hadn't heard that deep masculine voice in over sixteen years. Inhaling deeply, she snuck a glance at the man standing in the doorway of her office and was bowled over.

It was none other than Gage Campbell.

How? Why was he here at her office? A morass of feelings engulfed her and she tingled from head to toe. The last time she'd seen Gage there had been nothing but hatred in his eyes, not the amused expression he now wore. Fallon reminded herself to breathe in then breathe out.

Calm yourself. Don't let him see he's affected you.

So instead she took the offensive. "What the hell are you doing here?"

Two

"Hello to you, too, Fallon." Gage closed the door behind him and strode toward her desk.

Fallon regarded him from where she sat. Her blood pumped faster as she took in the sight of him. Time had been very good to Gage Campbell. Immaculate and imposingly masculine, he was utterly breathtaking. With his neatly cropped hair, warm caramel-toned skin, thick, juicy lips, bushy eyebrows and those brandy-colored eyes framed by black lashes that always drew her to them, he was impossible to ignore.

He was even sexier than the last time she'd seen him especially with those broodingly intense eyes. He reeked of money and looked as if he was born to wear the bespoke three-piece designer suit, cream shirt with striped tie and polished designer shoes. Fallon knew he hadn't always been this way. The Gage of yesteryear was happier in faded jeans and a wife-beater mucking out stables. The man in front of her was far removed from those days. He stood confident and self-assured.

"I hope I pass the mustard," Gage said after her long perusal.

Fallon blushed at having been caught openly staring and glanced up to find Gage's eyes trained on her. She blinked to refocus. "My apologies. I'm just surprised to see you after all this time."

"I'm sure," Gage responded as he unbuttoned several buttons on his jacket before sitting across from her. Fallon remembered how impossible it had always been to resist those dangerous gleaming eyes of his and today was no different. He looked intriguing, like a total enigma. "It's been what—sixteen years since we last saw each other? You're all grown up." He dropped his gaze and used the opportunity to give her a searing once-over.

Fallon was in her usual work mode. Her naturally wavy hair had been tamed with a flat iron until it lay in straight layers down her back while her makeup was simple: coal eyeliner, mascara, blush and lipstick. Having been blessed with her mother's smooth café-au-lait skin, she required little makeup. And although she was no clothesmonger like Nora, Fallon always managed to be fashionable. She was sporting linen trousers with a sleeveless silk top. She'd abandoned the matching jacket earlier in the day. She wondered what Gage thought of her.

"Oh, yes, you've definitely matured since I last saw you."

Fallon noticed his eyes creased at the corners when he spoke. The sly devil was actually staring right at her breasts and she felt her nipples pucker to attention in her blouse. Immediately she rose. "What can I do for you, Gage? I'm sure you didn't come here for a walk down memory lane."

His eyes narrowed and she could see she'd touched a

nerve. "Now that wouldn't be pleasant for either of us, would it?"

Fallon flushed. She'd never forgiven herself for the horrible action she'd taken that had caused his mother to lose her job. She wanted—no, she *needed* to apologize. "Gage, I'm—"

He interrupted her. "I'm here because Stewart Technologies is in financial trouble and I thought I could help."

Her brow furrowed. "And why would you want to do that?"

Gage laughed without humor. "Is that any way to treat a potential investor? Or don't you need an influx of capital to save your father's company?"

"My company now."

"I stand corrected." He inclined his head. "I thought perhaps we could discuss the matter over dinner. My afternoon is rather full and I barely managed to squeeze in this reunion."

"Dinner?" she choked out as she looked at him in bewilderment. Why would he want to break bread with her after their checkered past?

He tilted his head to one side and watched her, waiting for her to speak. "It's the meal commonly eaten after lunch. Or do you have a problem being seen with the former maid's son?"

Fallon looked him directly in his eyes and replied coolly, "Of course not. I'm not a snob."

"Really?"

"You sound surprised."

"If I recall, back in the day you wouldn't be caught dead with me except in the stables or when we were alone."

"That's not true." She felt the flush rise to her cheeks at the memory. "I didn't want us to be disturbed. If my mother found out, she would have forbidden it because…"

"Because I wasn't good enough for you." Gage finished the sentence.

Fallon lowered her head. He was right. It's what Nora had thought. But never Fallon. She'd been too much in love with Gage to see his class or station in life. Agreeing to dinner would show him he was wrong about her and that they were equals. It would also enlighten her as to his true motives.

Several seconds passed and she glanced up to find he'd leaned closer toward her. "Shall I pick you up?"

Fallon shook her head. "No, that's not necessary. I can meet you wherever you like."

"Still not wanting to be seen with me, eh?" Gage un-coiled his tall length, stood and rebuttoned his jacket. A deep chuckle escaped his lips as he made his way to the door. "I'll meet you at the Driskill Grill at seven."

And then he was gone, leaving Fallon to stare at the door. *What was his real agenda?*

Irritation fueled Gage as he headed for the elevator. He was offering Fallon a lifeline and she refused to even allow him to pick her up for dinner! Her arrogance irked him, but so did her beauty. He'd hoped to find a spoiled, selfish shell of a woman, but instead he'd found a stunning and fierce ice princess. Fallon Stewart wasn't the young teenager he remembered. She was a woman. And it angered him that he still found her so...so damned attractive.

When he'd walked through the door and seen her, blood had stirred in his veins and his belly had clenched instantly. He'd wanted to touch her. To refamiliarize himself with her exquisitely soft skin. To crush those sinfully pink-tinted lips underneath his and lose himself. But Fallon had cast her eyes down and acted as if she was unaffected by him.

But the willful sexy teenager who'd come to his bed in

the middle of the night wearing nothing but a teddy was still there. Gage was certain he'd seen a spark flare when her eyes traveled the length of him. Now they were both grown and consenting adults, and it was time they finished what they'd started sixteen years ago.

Resolve formed deep in the pit of his stomach. A twist of circumstances had turned the tables and the Stewarts were no longer on top and in a position of power. Gage was. Fallon was exposed, vulnerable and his for the taking. Last night he'd come up with a plan for revenge to finally get back at Fallon and the Stewarts for their treatment of him and his mother.

Stewart Technologies needed cash and Gage was the money man. He not only had loads of it himself, he knew how and where to acquire more. He would convince Fallon bygones were bygones and *help* the company with an influx of cash. Meanwhile he'd secretly purchase stocks until eventually he owned the lion's share and could take it away from them. The best part in this entire scenario was the chance to bed Fallon, the overindulged princess.

Today when he'd seen her, something indefinable had happened. It was as if the years had melted away. Gage had been hit in the gut with the incredible need to possess her. He didn't want any other man to have her, at least not until he'd had his fill.

When he exited the building and slid into the Bugatti waiting for him at the curb, a new idea began to form in Gage's mind.

What if he married Fallon! For his *help* in saving the company, he would become a member of the acclaimed Stewart family and finally not only have Fallon in his bed, but have the prestige he'd always wanted. Because, try as he might, no matter how much money he made, there was a certain echelon of society that still saw him as the maid's son. Wouldn't it get their goat to have him rubbing elbows with the lot of them? To show them he wasn't just the un-derprivileged kid-made-good? It was a brilliant strategy.

Fallon had no idea what was in store for her tonight.

As he started the engine, Gage's cellphone rang. The display read Mom. "Hey, Mama. How are you?"

"I'd be doing a lot better if you came to see me. You've been back for a while and I've yet to see you."

"I'm sorry. I've been a little busy, and you were away on one of your trips. But I'll visit this weekend."

"Good. It's good to have you back in Austin. It's been much too long."

"Yes, it has." He hadn't been home since he'd finished college and they both knew why. The Stewarts. Gage hadn't thought he'd get a fair break in a town where Henry Stewart had so much power. But the tide had changed, providing Gage the opportunity to put a plan in place to give the Stewarts the comeuppance they so richly deserved.

Fallon didn't have time to go home and change if she was going to be on time for dinner with Gage. A departmental meeting ended later than she'd anticipated, leaving her precious little time to shower in the private bathroom in her office and change into one of several dresses she kept on hand for such occasions. She chose a beaded champagne cocktail dress that accentuated her curves. Refreshing her makeup, she added a touch of blush to her cheekbones to go along with the mascara, eyeliner and pale pink lipstick.

Glancing at herself in the mirror, Fallon felt armed and ready for a night in Gage's company. And she felt like she needed every bit of armor for this unexpected invitation.

Throughout the remainder of the afternoon, Fallon had wondered why Gage wanted to help her family. She'd come up with only one reason: comeuppance. After the way he'd been treated by the Stewarts, he wanted to be the one to come in on the white horse and save the day. Him, the man her father had thrown out of the house because he'd dared to touch his daughter. Gage wanted them to *owe* him.

Fallon didn't much blame him.

Gage had every right to be angry over how he and his mother had been treated. But now the shoe was on the other foot. The Stewarts were the laughingstock of the business community, turned down by every bank in town because of her father's poor decisions and financial mismanagement. Fallon hoped seeing how far they'd fallen from grace would be enough to salve Gage's wounds.

She made it to the restaurant at seven o'clock on the nose.

The hostess led her to a secluded corner booth where Gage was already seated, wearing a fine, tailored suit. Had he booked this? Did he intend for it to be as romantic as it looked? A dark, quiet corner with a table for two?

He stood when she approached. "Fallon, you're looking lovely this evening." She was stunned when he kissed her on the cheek before she slid into the booth.

"Uh, thank you," she returned, her pulse thumping erratically from the contact of his lips.

"I took the liberty of ordering wine," Gage said, pinning her with his razor-sharp gaze. "A Montoya Cabernet. I hope that's all right?"

She nodded, somewhat amazed at how at ease he was in a restaurant of such wealth and sophistication. He poured her a glass. She accepted and tipped her glass to his when he held it up for a toast.

"And what are we toasting?" she asked.

"New beginnings."

Fallon sipped her wine. "Sounds intriguing."

He grinned, showing off a pearly white smile, and Fallon's stomach flip-flopped. "I've been away in New York and London the last decade. So, get me up to speed, Fallon. How did you end up as CEO of Stewart Technologies?"

"It's really quite simple. My father needed an heir apparent," Fallon said, "and I was the only one willing to step up to claim the throne."

"You make it sound so medieval," Gage responded, tasting his wine.

She smiled. "It isn't that elaborate, I'm afraid. My brother Dane wanted nothing to do with the family business, much preferring his acting career to being an active member of the Stewart family."

"Was it really so horrible growing up in the lap of luxury?" Gage inquired wryly.

Fallon detected the note of derision in his tone. "You'd have to ask him."

The waiter interrupted them to rattle off the daily specials. They both ordered the soup to start, followed by the spinach salad and fish for their entrée. It was all very civilized and Fallon couldn't understand Gage's agenda. Why was he treating her like an old friend when she knew that was far from the case?

Once the waiter left, Gage prompted Fallon. "Please continue with your story, I'm fascinated."

"After what happened between us all those years ago, my father was very unhappy with me."

"Explain."

She sighed softly but didn't stop. "You have to understand, I was his baby girl."

"Dressed like you were ready to take me to bed?"

Fallon didn't rise to the bait. "Seeing me like that made him realize I was growing up too fast and he didn't like it. And I was desperate to regain his affection."

"Had you lost it?"

Gage was perceptive, picking up on what she hadn't said. She didn't answer. "He sent me to a finishing school to ensure I was exposed to the 'right' crowd."

"And were you?"

Her lips thinned with irritation. "They were the snobbi-est, cattiest girls I ever met. The teachers were like prison wardens. The entire experience was unpleasant.

"When I returned home, I started accompanying my fa-ther to the office and soon I wanted to learn more. My fa-ther put me in the intern program and, much to his surprise, I soaked up everything like a sponge. I was interested in learning what it took to run a multimillion-dollar company, so I majored in business. During breaks, I worked at Stew-art Technologies, learning the business from the ground up while earning my MBA. Until, eventually, I proved to all the naysayers I had the chops to run the company.

"And, as it turned out, my father was ready to take a back seat. He's now chairman of the board. Of course, I had no idea of the financial straits he was leaving me to tend to. He'd leveraged the business and owed the banks a substantial amount due to projects he'd started but failed to get across the finish line."

"Very intriguing indeed," Gage replied. "And here we are."

Fallon took a generous sip of her wine. She hadn't planned on revealing so much, but Gage was looking at her so intently, as if hanging on her every word.

"And you? Fill me in on your time abroad."

Gage leaned back against the cushions. "I don't think my story is quite as intriguing as yours."

"But it clearly has a happy ending," she replied. "I mean, look at where we are. The roles have been reversed."

"Yes, they have," Gage said quietly. "But I won't sugar-coat it. After my mother and I were kicked off the Stewart estate, she had a hard time finding work, especially because your parents refused to give her a reference."

"Gage…"

"I was young and resilient, with only a year left of col-lege. I worked two or three jobs to keep us afloat. Once I finished school, I struck out on my own. A friend of mine worked on Wall Street and told me I could make a lot of money. The stock market had never really been my cup of tea but, lo and behold, I had a knack for it. From there I went to London, Hong Kong, making money in stocks and foreign trade. Until I settled on mutual funds and started my own business."

"So why come back here?"

"Simply put, I missed home," Gage replied. "I haven't been back since I graduated other than the odd trip. Mostly, I've sent Mom tickets to meet me at some exotic destination. She deserved it, after all her years of menial labor."

Although she'd never experienced the kind of hardship Gage mentioned, Fallon understood his drive to succeed because she shared it.

Over dinner they continued talking about his trading career, lifestyle and trips abroad before returning to the subject of Fallon. It surprised her how easy it was to talk to Gage, considering all that had transpired between them. It felt like a lifetime ago, but she was sure at some point Gage would be getting to the point of the evening.

"Are you having dessert?" Gage asked after they'd polished off nearly two bottles of wine with their meal.

She shook her head. "I couldn't eat another bite." She wiped her mouth with a napkin. "It's been a lovely evening, Gage, but I'm sure that's not the reason you asked me to dinner."

"What do you think the reason is?"

"Payback. What else?" Fallon asked with a shrug of her shoulders. "And although I'm not destitute and put out of the family home, we are in a bind. Surely this must delight you?"

"Not everyone is like you and your family."

Ouch. Fallon took that one on the chin because, after

all this time, he deserved to speak his mind. "Why am I here, Gage?"

Gage leaned forward, resting his elbows on the table and arresting her with his eyes. "I have a proposition for you."

"And what might that be?"

"Marry me."

Three

Fallon coughed profusely and reached for her water glass. Her hands trembled as she placed the glass to her lips and sipped. With all the wine they'd drunk, she must have taken leave of her faculties because Gage Campbell couldn't possibly have asked her to marry him. *Could he?*

"Are you all right?" Gage asked, his voice etched with concern.

"Y-yes." Fallon sipped her water again and placed the glass back on the table. "Can you repeat what you said?"

Gage's mouth curved in a smile. "You heard me, Fallon. Marry me and, in exchange, I'll give you the money you need to save your family business."

She had heard correctly. But he was dead wrong if he thought for a second she would take him up on his outrageous offer. "Gage! What you're suggesting is insanity! You didn't even give an expiration date for this union. How long would you expect this to last?"

"It's a business deal that will last as long as needed,"

he stated calmly. "You get the money you need to save a dying technology firm, while I get a wife from an upstanding Austin family. Think about it, Fallon. Our marriage would legitimize my social standing while simultaneously letting all those pesky bankers who have been hounding you know the Campbell/Stewart family is as solid as ever."

"That's real vague. Plus there's any number of society debutantes out there waiting to meet a catch like you, Gage. You don't have to marry me."

"But it's you I want," Gage responded. Within seconds he'd slid closer to her in the booth, until they were thigh-to-thigh.

Fallon flushed. "What are you saying?"

"A caveat to the marriage is it will not be in name only."

"Meaning?"

"Do you really need me to spell it out?" His piercing look went straight through her. "We would consummate the marriage and share the same bed. Become lovers."

Fallon sucked in a deep breath. *Sweet Jesus!* She had drunk too much wine because the words coming out of Gage's mouth didn't make any sense. She took another small sip of water.

"I think we would be quite good together," Gage said, picking up her hand and turning it over palm side up.

Immediately she tried to pull it back, but his grip was too strong. "How can you say such a thing? I haven't seen you in sixteen years."

"Yet, you still want me." His hold softened but he didn't let her go. Instead his thumb began circling the inside of her palm, making her pulse race erratically. "I can see all the signs of arousal in you, Fallon—the way your eyes dilate when you look at me, the way your breath hitches when I come near. Even the way your breasts peak with one look from me."

Fallon felt her cheeks flame. Was she so obvious that he

could read her like a book? It was as though he'd put her under some kind of spell, the same as when she'd been sixteen. And why oh why wouldn't he stop circling her palm with his thumb? He was teasing her and she didn't like it. She jerked her hand free. "Stop it, Gage."

"Stop what?" he asked so innocently she would have thought he meant it, but she knew better.

"Whatever game it is you're playing."

"No games. Just facts. I'm willing to give you millions to help Stewart Technologies, even though it's been hemorrhaging money. I'm willing to give my money to help save your company. And in return, I offer you the chance to be my wife. I think it's a fair trade."

"Of course you would." Fallon scooted out of the booth. "But I'm not a stock to be bought and traded. Furthermore, you got your signals wrong. I'm not interested in you in the slightest." She made it as far as the foyer of the restaurant before Gage caught up to her and swung her into a nearby alcove.

"You're not interested in me, eh?" Gage asked, stepping closer into her space. So close, her body was smashed against his. "How about we test that theory, shall we?"

She saw the challenge in his eyes seconds before his head lowered and he sealed his lips to hers. Fallon wanted to refuse him but the thrill of having his lips on hers again was too much to resist. Need unfurled in her, the likes of which she hadn't felt since…since the last time he'd kissed her. No other man had ever come close to making her feel this way.

This hot. This excited.

Gage's arm slid around her waist to the small of her back and he pressed her body even closer to his. Meanwhile his tongue breached her mouth, allowing him to increase the pressure, demand more and compel her to accept him. The kiss was hard yet soft, but also rough enough to thrill her.

Fallon's lips parted of their own accord and his tongue slid in. Teasing, stroking, tasting the soft insides of her mouth.

Fallon whimpered and her stance relaxed as the sheer power of his kiss enflamed her. Sliding her arms around his neck, she held his head to hers, reveling in the deeply carnal kiss. Gage ground his lower half against hers and she felt every inch of his hard body. Her tongue searched his mouth ravenously and he met her stroke for stroke. Her breasts rubbed against his chest and her nipples hardened. Fallon had never felt so desirable and could have gone on kissing him, but Gage pulled away first.

His breathing was ragged but he managed to say, "I've proven you are interested, but I'll give you some time to think about my offer."

Fallon looked up, dazed and confused. "Wait a minute." How could he compose himself after that kiss? "How much time?" she croaked out.

"Forty-eight hours."

She shook her head. "I can't make a decision about the rest of my life in two days."

"Well, that's too damn bad because that's my offer," Gage responded. "You can take it or leave it. It's up to you." He tapped the face of his Rolex watch. Then he reached inside his suit jacket and pulled out his business card. "My personal cell. Call me when you're ready to say yes."

A whirlwind of thoughts swirled around Fallon's mind as she somehow managed to drive herself home from her dinner with Gage. When she got back to the cottage she kicked off her heels, undressed and removed her makeup, and put on her old college T-shirt. Sliding into her king-size platform bed and falling back against the pillows, Fallon recalled the bombshell Gage dropped.

Marry me.

Gage had proposed marriage in exchange for saving

Stewart Technologies, the company her father started forty
years ago. Could she let it slip through her fingers without
a fight? But Gage wasn't offering a marriage in name only.
He wanted them to become lovers.

The thought both excited and terrified her, especially
after that hot kiss at the restaurant. Her attempt to appear
unaffected had been smashed to smithereens. The chemistry between them was off the charts. He'd smelled and
tasted so good. And the way he'd held her close, her heart
had fluttered unlike anything she'd ever felt with other
men. Had his one life-changing kiss all those years ago ruined her for anyone else? Because there hadn't been many
men. Since Gage she'd never succeeded in finding someone who could fulfill an ache. So instead she focused on
her career at the expense of her personal life. Work was her
baby, so much so she hadn't given much thought to marriage or children.

Would Gage want children?

No, no, no. She shook her head. She wouldn't have children with a man as part of a business arrangement or for
money like her mother had. She was no fool. She knew
Nora hadn't married her father for love. Instead she'd married him for the life he could give her. Fallon wouldn't
want that for herself or for Gage. And why would he want
to marry her anyway? She'd lied and cost his family their
livelihood. He should hate her but instead he was offering
her a way out. It didn't make sense. He could be setting
her up for failure so he could give her the comeuppance he
thought she deserved.

Was she honestly giving Gage's proposal serious consideration? She couldn't. Shouldn't. He'd been a brute, only
giving her forty-eight hours to make a life-changing decision. Marry him or risk losing the company. Marry him
and agree to be his wife, *his lover.* He could have been her
first if they hadn't been interrupted by her parents. Fallon

remembered the passion she'd felt in his arms then and now. Was it fate they would end up in this predicament? Was she always destined to be his?

Unable to sleep, Gage restlessly prowled his penthouse. Wondering. Wishing. Hoping.

Would Fallon say yes?

Would she agree to marry him?

He knew it was wrong to give her an ultimatum but he'd had to. Once she committed, he didn't want her to change her mind. When she agreed to be his and his alone, they would have a quick engagement, a big splashy wedding and a satisfying honeymoon. He wanted the entire community and all of Austin society to know *he*, the maid's son, had bagged Fallon Stewart, heiress to Stewart Technologies. He would rub it in all their faces that the young man they'd bullied because of his humble background had turned into a successful and wealthy entrepreneur.

Fallon *needed* to agree. She wasn't going to get a better offer. She'd exhausted every avenue. No one was going to lend her the amount of money required to turn the company around. A personal gift from him to Fallon would ensure Stewart Technologies stayed viable. In the meantime, since most investors were ditching shares, he would gobble them up until he owned the majority interest. Once he owned enough shares in the company, he would ensure it turned a profit or he'd die trying.

The best part of the deal was that he would finally take Fallon to bed. It was long overdue and very, very necessary. Tonight, when they'd kissed, he'd nearly combusted. She'd tasted exquisite and he remembered how her nipples had turned to stiff peaks against his chest. He'd wanted to break through the icy barrier she'd erected and find the passionate girl who'd stolen into his bedroom. And he had. When she'd opened her mouth to let him in, he'd taken all she'd had to give. He still had a thick, hard erection to prove it. If they hadn't been in a restaurant, Gage would have ravished her where she stood. But he was no animal. He was willing to wait. Hell, he'd waited nearly two decades to *be* with her—another few weeks wouldn't make much difference.

Four

"He did what?" With a look of shock on her face, Shana sat back on the couch in Fallon's cottage the following evening. She'd arrived a half hour ago. After the pleasantries were over, Fallon had uncorked a vintage bottle of Merlot and gotten right down to the matter at hand.

"There's nothing wrong with your hearing, Shana," Fallon replied. "I was just as floored as you were."

"When I mentioned Gage the other day, I was trying to get a rise out of you. I never dreamed he'd ever loan you the money let alone ask you to *marry* him. It's crazy!"

Fallon nodded. "I thought the same thing."

"Thought?" Shana peered at her strangely. "As in past tense?"

"Yes. But after considering it—and trust me, I couldn't sleep a wink last night—it kind of came to me."

Shana's eyes grew wide. "What came to you?"

"It makes an odd sort of sense in a way," Fallon responded. "Gage has always wanted to be part of the *in crowd*, but growing up on the estate, he was always thought of as the help. Marriage to me would be a way for him to even the scales."

"And make you pay on your back."

"Shana!"

"C'mon, doll." Shana scooted closer to Fallon on the sofa. "Don't tell me Gage didn't make a play for you. You're a grown woman now and a beautiful one, I might add. There's no way he's not trying to tap that." She patted Fallon on the behind.

"My God, Shana. Have you no shame?"

"Do you? Because it sounds to me like you're giving Gage's offer some serious thought."

"Wouldn't you?" Fallon asked. "A sexy, gorgeous, *rich* man is offering to solve my financial problem and save my family. How can I let the company fail under my watch?"

"See?" Shana pointed her index finger at her. "That's how he got you. He's tapping into all your fears and insecurities. Let it fail, Fallon. You didn't create this mess, your father did. You inherited it. And now you're supposed to—what? Give up your chance of finding Mr. Right and settle for Mr. Payback? Because that's exactly what this is. Mark my words. Gage wants revenge for how your family wronged him and he's using all the weapons in his arsenal."

"You make it sound like we're at war."

"You are. Think about all the anger, hurt and humiliation he must feel after *you* threw yourself at him and caused him and his mother to be kicked out on the street. The man must despise you, but clearly he wants you in equal measure. It's all kinds of messed up."

"You're not helping me, Shana."

"I have always been a straight shooter, Fallon," Shana replied. "It's what you love about me, so I'm telling you how I see it. I want you to consider what you could be getting yourself into before you make a life-altering decision."

"Aha!" Fallon said. "You've given me an idea."

"Oh, yeah? What's that?"

"If I agree, I can stipulate the marriage is temporary. I think six months is enough time to get Stewart Technologies back on its feet with an influx of cash and cement Gage's place in Austin society. What do you think?"

Shana shook her head. "I don't know, Fallon. You're playing with fire."

"Without risk, there can't be a great reward." Fallon sure hoped she was right because she was banking her future and Stewart Technologies on making the right call.

Gage couldn't wait forty-eight hours for Fallon to make a decision. He had to persuade her. All day in his home office he'd been thinking about her and he knew the only way to stop himself from going crazy was to see her again.

He picked up his cell phone and called her.

"Gage?" Fallon said. "Have you changed your mind? Did you come to the conclusion your arrangement was just as crazy as it sounds?"

"Quite the contrary. I wanted to *see you*."

"You told me I had forty-eight hours."

"And you do," Gage replied smoothly. "I'm going to do everything in my power to convince you to say yes. Starting with a date tonight."

"Tonight? I can't. I have to work."

"Excuses, excuses, Fallon. You're afraid to be alone with me after what transpired between us last night."

"That's not true." She paused for several beats. "I admit I find you attractive."

"Face facts, Fallon, if we hadn't been in public, the evening might have ended differently."

"You're very sure of yourself."

"I know what I want."

"And…oh, that's right, you want me," Fallon finished. "Well, I'm not that easy, Gage."

"I didn't think you were, but I admit I'd like to know more. Last night was the tip of the iceberg. Let me see you tonight."

"I need time to think, Gage. I don't appreciate the strong-arm tactics."

"I would think if you're going to agree to shackle yourself to me, you would want to get to know the man you'll marry. Or would you rather walk into this as strangers?"

"You seem to think it's a forgone conclusion I'll say yes to your outrageous proposal."

"I'm encouraged because you haven't said no."

"Fine. I'll meet you. Where and when?"

Gage shook his head. Oh, no, he wasn't falling into this trap again. He wanted a proper date. "*I* will pick you up at Stewart Manor. And, Fallon?"

"Yes?"

"Dress to impress. Because I'm taking you to the opera."

Gage ended the call with a smile on his face. That hadn't been as hard as he'd imagined. She was recalcitrant, but he'd convinced her it was in both their best interests to get to know one another. The problem was he didn't have tickets, but he'd heard from Theo that Puccini's *La bohème* was playing at Austin Opera and he knew anyone who was anyone would be there.

Austin society would see the former maid's son out on the town with Fallon Stewart. It was brilliant. He would kill two birds with one stone. Cement his place in society and spend time with the woman who would be his wife. Now he had to convince Fallon there was no way she could walk away from him.

Dress to impress.

Fallon stood in front of her gilded pedestal mirror and

glanced at the double-strapped, off-the-shoulder red gown with a deep side slit. The dress showed a generous amount of leg while the sweetheart neckline revealed a swell of cleavage.

She didn't want to give Gage any ideas that the evening would end differently than it had last night with them each going home *alone*.

After applying some red lipstick and a touch of blush to her cheeks, she was ready for an evening at the opera. *But was she really ready?* The remainder of the afternoon after Gage's call, she'd picked up the phone to cancel a half a dozen times. Yet she'd always stopped herself because maybe deep down she really did want to see him.

Fallon couldn't understand the pull Gage had on her after all these years. He'd awakened something in her and she wasn't sure how to get it back under control.

The doorbell rang and her stomach lurched. There was no turning back. Grabbing her matching red clutch purse and wrap, she made for the front door. When she swung it open, Gage stood there, resplendent in a black tuxedo with satin lapels. He was wearing a red tie that complemented her dress.

Fallon felt his eyes rake her up and down. It made her feel as if she was plugged into an electrical socket because currents were running through her veins. When she looked into those brooding brandy-colored eyes, her insides hummed.

"You look incredible!"

"Thank you," Fallon said coolly and wrapped her shawl around her shoulders.

Gage took her arm and led her outside to the waiting limo. He helped her inside, picking up the hem of her dress as she slid in.

Once he was seated beside her and the chauffeur closed the door, he reached across the short distance to the ice bucket and pulled out a bottle of Dom Pérignon. He uncorked it easily and poured them a glass. He handed her one and dinged his flute against hers. "To an unforgettable evening."

Fallon was sure it was going to be nothing but.

La bohème was everything. Gage had spared no expense. When they arrived, they were shown to box seats near the front of the opera house with a clear view of the stage. The singers were amazing and, by the end of the night, Fallon was on her feet along with the entire theater giving them a standing ovation.

"I didn't realize you were such a fan," Gage said from her side.

"I've come from time to time with my father," Fallon replied. "Mama couldn't be bothered. Said it was much too boring for her, but I loved it. Plus, it was something my father and I could do together."

"Must be nice," Gage said wistfully as he led her out of the theater and away from the throng.

"Did you know your father?" Fallon asked, turning to give him a sideward glance.

Gage's glare told Fallon she'd made a misstep in asking something so personal. Wasn't the point of tonight's exercise for them to get to know each other?

Their limousine was waiting by the curb. Fallon was thankful they didn't have to wait with the crowd lining the streets. Within minutes they were pulling away and Gage asked the chauffeur to raise the privacy screen.

"Where to next?" Fallon inquired. There had been an uncomfortable silence between them since she'd inquired about his father. It was clear Gage didn't wish to speak of him.

"I didn't know him," Gage said finally.

Fallon didn't need to ask what he meant.

"My mother never spoke of him. Only told me that he was an older gentleman who'd taken advantage of her youth and naïveté. Once she was pregnant, he turned his back on her and she never saw him again."

"That's why you pushed me away," Fallon replied softly. "Because you didn't want to be like him."

When Gage turned to her, his eyes were cloudy. "Very insightful of you. But know this, Fallon. If you had been a few years older, I wouldn't have turned you away."

"You wouldn't?"

"No. I would have taken what you offered."

"Why?"

"Because I wanted you. I wanted you *then* and I want you now."

His face was starkly beautiful in the dim light coming from the street and Fallon felt as if she were being hypnotized. Her hand went to her throat. Her mouth felt parched as if she'd walked hours in the desert with no water to hydrate her. She reached for the champagne bottle; a new one had miraculously appeared.

Gage grasped her arm and a tingling went straight to her core. "Does it scare you when I speak so openly?"

"You mean bluntly?"

"I was being honest. You should try it."

Her eyes flashed with anger. "I have been honest. I'm here with you now, aren't I? When every instinct I have tells me I should be running in the other direction, away from danger."

"You think I'm dangerous?"

"Hell, yeah! But I can't…"

"Can't what?"

"Can't seem to stop myself from wanting you, too. How's that for honesty?"

"It's great because I've been craving your sweet mouth all day," he growled. Within seconds he'd slid her along the seat until she was sprawled across his lap. The air around them was heavy and thick with desire. When Gage trailed a finger down one of her cheeks, Fallon felt her pulse beat hectically at her throat. "I know you don't want to want me, Fallon, but your body betrays you." With one arm securely around her waist, the other hand was free to cup her jaw and, with a surprising gentleness, Gage angled his head and his mouth closed over hers in the most persuasive of kisses.

Tender yet insistent, his mouth claimed hers again and again and her lips clung to his, seeking closer contact. Fallon gave herself permission to enjoy the taste and lush depths of his mouth. Gage gathered her to him, his fingers at her jaw, holding her captive as he lazily explored her mouth. His tongue teased and stroked hers, causing heat to pool low in Fallon's belly and spread like wildfire, incinerating everything in its path. Her breasts felt heavy and swollen. Gage sensed her ache and cupped the underside of one breast. His thumb grazed over the nub until it peaked and hardened.

Fallon moaned, loving the delicious yet tormenting strokes of his fingers. She wanted his mouth on her nipple, wanted him to feast on her. She became dimly aware of Gage pushing down the top of her dress and taking the rigid peak in his mouth. His mouth and tongue worked the nipple with licks, flicks, tugs and suction. The ache inside her intensified when Gage transferred his attention to her other nipple.

Hadn't she known they might end up like this? This was no longer about a kiss. It was about need. And now that the desire had been unleashed, she didn't know if it could be bottled up again.

Gage ran his hands down Fallon's body. Touching her in ways he'd imagined for far too long. Of course, now that he had her exactly where he wanted her, his brain had short-circuited. He was hardening underneath her sweet little bottom, and he was completely useless. All he could think about was how he'd love nothing better than to wrap her legs around his hips and take her right there in the limousine.

And her breasts. God, they tasted heavenly. It made him want more. He moved upward so he could slant his mouth over hers again. He loved the hot slide of her tongue in and out of his mouth and the way her hands clutched his tuxedo jacket as if she was seeking something to hold on to. But there was nothing. Nothing but this white-hot arousal between them. His free hand went up and undid her hair, which fell to her shoulders. Gage slid his hands through the tendrils and cupped the back of her head so he could give her another mind-numbing kiss.

But a kiss wasn't all he wanted. His hand moved lower until he came to the slit of her dress. He hiked it up to her waist and moved his hands up her bare legs. She trembled when Gage's finger found her thong and pushed it aside so he could trace the most intimate part of her. She was so wet for him. Her body was betraying her, showing him physical evidence of her arousal. And when he began to circle the top of her clitoris with a feather-light touch, she gasped. When he slid one finger inside her, her body tightened around him.

Gage watched Fallon's face as he worked her with his fingers. Slowly, deliberately, he brought her higher and higher. The sounds of pleasure she was making, and especially the way she writhed against his hand, turned him on. Her sexy bottom was brushing his erection and he was going mad. He added another finger and her eyes became hazy with passion.

"Come for me, Fallon," he commanded. She closed her eyes and he sensed her resistance, but his hands were insistent. He could feel it when she orgasmed and clenched around his fingers. Satisfied, Gage claimed her mouth with his, whispering his approval as aftershocks shuddered through her entire body. He kissed her through them until she eventually quieted.

Fallon's uninhibited response was more than Gage could ever imagine. Now he realized *he* needed her to say yes because they were far from over. In fact, they'd just begun.

Five

Fallon was embarrassed as she came back down to earth and registered what had happened. She'd allowed Gage to make love to her in the back of the limousine. Her breasts were bare, aching and wet from his mouth, while her dress was pulled down to her hips. Did he think she behaved this way with every man? Well, she didn't!

She quickly scrambled out of his lap to pull her dress up over her breasts and push it down her thighs.

"What's wrong?" Gage asked.

"How can you be asking me that? After I— After we—"

"Behaved like two consenting adults?"

Fallon flushed and moved as far away on the seat as humanly possible without falling out of the limo.

"Tonight was inevitable, just as it's inevitable that we'll become lovers. Marriage agreement or not."

The limo stopped and Fallon realized they'd made it to her cottage. She was thankful when the door opened and she was out in the cool evening air, briskly walking to her front door. Unfortunately she was not alone. Gage followed her.

"I'd like to walk you to your door."

Fallon spun around on her heel, "Oh, no, you don't." She held her hand up against his hard chest. "We'll say our good-nights here."

"All right." Gage handed Fallon her wrap. "You might want this."

"Thank you."

"Good night." He started back toward the limo but then turned around. "About tomorrow…"

"I'll call you," Fallon responded.

"Very well, I'll await your answer." He'd slipped inside and the limo took off down the gravel driveway.

Once inside, Fallon grappled with how the situation with Gage had escalated. One minute they were enjoying the opera and the next she was coming apart in the limo. How was it possible they still shared such a passionate connection after their storied past? Whenever he was near, she felt weak, fluttery and out of control. Her feelings for Gage had always been complicated, but adding sex into the equation would make it a hell of a lot harder to walk away from a marriage. Was she honestly considering going through with it and locking herself in unholy matrimony with Gage?

Yes.

The next day Fallon was as jittery as ever. She had a hard time focusing on work as the clock tick-tocked. The forty-eight-hour deadline Gage had given her loomed. And she couldn't get the man out of her mind or the way she'd burned up for him with every kiss and every caress. She was unnerved at how far things had gone. She was thankful it hadn't gone any further. She didn't need full-blown sex clouding the picture when she had such a momentous decision to make.

On the one hand, Gage was offering her a way out. It would save thousands of jobs and allow her employees to keep food on the table. She would show her father and all the naysayers that she had the expertise to run Stewart Technologies. On the other, marrying Gage and agreeing to his nonnegotiable terms would mean consummating the marriage. If she agreed, all the old feelings she'd once had for Gage could come bubbling back up to the surface, making her vulnerable. Because could she really trust him, given their history? And she doubted he trusted her, so what was in it for him?

She was reading through some reports when her baby brother, Dane, swept into her office and swung her out of her seat into his arms. "Fallon! Baby girl, I've missed you."

"I've missed you, too, you big oaf. Now put me down, so I can have a look at you." She hadn't been expecting a visit from him, but then again Dane danced to the beat of his own drum, doing things in his own way and his own time. "What are you doing here? I didn't know you were coming for a visit."

When Dane finally set Fallon on her feet, she peered up at him. Dane had inherited their mother's dark brown eyes instead of their father's hazel-gray ones like her and Ayden. His classical good looks, tawny skin, chiseled cheekbones and smile had won the world over, making him one of America's favorite actors. Today he was dressed casually in Diesel jeans, a black T-shirt and biker boots, and was rocking a serious five-o'clock shadow like he hadn't shaved in days.

"When did you get in?" Fallon inquired, leading him over to her sitting area.

"An hour ago, but I'm not staying long. I decided to lay over here for a couple of hours on my way to Mexico for a movie shoot."

"Dane? You promised me that the next time you came to town, you'd stay for a spell."

"I'm sorry, sis, but we have a tight schedule," Dane responded, flopping down on her sofa and putting his booted foot on her cocktail table.

Fallon came forward and knocked it off. "Have you forgotten your manners out there in LA?"

Dane grinned mischievously. "Not all of them. But I had to come. You sounded down the other week when I called, so I had to see for myself what all the ruckus was about. Everything looks the same."

"That's because I've been keeping the bankers at bay."

Dane frowned. "And now? Are they threatening to take the house? I think Nora would have a fit if she lost her gravy train."

"Must you call our mother by her first name?" Fallon replied.

"C'mon, Fallon," Dane said, "When has that woman ever been a mother to us? She was always pawning us off to a nanny or maid. Well, that was until you ran off the one good maid we had."

Fallon felt her face flush and cast her eyes downward. She wished Dane hadn't brought up Grace Campbell. It was still hard remembering how Fallon's actions had affected not only Gage but his mother, as well.

"Fallon." Dane scooted over on the couch and grabbed her hand. "I'm sorry, okay? I didn't mean to stir up the pot and bring back bad memories. Anyway, I realize I've been out of commission and on the sidelines in this family, but I know money is tight. How much do you need? I can liquidate some assets and get you probably a couple of million in a few days."

"It wouldn't be enough."

Dane's dark brown eyes grew large. "It's that bad? Why

didn't you tell me? I could have been helping instead of frivolously spending on houses, cars and trips."

"It's okay." Fallon patted his hand. "I didn't want to bother you. And, furthermore, it's your money. You earned it."

"But I'm your brother. I want to help."

"Ayden offered to help, as well."

"Ayden? Wow!" Dane shook his head. "I'm still in shock over your call. After all this time, he wants a relationship with us? Do you know why?"

Fallon shrugged. "Does it matter? We're family."

Dane was noncommittal. "Sure. And I can see how important it is to you, so I'll make the effort. All right?" He tipped her chin up to look into her eyes.

Fallon grinned. "Great! I'll plan something soon for the three of us."

"What are you going to do in the meantime about the company?"

"Don't you worry, your big sister always has a plan."

Why wasn't she here yet? Gage paced his penthouse like a panther stalking its prey. Fallon had called him earlier and asked to meet at his place, so he'd given her his address. And waited. But the call had been over an hour ago. Gage wondered if Fallon didn't want to be seen with him. Is that why she was coming to him? Did Fallon want to keep their association a secret from her family? Was she having cold feet?

He went to his subzero refrigerator and pulled out a beer. Unscrewing the top, he took a generous swig and slid open the sliding pocket doors to the balcony.

Gage was certain she would agree to his terms. Why else would she bother coming? If she wasn't interested, she'd have laughed in his face when he'd first made the offer and told him where to go. But she wouldn't. Not after last night. They'd given in to the fiery passion between them. And now she was coming to him. She'd be on his turf. *Did she know the danger she was in?*

Gage found himself wondering what it would be like when they were finally together. When there were no parents standing in their way or terms to discuss. Just a man and woman in the throes of passion. Blood rushed to his head and his groin, making him both dizzy and hard at same time. He still couldn't wrap his mind around why she affected him this way. It mocked everything he'd ever said about what he'd do to Fallon if he ever saw her again. He thought he'd throttle her for her careless behavior, but instead all he wanted to do was to drown himself in her. She was the key, the final piece to achieve all he'd ever wanted.

He already had money and power, but by marrying Fallon he would have the grudging respect and acceptance of society. He would no longer be living in the shadows and envying the Stewarts' charmed life, which had been utterly different from his humble roots. Instead he would be living it with them. But, unlike the Stewarts, he wouldn't take what he had for granted because he knew what it was like to go without.

The sound of his doorbell forced Gage from his thoughts. With a loose-limbed stride, he walked to the door and opened it.

Fallon was wearing a black sheath with a sharp asymmetrical collar. Her hair was pulled up into a high bun and she wore little to no makeup. She looked effortlessly beautiful. Gage yearned to touch her but her features were schooled.

"Come in." He motioned her forward.

"Thank you." She walked inside and paused when she reached his living room. It was large, with sweeping views of the capitol building and the University of Texas tower. "Great view."

"Yeah, I like it," Gage replied. "But I'm sure you didn't come here for the scenery. Have you made a decision?"

Fallon eyed him warily. "Yes, I have. But I have a few stipulations that aren't open for negotiation."

Gage chuckled to himself. *Did she actually think she was in a position of power?* He held all the cards and he was damn well going to play them. But he would humor her. "All right, let's hear them."

"I'll agree to marry you."

His mouth curved into a smile. Of course she would. She was desperate to save her father's legacy. Was that her only reason?

"But only for six months."

"Excuse me?"

"Six months is enough time for you to ingratiate yourself into Austin society and get the full benefit of the Stewart name and all its connections. I see no reason for us to continue the charade a moment longer than necessary. Wouldn't you agree?"

Gage had to admit he was surprised; he hadn't thought of making their arrangement temporary. The only thing on his mind was Fallon in his bed and getting a foothold into Stewart Technologies. "I can live with that. What else? Because I suspect there's more."

Fallon stood straighter and stared at him. "The marriage must be in name only."

Gage laughed. "Do you really think that's possible, Fallon, after the way you were crawling all over me last night?"

"I—I…" She stuttered but then stopped. It appeared as if she was regrouping. "I don't want to muddy the waters and complicate what is essentially a business arrangement. You must see that."

"No, I don't." Gage plopped his beer on the nearby cocktail table, causing some to spill over. "What I see is a woman afraid of taking what she wants. You and I know this isn't just about business, Fallon. It never was."

Her eyes narrowed. "What is it?"

"It's a reckoning. Between you and me. About what we both wanted but didn't get years ago. Don't you think it's time we find out what could have been?"

Fallon turned and walked onto the terrace. She was quiet, contemplative, as if she were battling herself, and Gage feared she would say no to him. It was imperative she agree. It would finally give him the means to avenge his mother while simultaneously getting Fallon in his bed.

Gage touched her shoulders and she jumped. Rather than touch her again, he placed his hands on either side of the railing, closing her in. She was out of options. He heard her sharp intake of breath as he inhaled the sweet fragrant smell of her perfume. "Fallon…"

"All right," she whispered.

Gage sucked in a breath and leaned in closer. "Say it again."

"I said, all right." Fallon turned around to face him and he appreciated how she looked him in the eye. She was no coward. "I'll agree to the stipulation we share a bed."

Victory surged through Gage and a large grin spread across his lips. "Then how about we get a head start." He hauled her to him. He was following his base instincts of taking her here and now. He didn't care. On the couch or his bed, it didn't much matter to him. She was his now. He lowered his head to finally have a taste of her delectable lips, when Fallon placed her hands against his chest.

"No."

"No?" Fallon made him feel a little wild and out of control while she still looked poised. "You said that you were agreeing to my terms."

"And I will." Fallon slid out of his grasp to walk back into the living room. "When we're married."

"You expect me to wait until our honeymoon?"

Fallon chuckled. "As shocking as that sounds, yes, Gage. You've called the shots up to this point, but not on this. I'm agreeing to marry you and to share your bed, but not until then."

Gage gave her an eye roll and sighed. Fallon played hardball and was a shrewd negotiator. He could see now how she'd climbed the ladder to become CEO of Stewart Technologies. "Fine."

"Good." She inclined her head. "I assume you'll have your attorney draw up a prenuptial outlining terms, including your *gift* to your fiancée?"

"Of course. The prenup will state the exact amount of funds I'm giving you to bail out your company. Other matters will be between us—a gentleman's agreement, if you will."

"Excellent."

"And as for the wedding, it needs to be arranged quickly yet lavishly so the entire community can see it."

"Why the rush?"

"You need a reminder of our explosive chemistry? Then let me remind you." He slipped his arm around her nape and covered her mouth in a searing kiss. She was stiff at first, but it didn't take long for her to warm up and to delve into the kiss. He angled his head for better access and reveled in how Fallon tasted like no other woman. Over the next six months he intended to get rid of this craving he'd developed for her.

His hands skimmed down her back to cup her bottom and she groaned. Jesus, if he continued, he would have her flat on her back despite her protests. Gage pulled away and took a shuddering breath. "You should go now while you still can."

"I think that's a good idea." Fallon grabbed her purse and was out the door, leaving only her scent in her wake.

Oh, yes, they needed to have a very short engagement.

Six

"Gage, darling. It's so good to see you." His mother enveloped him in a warm hug. Gage returned her affection, squeezing her small frame.

He pulled back and regarded her. She wore a simple shift-style dress and espadrilles, and looked youthful. The earlier years of hard menial labor couldn't be seen in her smooth caramel complexion. Her dark brown eyes were warm and inviting, reminding him he had been away from home far too long.

"C'mon in." She motioned him inside the five-bedroom palatial home he'd bought her a decade ago when his finances had begun booming. Gage had ensured that his mother could retire from a life where she worked late into the night cleaning other's people houses and looking after their children.

"The place looks great." Gage followed her into the sunroom where she had set a pitcher of sweet tea and her famous oatmeal-raisin cookies in the middle of the cocktail table. Gage snatched one from the platter and began munching away happily as they sat on the sofa.

"The interior decorator you hired had a great eye. Once I told her I wanted modern contemporary, she came up with this." Grace motioned to the sleek white furniture and the room mostly done in creams and light beige with a few colored throw pillows here and there. "Now, let me pour you some sweet tea."

"Good, you deserve it." He accepted the glass when she handed it to him.

"Tell me what's new. You must have something on the horizon. You wouldn't leave your precious London otherwise."

Gage shrugged, not meeting her eyes, and reached for another cookie. "Why don't you tell me about your next trip?"

His mother eyed him suspiciously and Gage squirmed in his seat. "Don't play with me, boy. Your mama can tell when you're not being forthright. So spit it out."

Gage sighed. He would have to tell her about Fallon, but he didn't relish her response. "I ran into an old friend recently and we reconnected."

"Really?" His mother poured herself a glass of tea. "Anyone I know?"

"Fallon Stewart." Gage didn't look up when he spoke. He didn't need to because the silence permeating the room was deafening.

"The Stewart girl who caused me to lose my job of ten years without so much as a reference?" his mother responded. "What in hell's name is going on, Gage? I thought you despised that family as much as I did."

"I do but…"

"But what?" Her fierce gazed rested on his. "Explain yourself."

Gage wasn't sure how much of his plan he wanted to tell

his mother, so he gave her a half-truth. "She's turned into a beautiful young woman."

"She's deceitful. Had Fallon Stewart spoken up years ago, she would have saved us years of struggle."

"She apologized and wants to move on."

"And you've forgiven her?" his mother asked incredulously. "After you vowed vengeance? I can hardly believe that."

"Believe it, because Fallon and I are getting married."

"What?" Her eyes grew wide. "Over my dead body."

"Mama, don't be melodramatic."

"I'm not. That girl is your Achilles' heel, Gage. She always has been. I remember how she used to fawn over you and follow you around like a little puppy dog and you never put her straight. And now you're turning the other cheek? Sounds to me like you're thinking below the belt and not with your head."

Gage reached across the sofa and grasped his mother's hand in his. "I know what I'm doing."

"Do you?" She gazed deep into his brown eyes. "Because I think the Stewarts will do nothing but destroy you. Mark my words. You're playing with fire, Gage."

"Trust me, Mama, I have the situation under control." *Or did he?* Was he blinded by Fallon's charms and headed for a fall?

"I don't think so, but then again you're a grown man and capable of making your own decisions."

"I'm glad you recognize that because I will make them pay dearly for how you were treated. I promise you." He would take sweet revenge on Fallon. In bed.

"Let me get this straight. After I told you the Stewarts' company was in trouble, you thought it would be a good idea to confront Fallon?" Theo asked when he and Gage met up to play pool late Saturday afternoon.

"Yeah," Gage responded. "I had to see for myself if she was still the spoiled, overindulged princess she once was."

"Well, apparently not, because you asked her to *marry* you," Theo said, taking a swallow of his beer. "Have you lost your mind?" He leaned over to feel Gage's forehead.

"No. I haven't," Gage said. "Fallon's not sixteen anymore, Theo." He used the cue stick to get the green ball into the corner pocket. Then he eased the cue into position for the blue ball and aimed for the middle pocket. He missed and it was Theo's turn. "She's a grown woman."

"Then sleep with her," Theo stated. "You don't have to marry her. I mean, I know she's hot and all." He glanced over at Gage and laughed when his best friend gave him a jealous glare from across the pool table. "Hey, I have two eyes, I'm not blind. But since it's clear you're the possessive type, I'll keep my opinions to myself."

"You do that."

"Answer me this. I get why she's doing it. You're offering her a ton of money to save her business and you two have a history, so I understand the attraction. But what do you get out of all this, because a bed partner seems like a flimsy excuse to tie yourself to another human being in holy matrimony."

Gage reached for his beer on a nearby table. After telling his mother, Gage had been shaken. But on his way over to meet Theo, he'd had to remind himself of why he was doing this and his resolve strengthened. "I told you. Fallon will secure my place in society and while she's so busy focused on the wedding, I'll be secretly buying up stock of Stewart Technologies until I own a majority interest."

Theo pointed at him. "I knew you had a trick up your sleeve, but this is pretty underhanded, even for you, Gage."

"Don't you think they deserve it?" Gage countered. "Henry Stewart threw us out on the street with just the clothes on our backs. We weren't even allowed to get our meager belongings. And after working for them for years, they wouldn't even give my mother a reference. All because she stuck up for me." He slammed his hand against his chest. "Do you know how the guilt ate me up at causing my mother harm?"

"I know it wasn't easy."

"It was hell. We had to scrape by with the little savings we had. I blame the Stewarts. And I will feel triumph the day I can ruin them."

"And Fallon. Even though she was a naïve young girl?"

"She was old enough to know better and she's no young ingénue anymore. She's well aware of what she's agreed to."

"She's not the only one," Theo responded. "I worry about you, Gage."

"Don't. I've been on a collision course with the Stewarts for sixteen years and the moment has finally come for me to get vengeance. And after telling my mama, I'm even more convinced I'm doing the right thing."

"You told your mother?"

Gage nodded. "And she pretty much blew a gasket."

"Can you blame her?"

"No. But I'm on track to get everything I ever wanted, including Fallon."

This marriage was one of the best decisions he'd ever made and the unexpected bonus was the sizzling sex awaiting him once he finally made Fallon his. He wasn't going to let up on the gas. Gage had to push forward until he took over the Stewarts' empire. Only then would he feel like he had avenged his mother.

Fallon was happy to receive a lunch invitation from Ayden. She arrived before him on Monday afternoon and had several minutes to settle her nerves. Their meeting would be very different from the tense scenario a couple of months ago. Fallon would get to know Ayden on a personal level. She didn't know why she was nervous at the prospect, but she was. She wanted this so bad and it had meant everything that Ayden extended the olive branch.

She noticed her big brother the moment he arrived. He was over six feet tall, bald with tawny skin, and impressively male in his tailored suit. He was impossible to miss. He waved when he saw her and stalked toward the table. His eyes creased into a smile and she was surprised when he leaned toward her and offered a hug. They were off to a good start.

"Sorry I'm late. A client meeting wrapped up later than I anticipated," Ayden said as he sat across from her. "How are you?"

"I'm good. Thank you for the invite." Fallon glanced over and found herself looking into the hazel-gray eyes they shared with their father.

"You're welcome," Ayden responded, unbuttoning his suit jacket and leaning back to regard her. "When I said I wanted a relationship, I meant it."

Fallon nodded and smiled. "I know. So did I."

"So, in the interest of family, I'd like to know how you're really doing. Any luck on getting a financial bailout with any of the banks I referred you to?"

After he'd told Fallon he wanted to forge a sibling relationship, Ayden had sent her some leads. As owner of Stewart Investments, Ayden's clients were quite wealthy and might be looking for an investment vehicle.

"No, I didn't get any bites," Fallon responded, reaching for her sparkling water.

His gaze bore into her. "What are you going to do then? You're running out of time."

"I've found a private investor."

Ayden frowned. "Who would have that kind of cash?"

"Gage Campbell. You may have heard of him."

"Yeah, I have. They call him the Wizard of Wall Street.

But usually he's making other people money, not investing his own." He peered at her with a strange expression. "What gives?"

"Gage and I have a personal connection," Fallon replied, forcing her eyes to meet her brother's. "And…" She tried to find the right words but it was hard with Ayden staring at her so intently. She could lie. Spin it that they were old acquaintances. But Ayden wouldn't believe it. And she didn't want to start out their newfound relationship that way. She had to tell him the truth. "We're getting married. And in exchange, Gage is giving me the money to bail out Stewart Technologies." Fallon shot Ayden a glance, but his eyes were blazing with fury, which stunned her. She didn't know Ayden cared.

"Marriage?" His eyes widened in concern. "Why would you agree to such a thing? I will *give* you the money. You don't have to marry this man."

She shook her head. "It's all right, Ayden. I've known Gage for years. We grew up together. And…"

"And what does he get out of this arrangement?" His eyes narrowed as he waited for her answer.

Fallon blushed and he caught it. "So you're willing to pros—"

Her eyes flashed a gentle but firm warning. "Don't you say it, Ayden, not unless you want this relationship to end before it's begun."

She heard his sharp intake of breath and his eyes were hooded when he spoke next. "You're my sister, Fallon. A fact I've been trying to hide from a long time but not anymore. I'm responsible for you taking such drastic action. I made you feel like you had no other choice."

Fallon leaned across the table and placed her hand over his large one. "Listen, I appreciated your offer. Ultimately it was my choice, Ayden. Not yours. You're not responsible for my actions."

"And you're not responsible for Henry running the company into the ground, especially after he frivolously spent money on new inventions that never went to market," Ayden responded hotly. "Yet you're willing to sacrifice yourself."

"Please respect my decision," Fallon implored. "I need your support on this."

Ayden sighed and sat back in his chair. "I'm worried for you."

"Don't be. I know Gage. He won't hurt me." Fallon certainly hoped that statement was true because she wasn't only risking her pride. Gage had the power to hurt her more than any other man because of the long-ago buried feelings she had for him. She had to protect herself at all costs. She might be giving her body, but not her heart.

Fallon was exhausted. It had been an emotionally draining day. All she wanted was to go home and soak in a long, luxurious bath. So much had happened in the last couple of days. Dane and Ayden were both so concerned for her well-being she needed to regroup, to make sure she could handle what she'd signed up for.

Seeing Gage again and finding out the passion she'd once had for him hadn't died but blossomed was disconcerting. Over a decade had passed. He should no longer cause her pulse to race, but he did. She was a bundle of tight emotions and lust. Whenever she was in his company she acted completely out of character, starting with the heated kiss at the restaurant then again in the limo after the opera.

Is that why she'd agreed to his marriage proposal? He was a rich and successful man with deep pockets that could help save her company, but was it more than that?

Her phone rang and she answered it from her car. "Fallon?"

"Gage. What can I do for you?"

"I'm here at Stewart Manor and thought you'd like to join me."

"You're at my house? Why?" Panic surged through Fallon. *What was he doing there?* They hadn't even had time to get their story straight. And then it dawned on her: he couldn't wait for the opportunity to rub it in her parents' faces. He was marrying their daughter. It was a *take that* to her father. It would serve him right if she told Gage to go to hell, but then she would still be in the same predicament tomorrow.

She heard his chuckle from the other end. "I thought it would be obvious. I'm here to share the news of our impending marriage with your parents."

Fallon sucked in a sharp breath. "You had no right to do that. *I* was going to tell them."

"*We* are going to talk to them, so meet me here." The call ended and Fallon glared at the display screen. Anger coursed through her and she let out several choice words. Who did he think he was, running roughshod over her? She had been planning to tell her parents in due time. What right did he have to force her hand like this?

Apparently, in his view, every right. He wanted to be able to rub the fact they were getting married in her family's face. The maid's prodigal son had returned and was there to save the day. This was all part of his retribution. She could only imagine what her mother's response would be: sheer and utter embarrassment at having to kowtow to Gage Campbell.

She was wrong.

After parking her red Audi in the circular driveway, Fallon walked into the manor expecting to hear loud voices, but she found Gage and her parents lounging on the sofa as if they were fast friends instead of known enemies.

She caught Gage's compelling stare the moment she entered the room. With his height and broad shoulders, he was beyond handsome. The words that came to mind were *potent*, *vital* and *commanding*. Fallon found herself mesmerized.

"Babe." Gage rose and strode toward her, a barely leashed tension radiating off him. He leaned forward and brushed his lips across her temple before circling his arm around her waist. Fallon allowed herself to be ushered to the sofa where they sat side-by-side, thigh-to-thigh.

"Fallon, darling." Nora was perched in a chair opposite her father while she and Gage sat on the sofa between them. "Why is this the first we're hearing that you've been seeing Grace's son?"

Fallon was vexed. The innocuous question made it seem as if Nora and Gage's mother were old friends rather than boss and employee with a bad history. She didn't get a chance to respond, though, because Gage was quick to answer.

"We were keeping it private, Mrs. Stewart. We re-connected some months ago." He turned to Fallon at his side. His eyes, fringed with long black lashes, held hers for several seconds before he faced her parents again. "We didn't want to let the cat out of the bag, so to speak, until we were sure of where the relationship was heading."

"But Fallon never keeps anything from me." Her father glanced in her direction.

Fallon attempted a half-hearted smile. "I'm sorry, Daddy."

Gage reached for her hand, which she'd kept firmly in her lap, and laced his fingers through hers. "Don't apologize, Fallon. We wanted privacy. Besides, it doesn't matter now. We're in love and we want to get married as soon as possible."

Nora gasped. "Why the rush? You aren't pregnant, Fallon, are you? I mean, what would everyone think?"

The horror in her mother's voice over the idea that *she*

would get knocked up by Gage of all people was clear to everyone and Fallon felt Gage stiffen at her side. She patted his leg and answered. "Of course not, Mother. We see no reason to wait. We're both very eager to tie the knot."

"Perhaps it would be best if you had a long engagement." Henry eyed them both. "It would give us time to get to know Gage again."

Gage looked at her father. "Oh, I'm sure you know me quite well, Mr. Stewart, considering I grew up in this household and you took me under your wing."

Fallon's stomach plummeted and her father bristled.

Her mother spoke first. "That may be so, Mr. Campbell, but—"

"Gage," he interrupted. "I mean, I am going to be your son-in-law, after all."

Fallon watched her mother plaster on a fake smile. "Gage, it's clear you've done quite well for yourself..." she began. Fallon knew her mother had noticed his Tom Ford shoes, Rolex watch and tailored designer suit, but did she have to be so *obvious*? "But we really know nothing about you."

Gage leaned back against the sofa, one arm draped casually behind Fallon. "Well, after my departure from Stewart Manor, I went on to graduate from the University of Texas with a degree in finance and economics."

"You were always a whiz with numbers," her father said.

Gage continued as if he hadn't spoken. "After college, I went to work on Wall Street, then in London and Hong Kong, where I made a number of substantial investments that have put me in the position I'm in today."

"And where is that exactly?" Her mother pursed her lips. "As you can see—" she swept her arms across the room "—Fallon has grown up in a certain lifestyle and we wouldn't want her to do without."

Gage's eyes narrowed as he sat forward. "As my wife,

Fallon would want for nothing. Money is no object for our wedding."

Her mother's finely arched eyebrow rose. "No object, did you say?"

"That's right."

"Well then, Henry." She turned to her husband. "Seems like our daughter has landed quite the whale. Having Gage here—" she inclined her head in his direction "—should most assuredly fix the company's dire straits."

"Mother, please."

"It's all right, Fallon." Gage patted her thigh. "I'm aware of the company's financial problems."

"And will you be assisting in that effort?" Henry responded. "Or is this all a ploy to get back at me? Do you even love my daughter? Because I'm finding it very hard to believe, after all these years, you're willing to let bygones be bygones."

Fallon could tell Gage was seething with rage. He slowly stood. "The time for me justifying myself to you, Mr. Stewart, is long since over. I suspect it's you who should be thanking me for even considering jumping onto this sinking ship." He buttoned his suit jacket. "Fallon?" He glanced down at her. She had no choice but to stand, as well. "If you'll excuse us."

"Wait just a second, Campbell." Her father jumped up. "I'd like to talk to my daughter *alone*."

"So you can talk her out of marrying me?" Gage asked with eagle-eyed precision. "I don't think so. Fallon is coming home with me."

Fallon looked at her father and then back at her fiancé. She could feel the hostility emanating from both men and realized she was caught in the middle *again*. If she went with her father, he would surely ask questions she wouldn't want to provide him the answers to. She had to go with Gage because she needed to lay a few ground rules on how this engagement and marriage were going to work. Gage couldn't have everything his own way. He would have to give.

She nodded her acceptance and Gage placed his hand at the small of her back and ushered her out of the room.

Seven

Gage fumed as he and Fallon strode toward the front door and he didn't say a word as he walked her to his car. He'd known facing the Stewarts after all this time wouldn't be easy. He'd hoped to get some satisfaction at seeing the shocked expression on their faces, but he hadn't expected the rage that had grown deep in his gut with each passing moment. Perhaps he shouldn't have been hotheaded and waited for Fallon. He'd been on edge because his mother had called him earlier and tried to talk him out of the marriage. He'd had to do something big so *he* wouldn't change his mind.

Once they made it to his Bugatti, Gage opened the door for Fallon and she glared at him. "Is this really necessary? I can go home. I'm right here."

"Yes, it is. Get in."

Fallon must have thought better of arguing with him and slid inside the vehicle. He closed the door behind her, came around to the driver's side and started the car. He didn't need to look at his passenger to know she was angry with him.

Once they pulled away from the estate, she turned to him. "There was no reason for you to behave like a caveman back there. My father gets we're together. He didn't need to know you were taking me back to your place."

"I had cause."

"You rose to the bait," Fallon said.

It galled Gage that she was right. He should have acted as if he couldn't care less about their disdain, but instead he'd shown his hand. "Your father needs to know I won't be pushed around, not again."

"Well, neither will I, Gage," Fallon replied, folding her arms across her chest. "I agreed to your terms, but I don't take orders from you or anyone. You got that?"

Gage glanced at her sideways. Fallon had guts and he liked that about her. Not to mention those luscious, ripe lips of hers. He felt himself getting hard.

"The light changed," Fallon commented.

Gage glanced up; indeed it had. He slid the car forward. "I'm sorry if I was a bit *heavy-handed*."

Fallon eyed him narrowly. "An apology? Wow! I'm surprised you could manage it."

"I can admit when I'm wrong." He heard her mumble something underneath her breath. "What was that?"

"Oh, nothing," she said. "Since we're going to your place, I hope it's your intention to feed me because I'm starved. I was looking forward to a meal and a hot bath."

Envisioning Fallon naked underneath a sea of bubbles was quite the erotic fantasy. "Both of those can be arranged."

"I'll take the meal now. Bath time will be later at my cottage alone."

"Damn." He snapped his fingers. "I was hoping you might want some company."

"Not a chance, Campbell. If you recall, our agreement was to wait until after the wedding."

"C'mon, don't tell me you're not tempted. I give great back rubs."

"I bet you do. Now, drive please."

"With pleasure," he replied.

When they made it to the penthouse, he started for the kitchen. He tossed the jacket he'd been wearing aside and rolled up his sleeves to rustle up some steaks and a salad for dinner. He noticed how Fallon made herself comfortable in his home and he liked it. She busied herself, taking off her jacket, kicking off her heels and following him into the kitchen. He watched her pull two wineglasses from the cupboard and a corkscrew from a drawer. Then she went over to the wine rack nestled in the living room corner and pulled out a bottle of his favorite red wine. Clearly she was as on edge as he was as she quickly set about opening the bottle. He stopped her.

Taking the corkscrew from her hands, he uncorked the bottle and poured them both a glass. Fallon moved over to the sofa and drank in silence while he prepared dinner.

"I'm sorry about my parents," Fallon said after some time had passed.

"Why are you apologizing for them?" Gage asked as he placed the steaks in the microwave to thaw and turned on the broiler.

"Because…"

"Just stop, Fallon." She had no idea what it was like to escape the dead-end world he'd grown up in. To claw his way out, inch by painful inch, to make something of himself. To achieve the heights he hadn't thought he could. And to have her parents look down on him angered Gage. Henry didn't think he was good enough for Fallon. Nora was a different story; as long as Gage kept their bank account flush, she was content to pawn her daughter off. It disgusted him. But Gage reminded himself of his end goal. Bed Fallon. Take away Henry's most prized possessions—his daughter and his business—and leave him with nothing.

He gathered the fixings for a salad from the refrigerator and began cutting up the vegetables.

"You sound as if you're angry at me," she said softly, turning to face him from the sofa. "It was your decision to go off half-cocked. I would have told my parents on my own. In *my own time.*"

"And when might that have been? On our wedding day?" he asked, taking the steaks from the microwave and liberally seasoning them.

She shot him a penetrating glare. "No, but you jumped the gun and now you're mad because you didn't like their reaction. Well, tough! You didn't give me time to set the stage. You went in guns blazing. If you'd given me time for a little diplomacy, I could have smoothed the waters."

"There's no time for diplomacy, Fallon," Gage said, placing the prepared salad in the fridge until the steaks were done. "They were never going to approve of you marrying me. What's done is done. They know. We set a wedding date." He placed the steaks in the broiler.

"Christ! Can you let me catch my breath?" Fallon implored.

No! he wanted to scream. If too much time passed, she could change her mind or his mother would change his. It was imperative the train left the station. He'd already contacted his attorney last night and told him to prepare the paperwork.

"I'm sorry if I'm being pushy here," Gage said, finally answering Fallon's question, "but I see no reason to delay the inevitable. I would think you would welcome a swift engagement and wedding to secure Stewart Technologies."

Fallon flushed. "Of course I want that. I just…" Her voice trailed off and she took a sip of wine.

"Just what?"

"Nothing." She reached for her purse on the cocktail table and pulled out her cell phone. "What date were you thinking of?"

"October first sounds great. A fall wedding would be brilliant."

"That's a month away!"

"I know, but your mother can help," he responded. Nora Stewart loved spending money. Although he wanted a big splashy wedding, he would have to keep Nora on a short leash because she was a notorious spendthrift. Did it really matter anyway? In the end, he'd have his way. Fallon in his bed.

"You still seem worried about the wedding," Gage said a few minutes later when they were seated for dinner.

"I have a lot on my plate right now." Fallon glanced down at the steak and spinach salad with a balsamic vinaigrette Gage had prepared. "No pun intended."

They both laughed. "How'd you learn how to cook anyway?" she inquired. She wasn't much of a cook herself and was surprised at Gage's talent. She told him so as she cut into her perfectly cooked steak.

"From my mom," Gage replied. "She didn't always have time to cook for me if she was at the main house. Some nights I had to fend for myself."

Fallon was quiet. She'd never thought about what happened to Gage when Grace was cooking all their meals. "I'm sorry, Gage."

"For what?"

Tears welled in her eyes and she said, "For everything. For how I treated you back then. For not thinking about you when your mother was at the house catering to mine, to me and Dane. I—I guess I didn't care about anyone else but myself back then. And I'm sorry."

Gage stared back at her, his expression unreadable, but Fallon wasn't stopping. She owed him this and it was long overdue. "I'm sorry I lied about you to my father and accused you of seducing me when we both know it was untrue. I was afraid. I didn't know what my father would do after he caught us. I didn't want to disappoint him and the way he was looking at me frightened me. I was afraid of losing his love."

"I doubt one mistake would have cost you his affection."

Fallon lowered her head. "Maybe. Maybe not. I'm trying to give an explanation for why I did what I did."

Gage stopped eating and watched her warily. "I'm listening."

"All my life I tried to be the son he never had because he and my brother were like oil and water from the day Dane was born. I knew Daddy wanted a son to follow in his footsteps, so I tried to be that person. Then one day I learned Dane wasn't Daddy's only son. He had an older son, Ayden, from his first wife, Lillian."

"I heard rumors Henry had another son. The papers alluded to it when they were covering Ayden Stewart of Stewart Investments, but he would never confirm it."

"Because Ayden hates our father. Wants nothing to do with him. Blames him for the awful childhood he had growing up."

"And you?"

"He knew of me, but I was the one who made contact with Ayden when I was eighteen. I was in college and away from my parents and wanted a relationship with the big brother I never knew existed."

"What happened?"

"Ayden wasn't interested in being a family and I accepted that. But things have changed. He's ready to put the past behind us and be siblings." Fallon didn't share that initially she'd gone to Ayden for help but upon further thought had realized she wasn't being fair to him. She couldn't ask Ayden to save a company he'd been cut out of. She'd agreed to Gage's marriage proposal and that's all that mattered.

"Then I'm glad for you," Gage replied. "I wish I had siblings growing up when I lived on the estate. It would have made it a lot easier to deal with the bullies. We could have double-teamed them. Instead it was just me. But eventually I grew up. Got taller. Stronger. And no one dared to approach me."

"Until the day a sixteen-year-old stole into your cottage and ruined your whole life," Fallon responded.

Gage glanced at her. "Fallon, I thought we agreed to let this go."

Like her father, Fallon had her doubts. She didn't want to be played. "So you've said, but I just poured out my guts to you and yet you haven't said whether you accept my apology."

"I accept. There, are you happy?"

"Only if you mean it. If you truly mean it."

"I can accept, but it doesn't mean I've forgotten. Is that fair enough for you?" Gage inquired.

Fallon nodded because she suspected she wasn't getting any more blood out of that stone. "All right. Now, about this wedding. You realize you told my *mother* you want something lavish."

Gage pursed his lips. "True. I'll meet with my accountant and we'll give her a substantial budget for the wedding. But in general you need to get her spending under control or you'll never stabilize the company."

They continued talking finances until they retired to the living room and killed off a second bottle of wine. At some point Gage swung her legs into his lap. He closed his hands around her heels and began massaging her feet. His long fingers slid from her heels to her toes as he encompassed them in firm, sure caresses. Fallon allowed herself to relax and rest her head back against the sofa. The slide of his hands against her skin felt so unbelievably good. Warm, gentle…and erotic.

"Mmm…that feels good," Fallon moaned as Gage used his thumb and fingers to hit the pressure points.

"My pleasure," Gage murmured. "Can you make that noise again?"

Fallon popped an eye open and caught his sly grin.

"C'mon, you must recognize how sexual that moan was," he said. "And I'm a man, after all." He pressed his fingers against the soles of her feet and Fallon's body arched off the sofa. "A man who's attracted to you."

Fallon straightened and wondered frantically how she'd got herself into this. When she looked up, she found him watching her intently. Desire had been awakened in the dark depths of his eyes; they glittered in a way that unnerved yet excited her, speeding up her pulse. She moved to turn away, but Gage wouldn't let her up. Instead he leaned forward. Her hands pressed into the silk of his shirt. She felt the solid wall of his chest and the rapid thump of his heartbeat.

She tried to push him away but somehow her fingers had a mind of their own and instead slid along his arms, molding his incredibly muscled biceps. Sensation coursed through her and she was transfixed as he lowered his head and kissed her with a thorough slide of his lips against hers. They traded kiss for kiss and Fallon clasped his face in her hands and angled her head for deeper contact. Gage plundered every inch of her mouth and she gave him full access.

How was it they always managed to end up here? Like this?

From her sensual fog, reason emerged. Then caution. If she allowed herself, she'd get caught up in the fervor because when they were together like this, Fallon was certain Gage had forgiven her and the past was long behind him.

But she was afraid to allow herself to believe it. As he'd said, he'd accepted her apology but hadn't forgotten what happened. It would always be between them.

Fallon pressed her hands against his chest and Gage stilled. He must have sensed her pulling back since he stopped and was already on his feet. She saw him rub his head in frustration.

"I think it's best if I leave." Fallon reached for her purse behind her on the console and stood. "We should refrain from spending too much time alone together until the wedding. I'm going to call an Uber."

"Fallon, you don't have to do that. I can drive you home."

She held up her hand. "Please, let me have some time alone, okay?"

"All right, all right. We'll talk soon?"

"Of course." Fallon knew Gage would make sure of that. He'd staked his claim not only on her but on her body. And if she didn't get some distance between them there was no way they would remain celibate until after the wedding.

Eight

"Care to tell me why you're marrying the housekeeper's son? A man who nearly assaulted you years ago?" Henry Stewart stood at Fallon's office door the next morning wearing a dark gray suit and a scowl.

"Daddy, what are you doing here?"

"I'm here to find out what the hell is going on." Her father closed the door and headed straight to her plush sofa.

Fallon released a deep sigh. She'd known this day was coming, but it was here. To move forward, she had to tell the truth about what really happened when she was sixteen.

"You have it all wrong, Daddy." Fallon came from behind her desk.

"What do I have wrong, pumpkin?" He patted the seat next to him.

Fallon sat beside him and looked into his hazel-gray eyes. "When I told you Gage came on to me, I lied. It was the other way around. I came on to him and *he* pushed me away."

"What?" Her father's eyes grew large with concern. "Why on earth would you do such a thing? Grace Campbell was good people and I threw her and Gage out on the street."

Fallon bowed her head and smoothed the pale pink dress she wore. "I know. And I've never forgiven myself for the pain I inflicted on their family. But in that moment I panicked."

"I see. And is this marriage some sort of penance? Because you feel like you owe him? Well, guess what? You can't make up for the past, sweetheart."

"It's not like that." She shook her head. "Gage and I... well, like he told you before, we've reconnected."

"If that's code for you slept together, I don't want to know." Her father bolted to his feet. Then he spun back around quickly. "But if you did, why marry? Although Gage may not be the scoundrel I thought he was, he still has to harbor resentment. There has to be more to the story because this is all too sudden."

Fallon wasn't going to explain the conditions under which she'd agreed to marry Gage. She'd already done enough to disillusion her father for one day. "There is no catch, Daddy. Gage and I are getting married and you'll have to accept it."

"I have to do no such thing. Gage Campbell isn't good enough for you, Fallon. I hope you see that before it's too late."

Gage hadn't seen Fallon in a week. He was anxious. The prenup was ready—his lawyers had couriered it over just this morning—and he wanted her to sign it before she changed her mind.

Although he'd agreed to her request for some space, it had been much harder to honor than he'd anticipated. Far too hard. Business was no longer paramount in his mind even though his attorney told him they were close to acquiring a big round of Stewart Technologies' stock through several different obscure holding companies. It would take someone months to discover that he owned all of them. It should make him feel good that he was achieving his goal to squash the Stewarts, but it didn't. His mother was disappointed he would even consider "marrying the enemy," as she put it. He'd tried to explain that he had a plan, but she would hear none of it.

Today, however, he and Fallon would cement their relationship by meeting for lunch at Capitol City, Austin's most exclusive country club. It was a blatant statement they were together and would certainly start the rumor mills churning. For privacy, he'd reserved the entire terrace for just the two of them. He glanced down at the manila envelope that held the paperwork formalizing the agreement between them. It was all in black-and-white. It laid out the monetary gift that would help her keep Stewart Technologies, some of the terms of their marriage, and the fact they'd each keep their individual assets in the event they divorced. Now all Fallon needed to do was sign.

He glanced at the entrance to the terrace. Fallon walked in wearing a simple navy sheath with a deep V, and desire flared hot in his belly. She smiled at him when she approached and he couldn't stop himself from grinning. She had a tantalizing figure with her long, shapely legs and pert breasts. His pulse quickened. He couldn't wait to find out firsthand how she would come apart when he had her underneath him.

Gage rose and schooled his features as he prepared to finally make Fallon his.

Fallon paused by the terrace doorway. The last week away from him had been good for her equilibrium. She'd been able to get her rampant lust for the man under control by explaining it away. Gage was a skilled lover. He knew how to seduce women and, given her limited dating experience, she'd been pulled into his web.

She wished her explanation to her father had gone equally as well. It hadn't. When she'd finally spoken with him after the night of their announcement, he'd been less than pleased, but Fallon had stood her ground. She'd even gone further and told him she was putting him and her mother on a budget. Stewart Technologies would no longer fund their lifestyle and their expense account would be shut down.

Her father had been furious and told her she had no right to do such a thing, but as CEO she had every right. Although he was chairman of the board and still had shares, Fallon wasn't going to kowtow to him anymore. She had the board on her side. Henry hadn't been pleased, claiming Gage was asserting undue influence over her, which was ludicrous. Fallon was finally doing what she should have done years ago when she'd been appointed CEO and realized the dire situation the company was in.

Meanwhile her mother was in serious spending mode. She'd already recruited Austin's top wedding planner to organize their hasty nuptials. She wanted to sit down with Fallon and go over color swatches, flower selections and cake choices, but Fallon wasn't interested. She'd told her mother whatever she selected was fine. Knowing her mother, it would not only be flashy, but lavish enough to appeal to Gage and ensure he got his money's worth because he wanted everyone in Austin to know he'd landed the golden goose. Her.

When she arrived at the table, Gage helped her into her seat. "Thank you. You're looking well," she commented when he sat across from her.

"And you're looking good enough to eat," he responded, placing his napkin in his lap.

Fallon noticed the amused expression on his face and realized how formal she'd been. Then she noticed the envelope on the table. "I take it that's the prenup."

"Yes."

"Hand it over." She held out her palm.

"In time. Let's have a drink." A waiter came forward and, after taking his wine order, departed. "We need to milk this." He inclined his head toward the window of the club dining room where several sets of eyes were watching them from inside.

She plastered a smile on her face. "Of course. I know how important appearances are."

His eyes narrowed. "Yes, they are. If you recall, that's one of the benefits of marriage *for me*."

She'd offended him, but it was too late to take it back now. "I'm well aware of the *mutual* benefits of this marriage. You don't have to remind me."

"Good."

The waiter returned with the wine and poured them each a glass. They both ordered the seafood entrée and the waiter left, giving them the privacy Gage craved.

Fallon didn't wait for a toast. She quickly took a long sip of her wine. She noticed Gage staring at her. "What?"

"Are you nervous?"

"Why would I be?" she asked tartly. "I'm just agreeing to bind myself to you, a man I hardly know, for the next six months."

"You didn't mind being with me last week." He drank some of his wine.

"How gentlemanly of you to remind me," Fallon answered. "We may not have a problem in that department, but I would have preferred it if we could have kept this strictly business."

"I'm sure you would," Gage responded, "but it's because of our *personal* connection the opportunity to save your company is even possible." He slid the envelope toward her. "You'll find everything is in order as per the changes requested by your attorney."

"You've already signed," Fallon commented as she flipped through the pages.

"I know what I want." The smoldering flame she saw in his eyes shouldn't have startled her, but it did. Fallon swallowed the frog in her throat.

"It appears in order. I should have my attorney review it one more time."

"That's a stalling tactic. Sign it, Fallon."

Her eyes flashed fire. "Don't bully me, Gage."

"We made the changes he requested, you can see for yourself. I want this settled between us." Gage sipped his wine again, watching her over the rim of his glass. "As you know, I don't have the full amount you need sitting in a bank account. I need time to make it happen. The sooner I get started, the better."

"You make it sound so easy. It's not." If she did this, there was no turning back. She would become Mrs. Gage Campbell and all that entailed, in and out of his bed. It was overwhelming. She sucked in a deep breath.

As if sensing her unease, Gage went in for the kill.

"If you don't sign, it's only a matter of time before you go belly-up. Think about all those lost jobs. It's a win-win for both of us, Fallon. Sign the document." Gage pulled a pen from the inside pocket of his suit jacket and handed it to her.

Fallon looked down at the pen in her hand for several beats. He was right. The sooner they got this over with, the better. Lives depended on her decision. She had to get the company back on its feet as soon as possible and Gage wouldn't turn over the money until Fallon walked down the aisle. Then, and only then, would Stewart Technologies be in the black.

Fallon scribbled her signature on several pages, slid the document into the envelope and handed it back to him.

"I imagine you should feel relieved," Gage commented.

"Not in the slightest." Her feelings for Gage were intensifying and now she'd agreed to marry him, to share his bed for six months. She feared for her heart because she could easily fall for him as she had in the past. And would he want her if she did? Gage had agreed to a temporary marriage of convenience. For him, they would be completing their unfinished history because, really, that's what this was. Somehow she would have to maintain her dignity.

"Be relieved," Gage suggested. "We're a team now. No matter how crazy life gets, you'll have me to rely on at least for the next six months."

"You make it sound so easy."

"There's no time for doubt or second-guessing, Fallon. It's done. Don't tell me you're not up for the challenge?"

"Of course I am," Fallon retorted.

Gage surprised her by reaching across the table, threading his fingers through hers and placing a kiss on them. "I promise you. We've got this."

Gage was on his way to the Stewart Technologies' barbecue the next Saturday to make an appearance as Fallon's fiancé. He was in the clear to attend because Henry had long since retired from coming to company functions, allowing Fallon to spearhead them. Now that the paperwork was signed, Gage felt like he was back in the driver's seat because he understood what was at stake. He doubted Fallon did.

She'd taken a calculated risk in accepting his offer without really understanding his motivations. His hatred of her family went deep. Deep enough he would do anything for revenge, including marrying the woman who'd started it all while secretly buying up shares of her company. Her apology for her actions had come a little too late in his opinion. For years all he could see was red and now he had the Stewart family right where he wanted them. Dependent on him.

My oh my, how the tables have turned, Gage thought as he pulled his Bugatti into a parking space at Mayfield Park. Stewart Technologies had rented the park for the company event, which would include food, games and prizes. He wore his favorite pair of faded designer jeans, a T-shirt and sneakers since they were experiencing a sort of Indian summer.

From the large cloud of smoke coming from several enormous grills and smokers, Gage could see the barbecue was already underway. There were large arrays of delicious fixings—including beans, macaroni and cheese, greens, potato salad and coleslaw—covering the large rectangular tables. At least two hundred people were milling around and getting involved in various activities. Men were on the football field while women played cards at a picnic table. Children tossed Frisbees or horseshoes. Quite an event to pull off for such a large group of people.

Gage was impressed by Fallon's managerial skills and her generosity, because Fallon was sponsoring the event from her personal finances. He found the lady of the hour passing out lemonade. It made his mouth water—not the delectable drink, but the outfit Fallon was wearing. She had on a crossover halter top showing off her sleek shoulders and buff arms while her cut-off jeans hugged her behind. Gage wanted to growl in protest because every man here could see what would soon be his.

Fallon turned around at that moment and saw him. She wiped perspiration off her brow. "Can you believe how warm it is today?" she said, smiling. "Would you like some lemonade?"

"I'd love some." He needed something to quench the desire that overtook him at seeing her half naked. She handed him a cup and he damn near guzzled the entire thing.

"Easy," she said, laughing. "You'll want to stay hydrated. Hey, Laura," she yelled to a woman standing nearby, "can you take over for me for a while?"

"Sure thing, boss."

Once Fallon came out from behind the table, he wasted no time circling her with his arm and giving her an open-mouthed kiss right in front of the entire table. When she pulled away she said, "What was that?"

"A proper hello."

She grinned and he allowed her some distance. "So, what do you think?" She motioned around the park. "Pretty awesome, huh?"

"You really know how to put on an event."

"Walk with me a minute." She surprised him by shoving her arm through his and leading him away from the group. Was it for his sake or their audience's? Because several people had watched their kiss. "I know you probably think we don't have the money for this, but morale has been at an all-time low. The employees heard rumors. They think we're going to fold. I want them to know we care."

"You mean *you* care," Gage corrected.

She gave him a sideward glance. "Yes, I do. Some of these people have been with us for years and have been loyal. I can't allow them to lose their livelihood."

"That's admirable."

Fallon snorted. "I know you think because of how I was raised I don't have a grasp on the plight of the everyday man, but I do, Gage."

She was right. He didn't think she understood, at least not entirely, but she was trying. "I can see that."

"Hey, you two lovebirds," a man wearing a T-shirt with

the company logo interrupted. "Would you like to join in? We have a friendly game of tug-of-war going."

Gage turned to Fallon. "You game?"

"Hell, yeah!"

And that's how they spent the afternoon, joined at the hip playing tug-of-war, hunting for treasure and tossing water balloons. The balloons were by far Gage's favorite activity of the day. He hadn't intended it to happen, but when he'd tossed Fallon a balloon, she hadn't caught it. Instead it exploded on her top and revealed her small round breasts to anyone with eyes. He'd immediately grabbed her by the arm and led her to a nearby tent being used as a diaper changing station for small children.

"What's wrong?" Fallon asked when she saw his thunderous expression.

He glanced down at her chest and she followed his eyes to see her nipples protruding through the thin material of her tank top. "Oh!" she exclaimed.

"Yes 'oh,'" he hissed. "Do you have a change of clothes? I can't have you out there looking like that."

She jutted her chin forward and with a smirk asked, "And why not?"

"Those are your employees out there." He pointed behind him. "I don't want the men ogling you."

"You mean, ogling what's yours?"

His eyes narrowed. "That's right, what's mine. Those—" he glanced down at her breasts "—are for my eyes only."

Color washed over her face and neck and Gage could see he'd gotten his point across. "If you were trying to seduce me, you win because," he said, taking a step toward her, "I'm willing to renegotiate our agreement to wait until we're married."

She bit her lip nervously and Gage caught the action. He wanted to soothe her lip with his tongue. But just then she reached inside her pocket and thrust her car keys at him. "I have a bag in the trunk with a change of clothes. Do you mind?"

He shook his head, eager to be out of the fog of desire he was in. "I'll be right back."

Fallon was contemplative after he'd gone. The naked hunger in Gage's eyes frightened her in its intensity because it mirrored her own. They were like two cats in heat, constantly circling one another. They couldn't be alone together. It wasn't a good idea.

Yet she'd enjoyed their day more than she thought she would. Gage was charming and engaging with all her employees. And there was more than one woman who'd given her an envious look throughout the course of the day. Fallon knew how lucky she was. Her eyes had drunk him in when he'd casually strolled to the lemonade stand earlier today. Tall. Good-looking. He looked sexy in his jeans and a T-shirt, with all that leashed testosterone. Fallon had to stop herself from drooling over him.

The games had been a welcome diversion from her riotous emotions and she'd been able to keep her feelings for Gage under wraps. But just now, when his intense dark eyes had landed on her breasts, she'd wanted to rip the damn tank off and beg him to take them in his mouth. That's how much she ached for his touch, for his mouth. Her body still remembered how he'd made her hum in the back seat of the limo.

Heavens. She needed to get a grip. He would be back any moment. He mustn't know the lustful thoughts going through her mind.

Gage returned several minutes later with her bag in tow. "Here you are."

"Thanks." She accepted the bag and rummaged through it, finding the extra tank she'd tossed in. She wanted to put it on, but Gage was staring at her. Awareness was burning in his eyes. "Do you mind turning around so I can put this on?"

"I've already seen it all before," he said, smiling.

"But you still have two more weeks to let the memory sustain you."

His eyes flashed but he spun on his heel, allowing her time to whip the tank over her head. "Damn the two weeks. If you would stop this madness, you and I could do what comes naturally instead of remaining in this constant state of arousal you have me in."

As Fallon adjusted her shirt, Gage's words sank in and she paused. *He was in a constant state of arousal?* It was news to her and she wondered if he'd meant to be so open with his *condition*.

Gage turned around then and caught Fallon in a half state of undress. His gaze met hers and held. Understanding passed between them, as loud and clear as church bells on a Sunday morning. Gage prowled toward her and Fallon sank into his arms. He ran his hands down her body, touching her in all the places she'd been thinking about, dreaming about. He adjusted his stance and shifted her until she was between his thighs and could feel the swell of his arousal at her core. Then he finally gave her what she wanted: his lips on hers.

Their mouths connected. They were hungrily kissing—deeper, harder and longer. Her arms clung tightly around his neck as she held his head in place, their lips meeting in a passion so strong it obliterated everything else. The world ceased to exist and their tongues tangoed and dueled for supremacy. They were both so caught up in the moment they didn't notice they had company until a very loud cough came from behind them.

Startled, they pulled apart and Gage stepped in front of her. It was one of her employees holding a baby in her arms. "I—I'm sorry. I didn't mean to interrupt. I needed to use the tent."

"Of course." Gage spoke up first. "Give us a moment, would you?"

The mother nodded and quickly hurried out.

"That was a close call," Gage said.

"Yeah." Fallon lowered her lashes. "We should go." She started for the exit but Gage stopped her.

"When we're finally together with no interruptions, it's going to be amazing."

And that's what Fallon was afraid of. Because she was starting to fall for Gage Campbell.

Nine

"When are you finally going to get excited about this wedding?" Nora Stewart asked her daughter as the limousine drove them to the bridal gown shop. "You do realize it's only a couple of weeks away? I can't believe you've pushed back getting a dress this long. You're going to have very little time for alterations. Thank God Gage said money was no object because it's going to cost a fortune to turn it around this fast."

"I know, Mother," Fallon said, clenching her teeth. The woman had been on a tirade since the moment they'd gotten in the vehicle, talking about flowers and centerpieces and the like. Fallon didn't care. It didn't mean anything because she wasn't marrying for love. This was an expedient marriage, a marriage of convenience. It wasn't some grand love story.

"Then act like it," her mother responded. "When we go into the bridal shop, you'd better act like the giddy bride. I won't have you embarrassing me with your somber mood."

"Duly noted." Fallon stared out the window. Heaven forbid she embarrass her mother in front of Austin's society ladies. She knew that's why Nora had chosen this particular store. It's where *everyone* went when they wanted a one-of-a-kind, jaw-dropping dress. And she was sure Nora wanted the same for her daughter.

When they arrived, they were immediately greeted by a sophisticated saleswoman. The blonde looked every bit the fashionista in a crepe sheath and Manolo Blahniks. She ushered them to a private area complete with a three-way mirror, pedestal and plush sofa. A bottle of Dom Pérignon was already chilling in a bucket nearby.

As her maid of honor, Shana was already waiting for them on the sofa. "Hey, cuz." She rushed over to give Fallon a hug and then glanced at Nora. "Auntie." Shana's new look consisted of kinky twists that hit her shoulders, a cold-shoulder top and ripped jeans. Fallon was sure her mother was horrified at her niece's appearance.

"Shana." Her mother was not a fan of Fallon's opinionated cousin and had no qualms about showing it. She left them to speak with the staff, allowing Shana to pull Fallon in for a private word.

"How are you doing, cuz?"

"I'm fine."

Shana stared at her. "Are you sure? You're marrying a man you hardly know. And you've allowed your mother to hijack the whole wedding like it's her own."

"It's fine," Fallon replied. "I told Nora she could plan to her heart's content."

"Because the wedding means nothing to you?" Shana asked. "It might not in theory, but it is legal and binding."

"I'm aware of that, Shana."

"I don't know if you are." Shana shook her head. "I think you're in way over your head on this one, Fallon. When I mentioned Gage to you, I thought you'd get a loan from him. Not go off and marry him."

Fallon shrugged. "What can I say? I like to live dangerously."

"Yeah, you must. Because Gage Campbell is dangerous to your well-being."

Fallon sighed. "You realize you sound ridiculous, Shana. Gage would never hurt me."

Shana folded her arms across her chest. "Maybe not physically, but he could emotionally. I know the huge crush you carried for this dude. Remember, I listened to you wax poetic about this man for years. And you're not like me, moving from man to man. Once you guys have sex, it's going to be a game changer."

"I may not have your vast experience, but I am capable of guarding my heart."

"You'd better be."

The saleswoman came over and interrupted their conversation. "Are you ready to find the dress of your dreams?"

Fallon feigned a smile. "Absolutely."

An hour later Fallon stood on the pedestal staring at herself in the three-way mirror. The wedding dress was everything she never thought she wanted. A shimmering tulle bodice accented in intricate beaded patterns trailed into a voluminous glitter tulle ball gown. Then there were the beaded spaghetti straps gliding from the sweetheart neckline to a sexy V-back with its crystal buttons.

The salesperson added another touch—illusion open-shoulder sleeves accented in beaded lace motifs—and the look was complete. Fallon was a princess.

"She's stunning," her mother cried from the sofa. "This is the one."

Nora had had Fallon try on nearly a dozen dresses before the beleaguered saleswoman had brought out this confection. Nora was right. This was *the one*.

"For once, I'm going to have to agree with Auntie," Shana said. "You've found your dress, Fallon. You look beautiful."

Fallon smiled genuinely for the first time all day. The wedding hadn't seemed real until this very moment. Until she was standing in this fairy-tale gown.

"Are you saying yes to the dress?" the saleswoman asked.

Tears sprung to her eyes and all Fallon could do was nod. She was just so overwhelmed and remained that way during the ride home as she tuned out her mother's non-stop chatter about how the dress would look lovely with the flowers she'd chosen. She was getting married. To Gage. Suddenly, Fallon wanted out of the limo as quickly as humanly possible. She was thankful when her mother exited after a quick kiss on her cheek.

Once she made it to her cottage, she went to her bedroom and fell across the bed. It was happening. She was going to be a wife. Gage's wife. His *lover*.

The implications were finally hitting home when her cell rang. It was Gage, as if he had ESP.

"Hello?" she answered.

"Hey, how'd it go today? Did you find a dress?"

"Yes."

He chuckled. "Are you not going to give me any more than that? No hint? Nothing?"

"I'm sorry. You're going to have to wait until the wedding day."

"Thank God that's only two weeks away. This is the longest month of my life. All the anticipation is driving me crazy."

Fallon sat upright. "Really?"

"Isn't it for you? Aren't you tired of waiting? Don't you want to know if we'll live up to the hype?"

"From what I've experienced thus far, I imagine you're

a very good lover," Fallon responded, priding herself on keeping her cool as they discussed their soon-to-be sex life with such casualness.

"I wasn't looking for a compliment," Gage murmured.

"Of course not." Fallon was sure he was very confident in his sexual prowess.

"But I would be lying if I said I wasn't looking forward to the day when you're my wife in every sense of the word."

When they ended the call, Fallon realized she was thinking the exact same thing.

The day of their wedding came much quicker than Fallon would have liked. It seemed as if she'd been trying on dresses with her mother and Shana only yesterday. But the day was finally here and she was a nervous wreck.

She woke up that morning in the Fairmont—where the wedding was being held—with a knot in the pit of her stomach. *Was she doing the right thing?* Logically, she knew that she'd done what she'd had to. Stewart Technologies and its employees depended on her making the right decision. Yet intuitively she knew today would change everything.

"Good morning." Her mother flitted into the room with a tray. "I've come bearing gifts." She approached Fallon and put the tray on the bed. "I have some tea and toast for you. Don't want you to bloat. And some cucumber slices for your eyes." She glanced at Fallon. "You did get some rest last night?"

Fallon nodded but she was lying. It had been hard to sleep. She'd been on pins and needles during the rehearsal dinner, afraid of some sort of outburst. How could she not be? Gage's mother had had to face her parents, the people who'd fired her and run her off the estate. Grace couldn't be happy her son was marrying the daughter of the man she surely despised. It was awkward to say the least.

Nonetheless, Nora acted as if it was water under the bridge and carried on as lady of the manor as she always did on such occasions. And if Fallon had wanted to confide in her cousin, that had been impossible because Shana had kept a steady drink in her hand all night while flirting with Theo, Gage's best man.

As for her fiancé, Gage had been surprisingly stalwart all evening. He'd kept his hands to himself the entire night and only showed signs of affection when he thought someone was watching. He wasn't his usual amorous self and it didn't help her mood. When the night finally ended, Gage had walked her to her suite and placed a quick peck on her forehead before leaving.

Was he regretting asking her to marry him?

Was that why she was having second thoughts this morning?

Fallon attempted to eat the toast, but it tasted dry in her mouth so she sipped on some tea while she slipped into her robe. One of Austin's top hair stylists and makeup artists would be here within the hour to begin working on Shana's, Nora's and Fallon's makeup for the big day. She wouldn't have much time to herself after that.

A knock sounded on the door and Shana walked in wearing sunglasses. "Rough morning?" Fallon asked.

"Yeah, you could say that," Shana murmured, snatching off her glasses. "How are you doing?"

"I'm fine." Fallon turned her back so her cousin couldn't read her true emotions. She busied herself with pulling out the new lingerie she'd purchased for the day. She was sure Gage would appreciate the silky, lacy pieces of fabric when he unbuttoned her.

"Fallon, are you sure?" Shana asked, touching her shoulder. "You don't have to do this. There's still time to change your mind."

"It's normal to have second thoughts," her mother interjected, apparently having overheard their conversation. "I had them when I married your father, but ultimately I knew I was making the right decision. And you are, too, Fallon. You're going to have an amazing life. With a husband as successful as Gage, anything you want will be at your fingertips."

"I thought you didn't like him," Fallon responded evenly.

Her mother chuckled. "I admit he isn't the man I would have chosen for you. But surprisingly he's done quite well for himself, so I have no reservations. Though I doubt Grace agrees. Did you see the evil eye she gave me last night? It was positively wretched."

Of course Nora would take Fallon's wedding day anxiety and make it about her. "Thank you, Mother. Now, if you'll excuse me, I'm going to shower before the dream team arrives."

Fallon quickly rushed off before Shana could say more. Too many thoughts were whirling through her head and she needed some breathing room.

"Are you sure you want to marry her, son?" Grace Campbell asked as she fixed Gage's tie and straightened the lapels of his custom-made tuxedo.

He was surprised she'd come. He thought she'd boycott the ceremony altogether, but she was here supporting him, so he tried to be gentle in his response. "We've already discussed this, Mother. I have my reasons." *Did she notice he hadn't said love?*

She eyed him warily. "I don't know, Gage. I feel like you're not being truthful with me and there's more to this story. I mean, you tell me you're getting married to the woman who caused us so much misery?"

"She was sixteen when it happened, Mama."

"True, but old enough to know right from wrong, Gage.

And she willfully lied about you and cost me my job. Have you honestly forgotten how hard it was for us back then?"

"Of course not."

"Then how can you do this?" She folded her arms across her chest, waiting for his answer.

"Trust me, okay, Mama?" He unfolded her arms and grasped her small hands in his. They weren't as pitiful and worn with cracks and calluses as they'd once been. When he'd made his first million, he'd made sure his mother never had to work another day in her life. "I know what I'm doing."

"I hope you do. Because if this is about revenge, it won't change the past. We have to make our peace with it. And apparently I have to make mine today as I make nice with the Stewarts and watch my only son marry their daughter."

"I don't know if I will ever be at peace after how you and I were both treated, but I've put some measures in place that will settle the score between our families." Theo walked in, breaking up their mother-son moment. "A word, Gage."

Gage nodded. "Be right back, Mama." He left her in the suite and closed the door behind him because he didn't like the look on Theo's face. "What's wrong?"

"I ran into Shana in the corridor."

"And?"

"She mentioned Fallon was having second thoughts."

"Second thoughts?" Anger blazed through him. "On our wedding day? Fallon had weeks to change her mind. Does she honestly think she can humiliate me and leave me standing at the altar? Where is she?"

"Gage." Theo placed a sobering hand on his arm. "Maybe it's best if you take a minute to cool down."

Gage shrugged his hand off. "Like hell I will. I will not be made a fool of again."

"I'm told she's still in her suite."

Gage wasted no time storming toward the elevator bank.

He and Fallon were staying on separate floors to prevent him from seeing her before the ceremony. But he couldn't care less about some stupid superstition. He was acting now. He jabbed the elevator button for the top floor and waited.

His nostrils flared when he thought about Fallon backing out. He simply wouldn't have it. She *would* marry him. He would not have his plans thwarted, not when he was so close.

The elevator arrived and he jumped in. Within minutes, he was knocking on her door. Shana answered and he must have looked thunderous because she immediately backed away. "Where is she?" Gage bellowed.

Shana pointed to the bedroom.

He stalked to the master bedroom and found Fallon seated in front of the mirror with several women surrounding her. She must have heard his voice because she turned and looked behind her. Her face blanched when she saw him.

"It's not good luck for you to see the bride," one of the women objected. But he didn't see them. His focus was on Fallon.

"Leave us," he ordered.

The women glanced at Fallon and she nodded her acquiescence, so they left the room, closing the door behind them.

Damn it. She was stunning with her hair in a mass of pinned-up honey-blond curls. And her face? Well, that was a work of art. Whoever those women were, they knew how to accentuate her best features—her high cheekbones, hazel-gray eyes and pouty lips.

"Are you having second thoughts?" he asked, his eyes never leaving her face. He was afraid to move closer because he feared he'd toss her on the bed and strip her naked and make her agree to be his.

She stared at him for several beats and he wondered if

she was going to be stubborn and not answer him. "Yes," she finally replied.

"Then perhaps this will make you reconsider." He pulled out the check he was giving her to save Stewart Technologies and handed it to her.

Fallon stared down at the figure. "I—I thought you weren't giving this to me until we were married."

"I'm not. I'm showing you I've kept up my end of the bargain. In my hands I have the means to save your company from ruin. Are you honestly going to turn your back on the men and women at the barbecue who depend on you, all because you're afraid to be my wife, my lover? You told me you cared about them and their well-being."

Fire flashed in her eyes. "That's not fair. I do care."

"Then prove it. Marry me."

Fallon turned and faced the mirror. He approached to stand right behind her where he could see her reaction. Her eyes were cloudy and he couldn't read her expression. "Fallon, you have a choice. You've always had a choice. Save your company. Or not. The decision is yours."

He turned on his heel and started for the door but she called out after him. "What are you going to do?"

Gage didn't turn around. "I'm going to walk down that aisle as I expect you to." He glanced at his watch. "In an hour."

Gage left the suite. Once he was outside, he leaned against the wall. He didn't know what he was more afraid of. That Fallon wouldn't walk down the aisle. Or that she would.

Ten

"Are you okay?" Fallon heard Shana's voice from behind her. Her hands were shaking so badly she had to clasp them together. She nodded quickly and then felt her cousin's arms wrap around her shoulders. "What did he say?"

"Nothing I didn't already know." She knew what she had to do, but it didn't make it easy. To survive marrying Gage, she'd have to bury her feelings so deep he wouldn't be able to use them against her. She took a deep breath. "Will you help me get into my dress, please?" She spun around and faced Shana.

The look of pity on Shana's face was nearly her undoing but she kept it together. "Yes, I will. If that's what you want."

"I do." Fallon moved toward the elegant princess dress hanging in the closet and pulled it off the hanger. "It's time."

Fallon didn't remember much else after that. Not removing her robe. Not Shana buttoning her into the delicate beaded fabric of her dress. Not her mother bursting in with the flowers, handing Fallon her bouquet and helping put on her veil. The next thing Fallon knew, she was in the elevator with Shana, her mother and the wedding planner, who held her train.

It was only when she was walking down the corridor and saw her father standing resplendent in a formal white tuxedo that she snapped out of it. He slid his arm through hers and looked down at her. "You've never looked lovelier, baby girl. Are you ready to do this?"

She nodded. And slowly the doors to the ballroom opened and they were walking down the aisle.

Fallon saw Gage standing at the end, waiting for her. He looked sinfully handsome, just as he had earlier when he'd walked into her bedroom and taken her breath away. He hadn't needed to show her the check. Although she'd had doubts earlier, she'd gotten through them and had already planned to marry him. But seeing how upset Gage was that she might back out showed her this marriage meant something to him whether he was willing to admit it or not.

Or at least that's the lie she fed herself as she made her way up the aisle to him. When she arrived at the altar, her father placed her hand in Gage's and her breath caught in her throat. He rewarded her with a smile, which she returned.

She could do this. Would do this. Why? Because Gage meant more to her than she was willing to admit.

Gage had never been happier than when he saw Fallon walking down in the aisle in that magnificent dress. He was glad he hadn't seen her wearing it earlier and they could retain some tradition because, quite literally, she was breathtaking. He found himself having to truly listen to the minister's words to be able to repeat the traditional vows to love, protect, honor and cherish her.

He sensed Fallon was nervous because her hands were

shaking as he placed the ring on her finger and she did the same to him. But she didn't back out. She honored her commitment to him and when they were pronounced husband and wife, Gage was beyond ecstatic. He slid his arm around her petite waist and pulled her to him. Then he softly kissed her before pulling away. They'd have all the time in the world later in the presidential suite when he would finally make Fallon his.

The reception was a blur. There were handshakes and hugs from friends, acquaintances and employees who were there to celebrate their wedding. There were frowns from Fallon's parents and Ayden, who were both there on sufferance. Ayden had only stayed for the wedding and stood in the shadows while her younger brother, Dane, chose to not attend at all. He only remembered the moments when it was the two of them.

Nora had transformed the ballroom into a winter fairyland. Crystal chandeliers hung from the ceilings, illuminating an explosion of beautiful white flowers. Frosted trees, sparkling crystal garlands and candles were everywhere. Nora had decorated each table in white and silver while their sweetheart table had two thronelike chairs.

For their first dance Gage held Fallon in his arms and she felt so good, but delicate in a way he couldn't quite put his finger on. Then there was the cake cutting. Rather than use a fork, he'd used his fingers to feed Fallon a piece. She'd been shocked at first, but had opened her mouth and accepted it, wiping his fingers clean with her tongue. It had been the most singularly erotic moment of his life.

He was thankful when the night began winding down. He made quite the show of going underneath Fallon's dress to get her garter, which Theo caught while her cousin Shana caught Fallon's bouquet. Gage sure hoped there wasn't a love connection there. He doubted Theo could handle Shana; she was a whole lot of woman.

Finally the night was over and he and Fallon were able to escape the ballroom to head upstairs as they were sent off with bubbles and well-wishes. They were led to an elevator exclusively for their getaway. Gage took her hand but it was a bit cold and clammy.

"Are you all right?"

"Yes."

"You haven't given me much tonight, Fallon," Gage said. "You've been quiet. Reserved, even."

"I kept up my end of the bargain, yes?" She turned away from him and Gage didn't like it.

"About earlier—"

"You made your point," Fallon interrupted, looking straight ahead. "And I heard you, okay? The day was a bit…overwhelming."

He squeezed her hand and she finally glanced in his direction. "It was for me, as well. I'm sorry, too, if I came across a bit…" He searched for the right word. "Rough. I always seem to be that way with you. Can we agree to put it behind us?" He needed things between them to be okay, because he was so ready to start their life together *in bed*.

She gave a hesitant smile. "Yes."

The presidential suite was a honeymooner's paradise complete with chocolate-covered strawberries, a bucket of champagne chilling in the living room and a trail of red rose petals leading to the master bedroom. Dozens of candles gave the room a romantic glow. Fallon stared at the enormous bed, picked up her train and came back into the living room. She wasn't ready to face the night ahead.

Once Fallon entered the room, Gage held up the bottle. "Care for champagne?"

"I'd love some." Fallon needed liquid courage for what was ahead. She didn't know how not to show her true feelings because her heart was involved now. Her whole heart.

Somehow she'd tripped into a state of love without knowing it and she knew with certainty Gage could break her heart. Because for Gage tonight was all about desire. Sexual desire. And she felt it, too. This raw, carnal, all-consuming lust. It was why she was so out of control whenever they were together. Even now her stomach was pulled tight in knots wondering what it would be like to *be* with him.

Gage made Fallon aware of her own body and she knew before the night was over he would become familiar with every inch of it. Of that she was sure. It was in the flare of his eyes as they drifted over her. He handed her a flute of champagne. She accepted and downed the entire glass in one gulp.

"There's no need to be nervous, Fallon," Gage assured her as he sat on the couch. "We have all night. There's no rush. Come here." He patted the seat next to him.

At first Fallon didn't move a muscle but when he gave her an imploring look, she relented and sat. "This feels a little surreal."

Gage reached for her hand and turned it over. When he did, the impressive six-carat diamond ring he'd purchased caught the light. He fingered it with his thumb. "I would disagree. It feels very real."

He cupped her face in one hand. "Is it really so scary to be married to me, Fallon?" His thumb swept across her lips, making her flesh tingle.

"I'm not scared," Fallon responded. "I made a choice and I stand behind it."

Gage straightened. "I'm glad. I would hate for you to regret the time we spend together."

Fallon had her doubts about the marriage but not about the pleasure she would find in Gage's arms. Leaning forward, his lips found hers. It wasn't a tentative kiss, nor was it a kiss meant to entice. The touch of his mouth was soft, yet it shot volts of electricity right through Fallon and she wanted more. When he lowered his head again it wasn't to her closed mouth—she'd already parted her lips. She gave in to his hungry mouth. Her hands moved to his chest and upward to link her arms around his neck to bring him closer, but Gage pulled away.

She didn't understand. "What's wrong?"

"I promised you we'd take this slow…"

Fallon rose and held out her hand. "I don't want it slow."

His dark eyes landed on hers and Fallon's breath caught in her throat. Slowly and seductively his gaze traveled over her face, searching her eyes. For doubt? He wouldn't find any. They were married and it was time. Gage must have seen her acceptance because he was on his feet within seconds and they were walking to the bedroom.

They stopped at the foot of the bed. Fallon felt Gage's hands on the back of her dress as he unbuttoned each crystal button until eventually she felt a cold gust of air against her back. Then Gage's fingers were on her shoulders, easing down the sheer gossamer straps until the dress fell to her waist.

She felt his mouth pressing soft kisses on her shoulder and tried to steady herself, but a dizzying current of attraction raced through her as he wet her neck with his tongue. He used his fingers to caress, tease and stroke her bare breasts. There hadn't been a need for a bra because it came built-in. She was naked and completely open to Gage, her husband. His palms cupped her aching breasts and when he skated his thumbs across her engorged nipples, she let out a low moan.

"You're so sensitive," he rasped and continued brushing his thumbs over her breasts. Fallon closed her eyes, allowing her head to fall back against the wall of his chest. Gage held her to him, pressing her hard against him and leaned down, rewarding her with a deep kiss, which merely increased their mounting desire. She spun around to face him.

"Tell me what you want," Gage rasped.

"I want you." To prove it she stepped out of the flowing dress, letting it pool at her feet until she was standing in nothing but her thong and bejeweled high heels.

"God, you're beautiful!" Before she could react, he sank to his knees in front of her and moved his hands to her hips until he arrived at her inner thighs.

"What are you doing?"

"Tasting you." He slid his finger along the edge of her lace thong and Fallon hissed out a breath. He pushed the fabric aside and his thumb traced along her cleft. Fallon jerked when his fingers delved and began gently exploring her inner folds. He lifted his head to look at her and smiled. "Hot *and* wet."

She was consumed with heat and when he slid one finger inside her, she shuddered. "Oh." But there was more to come, because he slowly withdrew it, only to add another finger. Meanwhile his thumb was working her clitoris. Pleasure was building, taking her to a fever pitch, making her want to whisper his name like some sort of mantra. "Gage, please—"

He wasn't listening, he merely plunged his fingers deeper inside her, filling her. "You like that?"

"Yes," she implored when he repeated the action, "but I—I need more."

"Like what?"

"Your mouth. I need your mouth on me." Fallon was embarrassed to say it out loud. She'd never been so vocal with her desires, but if she couldn't tell her husband, who could she tell?

Gage gripped her hips and within seconds had deposited her on the bed and disposed of her thong. Fallon shamelessly spread her legs and watched as he cupped her bottom and then raked her with his tongue. She arched off the bed, but Gage held her firm. His hands were against her pelvis, spreading her legs wide so his tongue could work her over and over again with such sensuous abandon that Fallon squirmed, begging him to end it.

He merely laughed and continued flicking his tongue over her core, laving her with deliberate yet feather-light movements. He had her wound so tight, she was aching for him to relieve the pressure building inside her. And when he circled her clitoris with his tongue while simultaneously pumping his fingers deep inside her, a scream rang out from deep within her.

"Omigod!" Fallon pressed her hands to her face, but Gage refused to allow her to hide.

Instead he crawled up her body and gave her an open-mouthed kiss. It was heady and erotic because she could taste herself on his lips.

"Don't hide. I want to see your face. I want to know you're enjoying our lovemaking."

Eventually, when her breathing returned, she smiled. "Don't you think you're wearing too many clothes?" She was naked while he was fully clothed save for the jacket and tie he'd discarded when they'd walked in.

"Indeed, I am, Mrs. Campbell. Care to help me with that?"

Gage sat upright and watched Fallon as she excitedly attacked the buttons on his shirt. When they didn't unbutton fast enough, she ripped it open and buttons went flying. He liked that she was as desperate and eager as he was for their union. The anticipation was heightened by the fact they'd waited a month—hell, years—to get here and he supposed that's why it felt so momentous. He was making love to his *wife*.

Fallon was his. There was no escaping it. She'd signed her name on the marriage certificate, sealing her fate. Be-

cause tonight he intended to possess her. Over and over
again until they were both spent.

As she pulled the shirt down his shoulders and he
shrugged it off his arms, Gage felt like a king. He moved
off the bed long enough to strip off his pants and boxers and
then, naked, he joined her on the bed. He reached for one
of her feet that were still encased in her bejeweled shoes.
"These are incredible," he said with a grin as he unbuck-
led the ankle straps.

"And they cost a fortune," Fallon responded as he removed one and then the other. He took the pins out from
the elaborate updo and ran his fingers through the mass of
honey-blond hair.

Finally he could feast his eyes on her with no barriers.
And he certainly looked his fill, from her round breasts to
her slim waist to her flat stomach to the curve of her hips,
before ending his tour with the patch of dark curls between
her thighs. He wanted to reach out and touch her, but Fallon took over. She pushed him back against the pillows
and straddled him. Her silky-soft hair slid onto his chest
as their mouths fused together, tongues tangling in heated
lust. Gage dragged his head back; he wanted to look at her.
Her eyes were wide and dilated while her lips were parted
and swollen. His need for her grew exponentially and he
reached for her again, this time putting his mouth on one of
her full, round breasts. His tongue swirled around her nipple, which tightened and puckered. She threw back her head
in abandon so he took his time worshipping the bud and
then paid homage to its twin with his mouth and tongue.

"Hmm…no fair," she murmured when he finally lifted
his head. "I'm on top. I'm supposed to be in charge."

"Oh, but you are," Gage said as his fingers moved between them to slip through her slick folds. He dipped inside
and found her as wet as when he'd made her come earlier.
It was time. He was throbbing with a need to be inside her

and now there was no need for protection. Last week, Fallon had asked whether he'd been tested. It was a fair question given they were becoming lovers and he'd answered honestly that he was clean. She'd shared the same news and they'd agreed she would be on the pill. Gage was happy because there would be no barriers between them. Just two people sharing the most sensuous of acts.

He grasped her hips and lifted her so the wide tip of his erection nudged at the entrance to her hot, damp flesh. She gasped, but he held her firm as she took him deep inside her. He loved the way her tight core clenched around his thick, hard, pulsating length, but he wanted more. He thrust his hips upward in one savage thrust and impaled her.

"Oh, God!" Fallon moaned, resting her palms on his chest. Her eyes were closed and he couldn't read her expression no matter how badly he wanted to.

"Look at me, baby," Gage urged and, when she did, he caught the passion in those hazel-gray depths and knew this was more than sex.

Fallon moved, lifting off him and then coming back down again. Over and over. She eased off and down onto him. Gage was blind with lust, gripping her hips and urging her on, but Fallon was in control, undulating against him, finding her own rhythm. He met her by pumping his hips up as his entire body stirred to life. He reached for her, his tongue raking her lips, demanding entry, and she parted for him. Gage thrust deep inside her mouth, mimicking the movements of their lower bodies. He heard Fallon's breath hitch and could feel her body tensing as if she was poised on the abyss. He wanted them to go over the cliff together so his thrusts became deeper, harder and more animalistic in nature.

Fallon moaned when he cupped her buttocks, so he drove harder until soon her body was clenching around him and pushing them both over the edge as he found his release.

Gage growled as the world righted itself and Fallon quivered over him, slumping against him. He'd suspected but hadn't been prepared for how sexually compatible they were. He was already feeling a resurgence of desire after being completely satisfied moments ago. The voracious hunger he had for her couldn't last, right? Because if it did, it would derail all of his best laid plans.

Eleven

Fallon woke with a start. Sunshine was streaming through the sheer curtains.

She'd succumbed to every illicit sensation Gage evoked throughout the course of the night. She wanted everything he had to offer. Gage understood and matched her in his unparalleled desire. Not once, not twice, but three times last night, their coupling had been wild and erotic. At one point he'd lifted her legs to his shoulders and she'd arched into him as he'd pumped into her, hard and fast, until she'd panted out his name.

Fallon hadn't known sex could be that good, that she could literally burn up with wanting for a man. But it was what Gage brought out in her. And that scared her because although it was thrilling, Fallon knew loving Gage was dangerous. They were in a temporary marriage of convenience, one that allowed them to both get what they wanted, though Fallon still didn't understand what she'd brought to the table. Status? Acceptance into Austin society? She would have given up her status in a heartbeat to have Gage fall in love with her.

Her husband stirred beside her. "Good morning," he slurred with eyes half open. "What are you doing up? Did I not wear you out last night?" When she didn't respond right away, he continued. "Then I didn't fulfill my husbandly duties."

Gage rolled over, positioning himself above her. "Gage..." she sighed as molten heat formed in her core.

"Hmm...don't worry. I'll be gentle." Slowly he nudged her entrance with his shaft, all the while looking straight at her. There was no hiding behind a façade. Fallon had no choice but to stare into his intense eyes as he thrust deep inside her.

There was a fierce need for possession in his eyes and Fallon was surprised by the depth of emotion she saw there. *Did Gage care for her more than she thought?* Fallon couldn't say because he gave her no reprieve. Instead he continued his merciless assault, molding her closer, pressing their bodies together so he could go deeper. Take her higher. Urgency expanded within her until Fallon's entire body erupted and she saw stars.

She struggled not to give away too much with her expression, but Gage surged inside her again and again and the delicious friction of their bodies caused her to come apart. She clutched at his biceps as another orgasm overtook her. Gage groaned in her ear and she tasted his passion as his tongue pressed past her lips to caress and stroke hers.

When he collapsed on top of her, his breathing slowly began to even out. Then he shifted to his side and relieved her of his weight. Fallon stroked his cheek and traced his mouth with her fingers. The uncontrollable lust and hunger for Gage was like nothing she'd ever known. This man was burrowing into her soul.

"Are you all right?" he asked, searching her face.

"Yes."

He touched the bridge of her nose. "But you're pensive. I can see the thoughts whirling around in your brain. Let them go, Fallon, and be present in the moment with me."

"I am."

"You're thinking about later and what comes next. About why it's so good between us. Isn't it enough that it is? Can't we enjoy each other?"

Until it peters out, Fallon wanted to add but didn't. She nodded.

"Good." Gage smiled.

Gage stared at Fallon from his poolside seat at the luxury resort in Punta Cana where they were staying for their honeymoon. He couldn't resist watching her every move as she made her way to him. His wife was a knockout. She wore a halter-style bikini held together by rings in the center of her bust and along the sides of her slim hips. It did wonders for her cleavage. Her round, pert breasts were pushed up and enhanced for the entire world to see. Although she'd wrapped a sarong around her waist, Gage knew men were looking.

The last several days they'd been soaking in the sun and swimming in the private pool of their beachside villa. Fallon had teased him he was keeping her naked and barefoot. They'd hardly left the villa except for a romantic candlelit dinner he'd arranged on the beach upon their arrival and the one day they'd spent sightseeing and snorkeling. Today they'd finally ventured out to the main building and now Gage wished they were in their private world again. He didn't like men wanting what was his. Because Fallon was *his*.

They'd been together in every possible position. He was very imaginative and Fallon had been enthusiastic about all of his ideas, adding a few of her own that had him begging and pleading with her for more. Her soft cries of delight, her hungry moans as their bodies moved faster and came together in mind-blowing release, were overwhelming. When it came to his wife, Gage was insatiable. But it was more than that. He'd thought that once they became intimate, his ache for her would go away. Instead it seemed to have metastasized and he was incapable of controlling himself. He wanted her all the time, but their marriage had an expiration date.

At least that was the verbal agreement they had. At the time, Gage hadn't seen a problem. He assumed he'd be ready to move on when the hunger and passion subsided. Plus, he had a plan in place to take over Stewart Technologies once he had enough stock. He'd already purchased a substantial amount on the open market with his holding companies. Now it was a matter of finding those investors who were eager to sell.

Gage tried not to think about how this would affect Fallon. He couldn't. Business was business. What they shared was something altogether different. Something that was just between them. Special, even.

"I arranged for our massages on the beach," Fallon said as they retreated to the loungers in their private cabana.

"Sounds marvelous." Gage eyed her as she removed the sarong from around her slim waist to reveal the barely there bikini that covered her curvy bottom and the patch of curls between her thighs. Thinking about when he'd been buried there this morning had his penis stiffening in his swim shorts.

Fallon reached for her drink, a fruity concoction inside a pineapple. He'd opted for a beer. "I had to do something. Otherwise, we'd never enjoy any of the resort's luxurious amenities."

"I have all I want right here." His eyes scanned hers. She blushed as she always did when he talked about their lovemaking. Over the course of the last four days, he'd made it his mission in life to help her shed her inhibitions. They'd made love in the shower, pool, hot tub, even on the beach near their villa. That had taken a little more coaxing, but once his hands and mouth had been on her, Fallon had given in and allowed him to have his way with her.

He smiled at the memory.

"What's so funny?" she inquired.

"Just remembering the other night on the beach."

Fallon's face flamed.

"And hoping for a repeat."

"You're terrible, Gage. And that's not going to happen. We could have been caught. If anyone had found us, I would have been so embarrassed."

"Trust me, babe. We weren't the only ones out there," he replied. "This is an adults-only resort, known for honeymooners and anniversaries."

Fallon shrugged, placed her pineapple on the table between the loungers and eased back. "We'll leave them to their shenanigans. I prefer the privacy of our villa."

"And where's the fun in that?"

Their butler, James, came to the cabana, interrupting the moment. "Mr. and Mrs. Campbell, can I get you anything? Another refreshment, perhaps?" He nodded to their drinks on the table. "Or a light snack?"

"I would love some fresh fruit," Fallon said. "And maybe some cheese and crackers?"

"Another beer for me," Gage answered.

Once James departed, Gage turned to Fallon. "I have a very special evening planned for our last night here."

"I can't believe the honeymoon is nearly over. Why did we only give ourselves five days?"

"Because someone—" he glanced in her direction "—is a workaholic and refused to take the entire week. But don't you worry, I will make tonight unforgettable."

* * *

Gage made certain the evening was beyond Fallon's wildest imagination. After their afternoon massages, they'd gone back to the room where her husband had turned showering into an erotic experience. He'd thoroughly soaped and washed her body with his hands before falling to the floor in the oversize super shower and loving her with his mouth. Then he'd hoisted her off her feet and made passionate love to her against the tiled wall while water pounded on his back. Fallon had melted into a sea of lust as she did whenever she was around him. His every touch, kiss and possession caused an inferno of passion to consume her.

Eventually they'd left their villa and ended up on a yacht for a sunset cruise Gage had arranged. It took them around the island while they enjoyed a four-course meal prepared by a private chef in the state-of-the-art kitchen belowdecks. The captain had given them a tour of the yacht's modern amenities when they'd come aboard; it had a kitchen, living area, dining room, two guest bedrooms and a master suite complete with a king-size bed and full-size master bathroom.

Now they were on the deck, lying on the plush recliners and stargazing while drinking Cristal. Fallon had chosen to wear a simple color-blocked maxi dress in deep orange, navy and white, pairing it with low-heeled white sandals. It was nautical and comfortable. Gage had opted for linen trousers and some sort of tunic shirt he'd picked up during their one and only sightseeing trip. But all she could see when she closed her eyes were those broad shoulders, chiseled eight-pack abs and trim waist.

Fallon felt fulfilled in Gage's arms. For the first time in her life, she was beginning to understand the addiction to sex. It hadn't even been a week and she wanted Gage with a pride-destroying hunger. She, who had never *needed* anyone, needed him.

Which was why Fallon was looking forward to flying home tomorrow. Life would go back to normal after the craziness of the wedding and honeymoon. She would dive back into work immediately. She had some thoughts on paring down the staff by retiring some of her father's old friends and bringing in new talent who were forward thinking.

"Penny for your thoughts?" Gage inquired.

"I'm thinking about going home."

Gage frowned. "I didn't realize spending 24/7 with me was such a chore."

Their eyes met.

"Of course not. I've enjoyed our time together."

"But you're ready to get back to work?" Gage finished.

Fallon shrugged. "There's much to be done to get Stewart Technologies back on track. I'll be very busy."

"Is that your subtle way of telling me that you'll be too busy or too tired to fulfill your wifely duties? Because that's not going to fly."

"No... I—" Fallon wasn't able to utter another word because Gage's long body came up and over hers, crushing her against the lounger as his heavy, muscular legs slid on either side of the thin fabric of her dress, caging her in. Her head fell back as Gage gave her a fierce, demanding kiss, plundering her mouth with his invading tongue. He was like a marauder, taking what he wanted.

She felt the weight of one of his palms at her ankles as he slid the maxi dress up her thigh.

"Gage, wait!" Fallon stopped his hand. "What about the staff?"

"They've all retired for the evening, per my instructions." Then he was underneath the hem, his hands searing every inch of her skin. Instinctively, she pressed herself further into his touch. Their bodies shifted and she was able to feel the hardness of his erection against her core. Fallon was needy and hungry—for him and no one else. His body was like a drug. When he touched her, what little was left of her functioning brain gave way to pure lust and all rational thought fled her body.

He lifted his mouth to trail kisses along her face and jaw, murmuring, "I had better get my fill now."

And so had she.

She feverishly tugged at his shirt. He had too many clothes on. Within seconds, he'd pulled it up and over his head. Electricity buzzed when she felt the crisp brush of his chest hair on her fingertips. She lowered her head and pressed her lips against the wall of his chest, tasting and tantalizing him with no restraint.

"Fallon…"

She liked how his voice was rough and raw with emotion, so she continued her ministrations. But Gage stopped her. Clenching his hands in her hair, he pulled her away so he could crush his mouth against hers in a hungry kiss turned sensual dance. She felt his urgent hands at her waist as he levered himself away long enough to remove the maxi dress and leave her naked save for the thong she'd been wearing. She'd taken to going braless the entire honeymoon.

"I want you so bad," he growled and cupped her breasts, teasing them into aroused peaks with swirls and flicks of his tongue and nips of his teeth.

"Me, too." She clenched her hands around the corded muscles of his biceps. The man had a wicked way with his tongue. She arched against his invasion, all the while feeling the hot moisture of need between her thighs that only he could assuage. She began shoving his trousers and his underwear down his legs. He stood long enough to rid himself of the offending garments before they were back together on the lounger.

"This has to go," he said and gave her thong a gentle tug, snapping the fabric asunder.

That was fine with Fallon; she didn't care about restraint. She wanted him right here, right now—regardless of who might find them. This is what he'd done to her: he'd made her a mass of need. His hands slid between them to brush the damp curls between her thighs. She was already wet and he easily slid not one but two fingers inside her. She encouraged him by moving with his hand. She was so desperate to come, but he didn't let her.

"I want to come with you," he murmured, removing his hands. His legs came between hers, nudging them apart. She spread her legs wider, inviting him in, and he surged inside her in one powerful movement.

Fallon let out a sharp, keening cry of delight and her arms went around his neck as she brought his mouth back down to hers. She was on fire. He pushed in again then withdrew. Fallon wanted to cry out in protest but he surged in further, deeper, than he had before. She wrapped her thighs around him and reveled in the way Gage took her higher, again and again, until there was only them, as connected as two people could be. Fallon arched her hips when he angled himself so he could take her harder and faster. The storm built, swirling until there was nowhere else to go but over the edge. Simultaneously they tumbled into ecstasy and cried out their release.

And Fallon knew, as she'd known for days, that somewhere along the line, passion had developed into love.

Twelve

After realizing the depth of her feelings for her husband in Punta Cana, Fallon hoped returning to Austin would give her peace. It didn't. The time they'd spent together during the honeymoon had been a revelation. Her husband wasn't the arrogant, bossy alpha male she'd thought she knew. Instead he'd been relaxed and easygoing, as if a weight had been lifted off his shoulders. And in bed he'd been a passionate yet tender and giving lover.

She was just as crazy about Gage as she'd been before except now, a month after the honeymoon, she knew even more about the man. It frightened her to know she could be in a love with a man who didn't return her feelings and considered her an added bonus to their business arrangement. Once they'd come back to the States, Gage immediately moved her into his penthouse and ensconced her even deeper into his world. Morning, noon and night, he was either in her head with constant calls or texts to check in to see how her day was going or making surprise visits to her office just to take her to lunch. And the nights…oh, the nights were something else entirely.

If Fallon thought she would get some sort of reprieve from their lovemaking, she'd been wrong. Gage was as hungry for her as he'd been on their honeymoon, maybe even more so. He seemed determined to not let her keep her distance. *Did he know that had been her goal?* On the plane ride home, Fallon had decided to limit sex between them, but Gage had seduced her nearly every night since. It was so intense, she'd had to beg off the other night, claiming it was the wrong time of the month. She knew her excuse wouldn't hold much longer, but the last few days had been bliss. She'd finally been able to clear her head of the sexual fog.

As she drove home late Friday evening, Fallon contemplated how she had to face facts. She was hopelessly in love with Gage. She'd been carrying a torch for him ever since she was a young girl. It had only grown when she'd thrown herself at him and he'd kissed her with such fervor. It was a double-edged sword knowing she was Gage's wife and loved him with heart and soul, but at the same time he didn't love her and had only married her for lust and acceptance into society.

How was she going to navigate the next five months feeling this way? It was going to be pure torture, but somehow she would. She had to turn off her emotions, not give herself completely over to Gage as she'd been doing. She had to focus on self-preservation because their marriage of convenience would end in the near term.

She pulled her Audi into the parking space next to Gage's Bugatti and turned off the engine. She inhaled, mentally steeling herself for the evening ahead, and eased out of the car. The ride to Gage's building had seemed like the longest ride of her life. But when she finally entered their living room, the atmosphere was relaxed. Jazz was playing softly in the background, candles were lit and the smells coming from the kitchen caused her stomach to stir. She'd only had a salad for lunch and that had been hours ago.

Gage came padding toward her barefoot, wearing low-slung jeans and a T-shirt, two wineglasses in his hands. "Thought you might need this after a long day of work." He handed her a glass, which she accepted.

"Thank you." Fallon had always imagined having a marriage like this one day, but she'd never dreamed of Gage in the role of caring husband. She followed him into the living room and plonked down on the sofa. She was about to remove her stilettos when Gage joined her and took over the task, removing one shoe and then the other. He helped her remove the suit jacket she'd worn, revealing the thin cami underneath.

When his gaze zeroed in on her breasts, Fallon felt as if she were naked because on cue her nipples pebbled at his searing gaze. She reached for her wineglass and liberally drank.

"Was it that bad at the office?" Gage asked, watching her intently. "I thought things were settling down a bit."

"They are," Fallon said. "I've settled some debts and made payment arrangements with other creditors. As we discussed last week, I want to use some of those funds for development to make Stewart Technologies what it once was."

"Did you meet with the head of R and D yet?"

Fallon was happy they were talking shop. She'd been nervous because he'd given her one of those hungry gazes when she'd come in, which usually ended up with her on her back. Or on top. Or on the side. Or the floor. It didn't much matter.

"Fallon?"

He was speaking to her. "Oh, yes, I did."

Over the delicious dinner a private chef had made for them, they continued discussing the viability of several options the department head had come up with. Gage opened up about some new deals he was working on and she offered advice Gage seemed to find valuable. Fallon relaxed as the evening progressed, especially when they retired to the sofa and streamed some television shows on Hulu. An hour in, Fallon couldn't help but stifle a yawn.

"Tired?" Gage asked.

She nodded.

"C'mon, let me put you to bed." Gage rose and helped her up.

Once they were in the bedroom, Fallon went about her normal routine of preparing for bed, but she felt Gage's eyes on her every movement. She knew she was pushing it when she reached for a sexy nightie. It had spaghetti straps and stopped midthigh, but it was clothing. Since their honeymoon, she'd forgone pajamas because she and Gage were so insatiable for each other.

After washing her face and brushing her teeth, she headed to her side of the bed. Gage was sitting upright with his phone in hand, but appearances were deceiving. Fallon didn't doubt for a second he hadn't noticed her attire. She slid in beside him, turned off the lamp and faced the opposite direction. She heard him move around before the room fell into darkness. Fallon tried to calm her breathing and act as if she were falling asleep, but Gage called her out.

"I know you're not asleep, Fallon."

"Nearly. I'm exhausted."

She felt his arms encircle her as he pulled her firmly to him until her backside was against his very hard shaft. She sucked in a breath.

"Too tired for this?" He planted hot, openmouthed kisses

on her neck until he came to her ear and gently tugged on the lobe with his mouth.

Sweet Jesus! He knew all her erogenous zones. Fallon closed her eyes and willed herself to stay strong. "Not tonight, all right?" Fallon managed to say despite her body's yearnings. "It's been a long day."

"That didn't seem to bother you before. Why now?"

Anger coursed through her and she spun around to face him in the darkness. "Really, Gage, I ask for one night to sleep and suddenly I'm in the wrong? Or am I supposed to be at your beck and call every night? Is that what you expected out of this arrangement? Because if so, you're in for a rude awakening. I'm my own person with my own mind, my own thoughts, my own feelings."

"I recognize that, Fallon. I didn't realize I was pressuring you. I thought the feeling was mutual and you wanted me just as much. Consider me duly warned off." He turned away and this time his back was to her.

Fallon felt terrible. She hadn't meant to hurt him, but she'd needed some breathing room because she was afraid of the tender feelings she'd developed. Afraid he might see them and then where would they be? She had to stay the course. It was best not only for her sanity but her pride.

Gage ran. On Saturday morning, he ran as fast as he could on the treadmill in his building's gym until he'd exhausted himself. He hadn't slept much last night because Fallon had shut him down. Literally. There was no mistaking the off-limits sign she'd been wearing for days, except last night she'd made it very clear she didn't want him. Before she'd been more than happy to sleep nude because they'd been so attuned to each other's needs.

Over the last month they'd awaken during the middle of the night and reach for each other. Sometimes he started it. Sometimes she did. They'd make love into the wee hours of the morning and *now* she was tired. Tired of him? Gage wondered.

He'd seen the way she responded to him. Felt her clench around his shaft when he'd been buried deep inside her. Watched the bliss come over her when she'd climaxed. Why? Because he'd felt it himself. An unexplainable ecstasy had plagued him since they'd become intimate. He'd thought he'd get the hunger for her out of his system, but he hadn't. And he'd tried. Perhaps he'd come on too strong? No. No. No.

He wasn't wrong about how Fallon felt about him. If he was honest, there were times another emotion had been visible in her expression. Something he was afraid to say out loud. She hadn't been able to hide it, but she'd tried to. And now she was acting as if their lovemaking had become burdensome when that was far from the case. She was feeling too much the same as him.

He was on the verge of everything he'd wanted in this marriage. The other day he'd secured another five percent of Stewart Technologies' stock, bringing his total to forty-five percent. He'd been slowly acquiring the stock through several holding companies to ensure it wouldn't be traced back to him. As for his wife, the attraction he'd felt for her had materialized into the most spectacular sex of his life. The problem was, the triumph he'd thought he'd feel as the moment of success got nearer left a bitter taste in his mouth.

Whoever said revenge was a dish best served cold had no idea what it would feel like mixed with white-hot sexual need. The anger he'd felt toward Fallon and her family was the reason he'd chosen to go down this path, but it was getting harder and harder not to want more out of this relationship than either one of them had wanted to give.

Gage stopped running and pressed the stop button on the treadmill.

The marriage was convenient. Fallon got her money and he got Stewart Technologies and Fallon in his bed. However, Gage wasn't satisfied. He wanted both, but deep down he knew there was going to come a time he would have to choose.

Thirteen

"Are you sure you want me to attend this dinner with you two?" Grace asked from the back seat of Gage's car. Gage had invited his mother to come to Thanksgiving at the Stewarts' with Fallon and him, because his wife had adamantly refused to miss it, claiming she always shared the meal with her parents.

"Of course. We want you there." He hazarded a glance at Fallon, but she was staring out the window. When Gage had first invited Grace, he'd been certain she would decline, but he'd been wrong. She claimed she hadn't seen much of him since the wedding and didn't plan on missing out on the holiday.

Gage wasn't looking forward to the hostility that could break out on all sides tonight. He and Fallon hadn't been on good terms in weeks. The night after she'd refused to make love, Gage had felt hurt and so he'd chosen to withhold any affection. The problem was, he was hurting himself in the process because he missed being close to his wife, but he was too proud to admit he was wrong and so their standoff had continued.

"I made one of my famous sweet potato pies," his mother said. "Wonder if Nora will mind."

"I'm sure Mother will welcome the pie."

She didn't.

When they entered Stewart Manor, the matriarch had air-kissed his mother and then handed the pie off to the butler, never to be seen the rest of the evening. From then on, Nora was overly solicitous, which made his mother uncomfortable. The night didn't get any better, especially when Dane called to inform them he'd missed his flight and wouldn't make it. Meanwhile Henry kept giving Gage the evil eye. And why wouldn't he? Fallon was being as warm as a lump of coal. Could her father sense their acrimony?

After dinner they retired to the family room and the night went further downhill.

"So what have you been up to, Grace?" Nora inquired.

"I wasn't cleaning houses, if that's what you're after. I've been retired for years because my son takes great care of me. He even bought me a house in Lost Creek." She winked at her son.

"You really have done well, Gage." Nora smiled. "You take care of your mother while our daughter harps about our spending and has placed us on allowance. Or was that your doing?" She eyed Gage suspiciously.

"No, Mother, it was mine." Fallon perked up after being surly all night. "Perhaps if you learned to curb your spending, I wouldn't be in the position I'm in."

"Married to my son?" Grace inquired. "You would do well to remember he forgave you your past transgressions, my dear."

"Leave my daughter out of this, Grace. Your beef is with me," Fallon's father interjected.

Grace glared at him. "Do you blame me, Henry?" She

used his given name, which she never would have years ago. "I'm still waiting on an apology."

"Mama…" Gage didn't need his mother to defend him.

"Don't *Mama* me." Grace stood. "You ask me to make *nice* with these people when they've yet to acknowledge the harm they caused both of us. And now…" Her eyes bore into Fallon, but one look at Gage made her not finish her sentence. "Please take me home."

"That might be best," Nora responded.

"Don't patronize me, Nora Stewart, when you can't be bothered to clean your own house or make your own meals. You would do well to learn a little humility as fortunes change." His mother walked to the exit and Gage made to follow her but looked at Fallon. "Are you coming?"

Fallon shook her head. "I'll stay here, if you don't mind. I'll get a taxi home."

Gage clenched his jaw. He didn't want to get into a fight in front of the Stewarts. "Fine. I'll see you at home."

On the way back to her house, his mother made it clear that, going forward, she wanted limited contact with the Stewarts. For his part, Gage was just glad they'd made it through the evening, though his thoughts kept circling back to the sullen look on Fallon's face and whether the chill between them would ever thaw.

"Can you help me with this?" Fallon asked Gage the following Saturday evening. It had been a tense few days since Thanksgiving and Fallon was hoping the ice would thaw between them. They were getting ready for a hospital fund-raiser where the crème de la crème would be in attendance. She would have to shine tonight. The Givenchy gown she'd chosen had sequins from top to bottom along with dramatic layers of silver and gunmetal fringe. It would certainly help draw attention to her and Gage. It fit perfectly with the nights' Roaring Twenties theme and, with her hair swept in a sophisticated updo, Fallon looked like a modern-day flapper.

"Of course." Gage came up behind her and studied her with his hawklike gaze for several moments. She froze, her breath jamming in her throat. Then he zipped up the dress and shocked her when he planted a kiss on her bare shoulder. The hairs on the back of her neck rose to attention and every muscle in her body tensed as the earthy, sensual scent of him slammed into her senses.

Gage hadn't touched her in over a month since their argument over her not being in the mood. For her, it had been as simple as needing space, but for Gage it was as if she'd mortally wounded him with her rejection and he'd avoided her ever since. Fallon had known Gage was upset—hurt, even—but she hadn't expected him to pull away from her so completely. Despite their lack of intimacy, they still played their newlywed role by attending charity functions, polo matches and art gallery openings where Gage could rub shoulders with high society. It was going rather nicely because he'd picked up several new clients.

The distance was palpable. When they did manage to sit together for a meal, there was an ever-present underlying tension between them. Fallon didn't know how to clear the hurdle and get back to how they'd been when he couldn't get enough of her. She literally ached with unrequited feelings because now she knew what she'd been missing all those years in the bedroom. She was addicted to Gage and she needed a hit, badly.

"I have something for you." Fallon realized he'd moved away while she'd been daydreaming about him. And how could she not? Tonight he was wearing a black, three-piece, pin-striped tuxedo with black wing-tipped shoes. He'd found a vintage fedora to complete the look. He looked every bit a gangster.

He handed her a large box imprinted with the Tiffany's logo. "What's this?" She glanced up at him.

"Open it."

She did as he instructed. Nestled inside the velvet cushion was the most stunning diamond teardrop necklace she'd ever seen.

Gage unclasped it and stepped in behind her to place it on her neck. How had he known this would complement the deep V of the dress so perfectly?

She touched the large diamond pendant. "It's beautiful."

"Just like you."

Fallon glanced into the mirror to find Gage's brandy-colored eyes raking her boldly. She hadn't seen that intense flare of attraction in his eyes in so long, her heart jolted. Did it mean he still wanted her? "So is this a truce?" she asked hopefully. "Because if not, I'd like it to be."

Gage offered her a smile, which had been rare of late. "Yes, let's consider it one. Now, c'mon, we should go. We don't want to be late."

"No, we wouldn't want that." Fallon knew making an impression tonight was important to Gage after his humble beginnings. She would do everything in her power to ensure the evening went well.

About forty minutes later their limousine pulled up in front of the Four Seasons. It had taken them some time because of the barrage of limousines filling the streets, but eventually they disembarked and headed inside. The venue décor was vintage art deco with a black-and-gold color scheme that was pure glitz and glam. There was even a photo booth so guests could grab a fedora, flapper hat, feather boa or fake gun and have their picture taken.

Fallon made her way around the room introducing Gage. Everyone was polite and charming, inquiring about their wedding and how they were enjoying married life. They even ran into her parents.

Her father gave her a hug while her mother blew her air kisses. "Don't want to ruin my makeup, darling," she purred. "You're looking well. Married life agrees with you. I love the gown. Givenchy, right?"

Trust her mother to know every designer. "That's right."

"But the true masterpiece is this diamond." Nora Stewart had no qualms about lifting the stone off Fallon's chest and admiring it. She glanced at Gage. "You outdid yourself."

"Thank you," he replied.

With that brief exchange, her mother grabbed her father's arm and continued on her socializing trek.

"Fallon? Omigod! As I live and breathe," a rather loud woman exclaimed from behind them.

Fallon spun on her heels to find Dani Collins a few feet away. She hadn't seen the buxom petite blonde since her parents had carted her away from Austin to boarding school all because she'd taken Dani's advice and tried to seduce Gage. Listening to Dani and their friend Millicent had been the reason why Fallon had ended up in Gage's room. Liquid encouragement of the alcoholic variety had also played a role.

"Dani Collins."

Dani smiled, showing a large, toothy grin. "I haven't seen you in ages." She pulled Fallon into an awkward hug. "Where have you been hiding yourself?"

"I've been working at my family's company, Stewart Technologies."

"Work?" Dani chuckled. "I would have thought you'd marry a filthy rich husband like your mama wanted before you ever worked your pretty little fingers to the bone." She held up Fallon's left hand. When her eyes landed on the six-carat ring, they nearly bugged out. "Wait a second, it looks like you have landed one."

A flicker of apprehension coursed through Fallon. "Yes, I'm married. You may remember him." She turned to Gage, who'd stepped away momentarily into another circle of partygoers. She touched his shoulder and he came forward. "Dani, this is my husband. Gage Campbell."

"What?" Dani's hand flew to her mouth. "You married the stable boy!" she shrieked.

Everyone around them turned to stare. The murderous look on Gage's face told Fallon that Dani had aroused his old fears and insecurities. Fallon could feel the deep red flush rising up to claim her cheeks.

"First of all, lower your voice, Dani," Fallon snapped. "Second, Gage is no stable boy. He's a grown man—"

But she never got to finish her sentence because Gage stepped in. "Who is, as you put it, Dani, filthy rich. So yes, I'm more than capable of looking after what's mine." His arm circled Fallon's waist. "Now if you'll excuse us…"

The lights blinked, indicating the event was about to begin. Fallon felt Gage's fingertips at her elbow as he guided her to their assigned table. He held her chair out and she sat. It was all so civilized, but when he deliberately brushed his fingers across her shoulders, Fallon shivered. *Had he intended to elicit a response?* She was sure he was upset over Dani's obnoxious comment from earlier. Tonight was his night to show society he'd arrived, and could Dani's outburst have marred that?

Once he took his seat beside her, Fallon leaned over. "You okay?" She watched him closely.

He winked but then sat with his back ramrod-straight and turned to face the front of the room. Fallon did the same, worried how the remainder of the evening would go.

Gage was fuming. Outwardly he portrayed the image of self-made millionaire, but inside he was still that twelve-year-old boy who'd come to live with his mother when she became the maid on a big estate. The same young boy who'd turned into a stable hand that silly rich socialites like

Dani Collins made fun of or bedded to show they were living dangerously.

Fallon was special. He'd watched her grow up from a spirited young girl into an attractive teenager with stunning hazel-gray eyes. He had been drawn to her. It's why he'd humored her, talked to her and let her follow him around. That night he'd thought to teach her a lesson, but it had morphed into one hell of a kiss. Gage had been ill prepared for the chemistry that had exploded between them. He'd ended it before they'd gone too far.

Yet in the eyes of Dani and some like her, he would always be a stable boy and that stuck in his craw. Gage lifted a hand to catch the attention of the waiter and requested a whiskey. He needed something stronger, less smooth than his usual brandy. Something to take the edge off to ensure he got through this night in one piece.

Three whiskeys and several hours later, Gage felt relaxed. The evening was nearly over. The hospital raised the requisite amount of money needed thanks to a last-minute, million-dollar donation from him, which had shocked the entire room, including his wife sitting beside him.

When the band finally struck up some lively tunes, Gage was ready to alleviate some tension. Fallon returned from freshening up in the bathroom with her mother and looked quite delectable in her metallic flapper dress. He couldn't wait to take it off her later and he'd be damned if she'd refuse him. He'd seen the look in her eyes tonight and knew she still hungered for him.

He stood and held out a hand. "Dance with me?"

Fallon slid her hand into his and allowed him to lead her to the dance floor, which was already crowded with couples. The song was a slow Etta James melody called "At Last." Gage eased his arms around Fallon's warm body and pulled her tightly to him. Then he leaned his forehead against hers and whispered, "I've missed you."

She was silent for several beats and Gage wondered if she'd heard him, but then she responded. "I've missed you, too."

Her words were like a match to his lust and Gage pressed his body closer so she could feel how he was straining in his trousers. "Will you let me have you tonight?" he growled.

"Yes."

Yes. The word had never sounded lovelier to Gage's ears. And once the song ended, he quickly danced them off the floor and back to the table so Fallon could grab her clutch and gloves. They were nearly at the door when once again Dani stepped in front of them.

She was weaving back and forth, looking like she'd had one too many drinks. "I have to hand it to you, Fallon. You certainly know how to pick them. Maybe I, too, should have gotten it on with our stable boy. Maybe then he would have become rich and famous and come back to bail my company out of trouble."

"You don't know what you're talking about," Fallon answered, a warning in her tone.

"D-don't I?" Dani slurred. "From what I hear, your daddy's company was about to go belly-up, until stable boy here—" Dani eyed Gage up and down "—came along. Did you finally have to put out?"

Fallon's eyes narrowed. "You're a witch, you know that?"

"I might be, but I'm a rich one," Dani returned.

"That no man wants," Fallon snorted. "It's no wonder you're alone. I, on the other hand, am not. I'm going home with *my man* and let me tell you something, Dani. He's the fantasy in bed we all thought he was." She didn't wait for another of Dani's catty responses. Fallon grabbed Gage's hand and stormed out of the ballroom.

"That was hot!" Gage couldn't help but comment. He loved Fallon's outburst. This was the second time she'd defended him tonight. Whatever residual anger he'd felt from the last month faded. Fallon was truly in his corner.

"Good." She stared at him boldly. "Because I need you bad. So, buckle up. It's going to be a long night."

A smile curved his lips. He was ready for whatever Fallon had in store because they had a month to make up for.

They didn't make it very far into the penthouse because Gage pressed Fallon against the wall of the living room as soon as they arrived. Then his lips found hers in the dark and he kissed her hard. Their mouths fused together in a tangle of tongues. Fallon didn't know who moved first. She knew her hand was sneaking under his tuxedo to push off the jacket. Gage pulled away long enough to shrug it off, undo his tie and unbutton his shirt. When her eyes landed on his flat brown nipples, she leaned forward and explored the salty taste of him.

She had a growing need to see him naked. When the buttons were finally free, Gage ripped the shirt off. Only minutes after they'd entered the apartment, he was naked from the waist up while she was still fully clothed. Gage reached for her, hauling her to him. He reached behind her, fumbling with the zipper on the back of her dress, but it wouldn't give.

"Damnation!" he cursed and then pulled one strap and then the other over her arms. Her breasts popped free and his mouth was on them in seconds, reducing her to writhing ecstasy. They were tight and puckered at his mouth and touch alone. Fallon's mind skittered as her insides fisted tight with need. She couldn't think of anything but Gage and how much she wanted him. She didn't care what anyone else thought; she would die if she didn't feel him inside her *now*.

She was sure Gage felt the same way because his erection had thickened. She reached between them to undo his belt and zipper, but he pushed her hands aside. In one fell swoop he pulled down his trousers and briefs and kicked away his clothes. He was gloriously naked and Fallon looked her fill. Then he was back, sliding his hands into her hair and kissing her. His hands roamed lower, hiking up her dress until it was bunched around her waist.

"Wrap your legs around me," he instructed roughly.

He didn't have to tell her twice. Gage hitched her up, resting her back against the wall, and Fallon wrapped her legs around him. Holding her with one arm, he reached between them to push aside her thong and slide a finger between her moist folds. She was already wet for him, as she always was, and without preamble he widened his stance and surged upward inside her.

Fallon had never felt so full, so taken, so possessed. She slid her arms around his neck and Gage thrust higher. Her breath hitched. He withdrew and thrust back in, this time going even deeper.

"Yes, Gage, oh, yes," she moaned and her head fell back against the wall. She closed her eyes, amazed at the fullness of having Gage inside her once again. Starbursts of blinding light exploded behind her eyes as pleasure washed over her.

"Look at me, Fallon."

She opened her eyes and found Gage staring at her. He cupped her bottom tighter in his palms and pushed higher. He was intent on pulling her apart, on dismantling every single one of her defenses. He accomplished his goal with single-minded purpose as he increased his rhythm and drove into her over and over.

"Gage…" Fallon's body grew taut and soon she felt herself clench around him as spasms overtook her. She heard his release in the distance as they both finally broke free.

Fourteen

"I have a lead for you," Gage's attorney told him over the phone the next morning. "The final shares you need to give you a majority in Stewart Technologies."

"What was that?" Gage asked absentmindedly. He'd been daydreaming about Fallon's uninhibited response last night. He should be satisfied he could bring her to that kind of climax, but he hadn't been unaffected, either. He had feelings for her, probably always had since he'd seen her fall off her horse when she was eight.

Being with Fallon had injected his life with meaning and made him feel emotions he'd never allowed himself to feel. The past two months had shown him she wasn't the strong woman she portrayed to the world. She was passionate. Vulnerable, even. There were so many layers to his beautiful wife he hadn't considered. He'd been so intent on taking her to bed, to claim what he hadn't taken sixteen years ago and unleash the chemistry between them, he'd failed to see the consequences of his actions. He was falling for his wife. *Hard.*

"I said I have a lock on those shares you need," his attorney repeated, clearing his fog. "Since the company is rebounding, stock prices are slowly starting to rise. You'll want to get these now, while you can."

Gage's chest tightened and guilt settled in his stomach as the heavy weight of what he'd been doing registered. He needed someone to absolve him of the guilt, to tell him he what he'd done was right. But that wasn't going to happen. If Fallon ever found out his true motives behind marrying her, it would crush her. She'd been so happy the last few weeks as she'd pulled Stewart Technologies from the brink of disaster. The projects she'd been working on would be coming to market in a couple of months. They were the brainchild of her new head of development and Fallon was excited to see what lay ahead.

"Are you ready to pull the trigger?"

A throb pulsed at Gage's temple and he massaged it with his fingertips, trying to alleviate the pressure, but nothing was going to do that. His feelings for Fallon ran deep and he was conflicted as to what to do next. "I—I…"

"If you don't act now, someone could swoop in and pick them up. You have to move."

Gage sighed. He couldn't allow anyone else to get those shares. They had to stay in the family. On the other hand, this enormous deceit weighed heavily on him. He would be crossing the line when he did this.

"Go ahead and purchase them."

"I'm on it. I'll let you know when it's a done deal."

"Thank you." Gage ended the call. He sat back in his seat and rubbed a hand across his brow. There was no denying the emotion he'd never wanted to claim; it was there mocking him because he'd thought he could skirt it. Thought he didn't need it. He certainly hadn't needed it before. Why? Because none of those women had been Fallon.

Yet, because of her, he'd wanted more. To *be* more. And

he'd accomplished that. But with it had come the all-consuming rage and quest for revenge. He now had the tools, the final nail in the coffin to get his ultimate revenge against the Stewarts, but it would cost him the woman he loved.

"What should I expect tonight?" Gage asked Fallon as they drove to the restaurant to meet Ayden and his fiancée, Maya, for dinner. "The firing squad?"

"Don't be so melodramatic." Fallon smoothed down her skirt.

"C'mon, Fallon." Gage took his eyes off the road to glance at her. "I know your brother doesn't like me. It was obvious at the wedding."

Gage recalled the killer look Ayden had given him when they'd been introduced. Ayden had warned Gage to take care of his sister or else.

"He doesn't know you. Give him a chance," Fallon said, obviously attempting to ease Gage's mind.

"If he affords me the same, I will," Gage responded, turning his eyes to the road again. He knew how important this dinner was to Fallon. She was forging a bond with her brother and he didn't want to get in the way, not when he wasn't on even footing himself.

"Good."

They pulled into the restaurant's valet parking twenty minutes later. Gage came around and helped Fallon out of the car, then laced his fingers through hers as they walked inside. The maître d' led them to a corner table where Ayden and Maya were already seated. Gage could see why Ayden had fallen for his fiancée. She was striking, with her mass of curly hair and flawless brown skin.

Ayden rose when they approached. He came over and kissed both of Fallon's cheeks and offered Gage a hand. Gage shook it before scooting Fallon into a chair across from them.

"Glad you both could join us," Ayden said. He glanced at Maya. "We're eager to get to know you."

"As are we," Gage answered. He offered them a smile.

"How about some wine?" Ayden asked. "I took the liberty of ordering a bottle of red."

"We would love some, thank you." Fallon patted his thigh. She knew Gage liked ordering their wine himself.

"How's married life?" Maya inquired. "I can't believe you two beat me and Ayden down the aisle."

"It certainly wasn't a shotgun wedding," Gage replied.

"Then what was the rush?" Ayden asked. "Were you afraid Fallon might change her mind?"

Gage felt Fallon's fury beside him rather than saw it. She didn't appreciate her brother's inappropriate comment any more than he did, so he reminded himself Ayden was merely concerned for Fallon's well-being. "No, I wasn't afraid. I knew Fallon would honor the commitment she'd made to be my wife." He reached for her hand and brought it to his lips.

"How is married life treating you?" Maya asked. Bless her heart, Ayden's fiancée was keeping the evening cordial.

"It's going well, thank you, Maya," Fallon responded. "Actually, better than I'd imagined. Gage even manages to keep the toilet seat down."

Fallon's joke lightened the mood and everyone began to relax. But Gage could see Ayden watching his every move. Could he see what Gage had yet to share with Fallon—that he loved her?

Fallon was overjoyed the dinner was turning around. It had started off rocky with Ayden giving Gage the death stare. She knew her brother wasn't happy about her arranged marriage to Gage, but he was going to have to live with it for another four months.

Her breath caught in her throat when she realized two

months had already come and gone. The first month with Gage had been sheer bliss. The way they'd connected on such an elemental level had surprised her. All her life she'd been searching for that elusive connection with another human being. She'd found it in Gage; it was as if he fit perfectly into the slot. With each passing day and all the intimacy they'd shared, it became harder to keep her true feelings from bubbling to the surface. It's why she'd pushed him away, making the last month hard. When Gage had felt rejected by her, he'd kept her at a distance, physically as well as emotionally.

His response had hurt, but she'd had to withdraw to save herself the pain she knew was coming. However, not being with him had hurt far worse than anything she could have imagined. Last night after the event, they'd given in and finally made love. It had felt so good and oh so right. That was why she'd felt in a good place to accept Ayden's dinner invite.

"Gage is treating you well, which I'm glad to see," Ayden whispered in her ear when they'd retired to the lounge to listen to a jazz quartet. Gage and Maya were engaged in a lively discussion on the latest mayoral candidate, while Ayden and Fallon stepped onto the terrace for a private conversation and some fresh air because Fallon had felt a bit queasy.

"He is."

"Is the fresh air helping?" Ayden asked.

Fallon nodded and inhaled deeply. The last week or so she hadn't had much of an appetite. And after seeing the crème brûlée Gage had ordered for dessert, she'd felt sick to her stomach.

"After hearing his story, I realize I misjudged him," Ayden said after a moment.

During the meal Gage had shared the story of his inauspicious start in life, from never knowing his father to being raised on Stewart Manor to branching out on his own after college to find success. Fallon could see how impressed Ayden was by Gage's determination. He respected her husband because he knew what it was like to make something out of nothing.

"I told you not to worry."

Ayden snorted. "It's an older brother's prerogative to worry, Fallon. It would be different if you'd married for love, but you didn't."

Color drained from Fallon's face and Ayden leaned in. "Omigod! You're in love with him, aren't you?" He glanced in Gage's direction and Fallon followed Ayden's gaze. Her husband was watching them and smiling.

She quickly turned around and tugged on Ayden's sleeve, leading him farther away. "Lower your voice, please."

Ayden looked down at her. His hazel-gray eyes pierced hers. "Does he know?"

Fallon shook her head. "And I don't want him to know."

"Why the hell not? I see the way he looks at you, Fallon. There's something there."

"Lust," she replied. "Lust is all that's there, Ayden. We're compatible in the bedroom."

"Are you sure? Because I would beg to differ."

"Trust me, I know," Fallon responded. "Let's keep this between us, okay? I don't want him to know."

"You don't want me to know what?" came the deep masculine voice from behind Fallon. Her heart thumped erratically. What had he heard?

"How I'm not that big a fan of jazz, but that it's your cup of tea," Fallon responded, turning to her husband with a smile.

Gage's arm snaked around her waist. "Babe, you should have told me. We could have gone someplace else."

She shrugged. "It's fine. Ayden said he'd been wanting

to come here for a while, too. Isn't that right?" She glanced up at her brother for support.

Ayden grinned. "That's right. So let's go back to our seats. The quartet is back."

The evening ended with Fallon and Gage saying their goodbyes and planning on another double date with Ayden and Maya. Afterward, in the car, Fallon was happy to hear Gage had enjoyed himself.

"That went well," he said on the drive home. "I like Ayden."

"You sound surprised."

"I thought he was going to treat me like your parents. Like I wasn't good enough for you."

Fallon realized how deep Gage's past wounds were when it came to being accepted. How her and her friends' treatment of him had had a profound effect on who he was today.

"But he didn't treat me that way. Instead he treated me with respect and I feel the same about him. What Ayden has been able to accomplish without any help from your father is nothing short of amazing."

Fallon beamed with pride. "He's pretty great, isn't he?"

"Yeah, must be something in the genes." Gage glanced in her direction.

A swell of rightness filled Fallon. If they had a *real* marriage, this would be the start of a great beginning for their family, but they didn't and it wasn't. What was she going to do at the end of six months when it was time to say goodbye?

"Fallon?" She heard the question in his voice. "You got silent on me all of a sudden. You okay?"

She nodded but deep down she was afraid of losing him.

Fifteen

"Why did I agree to do this?" Gage wondered aloud as he helped Theo drill nails into the new storage shed behind his home.

"Because you owe me one," his friend responded.

"What for?"

"For telling you about the Stewarts' plight," Theo replied. He glanced in the direction of the house where Fallon was talking with his girlfriend, Amanda, whom he'd started seeing a few weeks ago. "If I hadn't, you wouldn't be married now."

Gage laughed. "If I recall, you told me I was out of my mind to consider marrying my sworn enemy."

Theo shrugged. "Who knew you'd be the happiest I've seen you in years? You're a changed man, my friend."

"How so?"

"Lighter. Happy. And it's all because of the woman in there." He pointed to Fallon, whom Gage could see through the oversize kitchen window.

"She's certainly made an impact."

"Admit it, Gage. You have feelings for the woman. Probably always did, which is why it was so easy for you to make that offer."

Gage knew Theo was right. On some deeper level, he'd always wanted Fallon even when she'd been off-limits and too young to know any better.

"So what now?"

"What do you mean?"

"Didn't you only agree to a six-month arrangement? What happens when your time is up and Fallon wants out?"

Gage's eyes narrowed. He knew he was putting his head in the sand, but he refused to consider it. Fallon was happy with them, with their life. He was certain if he presented her with the opportunity to stay with him, she wouldn't leave. "I don't think that's going to happen, Theo."

"She signed documents. She doesn't owe you a thing."

"She owes herself," Gage responded quickly. "She owes it to us to see how this plays out. Instead of turning tail and running away."

"Sounds like you've gotten very comfortable being a married man," Theo noted. "I hope this doesn't blow up in your face. I mean, what happens when Fallon finds out your true motives for marrying her? How do you think she'll feel?"

Gage knew the answer. "She'll feel betrayed." She wouldn't be angry. She'd hate him for stealing her birthright like Henry did to Ayden. And it scared the living daylights out of him. But he was in so deep, there was no way out. By purchasing those final shares, he was sealing his fate and setting them on a collision course. But Gage was powerless to stop it.

"Then for God's sake, come clean with her, man. Tell her what you've done and maybe—maybe—you can work it out."

Gage stiffened. "I can't. I could lose her."

"You can lose her if you don't," Theo stated.

Gage looked toward the window and found Fallon watching and waving at him. His heart turned in his chest and Gage knew he would do anything to keep her.

"That was fun," Fallon said when she and Gage returned to the penthouse later that evening. He'd been very quiet during dinner and, on the ride back, she wondered if he and Theo had had some sort of disagreement outside.

"Yeah, it was good," Gage said absentmindedly as he headed to the kitchen and grabbed a beer out of the fridge. He twisted the top off, took a pull and leaned against the counter.

Fallon removed her leather jacket and boots and followed him, watching him closely. The last couple of months she'd picked up on Gage's mood. She knew when something was on his mind. "You can talk to me about whatever it is that's upsetting you."

"I'm fine."

Fallon nodded. He was stonewalling her and she didn't like it. "Suit yourself." She spun around and walked into the master suite. She was removing her jewelry and placing it in the holder when Gage came marching in behind her.

"We don't have to share our feelings all the time, Fallon," he snarled. "It's all right to keep something to ourselves."

"So you admit you have secrets?" Fallon responded, spinning around to face him. "That you're keeping something from me?"

"I never said that."

Her eyes narrowed. "You didn't have to. Because your answer just said it all."

"Damn it, Fallon. What do you want from me?"

"Everything! Nothing." She shook her head. "Hell, I don't know, Gage. I blindly agreed to this marriage to save my family's company but I had no idea what it would be like, how I would feel…" Her voice trailed off.

"And how do you feel?"

She stared at him incredulously. "You want me to lay my heart bare when you're not willing to do the same?" She shook her head. "I don't think so."

She moved away and headed into the bathroom to brush her teeth, but Gage was right there. "I want to know."

"Well, that's too bad. Because I have my own secrets."

His face turned to stone. "You're saying that to get back at me."

He was wrong. The last couple of weeks she'd felt off, as if something was wrong. She hadn't had much of an appetite and was nauseous the last few mornings. It was odd. When she'd spoken to Theo's girlfriend, she'd asked Fallon about her last period. That's when it dawned on Fallon: she hadn't had one since she and Gage were married. She'd been so enraptured with her husband it had slipped her mind. Amanda had gently suggested she get a pregnancy test to find out for sure, but Fallon was afraid.

A baby?

She was on the pill to guarantee there would be no strings once the marriage was over. *What could have happened?* Had she missed a day? A rising panic threatened to overtake her. Guilt. Regret. Fear. Love. Fallon was feeling too many emotions to share a potential pregnancy with Gage. Not until she was sure.

"Fallon." Gage's light brown gaze sharpened as he drew near. "What is it? What don't I know?"

"Don't turn this around on me, Gage," Fallon responded tightly. "You said you want to keep feelings and emotions to yourself. I merely expressed I'll do the same. If you don't like it, that's tough."

She knew before he moved that he was going to kiss her. Kiss away her insolence. And she would let him because a hot sea of need always seemed to be just below the surface with them.

"Don't think this changes anything," Fallon murmured before his lips covered hers and his hands began skimming her body. His fingers tugged on the narrow straps of her sundress until they loosened and he could tug it to her waist.

His response was a raw, shaken laughter. "Duly noted. Now, are you going to let me love you?"

"Yes…" Gage's mouth left hers and his tongue began trailing an erotic path of fire from her throat, neck and shoulders to her breast. When he reached one chocolate nipple, he lowered his head and took the turgid peak in his mouth. She released an audible sigh and gave in.

Long moments later, when they lay spent and wrapped in each other arms, Fallon stared up at the ceiling. They'd shared something special, magical even, and emotions swelled in her.

Gage seemed to sense it, too. As if reading her mind, he tried to verbalize it. "Fallon," he said huskily. "Fallon, I—I—"

Fallon touched his cheek because she understood how hard it was to say those three words out loud. So she said them to herself. *I love you.* And if they had created a baby, she would love it because it was a part of him. It would mean they would be inextricably tied together for years. Was she prepared for that? She knew she loved him, but it couldn't be just her. It took two people fully committed to make a marriage work, let alone to parent a child. Fallon wasn't sure they had what it took for the long haul.

Fallon had a splitting headache. She'd felt not quite right all day.

Lunch with her mother hadn't helped. Nora griped about the meager allowance she was being given for living expenses. Fallon had tried to politely explain she needed to curb her spending habits. The company was not out of the woods. Gage's influx of cash had certainly helped, but it was up to Fallon to get them back on course.

Nora hadn't liked what she'd said. She'd yelled and pitched a fit, accusing Fallon of being unfair. "You have a rich husband now. I would think you would be looking out for your mother. Instead you're selfish and want all the money to yourself."

Fallon had curtly reminded Nora she didn't live off Gage and wasn't going to take another dime from him just because Nora couldn't control her impulses. They'd ended the lunch on an unpleasant note. Fallon was thankful to return to the office and had planned to lie down, but then she'd received an urgent call from Ayden.

"Fallon, I have to see you. Can you meet me?"

Fallon agreed and was anxiously awaiting his visit. That's when the stomach cramps started. He'd sounded urgent, as if it was a matter of life and death, and she didn't have a clue what it might be. She hoped everything was okay with him and Maya.

When Ayden arrived dressed in his usual attire of suit and tie with designer shoes, he looked serious and his jaw was tight.

"Ayden, what on earth is the matter?" Fallon asked, closing the door behind him. She motioned him to the sofa in her office. "Please have a seat."

"I have some news and you're not going to like what I have to say," Ayden replied, sitting.

Fallon sucked in a breath and willed the cramps away. She joined him on the couch. "Hit me with it. It's already been a bad day. It can't get much worse."

Ayden peered at her strangely.

"For Christ's sake, Ayden. You're scaring me. What is it?"

He inhaled deeply. "I want you to know it gives me no pleasure in doing this."

Fallon searched his face for a sign but couldn't find one. A sense of foreboding came over her that the happiness she'd found with Gage could be at risk.

"You know I run an investment firm and many people come to me to manage their portfolios."

"Damn it, Ayden. Don't beat around the bush. Just tell me."

"I'm breaking a confidence in sharing this with you, but while reviewing one of my client's portfolios, I learned he'd offloaded a substantial amount of Stewart Technologies' stock."

A sharp pain hit Fallon deep in the pit of her stomach. She tried not to react, but it was significantly more than any of the cramps from earlier that day. Still, she masked the pain. She had to know what was happening. "Go on."

"There was one purchaser of the stock, Fallon." He paused several beats. "It was Gage. He used a holding company so it couldn't immediately be traced back to him."

"No, no." Fallon shook her head and tears sprung to her eyes. This couldn't be happening. Not now. "Are you sure it's Gage? Maybe you could be wrong."

"I wish I were, but when I noticed this holding company buying all of my client's stock, I decided to do some digging. That's when I found out Stewart Technologies' stock is owned by several different holding companies. So I dug deeper into the paperwork of each company and lo and behold, Gage was the president of each of those firms. Despite your claim that Gage's incentive for marrying you was acceptance by the upper echelon, I never entirely bought it and now I know why. He wanted Stewart Technologies. And he has it, Fallon. Based on his last stock purchase, he has the majority share in the company."

Majority share.

Another cramp seized her and she clutched her stomach. *Gage has a majority stake in my company.*

He could take it over at any time. Exercise his rights and boot her out of the company. Steal her birthright like Henry had done to Ayden all those years ago. By essentially not claiming Ayden as his son, their father hadn't allowed Ayden the chance to run the company. The shoe was on the other foot; now she knew what it was like to be in her big brother's shoes.

She rose even though the pain was excruciating. A cold sweat was forming on her forehead.

What a fool she'd been to believe a word that came out of Gage's mouth. This must have been his end game all along. Ayden was right. Gage didn't want acceptance. He wanted vengeance and he'd attained it at her expense. He must have laughed at how gullible and naïve she was. They just happened to be compatible in the bedroom and he'd gotten his jollies off.

"Fallon, are you all right?" Ayden was immediately on his feet and rushing over to her. "You're looking very pale."

"I—I can't." The pain was intense now and she clutched her stomach.

"I'm taking you the hospital." Within seconds Ayden lifted her into her arms and was striding for the door.

Gage stared down at the paper in his hands. This was it. He finally had a fifty-one-percent ownership stake in Stewart Technologies. After all these years he was finally in a position of power over Henry Stewart, the man who'd put him and his mother out on the street with no home, no job and only the clothes on their backs.

He'd blamed himself for what happened to his mother. Perhaps if he'd ignored Fallon, hadn't shown any interest, she would have never come to their cottage. Who knows where life would have led him if he hadn't been spurred to succeed? If he hadn't pushed himself to do more, be more, so no one could ever look down on him again?

Sharing one unforgettable kiss with Fallon had been a defining moment that had changed the course of his life. But now time had passed and he could see it had been for the better. He'd achieved the highest levels of success on Wall Street. He could afford anything and everything he'd ever wanted or dreamed of.

But what would it all mean if he was alone with no one to share it with? Getting involved with the Stewarts two months ago had altered his life once again. Marrying Fallon was the single best decision he'd ever made. The life they shared together was so rich, so full, so exciting, so passionate. Gage would never get tired of her eternal optimism, her bright smile, her easy nature. She truly was a rare diamond.

Quite honestly, she was everything he hadn't known he'd been looking for. He loved her. And he wanted *theirs* to be a real marriage. Not a temporary one. And although he excelled at managing people and situations, tonight he was going to be honest and tell her he'd been foolish thinking revenge was the answer. It wasn't. He was going tell Fallon he loved her.

"Fallon, oh, thank God." Ayden came into the hospital room and wrapped his arms around her. "Thank God you're okay. I was so worried. And the doctors—" he glanced behind him at the door "—wouldn't tell me anything. Even though I'm your brother, I'm not on your approved list to receive medical information, so they wouldn't—"

Ayden stopped rambling when he saw the tears streaming down her cheeks. "Fallon, what is it? Is it something serious? What can I do?"

Fallon laughed without humor. "There's nothing you or anyone else can do."

Ayden's eyes grew large with fear and he began grabbing at his tie as if it was too tight around his neck. "Is it bad?"

"If you mean being pregnant by a man who doesn't love you and used you for revenge against your family?" Fallon asked. "Then, yes, it's bad."

"Pregnant?"

The word hung in the air like the albatross it was. Fallon felt it around her neck and there was nothing she could do about it. Deep down, she'd known it was true, but had been afraid to take the test. Well, the stomach cramps and spotting had led her *here*, to the hospital, getting medication to help prevent a miscarriage.

"Yes," Fallon replied. "I'm pregnant."

Ayden rubbed his bald head and then turned to face her. "Does Gage know?"

"No."

"Did you?"

Fallon locked gazes with her brother. "I suspected." She wiped at the tears she couldn't stop. It had to be hormones—she hardly ever cried. "But… I didn't want to believe it, you know? We signed a six-month marriage contract. A baby wasn't part of the agreement."

"But it's here now."

"Your point?"

"You're going to have to face this, Fallon. Face Gage," Ayden responded.

"After everything he's done? How can I?" Fallon sniffed. She knew the truth now. The only reason he'd married her was for revenge. To stick it to her, to her father, for the wrongs against him and his mother.

And he'd achieved his goal.

He'd also single-handedly ruined any chance of saving their marriage. Of their being a family one day. He'd made a fool of her and she would never forgive him.

Fallon inhaled sharply. Her mama bear instincts kicked in and she rubbed her stomach, willing her nerves to subside. Gage may have won this round. Fallon hoped he enjoyed it because she was walking away with the most precious gift of all. Their child. And he would have no part of its life. She would see to that.

Sixteen

Fallon was in the hospital.

Gage's heart thumped in his chest as he frantically made his way there. When he'd stopped by to pick her up from work, her assistant, Chelsea, had informed him she'd experienced stomach pains and Ayden had taken her to the hospital. Gage was terrified. What could be wrong? Fallon was the picture of health. In their short time together he'd seen how she took very good care of herself. She ate right and went to the gym. Working out with his wife was one of his favorite pastimes. She was a great sparring partner, though it was difficult to focus when she wore workout capris and one of those sports bras that bared her midriff.

He was terrified something was terribly wrong. *But what?*

As soon as he pulled up at the valet stand, Gage quickly dispensed with his keys and rushed inside. After finding her room number, he took off running down the hall. What had stunned him was when the nurse had told him she was in the maternity ward. *Why in the hell would she be there?* The ride seemed interminable but eventually the elevator stopped and he disembarked. He found her room and strode to the door. When he arrived, she was sitting up in bed and Ayden was in a nearby chair.

"Thank God, you're all right," Gage said, hastening toward her. He bent his head to kiss her but she held up her hand and blocked him.

"Don't even try it." She lurched away from him as if he were contaminated with some virus.

Gage stepped back and stared at Fallon in confusion. He didn't understand the look of disgust on her face. He glanced at Ayden, but he had a stony expression. "Would either of you care to tell me what's going on? When Chelsea told me you were in the hospital, I was worried sick. You have no idea the crazy scenarios that were running through my mind. Do they know what's wrong? Why are you here in the maternity ward?"

Fallon turned to Ayden. "Do you mind giving us some time alone?"

Ayden glanced in Gage's direction and the dirty look he gave him told Gage that he was not pleased to see him. "Are you sure? I can stay behind."

She shook her head. "No, Gage and I need to have this conversation in private."

Ayden nodded and got to his feet. He leaned down and pressed a kiss against her forehead. "I'll be outside the door if you need me."

She attempted a half smile. "Thank you."

After giving Gage another fiery look that could have melted ice, Ayden left the room and closed the door.

Gage again moved toward the bed. "Fallon, please. Tell me what's wrong. What happened?"

She glared at him. "I don't know, Gage. Why don't you tell me since you decided to stab me in the back?"

"Pardon?"

Her hand slashed through the air. "Don't act coy. Now's your time to exact the revenge you've been plotting for months. I'm a sitting duck. Take your best shot."

A knot formed in his stomach. Surely Fallon couldn't know about the shares of Stewart Technologies' stock he'd acquired. *Could she?* "What are you talking about?"

"Really? Really?" She raised her eyebrows. "You're not going to admit it? You're going to make me spell it out for you? All right then, Gage. I'll bite. One question. How long have you been conspiring to take over my company?" She folded her arms across her chest and waited for his response.

She knew.

"Fallon, I can explain." His voice was low, tense.

"Ha." She laughed without humor. "I seriously doubt that." Her voice was tight. "But go ahead and try me."

Gage had an overwhelming urge to wrap his arms around her and hold her close. In the bed, she looked small and fragile wearing the hospital-issued gown, her hair hanging limply around her shoulders. Even her hazel-gray eyes seemed cloudy. Yet her voice was strong and fierce. He moved past her and walked to the window overlooking the street.

When he remained silent she said, "Well?" Her voice was cold and distant.

He spun around to face her. "I won't lie. I've been acquiring Stewart Technologies' stock for a couple months."

"So you admit it?"

He took a deep breath and nodded. "I was angry, Fallon. I wanted retribution for how your family treated us sixteen years ago. Your father threw us out with nothing but the clothes on our backs. He left us with nothing. No clothes. No money. Not even a reference for my mother, who'd worked for him for nearly a decade. You have no idea the trials and tribulations we faced starting over."

At her stone-faced silence, he continued. "I was angry. Rage coursed through my DNA and I vowed that someday I would get back at the Stewarts. After living on the estate and hearing the barbs from your wealthy friends, I recognized the reality of my life. I had to be successful. I promised myself I would elevate myself to a better station in life. One in which no one could ever treat me as anything less than an equal."

"And when did you decide to use me as a pawn in your revenge scenario?"

His gaze landed on Fallon. "You were never a pawn, Fallon. I wanted you. I've always wanted you. Even back then, when you were sixteen. But the timing wasn't right then. I had to push you away—but not before I kissed you. And it was that kiss that I've never forgotten."

"Oh, please, don't make it sound like it was more than it was. I was just a naïve girl making a play for you."

"It was more than that. It stirred something in me," Gage replied, "but I pushed it down. And after we were kicked out, I tried to forget you. And I did a good job of it with lots of women of all shapes and sizes. Beautiful women. But they weren't you, Fallon."

"Stop it, Gage. Don't act like we had some unrequited love because it doesn't ring true. You deliberately sought out retribution, against me and my family. Ayden told me everything. He told me how you've been purchasing shares of the company behind my back."

"Can you blame me?" Gage inquired testily. "I was angry. Angry about the raw deal we received."

"No, I wouldn't blame you if you hated me and my family, but I point-blank asked if you could put what happened behind you. You lied to me. Told me you could forgive but wouldn't forget." She sighed. "You let me believe…" Fallon's words trailed off.

"Believe what?" The tension that gripped her was vibrating through him, engulfing them in a volatile bubble.

"That you *cared*?" she yelled at him as her eyes swept downward. "This entire time I was drifting along in some fantasy world in which I thought you and I might actually last beyond the contract, but it was all a lie." She pierced him with her gaze. "It's all about crime and punishment with you, isn't it?"

"It may have started out that way, Fallon," Gage said. He came to sit beside her on the bed and this time she didn't move away. "But it quickly changed once I saw you again and the familiar visceral response I had to you wouldn't be denied. I admit, marriage was never my intention. I'd thought one night together would be enough and I would rid myself of this simmering attraction I felt for you. But that night in the car…you must remember how hot it was between us. We were a fuse waiting to be lit and, when we were finally together, it was incredible. More than incredible. I realized I'd grossly miscalculated my feelings."

"Feelings. We're talking about feelings," Fallon scoffed. "We've been married for two months, Gage, and this is the first time you mentioned those. But it doesn't matter because I don't believe a word you say. You've gotten what you wanted. Me in your bed, an introduction into Austin society and the Stewart family at your mercy with you calling all the shots. And now I want you out of my room and out of my life."

"Fallon…listen, I know you're upset and when you calm down we can talk rationally."

"I am rational and I want you gone. Go!"

"Not until I know you're okay," Gage responded. "You collapsed, for Christ's sake, and I'm not—" The words he'd been about to say cut off when he noticed the book on the bedside table.

What to Expect When You're Expecting.

Suddenly it became very clear to him why she was in the maternity ward. It was the same reason she hadn't been eating much lately and had gotten sick a couple of mornings. It was why her breasts had felt fuller and more sensitive during their lovemaking.

Fallon was pregnant.

Fallon knew the moment the truth hit Gage. Color leached from his face and he looked at her. "Are you…?"

"You know the answer to that question," Fallon responded.

"How?"

Fallon shook her head. "I don't know. I was taking the pills, but apparently that's normal. Anyway, it doesn't change the facts. I'm going to have a baby."

"You mean *we're* having a baby," he replied.

"This baby is mine," Fallon stated fiercely, clutching her stomach.

His gaze zeroed in on her action. "Fallon…"

"I don't need or want you, Gage. Neither does this baby."

Gage's face was drawn and tight, and Fallon knew she'd hit a nerve.

"A child needs its father. And I won't be separated from him or her." Gage's tone was vehement.

"You have no rights," Fallon stated. "My body, my choice. And right now I choose not to have anything to do with a liar for a husband."

"You're being unreasonable. You must know this changes everything between us, Fallon. It's not black-and-white anymore."

"You mean like it was for you when you conspired against me?" Fallon sat upright in the bed. "When you mercilessly seduced me night after night until I ended up here in this bed!" She pointed downward. "You used me for your own enjoyment and amusement. What was I to you but some pampered bed-warmer you could keep handy when you had an itch that needed scratching?"

"That's not true!" he retorted hotly. "I've never treated you with anything less than respect."

Fire flashed in Fallon's eyes. "Respect. You call lying and going behind my back respect? You don't know the meaning of the word and I won't let me or my baby be a pawn in your games any longer. I want you out. Now!" she yelled.

Suddenly the door to her hospital room swung open and Ayden walked in. His eyes were laser-focused on her. "I could hear Fallon screaming down the hall. What the hell is going on?" He looked at Gage.

"Please make him leave." Fallon turned onto her side and faced the window. She couldn't bear to look at Gage. Not knowing how incredibly foolish she'd been to fall for his lies. He'd set this course of events in motion and now they'd created a life. She placed her hand over her small, rounding belly.

Ayden walked over to Gage. "I won't have you upsetting Fallon anymore, Gage. She nearly suffered a miscarriage because of your lies and machinations."

"But the baby's okay?" Gage asked.

Fallon studiously avoided looking at him. "*For now.* I was having spotting and cramps. The doctor put me on some medication that will hopefully stop them, but I need to rest and be stress-free."

"Meaning you don't want me anywhere near you? Is that it?"

"That's right," Fallon responded hotly and turned to glare at him. "You can go back to your high-profile Wall Street existence making loads of money because I don't want or need you and neither does my baby. Consider the contract we signed null and void. Gather your team of highly paid lawyers and get them to send over whatever paperwork is necessary to end this sham of a marriage."

"Fallon, you can't get rid of me that easy. Not only did we sign a contract, but I own a majority stake at Stewart Technologies."

Fallon's eyes flashed fire. "So you're threatening me?"

"No, of course not." Gage sighed. "This isn't coming out right. I want you to calm down."

"Then let me show you the exit." Ayden motioned to the door.

Gage held up his hands in surrender. "Okay. I'll leave for now, but I will be back, Fallon. It isn't over between us."

When she finally heard the door click shut, Fallon fell back against the pillows. Holding herself up, being strong in front of Gage, had zapped all her energy.

"It's all right, Fallon. You can rest now." Ayden came forward and helped make her more comfortable on the bed. "I meant what I told Gage. You need to get some sleep."

"Are you leaving?"

Ayden shook his head. "No, I'll be right here by your side."

His words were one of the last things Fallon thought about as she drifted off to sleep, along with Gage's promise it wasn't over between them.

Pregnant.

Gage was still in shock over the news. He had absolutely no idea what to do with the information. He was equal parts overjoyed and scared out of his mind. He'd never thought about being a father because he'd never had one of his own. The closest he'd had to a father figure had been Henry Stewart and look how that had turned out.

But that didn't change the facts. Fallon was having his

baby. He wasn't sure how far along she was, because they'd had a very active sex life, but he suspected she could have conceived as early as their honeymoon. During those idyllic days in Punta Cana he hadn't been able to get enough of her. He'd had a ferocious, all-consuming need for her. A need that had led them to creating a child.

But Fallon wanted nothing more to do with him. *Ever.*

She knew the truth that he'd been seeking to right the wrongs from years ago by acquiring stocks in Stewart Technologies. But she was wrong about his feelings for her. They'd grown exponentially and he was no longer seeking revenge. All he could see was Fallon. And now their baby.

Flashes of the two of them together holding a beautiful brown baby with hazel-gray eyes struck Gage. He walked to the bar and poured himself two thumbs of whiskey. Padding to the terrace, he lifted the glass to his mouth and sipped. The spirits warmed his insides but nothing could smooth out the raw edges from his reckoning with Fallon.

The disappointment in her eyes, the hurt—it dug into his insides. The thought he might never know his child, as he'd never known his father, was too much to deal with. He stared out at the city and sipped the whiskey as night fell over Austin. Somehow, some way, he had to change her mind. Make her realize her future and their baby's included him.

Seventeen

Muted voices slowly pulled Fallon back into consciousness. At first she didn't know where she was but then it dawned on her. She was in the hospital, fighting to keep her baby after nearly suffering a miscarriage.

Fallon blinked and opened her eyes. Her mother and father rushed to her side.

Her father spoke first. "You're awake. When we heard you'd fainted, your mother and I were scared to death. Thank you for calling us."

Henry turned and Fallon looked to see who he was speaking to. She noticed Ayden standing in the corner of the room, a haunted look on his face. Seconds later he walked out the door. It had taken courage for her big brother to make that call after their father had essentially abandoned him as a child. Fallon would be forever grateful. And she would tell Ayden that as soon as she had the chance.

"So, you're going to be a mommy," her mother stated with a wide grin. Nora came forward and lightly stroked her cheek. "You know, you're making me a grandma way before my time."

Fallon couldn't resist a smile.

"How far along are you?" her father asked. "If you don't mind my asking."

"Two months."

"You certainly didn't waste any time, my dear," her mother said. "It will certainly ensure Gage is on the hook for taking care of you and my grandson or granddaughter for years to come."

Fallon sighed. Of course her mother thought in monetary terms. Fallon hoped Ayden hadn't told them Gage's true intentions and the reason she'd fainted. Her parents had no idea her marriage to Gage was over. Finished. She wouldn't stay married to someone who'd lied to and deceived her.

"Where's Gage?" Her father searched her eyes for an answer. "The mother of his child is in the hospital. Why isn't he here at your side?"

Fallon rubbed her temples. She was not in the mood for this. "Not now, Daddy."

"I agree, Henry," her mother said quietly. "Now isn't the time or place."

"Like hell it isn't. I smell a rat." Her father pressed on. "I had to hear about my daughter—" he pounded his chest "— from Ayden of all people. The son who hates me because I walked away from his mama. And you tell me I'm wrong?"

"What do you want from me, Daddy?" Fallon wailed. "For me to admit I made a mistake marrying Gage? Well, I did. There, I said it. Are you happy now?"

Her father's face clouded with unease and he came to sit by her bedside. "Of course I'm not happy to see my baby girl in pain. I only want what's best for you. That's all I have ever wanted."

Nervously, Fallon bit her lip and nodded as tears streamed down her cheeks. "Then let this go."

"All right." He nodded.

The nurse interrupted at the right moment when she came in with the cart to check Fallon's vitals.

"We're going to let you get some rest," her father said, giving her hand a gentle squeeze. "But we're a phone call away if you need us."

"Thank you, Daddy. And one other thing?"

"Anything, baby girl."

"It took a lot for Ayden to call you today, but he did it for me. Because he loves me. Please be kind to him."

"I will."

"Promise me."

"I promise."

After her parents departed and the nurse checked her blood pressure and pulse, Fallon glanced at her phone for messages. There was a text and a voice mail from Dane stating he was en route to Austin because Ayden had called him, too. Her big brother was pretty amazing. There were, however, no calls or texts from Gage. Had she been expecting one? She shouldn't. She'd made it crystal clear she didn't want him near her, but theirs was only a cease-fire. Gage had *chosen* to leave, but he would be back. Of that she was sure.

The door to her room opened and Ayden returned. He'd long since abandoned the jacket and tie he'd come to her office in and was drinking what she suspected was coffee in a foam cup. He glanced around the room.

She read his mind. "They're gone."

He nodded and was quiet as he came to sit on the bed with her.

"Thank you for calling them. I really appreciate it. It must have been difficult dealing with our father after all this time. I know you didn't stay for the reception."

Ayden's hazel-gray eyes rested on her face. "You have no idea how hard, Fallon. When he arrived, there was no tearful reunion. He was here for you and you alone. It didn't matter that I was here, because I mean nothing to him."

Tears sprung to her eyes. "I'm sorry, Ayden."

He shrugged. "It's okay. I made my peace with it a long time ago. I'm glad I have you and Dane."

"So am I." Fallon attempted a half smile. "I owe you a great deal for looking out for me and bringing me your findings on Gage even though you knew it would hurt me."

"Honestly, Fallon, I struggled with whether I should tell you. I'd seen how happy you've been with Gage with my own eyes. Ultimately, after talking with Maya, she advised me I had to tell you, but it was hard. He clearly adores you and vice versa."

"That's a lie, Ayden." Tears brimmed in her eyes and fell down her cheeks. "He was acting, giving me a false sense of security before he slipped the rug right out from under me. And as for me…" Her voice trailed off. "I foolishly thought somehow love would find a way. I thought in time my love might heal the pain and heartache he'd been through. I was wrong."

A wave of something close to desolation rushed through her. A sob broke free and she curled herself in the fetal position.

"It's okay, Fallon," Ayden whispered in her ear as he climbed onto the hospital bed and gathered her in his arms. "I'm here for you. Your big brother is here."

Days bled together in a dull gray jumble for Gage. He was trying not to mope and was focusing all his energy into work and managing his company's mutual funds. But it didn't lighten his mood. Instead he only grew bleaker as the days dragged on. Meanwhile he'd learned that Fallon had been released from the hospital with strict instructions to relax and avoid stress.

When he'd told Theo, his best friend had given him an

I-told-you-so speech. Theo had advised Gage to grovel at Fallon's feet and beg her to take him back, but that was hard to do because, true to her word, she wanted nothing to do with him. She'd ignored every call or text he'd sent since her release. As for his mother, he couldn't tell her about the baby, not until he made things right with Fallon.

She'd sent Ayden and Maya to pack up her belongings at his penthouse. Gage had been sure not to be there; he hadn't wanted to see the sad looks on their faces.

His marriage was over when it should be thriving because they were having a child together. But he couldn't confront Fallon now and beat his chest about his rights. The doctor had told him she'd nearly miscarried and, in another month or so, she'd be out of the woods. Then they could tell everyone their great news.

And so Gage was giving Fallon the space she needed to get stronger so she could carry their child to term. She and the baby meant more to him than anything. He knew he didn't deserve either of them, but he would do his best by them. If she needed to relax in a stress-free zone and be with her family, then so be it.

He wasn't prepared, however, for her brother Dane to make an appearance at his office. The youngest Stewart was known to been MIA on most occasions. He hadn't even made their wedding, citing the excuse that he couldn't leave the movie he'd been filming, even though he was one of Hollywood's A-list actors.

"Dane." Gage rose when the six-foot-tall man approached him. He was what the ladies called a Pretty Ricky with café-au-lait skin, dark brown eyes and a perpetual five-o'clock shadow. He was wearing faded jeans, a graphic T-shirt, black boots and a leather jacket. Dane's good looks must have gotten him past Gage's assistant even though he'd given strict instructions to not be disturbed. "What can I do for you?"

"I came here to give you a black eye," Dane responded, making a fist and punching his other hand. "I heard about what you did to the company, but most of all to Fallon, how you played her for your own gain. And I came here to give you a piece of my mind."

"By all means," Gage responded, widening his arms. "Take your best shot. I deserve everything you have to say and then some."

Dane frowned. "You're not supposed to be helping this along."

"Why not? I know what I did was wrong. I apologized. Told Fallon I made a mistake and I should have never lied to her."

"Yet you did." Dane glared at him. "She feels like you made a fool of her. How could you do that? How can you stand to look at yourself in the mirror?" He crossed to Gage's desk and slammed his large hands on it. "Fallon has had a thing for you for years, Gage. And you knew that. You took advantage."

"I admit my intentions from the outset weren't honorable, but they changed when I fell in love with your sister."

"Love?" Dane laughed as he stood to his full six-foot height. "C'mon, Gage."

"It's true, Dane. I love Fallon and I love our baby."

Dane stared incredulously. "Does she know that?"

Gage shook his head. "That night…at the hospital. She never gave me a chance to say more. She ordered me out."

"Can you blame her?"

"No, I can't," Gage replied. "It's why I've stayed away, so she can calm down and get some rest. I don't want anything to happen to her or our baby."

Dane eyed him suspiciously. "You should know she intends to divorce you. If you really love my sister, you don't have very long to fight for her."

"I know, but I will. You best believe that."

* * *

Fallon was ready to get back to work. Sitting on her bottom for the last two months had been sheer agony, but she would do anything to keep this baby safely in her womb. And she had. But she'd hated not being able to run her own company and be in the thick of the action.

Initially she'd been worried Gage would try to make a move on Stewart Technologies while she was out, but surprisingly it had been business as usual with no outside interference. It wouldn't last for long. One day soon Gage would make his move. In the meantime she enjoyed visits from her parents, Shana, Ayden and Maya. Even Dane had come during the early part of her convalescence to spend some time with her.

But she'd done as instructed and worked remotely from Stewart Manor to keep her stress level to a minimum. Initially she'd wanted to go back to her cottage, but her parents had been adamant that if something happened, they'd be too far away. They'd insisted she come home.

Nora fussed over her and was already knee-deep in discussion with an interior designer on decorating a nursery for when the baby came. Initially, Fallon was suspicious of Nora's motives. At the hospital her mother had made no secret of how her grandchild guaranteed Gage wouldn't be off the hook financially. But then Nora had surprised Fallon by offering to be her birth coach. It had been a rare mother-daughter moment, one that involved tears and hugs. But, of course, it was over much too quick. Nora wouldn't win mother of the year, but they were making inroads in their relationship. It seemed the baby was bringing them together.

Ayden and her father had gone from being civil to one another to actually having a conversation. They wouldn't be breaking into a hug anytime soon, but progress was being made. And if her personal suffering had caused a reunion between her big brother and father, then Fallon would gladly endure it.

Today, however, she was excited. After her checkup this morning at the four-month mark, she'd been given the green light to return to work next week. It felt like she'd been given a get-out-of-jail-free card.

She was leaving the doctor's office and heading to her car in the parking lot when she caught a familiar figure standing by her driver's-side door.

Gage.

She'd known it was possible he might show up. Although she didn't owe him a thing, she'd informed Gage of the doctor visit, but she'd urged him to stay away. When he hadn't shown, she'd thought she was in the clear. She'd been wrong.

Swallowing the lump in her throat, Fallon strolled toward him, hoping to give the appearance of nonchalance. Gage looked different. His eyes were haunted instead of intense as they usually were. He had on a leather jacket and faded jeans, which were hanging off him instead of clinging to his muscular thighs. *Had he lost weight?*

"How'd the doctor's visit go?"

"Fine."

"And the baby?"

"Is also fine," she replied. "We're both—"

"Fine, I know. I get that," Gage interrupted her. "Can we talk?"

"I believe your lawyers can handle whatever it is that requires discussion." Fallon used her key to unlock her door. "Can you step aside?"

Gage shook his head. "Fallon? We *have* to talk."

"Why? Because you say so?"

"Because we're having a baby. Do you honestly want other people deciding what's best for our child?"

Fallon sighed. "All right, there's a park across the street."

She began walking toward the crosswalk and noticed that Gage was still standing there. Had he been expecting her to hold his hand? He could think again. She watched him insert his hands into his pockets and move quickly to her side.

When they made it to the park, they sat on one of the many benches surrounding the playground. How apropos, considering one day they'd be watching a child of theirs running around and playing on the swings, slide and monkey bars.

Fallon turned to Gage. "Well, you wanted to talk. You have the floor."

Gage scooted around to face her. "Thank you for agreeing to talk to me."

"I doubt I had much choice."

"You have choices, Fallon," Gage responded, "and I'm sorry if I made you feel like you didn't. I forced you into marrying me and didn't give you a whole lot of options."

"No, you didn't. I had forty-eight hours."

"I was afraid if I gave you too much time, you'd turn me down. And I had a plan to bring you and your family down a peg. It was all so easy when you're looking at it on paper, but after seeing you again, I was undone. I hadn't expected to be so completely enamored with you. I wanted you for myself."

"Do you honestly expect me to believe that?"

"I do. Look at how bullheaded I was. I wouldn't give you an inch. I requested we get married in a month's time."

Fallon sighed. "All right, so you lusted after me. That doesn't change the fact that you lied to me."

Gage stared her directly in the eye. "I did. And I can't take back what I've done. All I can do is tell you how incredibly sorry I am for hurting you. I never thought we'd have a real marriage, but somewhere along the line…" He paused. "Fallon, I fell in love you."

Her eyes widened in disbelief.

"I know you don't believe me," Gage said quickly. "Because I haven't earned your love. I used and abused your trust. I can only hope one day you'll believe me and let me be a father to our baby." He glanced down at her stomach, which was starting to show signs of rounding thanks to the child growing inside.

"Gage…"

"I love you, Fallon," he said again. "I probably always have and I certainly know I always will." He rose and lowered himself far enough to plant a kiss on her forehead. "And I believe what we had together was precious, but it wasn't built on the right foundation. One day it will be. I will prove to you I'm worthy of your love. I promise."

Stunned, Fallon watched Gage walk away. She sat on the bench until she heard school bells in the distance. Gage *loved* her. Why had it taken him so long to say the words she'd longed to hear? The words she'd felt so long for him but couldn't express for fear he didn't feel the same? Was he expressing his undying love for her because of the baby? He'd lied too easily and believably before. He'd made her think he wanted acceptance into society, all the while seducing her, when all he'd wanted was to ruin her family. No, as much as it pained her, she needed to listen to her gut. Gage didn't deserve her love or her trust.

Fallon patted her stomach and spoke to their baby. "I'm sorry we've made such a mess of this, but I'll fix it." Somehow, some way, she would. She would carve out a life for herself and this baby even if it didn't include its father.

"I have to admit your call was a surprise," Ayden said when Gage met up with him for drinks at a swanky downtown bar near both their offices a couple of weeks later.

"Even though I'm persona non grata in the Stewart family, I was hoping we could talk," Gage responded.

"If you're looking for help with Fallon," Ayden began, "you can count me out. It's up to you to heal the wound in your relationship."

"Agreed. What'll you have?" He motioned to the bartender standing in front of Ayden.

"I'll have a whiskey." Ayden turned to Gage. "So, what's up? And has anyone told you that you look like hell?"

Gage smirked. He couldn't remember the last time he'd been to the barber for a haircut much less a trim to his beard. Nothing seemed to matter without Fallon in his life. He slid a large envelope toward Ayden.

Ayden's brow furrowed as he took it. "What's this?"

"Open it."

Ayden studied him for a long moment before sliding his finger under the flap and opening the envelope. He pulled out a stack of papers and read through them. Then those hazel-gray eyes so like Fallon's stared at him in shock. "Why would you do this?"

"To prove to Fallon I only want her and our baby."

"But why me?" Ayden inquired. When the waiter returned with his drink, he took a long swallow.

"Because they're rightfully yours. They belong to you," Gage responded. "Call it righting a wrong done to you and your mother. I know Henry cheated your mother out of her shares. I'm only giving you what you deserve."

"I can't let you do this, Gage," Ayden responded. "This is a fortune. I'm sure there's another way to prove yourself to Fallon. Plus, I'm not even sure how I feel about this. I mean, I'm not a part of the Stewart family."

"My spies tell me otherwise. I heard you've been visiting Stewart Manor."

"To see Fallon." Ayden's voice rose slightly. "Although Henry and I are polite to one another for Fallon's sake, we're far from bosom buddies. And even if I were to accept your generous offer, how would this look to Fallon? She might think you and I were in it together all along to get revenge against Henry because we both have a beef with him. I don't want to ruin the relationship we have. Fallon and I have grown close."

Gage slid off the bar stool and threw back the last bit of whiskey he'd been drinking. "You and I know the truth. We were never in cahoots to cheat Fallon. Just me. I'm the scoundrel and she knows that. You have to trust in what you've built with her. As for the others, do you really care what Henry thinks?"

Ayden gave him a sidelong glance. "Once upon a time I did, but not anymore."

"Well then, you're a Stewart, Ayden. Take what's yours. Take what should have been your inheritance. I have no right to it and neither does Fallon. I hope she'll understand the reasoning behind my decision."

"I hope to God you're right," Ayden said, grabbing the papers and scribbling his name on them. "And I don't regret this decision. But, yes, on my mother's behalf for everything she was denied from Henry, I accept."

Leaving the bar, Gage had never felt so good. The last two months he'd been tormented by his actions. Each morning he woke up feeling as if something had broken inside him. It had. But tonight he'd relieved himself of the one thing standing between him and a second chance with his wife. He hoped it was enough to prove he loved and wanted Fallon and their baby.

Fallon still couldn't believe what Ayden had shared with her. Gage had given Ayden all of the stock he'd acquired in Stewart Technologies. And he hadn't sold it to him. He'd *given* them to her big brother lock, stock and barrel, without asking for anything in return.

It was a generous gesture and Ayden explained that at first he wasn't entirely sure what to do. But then he told her why he'd said yes. His mother, Lillian, had helped his father start Stewart Technologies, but during the divorce she'd been outgunned by Henry's fancy lawyers and had walked away with a small settlement. Ayden felt it was okay to accept Gage's gift. And Fallon had agreed. He'd been surprised Fallon wasn't angry with Gage for not offering them to her first.

She wasn't. Yet Ayden had offered to share the stock Gage had given *him* with her. He wanted to prove he wasn't in cahoots with Gage on a takeover, but Fallon turned Ayden down and told him to keep the stock. She already ran Stewart Technologies and had shares in the company herself. She didn't need more. But Ayden? He'd been abandoned by their father. Fallon was ashamed Henry acted as if Ayden didn't exist. He'd never even paid child support, much less acknowledged Ayden's accomplishments. The shares were his just deserts. She was surprised Gage had understood that and hadn't wanted to keep them for himself. After everything that had happened to Gage and his mother, she was certain he felt entitled to them, but he hadn't. Instead he'd offered them to Ayden.

A man who, like Gage, had been looked down on.

She doubted her father would agree with her. He would be livid that Ayden, the black sheep, had leverage over him. But Fallon didn't mind if Ayden had a larger stake in Stewart Technologies than she did. She was CEO and running the company, after all. Ayden had his own company, Stewart Investments, to worry about.

What she couldn't get over was Gage's generous act. It gave her hope that there was some humanity left in him. That he was a man she could love. A man who could be a father to her baby.

And so today she'd decided to hop in her Audi and drive to see her bullheaded, arrogant and controlling husband to find out if she was still living in a fairy-tale world where love won out in the end.

She didn't waste time parking when she arrived at Gage's building; she merely tossed her keys to the valet, waved at the doorman and rushed to the private elevator. She pressed the code for the penthouse and impatiently waited for the car to ascend to the top. She paced the travertine-tiled floor until finally the doors opened into the penthouse.

The apartment was dark and Fallon wondered if Gage was home, but then she saw a figure in silhouette outside on the terrace. It was Gage's favorite place to go when he needed to think things over. The pocket doors were open so the click of her heels as she approached caused Gage to turn around in his chair. Her heart quickened at the sight of him.

"Fallon?" His voice was raspy.

When she was within a few feet of him, she answered. "Yes, it's me." She noticed the glass in his hand with a dark liquid she could only assume was brandy, his drink of choice.

"I thought perhaps I was dreaming like I have been the last couple of months, hoping you'd come home. That you'd come back to me. Is that why you're here? Are you back for good?"

Fallon stared at him from where she stood. He looked haggard, with lines around his eyes, and his beard had grown. When was the last time he'd shaved? "I don't know, Gage, that depends on how this conversation goes."

The hope she'd given him instantly caused him to straighten and he walked toward her until they were face-to-face.

"Why did you do it, Gage?" Fallon asked, searching his face. "Why did you give Ayden those shares?"

"Because they're rightfully his," Gage responded. "Always should have been. I had no right to them. I was angry and acquired them as a way to get back at your father. To strike him where it hurts. Then he would see I was good enough for you. But you know what?"

"What?"

"The person I hurt most was you. The woman I've come to love. And as a result, I hurt myself because you left me. Alone. How I've always been."

She dragged in a sustaining breath. "Gage…" Her heart broke for him even though he was the reason they were in this situation to begin with.

"I know I have no right to ask you this." His eyes pierced hers as he held her gaze. "Can you forgive me for being such a stupid, arrogant, bullish fool in search of power and prestige? I can't change the man I was, but because of you I can change and be the man you need me to be—a whole, mature man." He glanced around and his mouth twisted in pain. "Because none of it means anything without you, Fallon. I'm sorry. Your being here gives me hope that perhaps—perhaps—you might be willing to give us another chance. A chance to be a family. Because I want more than anything to be married to you."

Fallon didn't move. She stayed where she was. Her heart galloped in her chest. She was afraid to move, let alone speak, because her heart was so full. She felt the tears silently slide down her cheeks one by one. She felt the moisture against her skin but was suspended in time with Gage as she always was whenever he was near.

"Please don't shut me out of your life, Fallon. Please let me be near you and our baby." Gage reached out and cupped her cheek. "Don't cry, please. That's not what I want." Slowly he pulled her to him, cradling her in his arms.

It was her undoing. His words were scraping away all her defenses, all the walls she'd erected around herself. Fallon knew why Gage had been so generous and why he'd given those shares to Ayden. He wanted to prove that he wanted her more than his quest for revenge. The truth blazed in her heart, sure and true. Gage was the man she loved. The man she'd always loved. Whom she would love forever.

"I love you." The words escaped her lips before she had a chance to take them back. And as she said them, the heaviness she'd felt for weeks began to lighten.

It was an indelible fact. She could never stop loving Gage. He'd had her from the moment he'd helped her after she'd fallen off that horse. "Totally. Uncontrollably. And with all my heart."

"Oh, God, Fallon, I love you, too, so much." His voice sounded choked.

They reached for each other at the same time. Their eyes locked in a hot, heated moment before he bowed his head and he brushed his lips across hers. The slow, sweet kiss caused a low moan to release from her lips. Oh, how she'd missed this. And when he angled his head so he could deepen the kiss and take full possession of her mouth, Fallon was on board. She slid her tongue against his and the taste of him exploded in her mouth.

A slow curl of heat unraveled in her as she tangled her arms around his neck. It had been too long—far too long— since he'd touched her like this. Kissed her like this.

"Gage," she murmured when they came up for air. She took in large gulps, breathing in his dark, delicious scent that was so real and achingly familiar. Peace filled her as Gage held her to his hard, solid chest. "Make love to me," she whispered.

"With pleasure." In seconds he'd swept her into his arms and carried her down the hall to their bed.

Gage laid his beautiful wife down on *their* bed and smiled as she hurriedly removed her clothing and his until he could lie beside her. Catching a whiff of her delicate floral scent awakened every cell in his body and revived memories of how good it had been between them. It had been those images that had haunted him in the weeks they'd been apart, tormenting his mind and his body. He'd been unable to sleep and it showed in the tiredness he'd felt each day.

Until now. He considered himself lucky Fallon was forgiving him. He would have another chance to be a better husband and a father to their child.

He looked down at her in bewilderment. "Is it really possible we can try again? Start afresh?"

Fallon reached for him then, wrapping her arms around his neck and bestowing him with sweet, tender kisses. And Gage realized what true forgiveness looked like.

"Good. Because I want to give you everything," Gage said.

Their lovemaking that night was slow and worshipful because there was nothing but love and joy between them. They found their way back to each other's bodies, exploring every available inch while whispering loving words that would blanket them and last them a lifetime. Until, eventually, sleep claimed them as they lay in each other's arms.

Epilogue

A year later

Fallon emerged from the bedroom where she'd gone to change clothes—for the second time that day—after her son, Dylan, had chosen to throw up all over her baptism outfit. But she didn't care. Fallon felt as if she were the luckiest woman in the world.

She and Gage were as in love as ever. She never knew she could be this happy. This fulfilled. Months ago they'd renewed their vows. It had been just the two of them and they'd pledged to start over. And they had. They were rebuilding Stewart Technologies with some help from her big brother. Ayden had chosen to keep the stock and hoped to give it to his children someday. Her parents, her father especially, had initially blustered over Gage's gift, but eventually he'd piped down when he'd realized pitting Fallon against her big brother could cause him to lose her.

Fallon and Gage had been thrilled. And when they'd

attended Ayden and Maya's wedding on Valentine's Day, it had brought tears to Fallon's eyes. Gage had incorrectly thought she was upset over their first ceremony, but then she'd told him, she'd been in love with him even then and they'd kissed and made out like two love-struck teenagers in the back of the reception hall.

Fallon smiled at the memory as she walked down the corridor of their new house, which wasn't far from Stewart Manor so her parents could be close to their grandson. Before Dylan's arrival, she and Gage had decided they'd need more space, a house that was kid-friendly instead of Gage's ultra-chic penthouse. He kept it as an investment and for the nights he worked late in the city, but those days were over for Fallon. Once she'd had Dylan, she'd cut back on her hours. She wanted to be a better mother than Nora had been.

When she arrived at the terrace where they were hosting the reception after the baptism, Fallon glanced at her mother, who was in a battle with Grace for the title of most doting grandmother. Both women had called a cease-fire when Fallon told them in no uncertain terms she would cut them off from seeing the baby if they didn't behave. Nora and Grace would never be friends, but they'd learned to coexist. It surprised Fallon to see another side to Nora— a kind, caring, compassionate side she'd never had, but of which she was glad Dylan would be the beneficiary.

However, right now, he was getting a little fussy and was starting to cry.

"I'll take him." Fallon reached for her son.

"Are you sure?" Grace asked. "Because I don't mind holding him."

"Yeah, I'm properly prepared now," Fallon stated, having procured a burping cloth to lay over her shoulder. She accepted her son from his grandmother.

"He's so beautiful." Nora stroked her grandson's curly

black hair while Fallon held him and patted his bottom, soothing his loud cries.

"What'd you expect?" her father interjected from nearby where he was huddled with her husband, Dane, Ayden and Maya. It wasn't hearts and roses between the men she loved, but they were all trying to be cordial for her sake and for Dylan's. "He's a Stewart."

"And a Campbell," Gage said as he made his way over to Fallon.

She glanced up at her husband and love shone so clearly in his eyes. She couldn't believe how lucky she was they'd found each other again. It hadn't been an easy road getting here, but they'd made it through the storm.

Gage bowed his head and brushed a tender kiss across her lips. "Have I told you how much I love you?"

Fallon grinned and paused a moment. "No—" she shook her head "—I don't believe you have today."

"Well, then, let me remedy that. I love you, Fallon Stewart Campbell, and you're the only woman for me."

"And you, Gage Campbell, are all the man I need."

* * * * *

THE TYCOON'S
MARRIAGE DEAL

MELANIE MILBURNE

To the Dangerous Liaisons Divas, Margie Lawson
Advanced Immersion Class, Melbourne 2016 – Lauren
James, Kristin Meachem, Natasha Daraio, Michelle
Somers and of course the marvellous Margie!
A special thank-you to Kristin's parents, Bill and Anna
McKay, who hosted our class in their gorgeous home.

And another special thank-you to my dentist, Dr Jim
Rushton, for the use of his cute labradoodle's name!

CHAPTER ONE

IT WAS THE best wedding cake Tillie had ever decorated but now there wasn't going to be a wedding. Her dream wedding. The wedding she had planned and looked forward to for more years than she wanted to count. She looked at the triple-tier wedding cake with the intricate orange blossom petals she'd taken hours and hours to craft. They were so darn realistic you could almost smell them. The finely detailed lacework around the sides of the cake had all but made her cross-eyed. She had even given the marzipan bride on the top of the cake her chestnut hair and pale complexion and brown eyes, and used a tiny scrap of fabric from her own wedding dress and veil to make a replica outfit.

Although…she'd taken a little licence with the bride's figure and made her look as if she spent her life in the gym rather than hours in a kitchen surrounded by yummy cakes that had to be tasted to get the balance of flavours just right.

The groom was exactly like Simon—blond and

blue-eyed—although the tuxedo she'd painted on him was now pock-marked with pinholes.

Tillie picked up another dressmaking pin and aimed it at the groom's groin. 'Take that, you cheat.' Who knew marzipan figurines could make such great voodoo dolls? Maybe she could do a side line business for jilted brides, making break-up cakes with an effigy of their ex.

There's a thought...

'Uh-oh.' Joanne, her assistant, came into the kitchen. 'Your favourite male customer is waiting for you. Maybe I should warn him you're in your all-men-are-evil mood.'

Tillie turned from the cake to look at Joanne. 'Which male customer?'

Joanne's eyes sparkled so much they looked as if they belonged on a tiara. 'Mr Chocolate Éclair.'

Tillie could feel her cheeks heating up faster than her fan-forced oven. For the last two weeks, every time that man came into her cake shop he always insisted on being served by her. He always made her blush. And he always wanted the same thing—one of her Belgian chocolate éclairs. She didn't know whether to dislike him for making sport out of her overactive capillaries or for him being able to eat a chocolate éclair a day and not put on a single gram of fat. 'Can't you serve him just this once?'

Joanne shook her head. 'Nope. He wants to speak to you and informs me he won't leave until he does.'

Tillie frowned. 'But I told you I don't want to be interrupted this afternoon. I have three kids' birthday cakes to decorate and I have to squeeze in a visit to Mr Pendleton at the respite centre. I made his favourite marshmallow slice.'

'This guy is not the sort to take no for an answer,' Joanne said. 'Anyway, you should see how clock-stopping gorgeous he looks today. Where on earth does he put all the calories you sell him?'

Tillie turned back to the wedding cake and aimed a pin at the groom's right eye. 'Tell him I'm busy.'

Joanne blew out an I'm-so-over-this breath. 'Look, Tillie, I know Simon jilting you was rough on you, but it's been three months. You have to move on. I think Mr Chocolate Éclair fancies you. He's certainly paying you heaps of attention. Who knows? This might be your chance to get out and party like you've never partied before.'

'Move on? Why should I move on?' Tillie said. 'I'm fine right where I am, thank you very much. I'm over men.' Three more pins went into marzipan man's manhood. 'Over. Over. Over.'

'But not all men are like—'

'Apart from my dad and Mr Pendleton, men are a waste of time and money and emotion,' Tillie said. When she thought of all the money she'd spent on Simon, helping him with yet another start-up business that ended going belly up. When she thought of all the effort she'd put into their relationship, her patience over his commitment to not have sex before marriage because of his faith, only for him to have an affair with a girl he'd met online.

On a hook-up app.

Grr.

Years Tillie had spent being by his side, putting her own stuff on hold in order to be a good little girl-friend and then good little fiancée. Faithful. Loyal. Devoted.

No. Moving on would mean she would have to trust a man again and that she was never going to do. Not in this lifetime. Not in this century. Not in this geological era.

'So…do you want me to tell Mr Chocolate Éclair to come back some other time?' Joanne said, wincing when she saw all the pins sticking out of Simon.

'No. I'll see him.' Tillie untied her apron, tossed it to one side and stalked into her small shop front. Mr Chocolate Éclair was standing looking at the cakes and biscuits and slices in the glass cabinet underneath the shop counter. When he turned and made eye contact something zapped her in the chest like a Taser beam. *Zzzztt.* She double-blinked just as she did every time he looked at her. Was it actually possible to have eyes that unusual shade of blue? A light greyish-blue with a dark outline around the iris, as if someone had drawn a fine circle with a felt-tip marker. His hair was a rich dark brown with natural highlights as if he had recently spent time in the sun. Clearly not in England, given the summer so far had been dismal even though it was June. His skin was olive toned and tanned and the wrong side of clean-shaven, as if he had been too lazy to pick up a razor that morning. It gave him a rakish air that made her toes curl in her ballet flats.

And he was tall.

So tall he had to stoop when he came in the shop, and even now the top of his head was dangerously close to the light fitting.

But it was his mouth that drew her eyes like a dieter to her cake counter. No matter how hard she tried, Tillie couldn't stop staring at it. The top lip was sculpted and only a shade thinner than the lower one, suggesting his was a mouth that knew all there was to know about sensuality. Even the way it was curved upwards in a smile hinted at a man who was confident and assured of getting his own way in the boardroom and the bedroom or even on a park bench. If there were a blueprint for an international playboy he would be a perfect fit. He was so rampantly masculine he made the models in sexy aftershave ads look like altar boys.

'The usual?' Tillie said, reaching for a set of tongs and a white paper bag.

'Not today.' His voice was so deep it was clear he hadn't been at the back of the queue when the testosterone was handed out. Rich and dark, honey and gravel with a side order of smooth Devonshire cream. His eyes twinkled. 'I'm abstaining from temptation just this once.'

Tillie's cheeks were flaming hot enough to make toffee. 'Can I tempt you with anything else?'

Bad choice of words.

His smile came up a little higher on one side. 'I thought it was time I introduced myself. I'm Blake McClelland.'

The name rang a bell. Not a drawing-room bell. A Big Ben type of bell. Blake McClelland—international playboy, super-successful businessman and renowned financial whizz. McClelland Park was the name of the country estate Tillie was housesitting for the elderly owner, Mr Pendleton. The estate had been reluctantly sold by Andrew McClelland when his young wife Gwen tragically died, leaving behind a ten-year-old son. The son had certainly done a heck of a lot of growing up. He would be thirty-four now, exactly ten years older than her. 'How can I…erm… help you, Mr McClelland?'

He held out his hand, and, after a brief hesitation, she slipped hers into its slightly calloused cage. The brush of warm male flesh closing around hers was as electrifying as a high-voltage current. The air suddenly became tighter, denser.

'Is there somewhere private we can talk?' he said.

Tillie was rapidly going beyond being able to think, much less talk. Even breathing was proving to be a challenge. Even though she pulled her hand out of his, the sensation of his touch was still travelling through her body like hot tentacles. One of them coiling deep and low in her belly. 'I'm really busy right now so—'

'I won't take up too much of your time.'

She wanted to refuse but she was a businesswoman. Being polite to customers was important to her—even the most annoying ones. What if he wanted to order a speciality cake? Not that she made cakes that big-breasted bunny girls jumped out of, but still. Maybe he wanted her to cater for an event or something. It would be churlish to refuse to speak to him just because he made her feel a little…undone.

'My office is through here,' Tillie said and led the way back to the workroom, every cell of her flesh conscious of him only a few steps behind her.

Joanne looked up from the child's birthday cake she was pretending to decorate with the handmade marzipan toys Tillie had worked on every night for the past week. 'I'll watch over the shop, will I?' she said with a smile so bright it looked as if she were advertising toothpaste.

'Thanks,' Tillie said, opening the office door that led off the workroom. 'We won't be long.'

Well, she'd used to think of it as an office.

Now with Blake McClelland occupying a ridiculous amount of space inside it she rapidly downgraded it to the size of a cake box. A cupcake box.

Tillie waved her hand at the chair in front of her desk. 'Would you like to sit down?'

So I don't have to dislocate my neck to maintain eye contact?

'Ladies first.' Something about the sparkle in his eyes made her think of another context entirely.

She gritted her teeth behind her polite closed-lip smile, and instead of sitting on her own chair, held onto the back of it like a lion tamer about to take on a rogue lion. 'What can I do for you, Mr McClelland?'

'Actually, it's more what I can do for you.' There was an enigmatic quality to his voice and his expression that made the fine hairs on the back of her neck stand up and pirouette.

'Meaning?' Tillie injected enough cool hostility into her tone to have sent a pride of lions scampering for cover, chair or no chair.

Blake glanced at the stack of bills lying on her desk. Three of them were stained with a red stamp marking them as final notices. He would have to be colour blind not to have noticed.

'Local gossip has it you're undergoing a difficult financial period,' he said.

Tillie kept her spine straighter than the ruler on her desk. 'Pardon me if this sounds rude, but I fail to see how my current financial circumstances have anything to do with you.'

His eyes didn't waver from hers. Not even to blink. He reminded her of a marksman who had taken aim, his finger poised on the trigger. 'I noticed the wedding cake on my way in here.'

'Hardly surprising since this is a cake shop,' Tillie said, sounding as tart as the lemon meringue pies she'd made that morning. 'Weddings, parties, anything—it's what I do.'

'I heard about your fiancé getting cold feet on the morning of the wedding,' he said, still holding her gaze with that unnerving target-practice intensity.

'Yes, well, it's hard to keep something like that quiet in a village this size,' she said. 'But again—pardon me for being impolite—what exactly do you want to speak to me about? Because if it's to talk about my ex and his tarty little girlfriend who is barely out of preschool, then you'd better leave right now.'

His smile tilted his mouth in a way that made the base of Tillie's spine tingle and her hand want to rise up and slap him. She curled her fingers into her palms just in case. She was annoyed with herself for allowing him to see how humiliated she was by her ex's choice of partner.

'So here's your chance to get even,' Blake said. 'Pretend to be my fiancée for the next month and I'll take care of those debts for you.'

'Pretend to be your...*what*?'

He picked up the sheaf of papers off her desk and proceeded to read out the amounts owing, whistling through his teeth when he got to the biggest one. He tapped the bills against his other hand and looked at her again with that startlingly direct grey-blue gaze. 'I will pay off your debts and the only payment I want in return is for you to tell your old buddy Jim Pendleton we're engaged.'

Tillie widened her eyes until she thought her eyeballs would pop right out of her head and bounce along the floor like ping-pong balls. 'Are you out of your mind? Pretend to be engaged to *you*? I don't even know you.'

He gave a mock bow. 'Blake Richard Alexander McClelland at your service. Formerly of McClelland Park estate and now on a mission to buy back my ancestral home, which, up until twenty-four years ago, had been in the McClelland family since the mid-seventeen-hundreds.'

Tillie frowned. 'But why don't you make an offer to Mr Pendleton? He's been talking about selling since he had a stroke two months ago.'

'He won't sell it to me.'

'Why not?'

His eyes continued to hold hers but this time there was a devilish glint. 'Apparently my reputation as a love-them-and-leave-them playboy has annoyed him.'

Tillie could well imagine Blake McClelland had done some serious damage to a few hearts in his time. Now she realised why he'd seemed familiar the first time he'd come into her shop. She recalled reading something recently about him at a wild party in Vegas involving three burlesque dancers. He had a fast-living lifestyle that would certainly be at odds with someone as old and conservative as Jim Pendleton, whose only misdemeanours in eighty-five years were a couple of parking fines. 'But Mr Pendleton would never believe you and I were a couple. We're total opposites.'

His smile was crooked. 'But that's the point— you're exactly the type of girl Jim would want me to fall in love with and settle down.'

As if that would ever happen.

Tillie knew she wasn't responsible for any shattered mirrors about the place, but neither would she be asked to model a bikini on a catwalk. Her girl-next-door looks wouldn't stop a clock or even a wristwatch. Not even an egg timer. The likelihood of attracting someone as heart-stoppingly handsome and suave and sophisticated as Blake McClelland was as likely as her becoming a size zero. But she didn't know whether to be insulted or grateful. Right now, the thought of paying off her debts was more tempting than a whole tray of Belgian chocolate éclairs. Two trays. And even better, it would send a middle finger in the air to her ex. 'But won't Mr Pendleton suspect something if we suddenly come out as a couple? He might be elderly and suffering from a stroke, but he's not stupid.'

'The old man's a romance tragic,' Blake said. 'He was married fifty-nine years before his wife died. He fell in love with her within ten minutes of meeting her. He'll be thrilled to see you move on from your ex. He talked about you non-stop—called you his little guardian angel. He said you were minding his house and his dog and visiting him every day. That's how I came up with the plan. I can see the headlines now.' He put his fingers up in air quotes. *'"Bad boy tamed by squeaky clean girl next door."'* His grin was straight off a cosmetic orthodontist's website. 'It's win-win.'

Tillie gave him a look that would have soured her shop's week's supply of milk. 'I hate to put a dent in that massive ego of yours, but my answer is an emphatic, irreversible no.'

'I don't expect you to sleep with me.'

Tillie didn't care for the way he said it as if she was being a gauche fool for thinking otherwise. Why didn't he expect her to sleep with him? Was she *that* hideous? 'Good, because I wouldn't do it even if you paid those debts fifty gazillion times over.'

Something about the spark of light in his eyes sent a shuddering tremor over the floor of her belly. His slanted smile was star student of charm school. 'Although, if you ever change your mind I'll be happy to get down to business.'

Business? Tillie dug her fingers into the back of her office chair so hard she thought her knuckles would explode. She wanted to slap that I-can-have-you-any-time-I-want-you smile off his face. But another part—a secret, private part—wanted him. Wanted. Wanted. *Wanted* him. 'I'm *not* going to change my mind.'

He picked up a pen off her desk, tossed it in the air and deftly caught it in one hand. 'And when the time comes to end it, I will allow you the privilege of dumping me.'

'Big of you.'

'I'm not being magnanimous,' he said. 'I don't want to be run out of town by a bunch of villagers wielding baseball bats.'

Tillie wished she had a baseball bat handy right now to beat her resolve back into shape. But the chance to let her ex know she could land a guy was proving a little hard to resist.

And not just any old guy.

Someone rich and gorgeous and sexy as sin on a sugar-coated stick. It was only for a month. How hard could it be? Her thoughts were seesawing in her head. *Do it. Don't. Do it. Don't.*

'Think about it overnight,' Blake said, apparently undaunted because his smile didn't falter. 'I want a walk around the Park some time. For old times' sake.'

'I'd have to ask Mr Pendleton if that's okay with him.'

'Fine.' He took a business card from his wallet and handed it to her. 'My contact details. I've checked in at the bed and breakfast down the road.'

Tillie took the card from him, desperately trying not to touch his fingers. Those long tanned fingers. Those long tanned masculine fingers. She couldn't stop thinking about how those fingers would feel on her skin...on her body. On her breasts. Between her legs.

She gave herself a concussion-inducing mental slap. Why was she thinking about intimate stuff like that? The only person who'd ever touched her between the legs—apart from herself—was her gynaecologist.

'I wouldn't have thought cottage flowers and cosy fireplaces and fancy china teacups would be to your taste,' Tillie said.

Blake's eyes glinted again. 'I don't plan to stay there long.'

What was he hinting? That he would be staying with her? Tillie inched up her chin, trying to ignore the way the backs of her knees were fizzing in reaction to the satirical light in his gaze. 'I'm sure you'll find much more suitable accommodation for your... erm...needs in the next town.'

The less you think about his 'needs', the better.

'Perhaps, but I'm not leaving this village until I

get what I want.' Something about the set of his jaw made her realise he had the steely will and determination to achieve whatever he put his mind to. And the ruthlessness.

She kept her gaze on his. 'Haven't you heard that wise old adage you can't always get what you want?'

Blake glanced at her mouth, then to the swell of her breasts behind her conservatively buttoned cotton shirt, lingering there for a nanosecond before returning his gaze to hers in a lock that ignited something deep inside her body. It was as if his eyes were communicating on an entirely different level—a primal, instinctive level that was as thrilling to her as it was foreign.

No one ever looked at her like…*that*.

As if he were wondering what her mouth would feel like against his. As if he were wondering what she looked like without her practical, no-nonsense clothing. As if he were wondering how she would taste and feel when he put his mouth and tongue to her naked flesh.

Even Simon had never given her The Look. The I-want-to-have-bed-wrecking-sex-with-you-right-now look. She'd always put it down to the fact he'd staunchly committed to celibacy, but now she wondered if the chemistry had ever been there. Their kisses and cuddles seemed somehow…vanilla. Unlike her, Simon had had sex previously as a young teenager, but he'd felt so guilty he'd made a pledge not to do it again until he was married. They'd occasionally petted but never without clothes. The only pleasure she'd had during the last eight years had been with herself.

But nothing about Blake McClelland was vanilla. He was dark chocolate fudge and tantalising, will-power-destroying temptation. She couldn't imagine him being celibate for eight minutes, let alone eight years. Which made it all the more laughable he wanted her to pretend to be his fiancée.

Who would ever believe it?

'Just for the record,' Blake said in a voice so deep it made Simon's baritone sound like a boy soprano, 'I *always* get what I want.'

Tillie suppressed an involuntary shiver at the streak of ruthless determination in his tone. But she kept her expression in starchy schoolmistress mode. 'Here's the thing, Mr McClelland. I'm not the sort of girl to be toyed with for a man's entertainment. That's what this is about, isn't it? You're a bored playboy who's looking for the next challenge. You thought you could waltz in here and brandish your big fat bank account and get me to fall on my knees with gratitude, didn't you?'

His eyes did that twinkling, glinting thing. 'Not on our first date. I like to have something to look forward to.'

Tillie could feel her blush shoot to the roots of her hair. She almost expected it to be singed right off her scalp. She could barely speak for the anger vibrating through her body.

Or maybe it wasn't anger…

Maybe it was a far more primitive emotion rushing

through her in blazing, electrifying streaks. Desire. A pulse-throbbing sexual energy that left no part of her untouched. It was as if her blood were injected with its bubbling hot urgency. She shot him a glare as deadly as one of her metal cake skewers. 'Get out of my shop.'

Blake tapped his index finger on the stack of bills on her desk. 'It won't be your shop for much longer if these aren't seen to soon. Give me a call when you've changed your mind.'

Tillie lifted one of her brows as if she were channelling a heroine in a period drama. '*When?* Don't you mean *if*?'

His eyes held hers in an iron will against iron will tug of war, making her heart skip a beat. Two beats. Possibly three. If she'd been on a cardiac ward they would have called a Code Blue.

'You know you want to.'

Tillie wasn't sure they were still talking about the money. There was a dangerous undercurrent rippling in the air. Air she couldn't quite get into her lungs. But then he picked up his business card, which she'd placed on her desk earlier, and, reaching across the small space the desk offered, slid it into the right breast pocket of her shirt. At no point did he touch her, but it felt as if he had stroked her breast with one of those long, clever fingers. Her breast fizzed as if a firework were trapped inside the cup of her bra.

'Call me,' he said.

'You'll be waiting a long time.'

His smile was confident. Brazenly confident. I've-got-this-in-the-bag confident. 'You think?'

That was the whole darn trouble. Tillie couldn't think. Not while he was standing there dangling temptation in front of her. She'd always prided herself on her resolve, but right now it felt as if her resolve had rolled over and was playing dead.

She owed a lot of money. More money than she earned in a year. Way more. She had to pay her father and stepmother back the small loan they'd given her because as missionaries living abroad they were living on gifts and tithes as it was. Mr Pendleton had offered to help her but it didn't sit well with her to take money off him when he had already been incredibly generous by allowing her to stay at McClelland Park rent-free and to use his kitchen for baking when she ran out of time at the shop. Besides, he would need all his money and more if he didn't sell McClelland Park, because an old Georgian property that size needed constant and frighteningly expensive maintenance.

But to take money off Blake McClelland in exchange for a month pretending to be his fiancée was a step into territory so dangerous she would need to be immediately measured for a straitjacket. Even if he didn't expect her to sleep with him she would have to act as if she were. She would have to touch him, hold hands or have him—*gulp*—kiss her for the sake of appearances.

'Good day, McClelland,' Tillie said, as sternly as if she were dismissing an impertinent boy from the staffroom.

Blake was almost out of her office when he turned around at the door to look back at her. 'Oh, one other thing.' He fished in his trouser pocket and took out a velvet ring box and tossed it to her desk to land on top of her stack of bills with unnerving accuracy. 'You'll be needing this.'

And without stopping to see her open the box, he turned and left.

CHAPTER TWO

JOANNE CAME INTO the office before Tillie had time to pick her dropped jaw up off the desk, much less the ring box. 'Oh. My. God. Is that what I think it is?' she said.

Tillie stared at the box as if it were a detonator device. 'I'm not going to open it.'

I'm not. I'm not. I'm not.

Even though her finger still felt horribly empty after three years of wearing an engagement ring. Three years and another five before that wearing a friendship/commitment ring. But she had a feeling Blake's ring wouldn't look anything like the humble little quarter-carat diamond Simon had purchased. Actually, Simon hadn't purchased it. She'd put it on her credit card and he was meant to repay her but somehow never did. Another clue he hadn't truly loved her.

Why hadn't she realised that until now?

'Well, if you don't want it, give it to me,' Joanne said. 'I'm not against gorgeous men buying me expensive jewellery. What did he want to speak to you about?'

'You wouldn't believe me if I told you.'

'Try me.'

Tillie let out a gust of a breath. 'He wants to settle all of my debts in exchange for me pretending to be his fiancée for a month.'

'You're right. I don't believe you.'

'He's the most arrogant man I've ever met,' Tillie said. 'The hide of him marching in here expecting me to say yes to such a ridiculous farce. Who would believe it anyway? Me engaged to someone like him?'

Joanne's smooth brow crinkled in thought. 'I don't know… I think you're a little hard on yourself. I mean, I know you're not big on fashion but if you wore a bit more colour and a bit of make-up you'd look awesome. And you've got great boobs but you never show any cleavage.'

Tillie sat down with a thump on her desk chair. 'Yes, well, Simon didn't like it when women paraded their assets.'

And how could I have spent money on clothes and make-up while saving for the wedding?

'Simon was born in the wrong century,' Joanne said with a roll of her eyes. 'I reckon you're better off without him. He never even took you out dancing, for pity's sake. You deserve someone much more dynamic than him. He's too bland. Blake McClelland, on the other hand, is capital D dynamite.'

Blake McClelland was too darn everything.

Tillie eyed the ring box again, curling her fingers into her palms like hooks to stop herself reaching for it. 'I'm going to take it to Mrs Fisher's second-hand shop.'

Joanne couldn't have look more shocked than if she'd said she was going to flush it down the toilet. 'Surely you're not serious?'

Tillie left the ring box where it was and pushed back from her desk. 'I'm deadly serious.'

Blake drove the few kilometres out from the village to his family's estate in rural Wiltshire. He had driven past a few times over the years after leaving flowers at his mother's grave at the cemetery in the village, but he hadn't been able to bring himself to stop and survey the estate in any detail. To stare at the home that used to belong in his family had always been too painful, like jabbing at a wound that had never properly healed.

The bank had repossessed the estate after his father's breakdown. As a ten-year-old child it had been devastating enough to lose his mother, but to see his father crumple emotionally, to cease to function other than on a level not much higher than breathing, was terrifying. His mother's death from a brain aneurysm had shattered him and his father. The cruel unexpectedness of it. The blunt shock of having her laughing and smiling one minute and then slurring her speech and then stumbling and falling the next. Ten days in hospital on life support until the doctors had given them the devastating news there was no longer any hope.

The mother he'd adored and who had made his and his father's life so perfect and happy had gone.

Irretrievably gone.

But somehow some measure of childhood resilience had kicked in and he'd become the parent during the long years of his father's slow climb out of the abyss of despair. His dad had never remarried or re-partnered. Hadn't even dated.

But after his dad's recent health scare, Blake was determined to put this one wrong thing right; no matter what the cost or the effort. McClelland Park was the key to his father's full recovery.

He knew it in his blood. He knew it in his bones. He knew it at a cellular level.

His dad felt enormous guilt and shame about losing the property that had been passed down through the generations. Blake suspected his dad's inability to move on with his life was tied up in the loss of the estate. His dad would literally die a slow and painful death without it being returned to him.

It was up to Blake to get McClelland Park back and get it back he would.

He smiled when he thought of Matilda Toppington. Colour him every shade of confident but he knew he had this in the bag with a big satin ribbon tied around it. She was exactly the woman for the job. Old man Pendleton wouldn't stop gushing about her—how kind and considerate she was, all the charitable work she did in the local community, the way she took care of everyone. He'd seen it himself each time he'd been in the shop. Freebies for the kids, special treats for the elderly, home deliveries for the infirm. Tillie was such a do-gooder; he was surprised she hadn't sprouted a pair of wings and didn't carry a harp under her arm. When pressed on the aborted wedding, the old man had more or less hinted he was relieved it hadn't gone ahead. Apparently so was everyone else in the village, although, according to Maude Rosethorne at the bed and breakfast, most weren't game enough to say it to Tillie's face.

But Blake was certain Tillie would say yes to him about the pretend engagement, if not yes to sleeping with him. When had a woman ever said no? He was the package most women wanted: wealth, status, looks and skill in bed. Besides, he was giving her the perfect tool to get back at her ex by showing off a new lover.

And becoming Tillie Toppington's lover was something he was seriously tempted to do. From the first moment he'd met her gaze he'd been intrigued by her. She wasn't his usual type but he was up for a change. The way she'd blushed when he'd first spoken to her made him do it all the more. She pretended to dislike him but he knew she was interested. All the signs were there. She was responding to him the way he responded to her—with good old-fashioned, clothes-ripping lust.

Okay, so call him vain, but no woman had ever complained about not having a good time in his bed. Not that he let them spend much time in it. He had a policy of no longer than a month. After that things got tricky. Women started measuring him for a morning suit. They started dropping hints about engagement rings or started dragging their heels while going past jewellery shop windows.

The estate came into view and a boulder landed in Blake's gut. The silver-birch-lined driveway leading to the house brought back a rush of memories. The screaming siren of the ambulance as his mother was rushed to hospital. The drive home with his father, the night his mother died. The empty front passenger seat where his mother should have been sitting. How he had stared at that seat with his eyes burning and his stomach churning and his head pounding with a silent scream.

The horrible silence.

The silence that gouged a hole in his chest that had never properly closed. If he closed his eyes he could still hear the crunch of the car tyres on the gravel on that last drive out twenty-four years ago, that and the sound of his father's quiet but no less heart-bludgeoning sobbing.

Blake braked but didn't turn into the driveway. After a slow drive past his memories, he put his foot down and drove on with a roar of the engine.

He would wait until he heard from Tillie before he finally came home.

Tillie walked into her office to put another bill on the pile. She had kept out of there for most of the day, determined to resist peeking at the ring. And to avoid looking at the stack of bills on her desk. She put the overdue florist notice on top of the others and eyed the ring box as if it were a cockroach in cake batter. 'You think I'm going to look at you, don't you? You've been sitting there all day just waiting for me to break.'

Taking money from Mrs Fisher's pawnshop for Blake's ring was proving a little tricky for Tillie's conscience. He had given it to her but it was hardly a no-strings gift. There were conditions attached. Conditions that involved what exactly? He'd said *pretend* to be his fiancée. What would that involve? Hanging out with him? Would hanging out include kissing him? Touching him?

Him touching her?

He'd said sleeping with him wasn't mandatory but she'd seen the way his eyes darkened every time they met hers. Darkened and smouldered and made her body feel as if she were sitting too close to a fire. Naked.

Maybe she should have discussed the terms with him. Sussed out some of the details before she flatly refused. The bills weren't going away—they were mounting up like a croquembouche cake.

Tillie sat down, and after a moment, began tapping her fingers on the desk. 'It's no good looking at me like that. You could be the identical twin of the Hope Diamond and I still wouldn't look at you.'

After another long moment, she gently nudged the box, moving it a millimetre away as if she were pushing away a crumb. The box was plush velvet. Rich velvet. Luxury jeweller's velvet.

Hours had passed since Blake had given the ring

to her, but she couldn't help thinking about how that box had been in his trouser pocket right next to his...

Tillie snatched her hand back and tucked it in her lap, eyeballing the ring box as if it were a poisonous viper sitting on her desk. 'Thought you had me there, didn't you?'

Joanne came into the office. 'Who on earth are you talking to?' she said and then glanced at the ring on the desk, a smile breaking over her face. 'Ah.'

'What do you mean "ah"?' Tillie said, scowling.

Joanne's eyes were doing the tiara thing again. 'You want to *so* bad.'

'No, I don't.' Tillie folded her arms.

'Not even a little peek?' Joanne's hand reached for the box.

'Don't touch it!'

Joanne's eyebrows went up and her smile widened so far it nearly fell off her face. 'I thought you were going to take it to Mrs Fisher's?'

'Changed my mind.'

'Because Mrs Fisher is the village's version of Facebook?'

'Exactly.'

Joanne perched on the edge of the desk, her eyes on the ring. 'I wonder if he paid a lot for it?'

'I. Do. Not. Care.'

'Maybe it's not a real diamond,' Joanne said in a musing tone. 'Some of those zircon ones look pretty amazing. You'd never know it wasn't the real thing.'

'I hardly think Blake McClelland is the type of

man to buy a girl a zircon instead of a diamond,' Tillie said.

Joanne's twinkling eyes met Tillie's. 'True.'

Tillie frowned. 'Why are you looking at me like that?'

'How am I looking at you?' Joanne's tone was so innocent it would have made an angel's sound evil.

'Don't you have work to do?' Tillie said with an I'm-your-boss arch of her brow.

Joanne's cheeky smile didn't back down. 'Best not look at it, then. You might want to keep it.' And giving a little finger wave, she left.

Tillie rolled her chair closer to the desk and picked up the ring box. She turned it over and over as if she were about to solve a Rubik's Cube. What harm would one little peek do? No one would know she'd taken a look. She cautiously lifted the lid and then gasped. Inside was a stunning handcrafted ring that was set in a Gatsby era style. It wasn't look-at-me huge but its finely crafted setting gave it an air of priceless beauty. There were a central diamond and two smaller ones either side of it, and a collection of tiny diamonds surrounding them. The sides of the ring were inset with more glittering tiny diamonds.

Tillie had seen some engagement rings in her time but none as beautiful as this. Hopelessly impractical, of course. She couldn't imagine thrusting her hands into pastry while wearing it but, oh, how gorgeous was it?

You can't keep it.

Right now Tillie didn't want to listen to her conscience. She wanted to slip that ring over her finger and step out and parade it in the village to make sure everyone saw it winking there.

Take that, you cheating low-life ex. See what sort of calibre of man I can hook?

No one would be casting her pitying looks then. No one would be whispering behind their hands when she walked past them or into their shops, or asking each other *sotto voce*, '*How do you think she's holding up?*' and, '*Doesn't she look a little peaky to you?*' or, '*I never thought Simon was right for her anyway.*'

She took the ring out of the velvet-lined box and held it in the palm of her hand.

Go on. Put it on. See if it fits.

Tillie picked up the ring and, taking a deep breath, slipped it over her ring finger. It was a little snug but it fitted her finger better than the one Simon had 'given' her. She kept staring at the ring's dazzling beauty, wondering how much it was worth. Wondering if she should take it off right this second before she got too attached to it. She had never worn anything so gorgeous. Her late mother hadn't had much jewellery to speak of because she and Tillie's dad were always so frugal over money in order to help others less fortunate. They hadn't even bought an engagement ring but instead donated what they would have spent to their church's missionary fund. Some of that social ethic had rubbed off on Tillie even though she didn't even remember her mother because she'd died just hours after Tillie was born. But this was the sort of ring to be passed down generations from mothers to daughter to granddaughters and great-granddaughters.

Although Tillie had grown up in a loving home, largely due to her kind stepmother who was the antithesis of the wicked stepmother stereotype, she had still longed to belong to someone, to build a life together and raise a family. To have that special someone to be there for her, as her stepmother was there for her father, and Tillie's mother before her. Prior to being jilted, she'd been a fully signed up member to the Love Makes the World Go Around Club.

Breaking up with Simon after so long together shattered her dream of happy ever after. She had been cast adrift like a tiny dinghy left bobbing alone in the ocean without a rudder or even an anchor. Three months on, it still felt a little odd to go out to dinner or visit the cinema on her own but she was determined to learn how to do it without feeling like a loser. It felt a little weird to be cooking a meal for one person but she was working on that, too—besides, she could do with a little less eating.

Now she was a fully paid up member of the Single and Loving It Club.

Well…maybe the Single and Still Getting Used to It Club was more appropriate.

But she would learn to love it even if it damn near killed her.

Tillie was about to take off the ring when her phone rang. She picked it up to see the number on the screen was the respite facility Mr Pendleton was staying in. 'Hello?'

'Tillie, it's Claire Reed, one of the senior nurses on staff,' a woman's voice said. 'I'm afraid Mr Pendleton's had a nasty fall coming out of the bathroom earlier today. He's okay now but he's asking to see you. Can you come in when you get a chance?'

Tillie's stomach pitched. Mr Pendleton was already so frail; another fall would set him back even further. 'Oh, the poor darling. Of course, I'll come in straight away—I was on my way in any case.'

She hung up from the call and went to snatch up her bag and cardigan off the back of the chair, but then she noticed the ring still on her finger. She went to pull it off but it refused to come back over her knuckle. Panic started beating in her chest as frantically as her food mixer whipping up egg whites for meringues.

She had to get it off!

She tugged it again, almost bruising her knuckle in the process. But the more she tugged, the more her knuckle swelled until the joint was almost as big as a Californian walnut. And throbbing painfully as if she had full-blown rheumatoid arthritis.

Tillie dashed into the workroom and shoved her hand under the cold-water tap, liberally soaping up the joint to see if it would help. It didn't. The ring had apparently decided it quite liked its new home on her finger and was staying put, thank you very much. She let out a rarely used swear word and grabbed some hand lotion. She greased up her finger but the more she pushed against her knuckle, the more it throbbed.

She gave up. She would have to leave it and get it off later when the swelling of her knuckle went down.

When Tillie got to the respite centre, the geriatrician on duty informed her that, along with some cuts and bruises and a black eye, Mr Pendleton was also suffering some slight memory confusion as a result of the fall and that he might well have had another mini stroke, which might have caused the loss of balance. She told Tillie not to be unduly concerned about the fact he was acting a little irritable and grumpy but to go along with whatever the old man said so as to not stress him too much.

When Tillie entered his room, Mr Pendleton was sitting propped up in bed looking sorry for himself with an aubergine-coloured bruise on his left cheek and a black eye. He had a white plaster bandage over a cut on his forehead where his head—according to the doctor—had bumped against the toilet bowl.

'Oh, Mr Pendleton.' Tillie rushed to his bedside and carefully took his crêpe-paper-thin hand in hers. 'Are you all right? The doctor said you'd had a bad fall. What have you been doing to yourself? You look like you've gone a couple of rounds with a boxer and a sumo wrestler.'

The old man glowered at her instead of his usual smile of welcome. 'I don't know why you bother visiting an old goat like me. I'm ready for the scrap heap. If I were a dog they would've put me down long ago like the vet did with poor old Humphrey.'

'I come because I care about you,' Tillie said. 'Everyone in the village cares about you. Now tell me what happened.'

He plucked at the hem of the light cotton blanket covering him as if it were annoying him. 'I don't remember what happened. One minute I was upright and the next I was on the floor… I'm all right apart from a bit of a headache.'

'Well, as long as you're okay now, that's the main thing,' Tillie said. 'I would've brought Truffles in to see you but I haven't been home yet. I came straight from work.'

Truffles was Mr Pendleton's chocolate-coloured labradoodle who had not yet progressed from puppyhood even though she was now two years old. Tillie had helped name her when Mr Pendleton had bought the puppy to keep him company after his old golden retriever Humphrey had to be euthanised. But Truffles was nothing like the sedate and portly Humphrey, who had lain in front of the fireplace and snored for hours, only waking for meals and a slow mooch outside for calls of nature. Truffles moved like a dervish on crack and had a penchant for chewing things such as shoes and handbags and sunglasses—all of them Tillie's. Truffles dug so many holes in the garden it looked as if she were drilling for oil. She brought in sticks and leaves as playthings and hid them under the sofa cushions, along with—on one memorable occasion—a dead bird. Not recently dead. Maggot-stage dead.

Tillie often brought Truffles in to see Mr Pendleton, but not unless she'd exhausted the dog with a long walk and some ball play first. A bull in a china shop would look like a butterfly compared to that crazy mutt.

Mr Pendleton's gaze went to Tillie's hands where they were holding his and spied the diamond ring glittering brighter than a lighthouse beacon. His faded blue eyes suddenly narrowed. 'Don't tell me what's his name—Scott? Shaun?—has come crawling back?' he said.

Tillie's heart was giving a rather credible impression of having a serious medical event. She glanced at the resuscitation gear above Mr Pendleton's bed for reassurance. Why hadn't she thought to put on a pair of gloves? Although, given it was summer it might have looked a little odd. No more odd than wearing an engagement ring that looked as though it cost more than it would to feed a small nation. 'Erm… Simon? No. Someone…else gave it to me.'

Mr Pendleton's frown deepened and he leaned forward like a detective staring down a prevaricating suspect. 'Who?'

'Erm…'

'Speak up, girl,' he said. 'You know I'm a little hard of hearing. Who gave you that ring? It looks like a good one.'

Tillie swallowed. 'B-Blake McClelland.'

Mr Pendleton's bushy eyebrows shot up like caterpillars zapped with an electrode. Then he started laughing. Not chuckling laughing, but the sort of laughing you heard at an Irish comedy festival. He rocked back and forth against his banked-up pillows, eyes squinted, and guffawed for so long she began to worry he would do himself an injury, like rupture his voice box or something. 'Now that's just what I needed to lift my spirits out of the doldrums,' he said. 'Did the doctor put you up to it? They always say laughter's the best medicine. You've done me a power of good, Tillie. You, engaged to Blake McClelland? Funniest thing I've heard in years.'

Tillie shifted her lips from side to side, annoyed that he found it so amusing and unlikely someone like Blake would ever propose to her. Why didn't he think she was good enough for Blake? Was it because she wasn't exciting enough? Not attractive enough? She might not be classically beautiful, but so far no travelling circus had ever asked her to sit in a tent and charged an entry fee for people to gawp at her.

'No, this has nothing to do with the doctor. It's not a joke. It's true. Blake did give it to me. He asked me to—'

'You're a bit late for April Fool's day.' Mr Pendleton was still laughing. 'I might be a bit muddled in my head but I know it's June.'

The stubborn streak Tillie had worked for years to suppress while she was with Simon came back with a vengeance. Gone was the submissive anything-you-say-dear girl. In her place was Tenacious Tillie. She would *make* Mr Pendleton believe she was engaged to Blake. She would make everyone believe it. No one would think her not up to the task of hooking a hot man after she was done.

'We met a couple of weeks ago when he came into

the shop. It was love at first sight. On both sides. It was instant, just like in the movies. He's the love of my life. I know it as sure as I'm sitting here telling you. He asked me to marry him and I said yes.'

Mr Pendleton stopped laughing and began to frown instead. 'Look, I might be nearly ninety but I'm no old fool in his dotage. You're not the sort of girl who falls for men like him. You're too conservative to have your head turned by such a handsome devil. And he's not the sort to fall for someone like you.'

Pride made Tillie sit stiffly in her chair while her ego slunk away to hide weeping in the corner. *Too conservative?* She had only been conservative for all these years because Simon had insisted on it. Sure, she might not be going to rush off to steal cars or snatch purses off old ladies any time soon, but neither was she planning to sit at home every night in front of a PG movie with forty-seven cats for company. 'What do you mean Blake wouldn't fall for someone like me? He's in love with me and wants to marry me.' *What's wrong with me?*

'Tillie...' Mr Pendleton gave her hand a little pat. 'You're a good girl. You always colour between the lines. Blake McClelland on the other hand is too much for an old-fashioned girl like you to handle. You'd never be able to tame him. And you're too sensible to even try.'

Old-fashioned. *Sensible.* She would show everyone just how 'old-fashioned and sensible' she was— including Blake McClelland. 'Maybe I have already tamed him,' Tillie said, pulling her hand away.

'Maybe he's sick of being a playboy and wants to settle down and have babies. That's why he wants to buy McClelland Park because—'

'He wants to buy McClelland Park because he's filthy rich and thinks he can open his wallet and get anything he likes,' Mr Pendleton said. 'It's time that man learned a lesson. And you, my dear, are not the one to teach him. Stay away from him. You've already had your heart broken once.'

'But I love him,' Tillie said, mentally crossing her fingers for all the lies spouting out of her mouth. 'I really do. He's so much more exciting and interesting than Simon. I can't believe I ever fancied myself in love with Simon now. Blake is romantic and attentive in a way Simon never was nor ever could be. He makes me feel things I've never felt before. I—'

'Have you slept with him?' The old man's gaze was as direct as a laser pointer at a scientific meeting.

Tillie opened and closed her mouth, her cheeks feeling so hot she was sure they were going to scald the skin right off her face. 'That's a rather personal question to—'

'Has he moved in with you?'

'Erm…would that be okay if he did?'

Yikes! What are you doing?

Mr Pendleton was still looking at her as a cop did a sneaky suspect. 'He's not the marrying sort, you know, and good girls like you always want marriage. I'm not saying he isn't charming. He is. Just about every nurse in this place goes into a swoon when he comes in here. He's only put that ring on your finger to sleep with you. As soon as he's done that he'll be off in search of the next conquest, you mark my words.'

The nurse popped her head around the door. 'Everything all right, Mr Pendleton?'

'Tillie fancies herself in love with Blake McClelland,' he said with a snort. 'Says she's engaged to him. And you think I'm the one who's confused.'

The nurse glanced at Tillie with wide did-I-just-hear-that-correctly? eyes. 'Blake McClelland and… *you*?'

Tillie's ego had had just about enough bludgeoning for one day. 'Yes. He asked me yesterday. He's been coming into the shop every day for the last couple of weeks and we hit it off. I know it's a bit of a whirlwind, but when you've met the right one you just know.'

'Oh, Tillie, I'm so thrilled for you. Everyone will be when they hear the news,' the nurse said. 'When are you getting married?'

'Erm…we haven't set a date yet but—'

'It's fabulous you've found someone. Really fabulous. We've all been so worried about you.'

The nurse led Tillie out of the room and softly closed the door. 'Don't listen to Mr Pendleton. He's still a little out of sorts from his fall. He'll be delighted for you in a few days. Give me a look at that ring. Gosh, isn't it gorgeous? Much nicer than he-whose-name-is-not-to-be-mentioned.'

'Yes. I'm very happy.'

Who knew how easy it was to lie?

'I have a theory about playboys,' the nurse said. 'They make the best husbands in the end. They get all that running around out of their system and then they settle down.'

Tillie was pretty sure Blake McClelland had no intention of settling down and certainly not with someone like her. What was she going to do now? Mr Pendleton might doubt her engagement but the nurse clearly didn't. It would be all over the village within hours. Tillie was effectively engaged to Blake even though she'd adamantly told him no. She could almost see his sardonic I've-got-you-where-I-want-you smile.

She slipped out of the respite facility and back to her car. The ring was still stuck on her finger as if some mischievous supernatural forces had conspired against her.

How was she going to face Blake now?

Blake came back to the bed and breakfast after tidying his mother's grave at the cemetery. He hadn't stayed in a B&B since he was a kid on one of the rare holidays his father took him on. But the cottage had a nice vibe—an old-world charm about it that made his business mind spark with ideas.

However, he didn't get a chance to discuss a business proposal when he entered the cottage's rose-framed front door because Maude Rosethorne was standing there with a broad smile on her face.

'Congratulations, Mr McClelland,' she said. 'We're all so excited with the news of Tillie and you getting engaged. It's the most romantic thing ever. It's all over the village. We didn't even know you two knew each other and now you're getting married!'

Blake had counted on that ring changing Tillie's mind. What girl could resist a rock like that? It was worth a minor fortune, but he wasn't quibbling over the expense—no expense was too much in his quest to get back his family property. 'Thank you,' he said. 'What's that old saying? When you've met the right one you just know?'

'She's a wonderful girl—but you don't need me to tell you that,' Mrs Rosethorne said. 'Everyone loves Tillie. We've all been so worried about her after Simon jilted her. I suppose she's told you all about that? Terrible, just terrible to leave her to face all the guests like that. He sent a text message. A text message! Didn't have the backbone to see her face to face. He's no longer welcome around these parts, let me tell you. No one gets to break our Tillie's heart without all of us in the village having something to say about it.'

Blake went to his room feeling relieved he'd offered Tillie the chance to end their relationship once his goal of securing McClelland Park was achieved. He didn't want his father to feel unwelcome when he finally moved back home. Blake wasn't interested in breaking any hearts. Tillie hadn't bothered to disguise her instant dislike of him—a novel experience for him, as he usually had no trouble winning women over within seconds of meeting them.

Her reaction to him amused him. He liked nothing more than a challenge, and cute little Matilda Toppington was nothing if not an Olympic-standard challenge. She was feisty and quick-witted and sharp-tongued with a body as delectable as the cakes and slices in her shop cabinet. Not beautiful in the traditional sense, but with the sort of understated looks that held a compelling fascination for him. For years he'd been surrounded by stunning-looking women, so much so they were starting to look the same. Even their personalities seemed similar—or maybe that was his fault for only ever dating a certain type.

But when Tillie hitched her chin and glared down her uptilted nose at him with those flashing nutmeg-brown eyes, he couldn't help thinking how unique she was, how refreshing and unaffected. Her mouth was on the fuller side with an adorable little Cupid's bow. For the last couple of weeks he'd been fantasising about kissing those soft and pliable-looking lips. She might not like him but he knew raw physical attraction when he saw it. Such crackling chemistry would make their 'engagement' all the more entertaining. That was probably why she'd decided to run with the engagement in spite of telling him to take his offer and get out of Dodge before dawn. And why not? A fling between them wouldn't be hurting anyone.

He allowed himself a congratulatory smile.

The ring had been the bait and she'd snapped it up just as he'd planned.

Tillie was walking Truffles around the lake in front of McClelland Park still wondering how on earth she was going to face Blake. Her phone had been running hot ever since she'd left the respite centre. When she went back to her shop, she'd explained to Joanne what had happened, but, instead of being upset on her behalf, Joanne had seemed inordinately thrilled, spouting such idiotic statements as 'it's meant to be' and something about 'fate's meddling hand'. Joanne had even gone on to say how she thought Tillie was secretly in love with Blake but hadn't yet admitted it to herself.

In love with Blake McClelland?

What a flipping joke. Tillie had been so put off by her assistant's reaction she'd turned her phone off rather than face the barrage of hearty congratulations from everyone else.

Everyone apart from Mr Pendleton, that was.

How soon before Blake found out on the village gossip network? Should she text him or call him? She had his card somewhere…or had she thrown it out?

Truffles suddenly pricked up her ears and looked to the front wrought-iron gates where a low-slung sports car was turning into the driveway. It came up through the avenue of silver birch trees like a sleek black panther, the deep throaty roars of the engine making the fine hairs on Tillie's arm rise in a Mexican wave.

Blake's car was exactly like him. Potent. Powerful. Sexy.

Truffles decided the car was the perfect prey and took off like a supersonic NASA rocket. Tillie lunged for her collar but missed and ended up falling onto her knees on the rough gravel. She clambered to her feet and inspected the bloody grazes to her knees. Why hadn't she worn jeans instead of a skirt? She picked out a couple of stones and, taking a tissue from inside her bra, dabbed at the blood.

Tillie limped to where Blake was standing next to his car. Truffles sat next to him as if she were the star pupil at obedience school.

Blake glanced at Tillie's knees and frowned. 'Are you okay?'

'No—thanks to you,' Tillie said. 'You could have called or texted to let me know you were coming. Truffles has a thing about cars. If I'd known you were going to visit I would've put her on the lead.'

'Let's get you inside to clean up those wounds. They look painful.' He offered her an arm but she sidestepped it and shot him a keep-away-from-me glare.

'I think you've helped me enough for one day,' Tillie said. 'Do you realise the whole village is abuzz with the news of our engagement? I've had to turn my phone off because the calls and texts haven't stopped with everyone's congratulations.'

His expression went from concerned to puzzled. Then his gaze zeroed in on the ring. 'But I thought you accepted my offer and—'

'Accept?' Tillie snorted. 'I did no such thing! I stupidly put your ring on to see what it looked like and it got stuck on my finger. Then I visited Mr Pendleton because the centre called to say he'd had a fall and he saw it there and laughed at me when I told him who gave it to me.'

'Laughed?'

Tillie clenched her teeth so hard she could have moonlighted as a nutcracker. 'Yes. Laughed. Apparently I'm too old-fashioned and sensible for someone like you and I have zero chance of ever taming you. But while Mr Pendleton didn't buy it, the nurse came in and thought it was the best news she'd ever heard and has since told everyone and now I'm engaged to you and the whole damn community is clapping their hands in raptures of joy because poor jilted Tillie Toppington has got herself a new man. I swear to God I'm so furious I could scream loud enough to blow out my voice box.'

Blake's mouth did that trying-not-to-smile thing. 'So why did you tell the old man I gave you the ring in the first place?'

Tillie rolled her eyes as if she were in a movie about an exorcist. 'Because the doctor told me Mr Pendleton was feeling a bit low and irritable after hitting his head so she said not to stress him too much. He saw the ring on my finger and asked me if my ex had come crawling back. I told him someone else had given it to me but he insisted I tell him who that someone was. Then I had to sit through three and a half hours of his paroxysms of laughter when I told him it was you.'

'How did you explain our relationship?'

Tillie loaded her voice with I've-got-you-now. 'I told him you came into the shop and fell in love with me at first sight.'

His laugh made something in her stomach tickle.

'Don't you mean love at first bite? One taste of your chocolate éclairs and I was hooked.'

Tillie was annoyed he found this so amusing. That he found *her* so amusing. She stabbed a finger at his chest. 'This whole flipping fiancée farce is all your fault.'

He captured her hand as if he was worried she would bore a hole right through his chest. Not that her finger could ever get through the layer of marble-hard muscle he had going on there. She'd need a jackhammer for that. His pecs were practically as big as the flagstones in McClelland Park's front hall.

'Did he say he was going to sell the Park to me?' he asked.

'Is that all you can think about?' Tillie pointed at her own chest this time. 'This is *my* life we're talking about here. *My* reputation. What is everyone going to think?'

'They're going to think well done you for landing yourself a wealthy good-looking fiancé after that jerk screwed you over.'

'Yes, well, at least that's one thing he didn't get to do,' she said before she could filter her tongue.

A quick flash of concern crossed his features. 'What do you mean?'

'Never mind.' She turned to look at Truffles, who was now lying at Blake's feet like a devoted slave waiting to obey his master's next command.

Sickening. Just sickening.

'Traitor,' she said to the dog. 'I knew Mr Pendleton should've chosen the whippet.'

Truffles showed the whites of her melting brown eyes and gave an I'm-way-too-cute-for-you-to-be-angry-at-me whine.

Blake chuckled. 'Cute mutt.' Then he looked at Tillie. 'Aren't you going to ask your new fiancé inside for a drink?'

'No. I am not.'

He gave a look not unlike the one Truffles had done moments earlier. 'Come on, Tillie. We have to get our history straight otherwise Jim Pendleton won't be the only one who's not going to buy our engagement.'

She speared him with a glare. 'I don't want people to buy it. I want this ridiculous situation to go away.'

'It's not going away until I get back this property,' he said. 'And, by the way, people are going to wonder why I'm not living here with you instead of at the B&B.'

'If you move in here that doesn't mean you get to make a move on me. *Comprende?*'

That dark twinkle was back in his gaze. 'We need to work on the old man to convince him to sell the Park to me now we're engaged.'

'I am *not* engaged to you.' Tillie spat the words out like lemon pips. 'Anyway, it's probably not legal to get an old man with memory problems to sign anything legally binding.'

Another flicker of concern passed over his features. 'Has he got dementia?'

'No, just a bit of temporary confusion from his fall,' she said. 'But I still don't think it would be right to take advantage of that.'

'No, of course not.' He gave an on-off smile. 'I'll just have to be patient, won't I?'

He didn't strike Tillie as a particularly patient man—not after 'proposing' to her within a couple of weeks of meeting her. But she couldn't help noticing the way he kept glancing at the house where he had spent the first ten years of his childhood. The ten-bedroom Georgian mansion was positioned on woodland-fringed acreage with a lake in front. There were both formal and wild gardens and a conservatory that made the most of the morning sun.

Tillie had moved in after Mr Pendleton's stroke two months ago to take care of Truffles and now hated the thought of ever leaving. She could well understand Blake's attachment to the place. If she had to picture a dream home then this wasn't far off it. Was it mean spirited of her to stop him staying here instead of the B&B? She had never had a permanent place to call home because her father's work as a vicar always required him to move into a vicarage owned by the parish. She had lived in the gamekeeper's cottage at Simon's parents' property for seven years, because when her father had been transferred she'd no longer been able to stay at the vicarage and had wanted to finish her final year at the local school and then go on to catering college. But she could imagine for someone whose family had lived in a place like McClelland Park for generation after generation, the emotional attachment would be so much greater.

Blake's gaze returned from surveying the house

to the droplets of blood tracking a pathway down her shins. 'You really should get some antiseptic on those abrasions.'

Tillie had forgotten all about her knees. It was hard to concentrate on anything but the grey-blue of his eyes and the shape of his mouth when he spoke. She couldn't stop thinking about how his mouth would feel pressed to hers—whether it would be hard or soft or something in between. 'Yes, right, well, then... erm...would you like to come in and have a look around while you're here?' The invitation was out before she could stop it.

There was a spark of devilry in his gaze. 'Are you sure the old man won't mind an old-fashioned and sensible girl like you inviting a guy you only met a couple of weeks ago in?'

She held up her left hand, her expression wry. 'Why would he? We're engaged—remember?'

He grinned. 'How could I forget?'

CHAPTER THREE

BLAKE STEPPED OVER the threshold of his family's home and a wave of memories washed over him. For a moment—a brief moment—he had trouble controlling his composure. An ache spread from his heart to every corner and crevice of his chest—a tight, squeezing ache that snatched his breath away in degrees. Every room of this house contained memories—every window, every wall, every floorboard. He had spent the happiest years of his life here with the two people he'd loved more than anyone else in the world. This house epitomised for him that long-ago era of security and love and safety.

The colour scheme had been changed over the years and the furnishings, of course, but the overall structure was exactly the same. The mullioned windows that fed the light in from outside, the polished wooden floors that creaked now and again when you walked across them. The staircase that led to the upper floors, the bannister he had slid down too many times to count. He could almost hear his mother's light cheery voice calling out to him as he came in the front door. He could almost hear the click-clack of her heels on the floorboards and the smell of her flowery perfume, the gentle weight of her arms as they gathered him close in a loving hug…

'I'll leave you to have a wander around,' Tillie said. 'I'm going to clean up my knees.'

Blake was pulled out of his reverie. 'Let me help you. Besides, it was my fault you hurt yourself.'

'I can put on my own plasters.' Her voice had a note of icy hauteur he found amusing. But then a lot about her was amusing. Amusing and refreshing and tempting.

'I insist.'

She let out a *whatever* sigh and turned in the direction of the nearest bathroom. He couldn't tear his eyes away from her pert behind, the way her skirt swished from side to side over it as she walked.

He wondered if he could persuade her to let him stay with her here. He was reasonably comfortable at the B&B, if you could call comfortable a bed you disappeared into like a cloud—all except for his ankles and feet, that was. He almost gave himself concussion every time he walked through the door and Mrs Rosethorne and her all-you-can-eat breakfasts were doing their best to undo all the work he'd put in with his personal trainer.

What was Tillie's main issue? It was a big house. There were enough rooms for them to avoid contact if she preferred not to interact with him. Although, the sort of interaction he had in mind required close contact. Skin-to-skin contact.

Blake followed her into the bathroom and crouched down in front of her.

'What are you doing?' she said, wide-eyed.

He placed a gentle hand on her leg just above her knee. 'Inspecting the wounds.'

'Get your hands off me.' Her voice had that starchy schoolmistress-tone thing going on.

He glanced up at her. 'You've got a piece of gravel in your knee. Hand me some tweezers and I'll get it out for you.'

Indecision flittered across her features. Then she let out another sigh and rummaged in the cupboard near the basin and handed him a pair of tweezers, some antiseptic and some cotton pads. 'Go for it,' she said, sitting on the closed toilet seat. 'I never was one for playing doctors and nurses.'

Blake smiled and set to work. 'Am I hurting you?'

'A bit.'

'Sorry.'

Within a short time he had the grazes cleansed and covered with plasters and then got to his feet. Tillie rose from the toilet seat with twin pools of colour in her cheeks.

Damn, he loved to see a woman who could still blush.

'Thank you,' she said, avoiding his gaze.

'My pleasure.' He put his hand underneath her chin and raised her eyes to his. 'You have great legs, by the way.'

The colour in her face deepened three shades. 'Look, Mr McClelland, I—'

'That's a bit formal for an engaged couple, don't you think?'

Her brown eyes simmered like overheated cara-mel. Her gaze slipped to his mouth and she drew in a jagged breath and the tip of her tongue darted out and left a layer of moisture over her lips. 'B-Blake, then,' she said in a voice as raspy as the emery board sitting on the bathroom counter.

Blake slid a hand along the side of her face to splay his fingers underneath her cloud of springy chestnut hair that smelt of sweet peas. He felt her shudder as if his touch had set off an involuntary tremor in her body. She was so close he could feel her hips brush-ing against his, stirring his blood into doing push ups. Could she feel what she was doing to him? He looked between each of her eyes in a back and forth motion, watching as her pupils flared like spilled ink.

She could.

Tillie's hands came up to lie flat on his chest, her luscious breasts pressing against him until it was all he could do not to bury his face in the cleavage hid-den behind her conservative cotton blouse. He wanted to kiss her. Badly. But he wanted it to be her idea, not something she could accuse him of setting up.

He put his hands on her upper arms and gently put her from him. 'So, here's what I think we should tell people. We met a while back and recently fell madly in love.'

She gave him the sort of look a hardened sceptic gave a faith healer. 'Met where?'

'Where everyone meets these days—online.'

'I don't meet people like that,' she said. 'I prefer the old-fashioned way of actually seeing a person in the flesh first.'

Blake began to undo his top buttons of his shirt.

Her eyes rounded until her eyebrows almost met her hairline. 'What are you doing?'

'Allowing you to meet me in the flesh.'

She whipped around and stalked out of the bathroom. 'You're unbelievable. You think you're so damn irresistible, don't you?' She turned back around to flash him a glare as hot as a flame. 'Well, guess what, Blake McClelland? This is one scalp you won't be able to add to your well-worn bedpost.' She pointed her finger towards the front door. 'Now get out before I set the dog on you.'

Blake glanced at Truffles, who was lying on the floor chewing on a ballet flat that was looking more like a dead animal than a shoe. The dog stopped chewing and wagged its tail back and forth along the floor like a fluffy broom and gave a soft little whine.

Blake looked back at Tillie. 'Look, I'm fine with us not sleeping together during our engagement. It's not a mandatory part of the deal. But I still think I should stay here for the sake of appearances.'

There was a small silence.

'Why isn't it?' she asked, cheeks darkening again. 'Don't you…fancy me?'

He fancied her *too* damn much. He couldn't think of the last time he'd felt so turned on by a woman. Maybe it was because she was resisting him. Dating had become a little too easy over the years. It didn't take much of an effort to get a woman into his bed. Was that why he was feeling a bit bored by it all just lately? The dinner-drink-bed combo was foolproof but predictable. This whiff of a new challenge made his blood tick and his pulse race. Or maybe it wasn't so much the challenge, but the fact it was Tillie.

'Come back over here and I'll prove it,' he said.

She pressed her lips together until they were white. 'You're laughing at me. I know you are.' She turned her back and hugged her arms around her middle. 'Please leave.'

Blake came back over to her and stood behind her with his hands resting on the tops of her shoulders. She flinched like a flighty filly as if torn between wanting to be stroked and wanting to flee. 'Hey,' he said.

She dipped out from under his hold and cast him a look that would have stripped three centuries of paintwork off the walls. 'I want out of this engagement before I'm made a laughing stock. Again.'

'Declaring bankruptcy would be worse.'

Uncertainty passed over her features and her teeth sank into her lower lip. But then a defiant spark came back in her gaze. 'I'll sell your ring and pay off my debts that way.'

'You could,' Blake said, with a slow smile. 'But you'd have to get it off your finger first.'

Her anger was so palpable he could feel it crackling in the air like static. Her eyes blazed and her fists clenched and her body vibrated. She whooshed out a breath. 'It seems I haven't got much choice but to go along with this. Too many people already think we're engaged and I'll look an idiot if I retract what I've said so far. If you pay off my debts I'll agree to this stupid charade, but there have to be some ground rules laid down first.'

Blake wondered what had finally swayed her. Was it just the money she owed? It was certainly an amount that would be enough for the average person to lose a little sleep over. Was it about losing face in the village? Or was it because of her affection for old Mr Pendleton—she didn't want to upset him so was prepared to run with the charade? Or did she plan to resist Blake to prove a point? Who did she want to prove it to? To him or herself?

'Scan and email the bills to me and I'll sort them out this evening,' he said. 'And as to rules—the only one I insist on is whenever we're out in public you behave like a woman in love.'

Her eyes fired off another round of sparks. 'And what about when we're alone?'

'I'll leave that to you to decide.'

Her chin jerked up. 'I've already decided. I wouldn't sleep with you if you paid me.'

'I'm not in the habit of paying for sex,' Blake said.

Her teeth started to tug at her lower lip as if the mere thought of the money she owed was enough to send her into a spiralling panic bad enough to invite an axe murderer to move in as long as he settled her debt. She released her lip and returned her gaze to his. 'You can move in tomorrow once I've had time to prepare a room. But you need to know, I'm not usually the sort of girl to live with someone I've only just met.'

'Did you live with your ex?'

'No…not really.'

Blake frowned. 'What does that mean?'

'I rented a cottage at Simon's parents' estate but he didn't share it with me,' she said. 'His parents were a bit old-fashioned about that sort of thing.'

Why couldn't they have let it to her for free? Local gossip informed him Simon's parents weren't as wealthy as he was, but neither were they sitting on street corners with a tin cup in their hand. 'You *rented* it?' he said.

'Yes.' Her jaw clenched and her eyes flashed as if the memory annoyed her. 'And they didn't give me back the bond after I moved out. His mother said I scratched her precious walnut coffee table but I did no such thing. Not that I didn't wish I had afterwards. I wanted to take a pickaxe to the whole damn cottage until there was nothing left but kindling.'

Blake suppressed a smile. Tillie might have a reputation as a mild-mannered angel but it didn't take much to scratch that Goody Two-Shoes façade to find a passionate and feisty little virago inside. 'Sounds like you had a lucky escape. Once I move in tomorrow, I'll take you out to dinner. It'll be a way to let the locals know we're the real deal.'

Her brown eyes narrowed. 'Just dinner, right?'

'Just dinner.'

Once Blake had left, Tillie stalked back into the sitting room and let out a curse word. Three curse words. Words she had never said before. Words that

would have made her God-fearing father have a con-
niption if he'd heard her.

Blake McClelland was the most infuriating man
she'd ever met—infuriating and way too charming
and attractive. She had been so close to making a fool
of herself—acting like a gauche schoolgirl mooning
over his mouth as if she was gagging for him to kiss
her. She had been just about gagging, but that was
beside the point.

Truffles came into the sitting room and jumped
on the sofa to look out of the window as if checking to see where Blake had gone and started whin-
ing piteously.

'Oh, for pity's sake,' Tillie said to the dog. 'Did
you have to make such a fool of yourself with him?
You're supposed to be on my side.'

Truffles gave a doggy sigh and flopped down on
the sofa, resting her muzzle on her paws and giving
another my-world-is-over whine.

Tillie flicked her eyelids in disdain. 'You might
think he's the best thing since those dog treats I baked
for you, but I know what he's up to. He thinks he can
hook me like he hooks all his other lovers. Well, he's
in for a big surprise because he could crook that little
finger of his all he likes. Unlike you, I *can* resist him.'

She had the willpower. She had the discipline. She
had the self-control.

He thought he could toy with her to fill in the
time until he secured his deal over the property. She
was going to give that overblown confidence of his a
wake-up call. If he thought he could stride into town

and pick her up like a cake off the counter then he was in for a big disappointment. He could take her out to a hundred dinners—a thousand. He could move into the house but she was *not* going to sleep with him.

But she would make everyone think she was.

Tillie was determined to show everyone in the village she had the ability to attract a full-blooded man. Even Mr Pendleton would be convinced once she executed her plan. No one would call her old-fashioned and too conservative once she had been seen out and about with Blake McClelland. Her Goody Two-Shoes reputation was in for a rapid makeover.

She would continue to hate him behind closed doors. Hate and dislike and loathe him. A pity about the issue of her physical attraction to him, but still—she couldn't win them all. He could pay her debts and she wouldn't suffer a flicker of conscience about him doing so. If he wanted her to act like a woman in love in public then that was what she would do—with bells and whistles and hearts and flowers.

Tillie turned back to the dog and smiled a witch-stirring-a-cauldron smile. 'I'm going to lay it on so thick and so cloyingly sweet he won't know what hit him.'

Blake visited Mr Pendleton the following day with a gift of a new bestseller and a small bottle of Scotch. The old man narrowed his eyes when Blake came in. 'I wondered when you were going to show up again. What's this I hear about you giving Tillie an engagement ring? You think I'm so stupid not to see what you're doing?'

Blake sat in the chair beside the bed and crossed one ankle over his thigh. 'And here I was thinking you were a romantic. Didn't you tell me you fell in love with your wife within minutes of meeting her?'

Mr Pendleton's features softened a fraction at the mention of his wife. 'Yes, well, they don't make women like my Velma these days… Mind you, Tillie comes close.' His expression sharpened again and his eyes bored into Blake's. 'She's a good girl. Too good for the likes of you.'

Blake couldn't help feeling a spike of irritation. Admittedly he had a bit of a reputation as a playboy, but neither was he out there robbing banks or ripping off little old ladies. 'Surely Tillie should be the judge of that, not you or the rest of the village.'

The old man shook his head. 'Thing is… I'm not sure Tillie knows what she wants. She saved up for years for that wedding. The dress alone cost a fortune and I have it on good authority she only chose the design because Simon's mother pressured her. I offered to help her with the money she owes but she won't take it off me.'

'I've sorted out all that for her,' Blake said. 'You don't have to worry about it any more.'

Mr Pendleton's gaze still contained a glittering sheen of you-can't-fool-me cynicism. 'Have you moved in with her yet?'

'I'm heading over there tonight. Thanks for giving the okay about it, by the way.'

'You must be more charming than I thought. Have you set a wedding date?'

'We're still getting used to being a couple,' Blake said. 'I don't want to rush her after her last relationship.'

Mr Pendleton made a *phhfft* noise. 'Call *that* a relationship? That boy didn't even sleep with her. She's as untouched as a nun.' He gave Blake another probing look. 'I bet a man like you wouldn't settle for a peck on the cheek and a bit of tame handholding. That's how I knew he wasn't right for her. I know he's a man of faith and all that, but chemistry is chemistry. You either have it as a couple or you don't.'

Blake was doing his level best to disguise his shock. *Tillie was a virgin?*

How had she got to her mid-twenties without having sex? He'd heard via Mrs Rosethorne at the B&B Tillie had been engaged to her fiancé for three years and dated him since she was sixteen. Surely her fiancé would have pushed for more? Even a man of faith had hormones, didn't he? Was that why she reacted to Blake the way she did? With that hungry look in her eyes, as if someone was offering her something she had longed denied herself?

Wait a minute.

Blake wished his conscience hadn't shown up for duty. How could he have a fling with her if she was a virgin? He didn't do virgins. Virgins were rosy-cheeked princesses waiting for princes to show up on a white horse. Virgins wanted the whole package: marriage and babies and a white picket fence.

He wasn't signing up for any of that.

Not one bit of it.

Mr Pendleton gave Blake the squinty eye. 'Everything all right? You want me to call the nurse? You're looking a little pale.'

Blake forced a smile and got to his feet. 'I have to get going. Call me if you change your mind about the Park.'

Mr Pendleton snorted. 'Tillie might fall for your charm but I'm not so much of a pushover. I'll sell when I'm good and ready and not a moment before.'

Blake stalled by the end of the old man's bed. 'Will you at least give me your word you won't sell it to anyone else?'

The old man's gaze was unwavering. 'Will you give me your word you won't break Tillie's heart?'

Blake tried not to flinch under the old man's piercing scrutiny. 'You never know—she might be the one to break mine.'

Mr Pendleton gave a mercurial smile. 'I hope so.'

CHAPTER FOUR

TILLIE WAS IN the shop serving one of her regulars when Blake came in that afternoon. She had so far survived Mrs Jeffries's questions about how she had met Blake and how he'd proposed—with a good bit of embellishment, of course.

She handed Mrs Jeffries her date and ginger scones over the counter. 'Ah, here he is now.' Tillie sent Blake a dazzling smile and gave him a little finger wave. 'Hello, sweetie pie. I was just telling Mrs Jeffries how romantic your proposal was. How you got down on bended knee and begged for me to say yes. I told her you had a little cry when I did. Well, not just a *little* cry.' She looked at Mrs Jeffries again. 'He was bawling his eyes out. I was about to call for sand bags to stop him flooding the joint. I've never seen a man so in touch with his emotions. Wasn't that awfully sweet?'

Mrs Jeffries made oohing and aahing sounds. 'Everyone's so happy for you, Tillie.'

Blake was a terrifyingly good actor, for he simply smiled. Tillie knew he wouldn't let her get away

with it for too long, but, in a way, that was part of
the thrill of doing it. She *wanted* to spar with him.
Their verbal exchanges excited her in a way no one
else's conversation had before. She saw the I'll-get-
you-for-that-later glint in his grey-blue eyes and a
shiver coursed down her spine like the tickle of a
strip of tinsel paper.

'Aren't you going to kiss me hello, babe?' he said.
'I'm sure Mrs Jeffries won't mind.'

'Of course not,' Mrs Jeffries said, smiling indul-
gently.

Tillie came from behind the counter. What harm
was there in a chaste brush of the lips? Actors did it
all the time and much more than that, too. She came
to stand in front of him and planted her hands on
his chest and looked into his wickedly glinting eyes.

Better get it over with.

She closed her eyes halfway and lifted her mouth
to his descending one.

The first brush of his mouth against hers sent a
frisson of heat right through to her core. The second
brush wasn't a brush—it was a lingering pressure that
made her lips open on a gasp and allow his tongue
to glide in with such toe-curling expertise every cell
in her body jerked upright as if jolted awake from
a long sleep. His tongue grazed hers, calling it into
a sexy duel that made her knees feel as if someone
had taken her bones out. She leaned into his embrace, another cascading shiver going down her spine
when his strongly muscled arms gathered her closer.
His hands moved from the small of her back to cup

her rear, bringing her flush against him. She could feel the growing ridge of his erection, thick and urgent, speaking to her feminine form with such primal power it was almost shocking.

How could she be responding to him like this? She didn't even like him and yet her body craved his as an addict did a forbidden drug.

Tillie wasn't sure who broke the kiss but she had a sneaking suspicion it might have been him. She lowered herself off her tippy toes and smiled. 'Well, nice to know you're pleased to see me.'

Blake's smile told her he wasn't finished with her yet. 'Always, babe. Always.'

Mrs Jeffries left the shop just as Joanne came in from her lunch break. Joanne's face broke into a wide smile. 'Hi, Blake. Congratulations, by the way. Best news ever.'

'Thanks,' he said. 'I think so too. I've called in to take Tillie out for a drive. Can you hold the fort for half an hour?'

'But I've got to—' Tillie began.

'Sure, no problem,' Joanne said. 'Tillie was about to have a break anyway. Have fun!'

When they stepped outside, Blake held out his hand and Tillie had no choice but to slip hers into it because there were villagers about doing their errands at the various shops along her section of the street. His hand was warm and dry and almost swallowed hers whole. There was a faintly erotic undercurrent in the way he held her hand. His thumb was absently—it might not have been absently but deliberately—stroking the flesh until every nerve was tinglingly aware of each back and forth movement of his thumb-pad. She was annoyed with herself for being so damn responsive to his touch. Surely there was something wrong with her? It wasn't normal to be so…so…*sensually aware*…was it?

Tillie walked with him to where his car was parked a couple of spaces down from her shop. 'Where are we going?'

'A drive.'

'Where to?'

'Just a drive.'

She frowned at him once he'd taken his place behind the wheel after settling her in the passenger side. She couldn't read his expression for it seemed a shutter had come down now they no longer had an audience. She turned back to face the front and didn't speak again until they were clear of the village and out on the country lane that led past McClelland Park. 'I do have a job to do, you know. I run a small business that requires me to be there eight to ten hours a—'

'Why didn't you tell me you were a virgin?'

Tillie blinked in shock. How on earth did he know that? Who else knew? It wasn't something she talked about with any of her friends. Although, come to think of it, a few months ago Simon had been prone to lecturing anyone who would listen about the benefits of being celibate. She wondered now if he'd done that because he'd been sleeping with his new girlfriend at the time. Or was it because everyone in the village saw Tillie as conservative and old-fashioned? A nineteenth-century throwback too prudish to show an ankle in public. Maybe they secretly blamed her for Simon running off with someone else. 'I can't imagine how you came by that information or how you could possibly believe it's true.'

'Is it?'

Tillie folded her arms across her chest and stared straight ahead. 'I'm not going to answer such an impertinent question.'

The car slowed to a stop by the side of the road and Blake turned off the engine and swivelled in his seat to look at her. 'So it *is* true.'

She chanced a glance to find him watching her with a thoughtful expression. 'So what if it is?'

'How old are you?'

'Twenty-four.'

'A bit old to be a virgin in this day and age, isn't it?'

Tillie looked at the cows snatching mouthfuls of lush green grass in the field nearby. It was a bit old, but she'd only agreed to it because Simon had insisted. She hadn't questioned it because she knew her parents, and then her stepmother too, had also abstained before marriage. It was common with people of faith; there were even celibacy movements amongst young people all around the globe. But she couldn't help wondering if Simon had never truly wanted her but had been using her as a back-up plan until someone more attractive came along. The absence of a strong pull of attraction in her relationship with Simon was only apparent to her now she had met Blake. No amount of mountain-shifting faith, no strength of conviction could withstand the incendiary heat that flared between her and Blake.

'Simon didn't believe in sex before marriage,' she said. 'Not unless it was with a size zero blonde who looked like she should still be in school.'

'You didn't...try and change his mind?' Blake asked after a small silence.

Tillie had tried that once and it had spectacularly failed. She still cringed in embarrassment thinking about it. Simon had gone all preachy on her and made her feel abnormal for giving in to 'base desires', as he'd called them.

'You mean seduce him?' She gave a snorting laugh. 'Not my forte at all, I'm afraid.'

'I don't know about that.'

She couldn't stop her gaze going to the curve of his mouth. She swallowed and dragged her eyes back to his. 'Can we talk about something else?'

He reached out a hand and picked up a loose curl and slowly but surely wound it around one of his fingers. 'You're a beautiful woman. Don't let anyone tell you you're not.'

Tillie leaned closer as if to inspect the function of his eyes. 'Do you need glasses? Because I'm not sure what school of beauty you subscribe to but no way would I ever describe myself as beautiful. Passable maybe, but not beautiful.'

He still had hold of her hair, inexorably drawing her closer and closer as if reeling her into his orbit.

His gaze kept going to her mouth as if, like her, he couldn't stop himself. 'You're too hard on yourself. I find intelligence enormously attractive. Sexy too.'

So did Tillie. But then, she found everything about Blake McClelland attractive and sexy. 'Right, well, thanks for the compliment but I have a business to run so if you're done with talking then—'

'When I asked you to play this charade with me I intended to sleep with you,' Blake said, releasing her hair to sit back against his seat.

Tillie gave him a pointed look. 'Was my consent a part of your plan?'

A frown snapped his brows together. 'Of course it was. I'm not the sort of man who forces himself on a woman.' He let out a gust of a breath and the frown relaxed but only slightly. 'I'm also not the sort of man who gets involved with virgins.'

All virgins? Or only plus-size ones who aren't considered classically beautiful?

'So what's with the anti-virgin bias?' she asked.

'Women who've waited to have sex until they meet the right person are usually waiting for the fairy tale,' he said. 'It wouldn't be fair to sleep with them and then ride off into the sunset without them.'

'You don't see yourself getting married one day?'

'No.'

'Better not tell the rest of the village that or they'll be after you with feathers and a pot of tar,' Tillie said.

He gave a soft laugh that didn't sound all that amused. 'Yes, well, you think I don't know that? Which is why we're not going to get down to business.'

She arched her brow. 'Did I say I was going to sleep with you?'

The look he gave her made her want to tear off her clothes and throw herself at him then and there. 'I haven't had anyone turn me down before.'

Tillie felt a faint thrill at being the first. Faint because she didn't want to turn him down. She wanted to crush her mouth to his and open her lips for the smooth thrust of his tongue, to push her breasts up against his chest, to push her hips against his and feel the stirring of his arousal in the throb of his blood.

She wanted. She wanted. She wanted.

The air seemed to pulsate with the sexual energy that flared between their locked gazes.

'Don't even think about it.' His voice had a note of stern authority.

'You don't know what I'm thinking,' Tillie said, quickly schooling her features.

One corner of his mouth came up. 'Don't I?' He reached out a fingertip and traced the line of her mouth like someone reading Braille—the top lip and the lower one, as if memorising their contours.

Tillie hadn't known how many nerve endings were in her lips. She hadn't known how hard it would be to resist such a caress. She hadn't known she didn't have the willpower to. *Where was her willpower?* 'Tell me what I'm thinking, then.'

His finger grazed the curve of her cheek. 'You're thinking how it would be—you and me—getting it on.'

'Actually, I'm thinking of the christening cake I have to decorate before the weekend,' Tillie said.

'Liar.'

His fingertip found her ear and did a slow circuit of her cartilage until she had to hold her breath to stop from whimpering in delight. His mouth came closer as if in slow motion, his warm hint-of-cinnamon-scented breath mingling with hers in the tiny space that separated their mouths. She closed the distance and touched her mouth against his with a feather-light brush, but it wasn't enough. She wanted more. She pushed her lips against his in a playful nudge, a part of her looking from above and wondering where she had been hiding this sensual side of herself for all these years.

Blake took control of the kiss with a muttered groan, his arms gathering her closer, almost crushing her as his mouth moved with passionate urgency against hers. She opened to the commanding thrust of his tongue, welcoming it into the cavern of her mouth, tangling with it in a cat and mouse caper that made the desire deep in her core break free from its restraints. It flooded her body like a sizzling hot tide, sweeping away all the reasons why she shouldn't be encouraging this sort of interaction with him. Right now all she could think about was how amazing his mouth felt on hers. How thrilling it was to have him as turned on by her as she was by him. The guttural sounds he was making made her shiver all over as if someone had dusted her body with sparkly glitter and filled her blood with bubbles.

No one had ever kissed her like this. Not with such heat and intensity. Not with such ferocious desire that matched her own. She could feel her body preparing itself—her female flesh aching for friction to bring the release it craved.

She could hear the noises she was making. Primal noises. Noises of encouragement and approval. Noises of pleasure—whimpers and gasps and little groans that sounded nothing like her. She linked her arms around his neck, pushing her breasts as close to him as the gear console allowed, her fingers toying with the wavy ends of his dark brown hair that were brushing against his collar. She breathed in the clean male scent of him, the notes of lime and citrus, tasted the hint of mint on his tongue, ached for him with a pulse throbbing like a drum beat between her thighs. Desire hijacked her body, making it a slave to the sensations powering through her body—shockingly addictive sensations his touch evoked. Every movement of his mouth, every thrust and glide of his tongue, every nip and nudge of his teeth stirred her senses into a fireball of longing, sending arrows of heat to her core.

Blake suddenly pulled away, breathing heavily. 'Okay. Time out.' He sat back against his driver's seat and took a steadying breath, his hands gripping the steering wheel as if to anchor himself.

Tillie sat back and smoothed her hands down her skirt, trying to get her body to settle down but it wasn't listening. Needs she hadn't been aware of were thrumming inside her—deep, deep inside her. If she squeezed her legs together it only made it worse. It was a shock to realise how close she'd been to begging him to finish what he'd started.

Or had he started it?

There was a painfully long silence.

'Aren't you going to say anything?' she asked.

He opened and closed his fingers on the steering wheel for a moment, his brows still jammed together over his eyes. 'I'm not sure it's a good idea for me to move in to the Park straight away.'

Not a good idea? It was a brilliant idea. No one would think she was too old-fashioned once she had Blake installed at the house. 'But you have to. I've told everyone you're moving in tonight.' She gave him a probing look. 'You *do* want McClelland Park back, right?'

'You know I do. But I have some business to see to in Edinburgh for a few days.'

'You didn't mention anything about business yesterday when you came to see me at the house. We were going to go for dinner.'

His face got a boxed-up look about it. 'It's come up since then. It's...urgent.'

What was urgent? His business or his need to get away from temptation? It was weird thinking of herself as a temptation. She had never tempted Simon beyond his control. Not once in eight years. A thrill trickled through her body at the thought of Blake wanting her so badly he felt the need to distance himself.

Maybe size zero blondes didn't have all the fun after all.

He turned over the engine. 'I'd better get you back

to work.' And glancing over his shoulder, he drove back out into the lane, spraying arcs of loose gravel out from under the spinning tyres.

Okay, so that went well.

Blake drove away after dropping Tillie back at her shop. He couldn't get that kiss out of his mind. He'd been like a horny teenager necking by the side of the road. He was supposed to be putting the brakes on now he'd found out she was a virgin. But as soon as her lips met his it was all he could do to keep his hands off her. Her inexperience was supposed to be helping him keep his distance, but instead it was drawing him to her like an alcoholic to a free wine tasting.

Her mouth was so soft and sexy beneath his. It responded to his as if he were feeding her the air she needed to stay alive. It had damn near killed him to pull back. He'd wanted to keep on kissing her, to touch her, to peel those clothes off her and put his mouth on those gorgeous breasts he'd felt crushed up against his chest.

He had to get control of himself. He was supposed to be focussed on getting McClelland Park back, not having a fling with a girl who had been saving herself for Prince Charming. Tillie responded to him as if she had never been kissed properly before. But then, maybe she hadn't if her ex had had his interest invested elsewhere. She kissed with her whole body, throwing so much passion into the mix he could only imagine what it would be like to make love to her.

You could offer her a fling.

The thought nibbled at the edges of his conscience like a mouse at wainscoting. Tillie was attracted to him; there was no doubt in his mind about that. But would she agree to a short-term fling when she had the fairy tale as her ultimate goal? Girls like Tillie did not do flings. Girls like Tillie waited years for the right guy to put a ring on their finger and promise them for ever.

Blake was a for-now guy. He had a mission and once it was completed he would be moving on. And he wasn't taking anyone with him when he left. No baggage meant exactly that: No. Baggage. He travelled light when it came to his emotions because that was the way to keep control. Control was his thing. He didn't need to sit on some therapist's sofa to know it had something to do with losing his mother when he was a kid. He'd seen what happened when emotions took over. They stopped people thinking clearly. They confused and distorted things.

He kept his head clear by focussing on the task. So what if he was a workaholic? It was his determined focus that had clawed back the wealth—and more—that had been lost when his father had his breakdown. Blake's ability to make tough business decisions without involving emotion had been the blueprint for his success. As soon as people allowed feelings into the mix things started to get messy. He had seen previously successful companies fall over as soon as feelings started flirting with the numbers. It was numbers you could rely on, not spur-of-the-moment impulses.

He'd thought it would be so simple talking Tillie

into helping him to get McClelland Park back. When he'd heard on the village grapevine about her being jilted and the debt she was in, he'd thought he could use her situation to his advantage: a month pretending to be his fiancée in exchange for clearing her debts. Too easy…or so he'd thought. But he hadn't considered the aftermath of such an arrangement. He planned to have his father live at the Park in the not too distant future. If Blake messed with Tillie the whole darn village would run him out of town and perhaps make things awkward for his dad. She was the village saint and he would be asking to have his kneecaps taken out with a cricket bat if he did the wrong thing by her.

Although she wasn't averse to messing with him, the cheeky little minx. The way she'd laid it on with a trowel in front of her customer with all that rubbish about him weeping over his proposal. He had nothing against men crying, but it had been a long time since his tear ducts had had a workout.

But that was what he liked about Tillie. She wasn't a pushover. She gave as good as she got and didn't seem in the least fazed by being outmatched by her opponent. He was looking forward to further interactions with her, even if it meant he'd have to shackle and double padlock his desire.

Anyway, a bout of celibacy might do him good.

Really looking forward to that.

Not.

CHAPTER FIVE

TILLIE HAD TAKEN Truffles to see Mr Pendleton and was back at McClelland Park keeping an eye on some cookies she had baking in the oven. She hadn't seen Blake for almost a week. When he'd first told her he was going to be away she'd been worried about what people would think given she'd announced to everyone he was moving in with her. But as each day passed with little or no contact from him, she felt strangely deflated, like a solitary balloon left behind after a party. She didn't want to admit how much she was looking forward to seeing him. Nor did she want to admit how boring her life was without him coming into the shop and giving her those glinting looks across the counter. She couldn't even look at a chocolate éclair now without a frisson passing over her flesh.

Tillie sent a text to Blake saying she'd leave a key to McClelland Park under a loose flagstone near the front door for when he got back in case she was still at work.

Mr Pendleton was still refusing to believe she

was really engaged to Blake. And it certainly hadn't helped when he'd heard Blake was in Scotland. But because of his memory issues, the staff at the respite centre reassured her it was just a phase and he would hopefully come out of it soon.

Every person who came into the shop stopped to chat about how wonderful it was she had found true love at last. Tillie was so good at lying now even *she* was starting to believe she was actually in love with Blake. The flutters in her tummy every time his name was mentioned made her wonder if her mind and her body were playing tricks on her. Surely you couldn't *act* your way into feeling something?

Tillie couldn't decide whether to be embarrassed everyone thought she was 'doing it' with Blake or disappointed she was not. Ever since those kisses her body had been feeling restless. It was as if a hunger had been awakened and nothing but him would satisfy it. If she closed her eyes she could recall every second of his mouth on hers, the way it felt, the way it tasted, the way his stubble left graze marks on her skin that she had to use make-up to cover.

When he'd first come to her with his plan, his intention had clearly been to seduce her into the bargain. But since finding out she was a virgin he had pulled back...apart from that kiss, that was. Could she indulge in a little fling with him? It wasn't as if she was going to fall in love with him. Her mind could play all the tricks it liked on her. She wasn't going to fall in love with anyone. No, siree. Not after the last time. Blake would be a means to an end just as he'd intended her to be for him.

What was the point of abstaining from sex when she had no intention of ever marrying? Not now. Not after being publicly humiliated at the wedding she had planned and looked forward to with such hope for the future. That was why she kept her wedding cake and dress as a reminder of her foolishness. A reminder of how stupid she had been to believe in the fairy tale.

The fairy tale sucked.

It was a big fat double-crossing lie.

It was a trap for romantic fools who thought life wasn't fulfilling without a partner. She could do just fine without one. Coupledom wasn't for her any more. No more pandering to a man. No more cooking meals she didn't like just because he liked them. No more watching bloodthirsty action movies or tediously boring sporting matches.

Single and Loving It. That would be her...*eventually*.

The engagement ring was still on Tillie's finger so she figured she might as well make the most of it. She suspected she would have to go on a crash diet for a month to get it off. No amount of hand cream or soap or butter would make it budge. She had to put on sterile gloves when she worked with pastry or cookie dough because she didn't want to get it dirty. But once the month was up that ring would be cut off and her ties with Blake cut, too.

But not before she had a bit of fun first.

Tillie took out the first batch of peanut butter cookies and slid in the next tray of chocolate chip. Truffles pricked up her ears, gave a bark and bolted out of the kitchen and started to scratch at the front door to be let out. Tillie pulled off her plastic gloves, wiped her hands on her apron and went to open the door to see Blake's black sports car coming to a stop in front of the fountain on the circular driveway in front of the house. He unfolded himself from behind the wheel with the sort of athletic grace she could only envy. When she exited a car, she looked like a baby elephant trying to squeeze through a cat flap.

Blake was carrying a bunch of pearly pink roses, not quite white but not fully pink, either. He handed them to her with a crooked smile. 'Thought you might like these.'

Tillie buried her face in the fragrant blooms, suddenly embarrassed at the thought of him moving in with her. Had she done the wrong thing agreeing to it? What if it got…awkward? She had never lived with anyone other than her father and stepmother. What if Blake didn't take up her offer of a fling? The house might be big, but it wouldn't be big enough for her to avoid him then. 'They're gorgeous. I love the colour.'

'That pink reminds me of your cheeks when I make you blush.'

She could feel her cheeks doing exactly that. No one could make her blush more than him. He only had to look at her with those twinkling grey-blue eyes and her face would be aflame. Had he thought about the kisses they'd shared? Had he relived every second of them or had he occupied himself with someone else?

The thought was jarring. Like finding a fly in the cookie dough. There was nothing to stop him carrying on with his freewheeling playboy lifestyle. Their 'engagement' was a charade. No one had made any promises.

But if he was going to sleep with someone, why couldn't it be her?

The more Tillie thought about it, the more sensible and convenient it seemed. It would be a chance for her to finally get her V plates off. She could indulge in a hot, no-strings fling with him as a way to celebrate rather than bemoan her single status. That was what singletons did, wasn't it? Had heaps of fun sex without the pressure of a relationship with expectations and responsibilities.

'So, how was your trip up north?' Tillie asked.

'Boring, actually.'

'So, they don't have burlesque dancers in Scotland?' The smile she gave him would have made a fox envious.

Blake sent her a mock glower but she could see his eyes were smiling. 'That was a stitch up by a mate of mine—a drunk mate of mine. He thought it'd be funny to have some scantily clad dancers hang out in my room while we were at an investment conference in Vegas. The press made a big thing of it, of course.'

His explanation pleased her in a way she couldn't quite explain. Or maybe it was because she was secretly glad he wasn't the sort of man to have sordid parties with Vegas showgirls.

'Would you like some dinner?' Tillie asked after

a slight pause. 'I've got enough for two. Actually, I always have enough for two. I'm still learning how to cook for one person.'

'Sure, if it's no trouble? We could go out if you'd prefer.'

Tillie flashed her best wry smile. 'Cooking is my thing. It's the one thing I'm good at.'

'I'm sure you're good at lots of things.' Blake's gaze went to her mouth for a nanosecond. 'Not just good—excellent.'

'I'm…erm…just going to put these in some water,' she said. 'Why don't you make yourself at home? Sorry, that must sound weird, someone telling you to make yourself at home in what used to be your home. I've given you one of the larger spare rooms. I haven't moved Mr Pendleton's things out of the master suite because, well, it didn't seem the right thing to do just yet.'

'That's fine, I wasn't expecting to move in there yet.' He sniffed the air. 'The house looks and smells the same, too. What are you making?'

'Cookies. I do a lot of my baking for the shop here as it keeps the workspace clear for my decorating.'

Tillie was expecting him to go get his bags from the car and head upstairs to settle in, but instead he followed her into the kitchen. He pulled out and sat on one of the chairs at the large scrubbed pine table in the centre of the room, crossing one ankle over his knee, his gaze moving about the room as if recalling the times when he'd sat there as a child. She wondered if coming back here was difficult for him, stirring memories of his childhood and the loss he'd suffered.

Tillie sorted out the flowers but became conscious of his gaze resting on her. She glanced up from the roses and gave him a lopsided smile. 'You can have one if you like. You're not allergic to peanuts, are you?'

'No.' He took one of the peanut butter cookies off the cooling rack and bit into it and chewed, making *mmm, it's good* noises as he did so.

The oven timer sounded and she snatched up her oven mitts and bent down to take out the next tray.

'My mother used to bake,' Blake said into the silence. 'She used to let me help her.'

Tillie put the cookies on the cooling rack and looked at him. 'You must have been devastated when she died.'

He didn't speak for a moment, but stared at the half-eaten cookie he was holding as if wondering how it got there.

'It hit my father hard,' he finally said. 'His work suffered. Lost heaps of money in bad business decisions. Got exploited by people who should have been helping him, not ripping him off.'

Tillie couldn't believe how tragic it all was. She could picture Blake as a small bewildered boy, shattered by the grief of losing his mother, struggling to support his grieving father, only to lose his family home. No wonder he was so determined to get it back. He couldn't bring his mother back but this was one thing he could do. 'Did your father ever remarry or—?'

The rueful twist was back on his mouth. 'He hasn't even been on a date.'

The strength of Blake's father's love for his mother made what she'd felt for Simon look like a school-girl crush.

Maybe that was what it had been...

'He must have loved her so very much.'

Blake's eyes moved away from hers, a frown settling between his brows. 'I wouldn't have thought it was possible to love someone that much if I hadn't witnessed it first-hand. He literally couldn't function without her. He barely functions now, especially after his recent heart surgery. He wouldn't have needed it if he'd been taking better care of himself over the years. But I'm hoping getting this place back for him will be a step in the right direction.'

'You're doing it for *him*?' Tillie asked.

His gaze came back to hers, a cynical smile tilting the edges of his mouth. 'What? Did you think I wanted to set up a playboy mansion for myself?'

She bit her bottom lip. That was exactly what she'd thought. 'It was an easy assumption to make, especially the way you went about it. Demanding I pretend to be your fiancée as if I would jump at the chance.'

He gave a soft grunt that might have been his version of an apology. 'I see you're still wearing my ring.'

'That's because the only way to get it off would be cut it or my finger off.'

There was another moment or two of silence.

Tillie started sweeping away invisible crumbs. 'I've been thinking about this arrangement we have between us...' she began.

Blake's gaze was steady and watchful. 'And?'

She licked the sudden dryness off her lips. 'Well, I might be mistaken about this but I got the feeling when you kissed me the other—'

'Don't do this—'

'Thing is… I haven't had a relationship… I mean a physical relationship…so—'

'No.' The word was flatly delivered, sounding like a punctuation mark driven in by the very determined nib of a pen.

Why did he keep saying no?

Tillie took a moment to pick up her splintered ego. 'Why is that? Because you don't fancy me or—?'

He rose from the chair with a jerky movement. 'I'm not going to sleep with you, Tillie. It wouldn't be…right.'

'Oh, so you've suddenly developed a conscience, have you?' Tillie said. 'Pity you didn't have one with you when you blackmailed me into being your fiancée.'

His jaw grew tense as if he was biting down on his molars. 'My *pretend* fiancée. I'm not intending it to become official. One month, that's all. One month.'

'Did I say I wanted you to make it official?'

His frown flickered as if not sure whether to deepen or relax. 'What exactly do you want?'

Did he have to make her spell it out? 'I just thought since we…erm…got on okay you might be able to help me with my…erm…little problem.'

His eyes were the darkest she had ever seen them, a smoky grey as deep and mysterious as the lake outside. 'What little problem?'

Tillie interlaced her hands in front of her body, reminding herself of when she was a tongue-tied schoolgirl standing in front of a stern headmaster over a uniform code violation. 'As you said the other day, it's unusual for a woman of my age to still be a virgin, so… I wondered…if you would consider helping me to not be a virgin any more.'

There was an echoing silence.

Blake's frown dug a deep trench between his eyes. 'You're not serious…*are you*?' The incredulous tone of his voice made it sound as if she were asking him to make a human sacrifice of her and then grind her blood and bones and feed them to the jackdaws.

'Of course I'm serious,' Tillie said. 'I'm sick of being a virgin. I only agreed to remain celibate for Simon's sake and then he went off and had sex with someone else behind my back. That's what made me the angriest. Do you know how that made me feel? Worthless, that's how. Hideously undesirable and worthless.'

Blake drew in a breath and then released it in a ragged stream. 'Look, here's the thing. I admit I was thinking about sleeping with you, seriously thinking about it, but when I found out you hadn't been with a guy before it changed everything. I'm not the white-picket-fence man you're after. It would be wrong to sleep with you knowing I couldn't offer you the whole package.'

'But I don't want the whole package,' Tillie said. 'Been there, done that, got the wedding dress and cake to prove it.'

His frown resembled isobar patterns on a map. 'What are you saying? You don't want to get married one day and have a family?'

Tillie wasn't so sure about the family part. She hadn't quite ruled out a rosy-cheeked kid or two. With IVF technology women didn't need a husband to become a mother. But marriage she had ruled out with a thick red pen. 'I'm open about having a child but not about having a husband. I can safely say no man will ever get me to put on a white dress and veil and turn up at church ever again.'

'People don't always get married in a church—'

'It's not the venue that's the problem,' Tillie said. 'It's the institution of marriage I'm shying away from. I want to have the life I missed out on while I was saving myself for Simon. I want to make up for all the opportunities I lost.'

Blake rubbed a hand down over his face until it distorted his features. 'This is crazy.'

Tillie wasn't sure what to make of his response. She'd thought—hoped—he'd jump at the chance to sleep with her. Now she wondered if it wasn't so much about her being a virgin but more about her being unattractive. All her self-doubt and insecurities came back like ants to a pile of spilled sugar. She wasn't model thin like the women he dated. She wasn't fashion conscious. She didn't wear enough make-up. She didn't show enough cleavage. The list went on and on.

'Fine,' she said. 'I get the message loud and clear. It was dumb of me to think someone like you might be remotely interested in someone like me.'

Blake came over to where she was standing and took her by the upper arms, his frowning gaze holding hers. 'You should think about this for a day or two before you rush into something you might regret.'

It was Tillie's turn to frown. 'Why would I regret doing what every other girl my age does without blinking an eye?'

His hands slipped away from her arms and he stepped back out of her personal space. 'I just think you need to put the brakes on, that's all.'

Tillie pressed her mouth flat, her arms folded in front of her. 'I'm starting to regret my invitation for you to come and stay here.'

'Is that why you issued it?' His tone had a sharp edge to it that scraped her already raw nerves. 'So I could help you with your "little problem", as you call it?'

'No. I do think you're right—people will wonder why if we're not under the same roof, especially since everyone knows you're not a saint. They expect us to be sleeping together. It wouldn't be normal for you not to.'

He pushed back his hair with a distracted hand. 'Just give it a day or two, okay? Think of it as a cooling-off period. The best business decisions are made that way.'

'Is that how you see this? As a business decision?'

A shutter came down at the back of his gaze like a vault being sealed off. 'My goal is and always has been to get this place back into my hands. You became a part of that plan when I struck that deal with you over the money you owed. But if you would prefer me to call our pretend engagement off then that's what I'll do. You won't owe me a penny. It's your choice.'

Was he testing her?

But even if he wasn't how could she walk away and see him lose the house he loved so much for a second time? He hadn't told her anything much about his mother, but the little he'd told her about his father made her realise how deeply he loved his dad and that he saw the return of the estate as essential to his well-being. She might have been able to walk away before, but not now. Not now she realised how important McClelland Park was to him and his hopes for his father's recovery.

'No. I want you to get your house back,' Tillie said. 'It's the right thing to do even if the way we're going about it is a little unconventional.'

If he gave a sigh of relief he hid it well for barely anything showed on his expression. 'Thank you.'

Blake brought his things in from the car while Tillie got working on dinner. A part of him insisted he repack the car and head out of that driveway before any more damage was done. But right then, her offer of a no-strings fling was far more tempting than the strength of his convictions. Would it be wrong to have a physical relationship with her?

He had never made love to a virgin before, but he knew enough about the female form to know the wrong handling or rushing her before she was ready could be not only painful but emotionally scarring as well. He hadn't thought he was one of those men who held female sexuality to different standards from men. He wasn't so draconian to think a woman was less of a person for having been sexually active. Sexual desire was a normal human process and why shouldn't women experience it in the same way men did without feeling guilty?

But the fact Tillie was a virgin did make him feel… special was not the right word. Privileged, honoured that she had decided to ask him to be her first partner. It wasn't because she held any true affection for him; he wouldn't agree to do it if she did. Feelings got in the way when it came to having casual sex. He was a master at blocking his. Now and again he would get the odd vague stirring over a particular partner, but he always moved on before it had time to take hold.

Tillie's attraction to him was purely physical—the best sort of attraction when it came to negotiating a no-strings fling. It wasn't as if his relationship with her was going to last longer than those he'd had with other women. A month was the longest he'd been involved with someone, although he had never cohabited with a partner before.

Would it be stepping over a boundary too far? Sharing a house this size shouldn't be an issue, but this wasn't just any house. This was a treasure trove of deeply emotional memories for him, a place where he had experienced love and happiness and a deep sense of belonging unlike anything in his life since.

Once Blake had put his things in the room Tillie had prepared, he walked a few metres further down the wide hall and opened the door of the bedroom he had occupied as a child. The bed, the furniture and curtains and paintwork were all different, leaving no trace of the boy who had spent the first ten years of his life there.

But when he walked over to the window and looked at the view, he was thrown back in time to that last day when he'd stood in this exact spot, his heart a bruising weight in his chest. From this window he could see the old elm tree with its limbs spread like the wings of a broody hen sheltering her chicks. He had carved his name where no one could see on that ancient elm tree that had watched over so many generations of McClellands.

His name written there was a secret promise to his ancestors that one day he would be back to claim the only true home he had ever known.

Tillie came up the stairs a while later to tell Blake dinner would be in ten minutes. She couldn't find him at first. He wasn't in the room she'd prepared for him, although his bags were. She walked further down the corridor and came to a smaller bedroom where she found him standing in front of the window with his hands in his trouser pockets, staring at the view of the lush green rolling fields and acres of woodland beyond.

He must have sensed her watching him for he turned and gave her a vague-looking smile as if he was lost in his thoughts. 'Sorry, did you say something?'

Tillie came further into the room, stopping when she got to just in front of him. It was hard to read his expression but she sensed he was struggling to keep his emotions locked away. 'Was this your bedroom when you were a boy?'

His eyes moved away from hers to gaze out of the window again. 'See that old elm tree in the distance?' He pointed to a gnarled tree Tillie had sat under many times playing with Truffles. She'd always thought it a magical sort of place, the kind of tree she had read about as a child in her favourite Enid Blyton books.

'Yes,' she said, acutely aware of the way his shirt-sleeve brushed the bare skin of her arm as he pointed.

He dropped his hand, his gaze still on the elm. 'I broke my arm when I fell out of that tree when I was nine years old. I got the plaster taken off just before my tenth birthday.' He paused for a nanosecond. 'If only I had known that was the last birthday I would ever spend here with my mother.'

Tillie slipped her arm through his to offer what comfort she could. 'I'm sure your mother would be very proud of the man you've become, especially as you're doing all you can to help your dad.'

He made a sound that was somewhere between a sigh and a grunt. 'It would've broken her heart to know we had to leave this place.'

'It's an easy place to fall in love with.'

He turned and gave her one of his half-smiles. 'Where did you grow up?'

'Not in a place as nice as this,' Tillie said, slipping her arm out of his. 'We only ever lived in vicarages attached to parishes so I never knew any place as home in that sense. The longest we lived any place was right here in this village but that was only for four years before dad was transferred to another parish in Newcastle. That's why I stayed with Simon's parents because I didn't want to interrupt my final year of school. I secretly hoped my dad and stepmother would change their mind about going but they didn't seem too worried about leaving me behind. They aren't really interested in First World problems. They live by faith.'

His grey-blue eyes held hers. 'Did your father have to accept the transfer or could he have asked for an extension?'

Tillie had always struggled with her father's decision to move but, being an obedient daughter, had never said anything. It felt a little strange to be confessing what she felt about that time to someone as worldly as Blake. 'He would never have questioned the decision because he believed it was a calling. I had to accept it but I can't say it was easy.'

'Do you live by faith too?'

Tillie's look was sheepish. 'Please don't tell my father and stepmother but I'm not very good at it. I like to know there is plenty of money in the bank and that all the bills will be paid on time.'

'Seems fair enough to me.'

There was a little pause.

'What about you?' Tillie asked. 'Do you believe in a higher power who is watching over you all the time?'

His eyes suddenly darkened and one of his hands

went to her face and trailed a nerve-tingling pathway down the slope of her cheek. 'If there is, then what I'm about to do is going to send me straight to hell.'

Tillie disguised a gulping swallow. 'Wh-what are you going to do?'

'Guess,' he said and brought his mouth down to hers.

CHAPTER SIX

BLAKE'S LIPS WERE strong, determined—hard, almost. As if he resented the attraction he felt for her and was fighting it to the last. Tillie didn't want him to fight it, she wanted him to embrace it the way she was embracing the fiery attraction she felt for him. The heat in his mouth spread to hers like combustible fuel, sending tingling sparks of feeling from the nerves of her lips that travelled through her body like flicking, licking flames. His tongue found hers in a single thrust, curling, duelling, teasing it into intimate play.

She pressed her body into his tall, hard frame, opening her mouth to his exploration, her tongue becoming bolder with every heart-stopping second. He tasted of mint and coffee and desperation, his lips moving on hers with exquisite expertise until her senses were singing like a symphony choir. How could a kiss stir her into such raptures of feeling? The sensations travelled in a hot rush from her mouth to her core as if his kiss had programmed a secret pathway through her body.

His hands went to her hips, holding her against

the surge of his male flesh, leaving her in no doubt the desire she was experiencing was in no way one-sided. His body was as turned on as hers.

He lifted his mouth off hers to blaze a trail of kisses down the side of her neck. 'You have to tell me to stop.' There was almost a pleading note to his tone but there was no way she was going to do any such thing.

Tillie traced the dip in his chin below his mouth where his stubble was rich and dense and arrantly male. 'What if I don't want you to stop?'

His hands tightened on her hips, his eyes pools of smouldering smoky grey. 'You're not making this easy for me.'

She lifted up on tiptoe to press her mouth to his in a series of feather-light touchdowns. 'I want you to make love to me.'

His mouth responded by kissing her with the same hot pressure, making every nerve in her lips tingle. 'I've wanted you since the first day you served me in the shop.'

Tillie pressed another kiss to his mouth. 'Why? Because of my chocolate éclairs?'

He smiled against her mouth. 'That and other things.'

She eased back to look up at him. 'What other things?'

He sent a lazy fingertip over the shape of her eyebrows. 'When you handed me my change, I knew we would be dynamite together.'

So he'd felt that zapping tingle, too? Tillie had

tried not to touch him all the times she'd served him since but he always made sure their hands came into contact. Was that why he always insisted on being served by her and not Joanne? 'Did you eat all those éclairs or were they just a ruse to get my attention?'

He gave her a crooked smile. 'Of course I ate them. There's only so much temptation a man can stand.' He brushed a strand of hair off her face. 'Are you sure about this? Really sure?'

Tillie slid her hands up his chest to link her arms around his neck. 'Absolutely.' She leaned closer, pressing her breasts into the wall of his chest, her mouth connecting with his in an explosive kiss as if the final bolt on his restraint had popped.

His hands cupped her bottom to hold her to his hard heat, his tongue tangling with hers in a sexy dance that made her insides shudder in delight. This was how a kiss was meant to be: passionate, unstoppable. Irresistible.

Tillie sucked in a breath when one of his hands moved from her bottom to slide up to just below her breast. It was as thrilling as if he had cupped it naked in his hand. But he seemed to be taking care not to rush her and instead kept kissing her slowly in a way that made her senses swoon as if she'd been given a powerful drug. She made little noises under the sensual play of his mouth, greedy, needy noises that signalled her desire for him as blatantly as the surge of his body against hers. Never had she felt anything like this tumultuous fever in her flesh. Every nerve of her body was activated, on high alert, anticipating the next brush of his mouth, the next glide of his hand, the ultimate possession of his body moving with heat and urgency within hers.

Blake walked her backwards to the bed, his mouth still locked on hers in a blistering kiss that made the base of her belly quiver like an unset jelly. His tongue was moving in and out of her mouth in an erotic mimic of his carnal intent.

Tillie began to work on his clothes, keen to get her hands on his naked flesh. She undid a couple of buttons on his shirt but her fingers were all but useless. He undid the rest and hauled it over his head and tossed it to the floor beside the bed. She planted her hands on his chest, running her palms over his toned muscles, wondering again where he'd stored all those calories she'd sold him.

Sudden shyness gripped her.

Would the little bulge of her tummy that no amount of sit-ups had ever been able to shift put him off? Her dimpled thighs? What if he was completely turned off by her body? She wasn't anything like the svelte model types he dated.

He must have sensed her change of mood for he stilled his movements and searched her gaze. 'It's not too late to change your mind.'

Tillie lowered her eyes and snagged her lower lip with her teeth. 'It's not that…'

He cupped her cheek in one warm dry hand, holding her gaze steady. 'Are you nervous?'

'A little…'

His thumb began a slow stroking motion across

her cheek. 'You're a beautiful, sexy woman, Tillie. You have no need to doubt yourself.'

Was he a mind-reader or what?

'I've always been a bit self-conscious about my body,' Tillie said. 'Simon made it worse by insisting I cover it up all the time. I started to see it as problematic, something to be ashamed of, to hide away instead of being proud of my curves.'

Blake's hand gently cupped her breast through her clothes. 'I've been having fantasies about your curves since the first day I met you.'

'You have?'

His eyes gave a sexy twinkle and he started to undo the buttons on her top. Her skin tingled when his fingers brushed against her and her inner core clenched with a spasm of desire so strong it threatened to take her legs out from under her. He peeled away her dress and let it fall to the floor next to his shirt. His fingertip skated over the twin upper curves of her breasts still encased in her bra. The sensation of his finger grazing her was electrifying, making her nipples stand up and cry, *Touch me!*

'So beautiful.' His voice was a low deep murmur that made her skin break out in goose bumps. Then he bent his head and sent his tongue over each of her breasts in a slow lick that made her spine feel as if someone had undone each and every one of her vertebrae. Who knew there were so many nerves in her breasts? That the lazy stroke of his tongue would make her tingle from the top of her head to the balls of her feet?

Tillie heard a pleading sound and then realised it had come from her. His teeth grazed her nipple in a gentle bite that made her hair lift away from her scalp. His tongue circled, tracing the darker skin of her areole and then moving to the sensitive underside of her breast. He did the same to her other breast, pushing it up to meet his mouth with one of his hands, the sensations so powerful, so entrancing her whole body quivered. Need clawed at her insides, clenching, aching need that was being fuelled by every touch and press of his mouth and hands.

He moved down her body, kissing her sternum, her belly button, gently peeling away her knickers so he could access her most intimate flesh. She automatically tensed, but he calmed her by placing his hand on her stomach just above her mound, soothing her as a trainer did a flighty horse. 'Relax, sweetheart. I won't hurt you.'

Tillie slowly let out the breath she was holding, forcing her spine to ease back against the mattress. He began to stroke her with his fingertips, gauging her response, encouraging her to tell him what worked and what didn't. And she would have told him if she'd been capable of speech. All she could manage was a breathless gasp as her sensitive nerves flickered like a struck match. He brought his mouth to her and began a slow exploration of her, soft little licks and nudges opening her like a flower, allowing her time to get used to his touch, to the feel of his breath moving over her.

The sensations were building in a powerful wave,

pulling all her flesh to one single delicious point at the swollen heart of her body. She could even feel the tension in the arches of her feet. It was like a terrifyingly savage storm approaching. She felt it coming but pulled back from it, afraid of its impact on her, of what it would do and how, or even whether, she could control it.

'Go with it, Tillie,' Blake said. 'Don't be frightened of it.'

'I—I can't.' She put a hand up to cover her face, suddenly embarrassed at how gauche she must seem to him.

He gently brought her hand away and gave it a soft squeeze. 'You're doing fine. It's hard to orgasm with a partner for the first time. But I've got you. I won't let anything bad happen to you. Roll with it. Let it take you.'

Tillie lay back and closed her eyes, letting him caress her with his lips and tongue. It was as if he was reading her body, letting it tell him what it needed. The pressure built again and this time there was no escaping the waves of pleasure, they seemed to crash into her and over her, spinning her into a vortex where she was beyond thought, her body so intensely captivated by feelings she had never experienced with such spectacular force before. Cascading, undulating waves moved through her body, leaving her limbless, boneless in the golden aftermath.

Blake stroked the flank of her thigh. 'See? I knew you could do it.'

Tillie reached for him, drawing him closer so she

could touch him. 'That was…amazing. But you have too many clothes on.'

'I got a little distracted there for a moment.' He stood from the bed and slipped out of his trousers and undershorts, before reaching for a condom from his wallet.

He came back to her on the bed, lying beside her so as not to overwhelm her. 'We don't have to do this if you don't feel ready.'

Tillie stroked his length. 'I'm ready. More than ready.'

I've been ready since the day I met you.

His features flickered with pleasure as her hand began moving up and down his shaft. The erotic power of him thrilled her, making her inner core tighten in anticipation. 'Am I doing it right?' she asked.

'You can do it harder. You won't hurt me.'

She squeezed her fingers around him and moved faster, delighting in the way his breathing changed. He brought his mouth down to hers, kissing her long and deep, his tongue mating with hers in a sexy mimic of what was to come.

Tillie moved her pelvis against him, letting her body communicate its need. He positioned himself over her, taking his weight on his arms so as not to crush her, his legs angled around hers.

He brushed her hair back from her face, his eyes dark with desire. 'Still okay with this? It's not too late to say no.'

Tillie touched his face, the rasp of his stubble

against her fingertips reminding her of how different his body was from hers. 'I want you.'

He dropped a soft kiss to her lips. 'I want you, too.' Then he slowly moved against her entrance, allowing her the feel of him without going any further. 'Tell me if I'm hurting you.'

Tillie brought her hand to him to guide him, not that he needed any directing. He was being so considerate but her body didn't want his consideration. It wanted him. Now.

He glided in a short distance, giving her time to get used to him. Then he moved deeper within her, a little bit at a time until she was comfortable with his presence. 'Still okay?' he asked.

'More than okay,' Tillie said, stroking her hands over his back and shoulders. 'You feel amazing.'

'You feel pretty damn amazing yourself.' He brushed her lips with his, softly and then with firmer pressure as if the need pounding in him was urging him on.

It was urging her, too. The primal power of it was surging through her body, making her gasp and groan and whimper as he began a slow rhythm of thrusting and retreating and then thrusting again.

There was none of the awkwardness she'd been expecting. None of the shame about her not so perfect body. She was swept up in the magical momentum of discovering the pleasure spots and erogenous zones of her body and feeling proud of how it responded to him. Like how her breasts became super-sensitive when he swirled his tongue around and over her nipples. Like how her neck and underneath her earlobes had thousands of nerves that danced and leapt under the glide and stroke of his mouth and tongue.

Tillie could feel her body swelling with need, a deep ache throbbing in her flesh, but she was unable to get to the final moment of lift off. She moved beneath him, searching for that little bit extra friction, finding it and then losing it just when she needed it most. 'I can't... I can't...'

'Yes, you can,' he said and brought one of his hands down between their bodies and stroked her intimately. It was all she needed to fly. The shimmering, shuddering sensations ricocheting through her from head to toe, leaving no part of her unaffected. She clung to him while the tumult thrashed her about, digging her fingers into his buttocks, feeling a little shocked by the way her body was so out of her control. Making love with someone was so different from self-pleasure. The skin-on-skin contact, the scent of arousal, the giving and receiving of pleasure made the experience so much more satisfying.

Blake waited until she was coming out of her orgasm before he took his own pleasure. She felt each of his shudders, heard his guttural groan that seemed to come from a deep dark cavern inside him. The power of it moving through him amazed her. Had he experienced the same earth-shattering sensations? Had she really done that to him?

He lifted his head and met her gaze. 'It will get better the more we do it.'

Tillie traced the line of his lower lip. 'I can't imagine how it could get better for me. I didn't know my body was capable of that.'

'You have a beautiful body that is capable of dismantling every bit of self-control I muster.'

She searched his face for a beat or two. 'Was it good for you?'

He pressed a kiss to her mouth. 'Better than good. Amazing. I've never slept with anyone like you before.'

'You mean a virgin?'

He played with a stray strand of her hair, winding it around his finger and letting it go, only to wind it back up again. 'Not just that.'

'Because I'm fat?'

A frown formed between his eyes. 'You aren't fat. You've got a gorgeous figure.'

'Have all your other lovers been slim?'

He did a slow blink and let out a long breath as if summoning his patience. Then he rolled away and dealt with the condom before he sat on the edge of the bed, one of his hands coming to rest on the side of her thigh. 'Listen to me, Tillie.' His voice had that stern schoolmaster tone going on. 'I understand that years of being engaged to a guy who never even tried to consummate the relationship would do a fair bit of damage to a girl's self-esteem. But I hate hearing you being so negative about your body. You have nothing to be ashamed of.'

Tillie let out a sigh. 'I'm sorry for spoiling the moment.'

He gave her a half-smile and leaned down to press

another kiss to her mouth. 'Repeat after me. I am beautiful just the way I am.'

She turned her head away. 'No! That sounds so ridiculously vain.'

Blake turned her face back so she had to meet his gaze. 'Say it.'

Tillie looked into his eyes and for the first time in her life felt beautiful. Beautiful and desirable. 'I am beautiful just the way I am. There, I said it. Now will you let me go?'

He trailed a lazy fingertip down between her breasts. 'Is that what you want me to do? Let you go or play with you some more?'

A shiver raced over Tillie's flesh at the sexy glint in his eyes. 'You want me again?'

He took one of her hands and brought it to the swell of his erection. 'You turn me on, Tillie Toppington. Big time.'

She stroked the proud heft of him, delighting in the way his expression contorted with each movement of her hand. 'Will you promise to stop treating me like I'm made of glass?'

'Are you sore?'

Tillie squeezed her legs together but while there was a slight twinge it was more pleasure than pain. 'Not a bit.'

He came back down beside her, lying on his side with one elbow propping him up. His other hand slowly caressed her thigh, a small frown interrupting his features. 'I was so determined I wasn't going to do this. I don't want you to get the wrong idea about us going forward—'

Tillie pressed a fingertip to his lips to silence him. 'Will you repeat after me? I am having a no-strings fling with you and I am completely okay about it.'

His expression flickered as if he was struggling with his conscience. 'I'm having a no-strings fling with you and I am completely okay about it.'

'You don't sound very convincing,' Tillie said, stroking the crease of his frown away without much success. 'Your eyes were saying, *what the hell have I done?*'

His mouth tilted in a rueful manner but his eyes still contained smoky grey shadows. 'As long as we're both clear on the boundaries.'

'I'm perfectly clear on the boundaries,' Tillie said, holding her fingers up as if to check off a list. 'We are going to have heaps of hot sex. We are not going to fall in love. And as soon as you get McClelland Park back we will end our fling.'

He tapped her on the end of her nose. '*You* will end it.'

'Oh, yes. I get to do the honours this time,' Tillie said. 'Will I do it in person or would you prefer a text?'

His frown came back. 'If ever I run into your ex I'm going to tell him what a pathetic yellow-bellied coward he is.'

Tillie couldn't help feeling a thrill at his comment. While everyone in the village had supported her in her disappointment when Simon jilted her, her father and stepmother had taken the 'forgive and forget' approach. Their lack of anger at Simon had made her feel as if they weren't listening to her, as if they were completely unaware of how deeply hurt she felt about being left in the lurch like that.

'You know something?' she said, toying with a whorl of Blake's chest hair as if it was the most fascinating thing she had ever seen, which, quite frankly, it was. Simon hadn't had a single hair on his chest and not from waxing them off, either. 'I was really disappointed when my father and stepmother refused to be angry with Simon. They kept carrying on about how I should forgive and forget as if he'd simply cancelled a date. I found it upsetting they thought it was far more important to forgive him than to let me express how hurt I was. I stopped talking to them about it because I know it disappointed them to see me so bitter and angry.'

Why are you telling him all your stuff?

Tillie knew exactly why. Because he listened with a concerned look on his face as if he were putting himself in her shoes and feeling hurt and betrayed on her behalf.

'Are you close to them?'

Tillie had always thought she was up until Simon had jilted her. 'I was hurt by the way they hadn't seemed to fully understand how devastated I was the day of the wedding. I expected them to be furious on my behalf. They had flown thousands of miles to be there, and at great cost, and yet when it was called off they simply shrugged as if a tea party had been cancelled.'

His expression was not only concerned but she was almost certain she could see a flicker of anger lurking in the back of his gaze. Anger on her behalf. 'That's terrible. They should've supported you better than that. Don't they know you at all?'

What was he saying? That *he* knew her better than her own family? Weird. Nice weird. 'I guess if I was truly close to them I would have told them the truth about you and me. But I didn't. I didn't feel comfortable lying to them but it was easier than admitting I was pretending to be engaged. They hold marriage as sacred so it would appal them that I was acting the part of your fiancée with no intention of it ever being real.'

Blake's frown dug a little deeper on his brow. 'What will they think of us living together?'

'I'm not sure they'll find out unless someone else in the village mentions it if they were to write or email them. I only told them we were engaged. They're on a remote mission posting in Uganda. The Internet and phone coverage is patchy and unreliable so I haven't heard back yet. Sometimes it can take days or even weeks to hear back from them.'

He threaded his fingers through hers, bringing up her hand to his mouth, holding her gaze with his thoughtful and serious one. 'It's never been my intention to come between you and your family.'

'You're doing no such thing,' Tillie said. 'I'm not a

child. I'm twenty-four years old and if I want to live with a man for a few weeks then that's my business.'

'You're not worried they might be disappointed you didn't—?'

'What? Wait for another Simon to come along and keep me in an ivory tower for years and years only to run off with someone else?' she said. 'No, thanks. I'm done with weddings.'

'So what's with the wedding cake in your back room at the shop?'

'I'm using it as therapy. I figure it's cheaper than seeing a therapist. Every day I stick a dressmaking pin into Simon's marzipan figure.'

'Is it helping?'

Tillie thought about it for a moment. Funny, but she hadn't stuck a pin in Simon since Blake had 'proposed' to her. 'Yes and no. I still have to do something about the wedding dress. It's taking up too much room in the wardrobe. It's like a cumulonimbus cloud crammed in there. I've thought of selling it, but I think it would be much more satisfying to cut it into ribbons.'

A flicker of amusement flirted with his mouth, but then his expression became serious again. 'Jim Pendleton told me you didn't get much say in choosing it.'

'No…but that was my fault for not standing up to Simon's mother,' Tillie said. 'That's the problem with wanting to belong to someone. You don't just belong to them but to their family, too. But I can see now Marilyn never accepted me as a future daughter-in-law. Nor did Simon's father. They tolerated me.

I can't help wondering how they're getting on with his new partner.'

'Would you ever go back to him if he—?'

'No. Absolutely not.'

Blake's frown hadn't quite left his forehead. He traced a pathway around her mouth with one of his fingertips. 'You were too good for him. Way too good.'

Tillie screwed up her face and then tiptoed her fingers down his sternum. 'I wish you'd stop calling me good. I want to be bad.'

His smile ignited a spark in his eyes and he brought his mouth down to hers. 'That's what I'm here for, sweetheart.'

CHAPTER SEVEN

BLAKE KISSED HIS way down her body, his hormones going nuts over the swell and shape of her curves. Why had he always dated stick insects when he could have had this? Her body was his every secret fantasy. The way she responded to him, the way she moved against him, the way she held him as if she never wanted to let him go. He couldn't remember a time when sex had been more satisfying.

Or more terrifying.

He had been so determined to keep control all the way through but in the end he'd blown like a bomb. That she could do that to him was a little unnerving. He was supposed to be the one at the control panels but every time his mouth met hers, he felt that control slip further out of his reach.

He came down to her breasts and swirled his tongue over her right nipple, taking the tight bud gently between his teeth, his blood pounding in his groin when she gave a breathless little gasp and clutched at his shoulders as if torn between wanting more and pushing him away.

He knew the feeling. The tug of war between common sense and a desire so raw and primal it took control of his flesh, made him a pawn to its needs—needs that he normally had firm discipline over, but not now. Not with her.

This was different.

Tillie was different.

She awakened something in him that up until now had been lying dormant.

He liked the closeness of making love to her. Coaching her into the magic of physical pleasure had intensified his own. He felt sensations he had never felt before. He had let go in a way he never had before. He hadn't had any choice. It was as if her body had triggered something in his—something dark and unknowable, a force he had fooled himself he didn't possess.

But it was there.

Lurking deep and secretively inside him.

The need to be close to someone, not just physically but enough to tell them about the things that weighed him down or buoyed him up.

When Tillie had told him how disappointed she'd been when her father and stepmother hadn't seemed to understand her devastation at being jilted, he'd felt a striking sense of commonality. A bond he hadn't felt with anyone else. The sense that someone else understood isolation and loneliness. Understood the hurt that couldn't be erased with a few casually flung platitudes.

Tillie was nursing her own hurt, but was a fling

with him the way to go about eradicating it? She said she no longer wanted the fairy tale. Could he believe she had changed so much in a matter of months? She still had her wedding cake and dress, for God's sake. She might say she was keeping them as part of her getting-over-her-ex therapy, but how sure could he be she was telling the truth? Even to herself?

He knew all about the lies people told themselves when they didn't want to face stuff. Hadn't he been lying to himself all these years about his father? Thinking, hoping that *this* year things would be different. Better. That his dad would finally emerge out of the well of grief he'd been drowning in for the last twenty-four years.

But had it happened?

Not yet, but Blake was determined he would make it happen.

Tillie's hand glided over his chest, her mouth fused to his in a passionate kiss that made the base of his spine tingle. She made soft little whimpering noises and opened her mouth for the entry of his tongue. Her tongue played with his in a dart and retreat dance that made the blood in his veins pound. What was it about her mouth that made kissing so damn exciting? Every nerve in his lips was on high alert, the shape and mould of her mouth against his delighting him as if this was his first ever kiss. He could feel every movement of it as if it had been magnified through his senses. The way she licked his lower lip and then took it between her teeth in a kittenish bite, before releasing it to sweep her tongue back over it, made every other kiss he'd experienced feel like a platonic peck in comparison.

Her touch was soft and yet electric, her hands moving over his body in an almost worshipful manner. His skin lifted in goose bumps when she sent her hand down in search of his erection. Her shyness was as endearing as it was exciting. But there was nothing lacking in her caressing of him. She responded to his sounds of pleasure as if they had their own secret language that no one else knew. Reading his body, stroking it with increasing confidence and boldness, making his senses go haywire.

Blake pulled away so he could concentrate on giving her pleasure. He moved down her body, kissing her stomach and then lower to her feminine mound. She was so responsive to him, so relaxed now under his touch it made him feel a level of trust had developed between them unlike anything he had experienced in his other relationships.

With Tillie, sex wasn't just sex. It was a discovery of the senses, a sensual journey with unexpected and thrilling results.

She came under the ministrations of his tongue, her hands gripping his head to anchor herself until the storm abated. 'Wow…just wow…' she said, her cheeks and décolletage still flushed with pleasure.

Blake smiled and moved up her body, turning her so she was straddling him. He reached for a condom but before he could put it on, she took it from him.

'Let me,' she said.

He glided his hands up and down her arms while

she put the condom on him with smooth strokes down his shaft that nearly took the top of his head off. She wriggled her body, taking him deep inside with a part-groan, part-gasp that thrilled him as much as the feel of her body gripping him so tightly. 'This way you can set the pace,' he said. 'Slow or fast, whatever you need.'

'I need you.' She lowered her face to his to kiss him.

Blake feasted on her mouth, tangling his tongue with hers, his lower body in raptures over what was going on down there. Tillie was riding him slowly, moving her body up and down and round and round until he was fighting to stay in control. Being able to see her joined to him so intimately ramped up his excitement. The pleasure rippling through him was played out on her features as if their bodies were tuned to report what each was feeling.

'You can do it,' he said when he could see she was close to orgasm. 'Don't hold back.'

She gave a sharp cry and then shuddered and shook over him, triggering his own release until his groans joined hers. Finally, she slumped over his still-tingling body, her hair tickling his face and neck, her chest rising and falling against his.

He stroked the silky-smooth skin of her back, enjoying the feel of her curves pressing into the harder planes of his body. 'You're not going to go all shy on me now, are you?' he said.

Tillie turned her head so she could access his neck,

sending her tongue out to lick just below his ear. 'I did feel a little bit…exposed doing it like that.'

Blake turned his head to look at her. 'You look beautiful when you come.'

Her cheeks went a faint shade of pink and her fingertip came up and passed over his stubbled jaw all the way to his mouth, her gaze lowered to follow its pathway. 'I knew sex would be good, but I didn't realise it would be this good.'

He lifted his hand to sweep her disordered hair back off her face. 'It's not always this good.'

Her eyes flickered with surprise. 'Even for you, you mean?'

'Yeah,' he said, realising with a strange little jolt it was true. 'Even for me.'

She propped herself up on her elbows, her eyes meeting his and her naked breasts with their tightly budded nipples tantalising him all over again. 'I have nothing to compare it with other than…you know…' Her cheeks fired up again and her gaze slipped out of reach of his.

Blake brought her chin up with the end of his finger. 'There's nothing to be ashamed about. Self-pleasure is the key to finding out what works for you and what doesn't and it's particularly important for women.'

She pressed her lips together for a moment. 'I know…but it's hard to shake off the repressed attitudes you've grown up with. I often wondered if it was somehow breaking the abstinence rule.'

'Is that what your ex thought?'

'Simon hardly ever talked about things like that,' she said with a little laugh. 'I asked him once if he ever relieved himself but he got all touchy about it, saying it was wrong of me to talk about sex when he was trying not to think about it.'

Blake frowned. 'And you were seriously going to marry this guy?'

Tillie's mouth flattened and two little circles of pink formed on her cheeks. She moved away from him and went in search of her clothes. 'I know it's probably hard for someone like you to understand my reasons for wanting to be with Simon, but—'

'Why someone like me?' Blake asked, swinging his legs over the side of the bed.

She snatched up her clothes and held them against the front of her body. 'You're good-looking and successful and can have anyone you want. It's different for people like me.'

'I'm not following you,' Blake said. 'You have just as much right to a good relationship as anyone else. Why would you settle for anything less?'

She sent him a pointed glance. 'Why do you settle for casual relationships and not something a little more lasting?'

He kept his expression blank. 'We're not talking about me. We're talking about you.'

She slipped her dress over her head without putting on her bra, smoothing the fabric over her hips that minutes ago had been pressed against his. Her features relaxed on a confessional sigh. 'I was never the popular girl at school. I made friends easily enough, but because we moved every few years I had to leave them and start all over again. I taught myself to fit in where I could.'

'That would've been tough on a shy girl.'

Tillie gave a little you-can-say-that-again eye-roll. 'It was. But when I met Simon when I was sixteen… well, I gravitated towards him because he seemed sensible compared to the other boys at school. He wasn't into drugs or partying and he had strong values. He was conservative, yes, but I liked that about him. It was what I grew up with so it was familiar. We started hanging out together and then we became a couple and were together until the day of the wedding.'

'When did he propose to you?'

She bit down on her lower lip and averted her gaze to scoop up her knickers off the floor. She bundled them into a ball and held them in one hand. 'When I was twenty-one, but it wasn't a proposal as such… more like a discussion.'

'You never had doubts he wasn't the right one for you? Especially given his parents were mostly negative about you?'

A shadow of something that looked like regret passed over her face. 'Looking back, I think I ignored all the things that weren't working between us and focussed on what was working. I wanted him to be my soul mate so I only looked for things to confirm that and disregarded anything that didn't.' She did a cute little self-deprecating lip twist and asked, 'I guess you don't believe in everyone having a soul mate?'

Blake thought of his father and mother. They had been a solid unit, a perfectly balanced couple who had always brought out the best in each other. He often wondered if things had happened the other way around—his father dying instead of his mother— would his mother have struggled as much as his father? He got off the bed and stepped back into his trousers. 'If there is such a thing, I'm not sure I'd want one for myself.'

'Why not?'

Blake shrugged, wishing he'd kept his mouth shut. 'I just don't, that's all.'

Her smooth brow furrowed into fine lines. 'Because of what happened to your father when your mother died?'

Bang on the money, sweetheart.

He kept his expression masked but he could feel Tillie's brown gaze bearing down on his resolve to keep that part of his life closed off like a persistent file picking at a lock. 'Hey, I thought you were going to cook me dinner?' He kept his tone light, even managed to crank out a smile.

She continued to hold his gaze. 'You don't like talking about her, do you?'

Damn right I don't.

What good did talking do? It hadn't changed a thing in twenty-four years. As far as he was concerned, two people had been put in that coffin that day and he had been left to carry on alone. His dad had all but died with his mother and Blake had had to grow up overnight. He had borne way too much responsibility for a child of that age.

And that responsibility had continued well on into adulthood.

He didn't tie himself down to any one place or any one person because of it. For he knew, at a moment's notice, his dad might need him.

He never wanted to need someone like that.

As his dad had needed his mum. Having a soul mate might sound great in theory, but in practice it sucked if and when that person left you or died.

Blake was the one who left his relationships. He started them. He ended them. He moved on from them without regret.

But something about Tillie's gaze got to him. The way it was both soft and direct, as if she knew how painful his past was and yet was determined to get him to air it like a musty sweater that had been shoved at the back of the wardrobe.

He let out a long sigh that made something tightly knotted in his chest loosen just a fraction. 'No. I don't.'

Tillie came over to sit on the bed right in front of where he was standing, looking up at him with those doe eyes. In spite of the sombre nature of their conversation, he couldn't stop thinking about the fact she wasn't wearing underwear under her dress.

'I've often wondered if it's harder to lose a mother you've never known or one you knew and loved,' she said.

Blake blinked away the memory of his mother's

death. How he had stood outside ICU the day her life support machine was turned off—because everyone had thought he was too young to be in there with her in her final moments—and prayed for and willed her to keep going even though the doctors said it was hopeless. But when his father had come out, Blake had known prayers rarely, if ever, got answered.

But then he thought of what Tillie said, and realised she must have lost her mother even earlier.

'It's hard on both counts,' he said. 'At least I have some memories. Do you have any of your mother?'

Her mouth rearranged itself into a wistful, almost-smile and her fingers absently plucked at the bedcover. 'She died within hours of my birth. I know it sounds a bit weird since I don't remember her at all, but I miss her. I miss the concept of her. My stepmother is lovely and all that but she can't tell me what it was like to carry me for nine months. What it was like to find out she was pregnant and all the hopes and dreams she had for me while she carried me in her womb. No one can do that but my actual mum. Every time Mother's Day comes around I feel like something—someone—is missing. It used to be awful at school when we made gifts for Mother's Day. I was always the only one without a mum. I would always make something I could leave on her grave, flowers and card or, once, a little pottery vase. Not that we visited her grave much. I think my dad found it difficult. Understandable, I guess. It wouldn't have been easy to lose his young wife that way.'

'Do you have any half-siblings from your father's marriage to your stepmother?'

'No. My stepmother couldn't have children,' Tillie said. 'She was so grateful for the chance to be a mum to a small child. I'm sure she was more in love with me than my dad at first.'

'Are they still happy?'

'Very,' she said. 'They have a lot in common. They both have strong faith and love working abroad on the mission field. They both felt called to do it since childhood.'

There was a small silence.

'I couldn't drag my father away from my mother's grave the first time we visited after the funeral,' Blake said. 'I didn't come with him much after that. I couldn't bear seeing him in so much distress. Once I was old enough to drive I came alone. I felt guilty about it. I still feel guilty about it, but I just couldn't hack it. Every birthday, every Christmas, every anniversary, every excuse he could think of, he'd want me to come down with him. I would've gone if I'd thought it was helping him. But I had my doubts.'

Tillie stood from the bed and slipped one of her hands into one of his. 'You shouldn't feel guilty. You did all you could to support him. Anyway, you were just a child. And having to be strong all the time wouldn't have helped your own grieving process.'

'No,' Blake said, vaguely registering how good… how *freeing* it felt to talk so openly about something he had locked away for so long. 'It didn't. I couldn't mention my mother without it causing my dad to fall into a deep depression that would last for days, if not weeks. I more or less taught myself not to think about her. It was as if she had never existed.'

Tillie moved closer so that the front of her body brushed against his, her arms going around his waist. 'Thanks for telling me about her.'

Blake wrapped his arms around her to draw her closer, resting his chin on the top of her head. 'It felt good. I haven't spoken to anyone about her, including my father, for a long time.'

She tilted her head back to look at him. 'Does he know you're trying to buy back McClelland Park for him?'

'No, I'm keeping that as a surprise,' Blake said. 'I didn't want to get his hopes up if it falls through. But I think it will be the key to his full recovery. He never forgave himself for losing this place. If he gets it back, I'm hoping he'll get his mojo back as well and finally move on with his life.'

She stroked a hand from the hinge of his jaw to his chin. 'I hope Mr Pendleton sells it to you. He doesn't have a direct heir because his only daughter died when she was sixteen in a car accident with her boyfriend. He has a couple of nephews but they never visit him. I'm going to try and convince him you're the only one who should own McClelland Park.'

'Let's hope he agrees, otherwise all this will have been for nothing,' Blake said.

Something flickered across her features and her arms around his waist loosened slightly as if she was withdrawing from him. 'All this? You mean…us?'

Maybe his choice of words could have been a little better, but there was a part of him that felt worried he had stepped over a boundary too far. He gave her waist a quick squeeze before he released her from his hold, stepping back to allow her some space…or maybe it was him that needed space.

'I can't help feeling you're the one who's going to lose in the end,' he said.

'Why would you think that?' she said. 'We agreed on the terms. You paid off my debts so I would pretend to be your fiancée for a month and a month only. The only thing I've lost is my virginity, which is exactly what I wanted to lose.'

Blake searched her features for a long moment. Her eyes were clear and honest, her expression open and unguarded. Was he worrying about nothing? Why then this little niggling sense of unease? 'What if you fall in love with—?'

'Will you listen to yourself?' she said with a half-laugh. 'Does every woman you have a fling with fall in love with you?'

'No, but—'

'Then you don't have to worry about me.' She gave him a pert little glance. 'Or maybe it's not me you're worried about. Maybe it's you.'

Blake gave his own version of a that-will-never-happen-to-me laugh but somehow it didn't sound half as convincing as hers.

CHAPTER EIGHT

TILLIE AND BLAKE enjoyed dinner together in the dining room with Truffles sitting at Blake's elbow waiting politely for titbits. They hadn't returned to the subject of Blake's concern over her falling in love with him during the course of their short fling. She was quite proud of the way she'd handled his concern with a quip that flipped his question back at him.

She liked him.

She liked him a lot.

He was the dream fling partner: kind, funny, generous, sexy and intelligent. But falling in love was something she was guarding against. Blake wasn't interested in commitment and nor was she. She had spent too many years of her life in a relationship she believed was the real thing only for it to fall over when she least expected it.

Or had she expected it?

It was an unsettling thought, but a part of Tillie—a secret part—hadn't been one bit surprised when she'd received Simon's text just as she'd arrived at the church. Hadn't she felt for weeks, if not months, he was moving away from her? But she had doggedly continued with the wedding arrangements, ignoring the fact Simon wasn't as involved in the plans as he had been. That he spent more time at his parents' house than he did at the cottage with her. That he always had something pressing he had to see to on their date nights. All the clues were there but she had refused to see them. For the last three months she had been angry with him for leaving her, but now she was angry with herself for allowing things to go on so long without speaking up.

But not this time.

This time Tillie and Blake were in mutual agreement on the course of their fling. One month. No one was going to get hurt. No one was going to shift the goalposts. They were both gaining from the arrangement, and contrary to Blake's concerns, there wouldn't be a winner or a loser when it came time to end it.

But when Blake reached across to refill Tillie's wineglass, something about the way his grey-blue eyes caught hers made her heart trip like a foot missing a step. She glanced at his hands—those clever, capable hands that had explored every inch of her body—and her belly fluttered like a breeze moving over the pages of an open book. She pressed her knees together under the table, the tiny twinge of discomfort an erotic reminder of the workout her inner muscles had been given.

He must have read something on her expression

for he put the wine bottle down and frowned. 'What's wrong, sweetheart?'

'Nothing.'

His frown stayed put and he narrowed his gaze and reached for her hand, stroking it so gently it was as if he were petting a tiny, much-adored kitten. 'Sure?'

Nerves Tillie hadn't even known she possessed danced under his touch. 'Do you know something funny? Simon always called me "dear". Like we were an old married couple in our eighties or something. It used to really annoy me, but for some reason I never said anything. Kind of pathetic, really.'

Blake's thumb stroked each tendon on her hand in turn. 'Why did you feel you couldn't express yourself with him?'

Tillie gave a one-shoulder shrug. 'I guess because deep down I was worried about him leaving me so I put up and shut up. I'm not going to make that mistake in future relationships. I'm going to speak up if something's worrying me.'

'Does it bother you when I call you sweetheart or babe?'

'No,' Tillie said. 'I like it. And anyway, you have to sound convincing if others are around so it's probably a good idea to keep doing it.'

'My dad called my mother darling,' he said after a long moment. 'I don't think I ever heard him call her Gwen—not until after she died.'

'What did she call him?'

A smile flickered across his mouth. 'She called him darling, too. But occasionally she called him

Andrew if she was annoyed with him. Not that they argued much. I only saw them disagree about something a couple of times, or maybe that was because they mostly discussed stuff in private.'

'Were you an only child by choice?' Tillie asked.

'No.' He let out a sigh. 'Apparently my mother lost a baby—a little girl—seven months into the pregnancy when I was two. I don't remember anything about it, as I was too young.' A frown interrupted his features like a wind pattern on sand. 'My mother used to talk about her now and again. I realised later that would have been on my sister's birthday each year. She was called Lucy. After she lost her, Mum had to have a hysterectomy. I think it grieved her terribly. She was the sort of woman who would have loved a large family. But my dad used to always tell her he would rather have one child and her than to have more children and lose her. And then guess what happened.'

Tillie was glad he was talking more openly about his tragic background. It gave her the sense he was starting to trust her. That he was feeling close to her. Somehow that was important to her. They might be having a simple fling but it made her feel better to think he was not treating her as a come-and-go lover, but as someone he shared not just his body with but his thoughts and feelings and disappointments, too. In spite of his charming laugh-a-minute persona, she suspected he was quite a lonely man inside. Used to keeping his own counsel. Having to be strong for his father, to cope and shoulder far more responsibilities than he ought to have done. Had it isolated him? Made him lock down his emotions so no one got close enough to truly know and understand him?

'How did your dad deal with the loss of your sister?' she asked.

Blake examined the contents of his glass. 'A lot better than he handled Mum's death, that's for sure. He hasn't mentioned Lucy in years. But I guess it's different for expectant fathers. They aren't as closely bonded to the child as to the mother who's carrying it.'

'Maybe,' Tillie said and paused for a beat. 'You don't see yourself becoming a father one day? Even if you don't officially marry someone?'

He did a lip movement that was part-smile, part-grimace. 'It's not something I've thought about too much. I've had to concentrate on taking care of my father for so long I can't see myself signing up for more caretaking duties in a hurry.'

'You don't want an heir to inherit McClelland Park?'

'That's assuming I get it back. Nothing is certain yet.'

'But if you do,' Tillie said, 'wouldn't you want your own flesh and blood to carry on ownership rather than to have it sold to someone outside the McClelland family again?'

His expression lost some of its openness; it was as if shutters were being drawn down over a window. 'My goal is to get the Park back for my father. That's all I'm focussed on right now.'

Tillie could sense he wouldn't be pressed further on the subject. She wondered if his reasons for not settling down and having a family were because of his sad background or whether he truly didn't want to be tied down. A lot of modern men were fronting up later and later in life for fatherhood. But while men had the luxury to become fathers at just about any age, the issue was much more pressing for women. She didn't feel the pressure just yet, but she knew once she turned thirty it might be a different story. There had been a time when getting married and having a family were all she could think about. But now she wanted to concentrate on building up her business and getting her life back on track.

Blake pushed back from the table and began clearing the plates. 'Why don't you take Truffles out for a walk and I'll join you once I've cleared away here?'

Truffles sprang up from the floor and did a mad spin and gave a loud volley of barks as if to say, *Yes, please. Take me for a walk!*

The moon was a golden ball shining over the lake, a light breeze crinkling the surface of the water like wrinkles in a bolt of silk. An owl hooted and in the distance Tillie heard a vixen fox calling for a mate. Truffles had her nose to the ground and her tail in the air as she followed a scent in the garden and Tillie followed so as not to lose sight of her.

Within a few minutes, Tillie heard Blake's footsteps on the gravel pathway and then the softer tread of him moving across the damp velvet green lawn. She turned to look at him, her heart doing that funny tripping thing again. His shirtsleeves were rolled back to his elbows from clearing away the dinner things, and his hair looked as if he had sent his hands through it for it looked more roughly tousled than it had earlier. He came to stand beside her, his shirt-sleeve brushing her arm. It was barely touching her and yet it felt as if a strong fizzing current was being sent from his body to hers.

'So peaceful at this time of night,' he said, looking at the moonbeam shining over the lake.

'Yes… I'm going to find it hard to leave when the time comes,' Tillie said, and then wished she hadn't because of the passage of silence that ensued. Did he think she was fishing for an invitation to stay indefinitely? That she wanted their fling to go on and on?

But you do want it to go on.

She quickly barricaded the thought. She didn't want the same things as before. She was a changed woman. A single-and-loving-it woman. A woman who was embracing her passionate side without the restrictions of marriage and commitment. Their fling had just begun. They still had another few weeks to explore everything about each other. But once it was time to move on, she would move on as agreed.

Blake turned and looked down at her. 'What are your plans once you leave here?'

Tillie refused to acknowledge the twinge of disappointment his words evoked. She had no right to be disappointed he hadn't issued an invitation to stay on at the Park as long as she wanted.

'I haven't thought that far ahead,' she said. 'I only

moved in here because Mr Pendleton's housekeeper retired just as he had his stroke and I had to move out of Simon's parents' cottage at short notice. It was never a long-term thing.'

'What will he do with Truffles if he moves into a care facility?'

Tillie glanced at the dog, who was busily chasing a moth. 'I don't know… I haven't discussed it with him. He loves that dog but I can't see him being able to take care of her properly now he's so frail.'

The dog came over to Blake and he leaned down to ruffle her ears. 'It must be hard growing old and losing control of all the things that are important to you,' he said.

'Terribly hard. I think that's why Mr Pendleton is so grumpy just now. He's struggling to come to terms with the limitations of aging.' Tillie rubbed at her upper arms to ward off a shiver from the cool breeze that had whipped up.

'Cold?' Blake asked, moving closer to put his arms around her.

'Warmer now.' She smiled at him. 'Much warmer.'

His eyes glinted in the moonlight. 'Let's get you inside where I can guarantee it's going to be hot.'

And it was.

Blake woke early the next morning and took Truffles for a long walk to allow Tillie time to get ready for work. He did a circuit of the lake and then went to the elm tree where he had carved his initials all those years ago. His fingers moved over the deeply grooved childish letters, remembering the heartache he'd felt as he'd carved them there. The heartache he still felt and would always feel until he could return this property to his father where it belonged.

The slight complication of where Tillie would live after he got the property back had kept him awake last night. He didn't want to turf her out on the streets or anything, but nor did he want to give her the impression this thing they had going could be anything more than it was. She kept insisting she was happy with a short-term fling. But where would she go after here? Her cake-decorating business was in the village, but there weren't many good quality rental opportunities available. He had already checked when he'd first come down to suss out the territory earlier that month. There was the bed and breakfast, but she wouldn't want to stay there unless she had the place to herself…

Blake let his mind run with the possibilities. When he'd checked out the other day, Maude Rosethorne had mentioned something in passing about retiring. The B&B would be a perfect set-up for Tillie to live and work from. The top floor could be her living space and the downstairs could be divided into kitchen and shop front with two rooms spare for a tearoom complete with cosy fireplaces. It was a perfect solution. What if he bought the B&B and gifted it to Tillie as a goodwill gesture? An end-of-the-affair thank-you gift?

Don't you mean a conscience-easing gift?

He wasn't listening to his conscience this time. This was about common sense. Sound business sense.

Tillie would be able to expand her business and stay in the village where she was known and loved by everyone. She wouldn't have to worry about rent hikes and baking off site due to space issues.

Why hadn't he thought of it earlier? He would have to be careful how he broached the subject, however. She had a streak of stubborn pride he privately admired.

No, he would wait for a suitable opportunity to raise the topic with her and take things from there.

It being summer, Tillie had a rush of wedding cakes to see to at work. It meant her time with Blake over the next week or so was a little compromised, as she had to work at night on some of the more intricate decorations in between visiting Mr Pendleton as often as she could. It was frustrating because she knew her work time could be better managed if she had more revenue coming in, but her plan to relocate and expand her business to include a tearoom component had been shelved after she'd got into debt after her wedding was cancelled.

But rather than be put out by it, Blake simply took over things at the house. He had set up an office for himself where he conducted his business work, but he also spent time fixing things that were in need of a bit of maintenance in the house or on the property. When she came home each night after working, she found dinner cooked and ready to serve, and an exhausted Truffles, who had been exercised and fed and was usually lying on her back on her bed, with her head lolling to one side and with all four paws in the air in a state of complete and utter relaxation.

After her fourth and final day of working late, Tillie took the glass of wine Blake greeted her with and sank to the nearest chair and took three generous sips. 'You know, you'd make some lucky girl a wonderful husband one day. I mean, obviously not me since I'm not in the market for a husband, but someone. You cook, you clean, you're good with dogs and fixing broken stuff.'

Oops. Maybe I shouldn't drink on an empty stomach.

Blake's crooked smile didn't reach his eyes. 'Not going to happen.'

Tillie took a much more cautious sip of wine for something to do with her hands. 'I got rid of my wedding cake today.'

'You did?'

'Yeah. I'm quite proud of myself, actually.' She rose from her chair to fetch a glass of water. 'Next is my wedding dress. One of the brides who came in to order a cake today was interested. I might even make some money out of it. Who would've thought?'

When Tillie turned around from getting the water from the kitchen tap, he was leaning against the bench on the other side of the kitchen near the cooker, watching her steadily. She gave him an over-bright smile. 'Is something wrong?'

'What are your plans for your business?'

'Plans?'

'Do you have any expansion plans to increase your profit margin?'

Tillie put her water glass back down in the sink. 'You know, you really scare me sometimes with your mind-reading ability.'

'What would you like to do with the shop?'

Should she tell him of her hopes and dreams for her business? Why not? He was a smart businessman. Maybe he had some hints for her to make the most of her current position, limited as it was. 'I'd like it to be bigger for one thing. And I'd like to have a tearoom attached so that when people come in to order cakes they can also sit down and have lunch or high tea.'

'What's stopping you from acting on those plans?'

Tillie sighed. 'The M word.'

'Money?'

'Yup.'

'I could help you with that,' Blake said.

Tillie blinked. 'Pardon?'

He pushed himself away from the bench and came over to where she was standing. 'Maude Rosethorne wants to sell her B&B. I talked to her about it the other day. It would make a great venue for your shop.'

'I can't afford a place that size!' Tillie said. 'I'd never be able to manage the mortgage. I'm barely breaking even as it is.'

'I'm not talking about you taking out a mortgage.'

She licked her suddenly flour-dry lips. 'What are you talking about, then?'

His expression was as unreadable as the wall behind him. 'I would buy it for you.'

Tillie's mouth dropped open so far she thought she would crack a floorboard with her chin. 'You'd do…*what*?'

Still nothing showed on his face. If anything it became even more inscrutable as if every muscle had been snap frozen. 'It'd be a gift for—'

'For?' She leaned on the word, driving it home with a look.

'Tillie, think about it,' he said, some of the tightness of his face relaxing. Some. Not all. 'You're doing me a huge favour by helping me get back my family's home and I want to repay you.'

'No.' She moved to the other side of the room and folded her arms to glare at him. 'Seriously? What are people going to think?'

'They can think what they like,' he said. 'You don't have to tell them I bought it for you.'

Tillie gave a scornful laugh. 'I won't need to because Maude and her cronies will tell everyone for me. It'll be broadcast from every outpost. Everyone in the village will be talking about how you paid me off at the end of our affair like a mistress you want to keep sweet. No, thanks. I'll expand my business if and when I can do it under my own financial steam.' Even if the only financial steam she had going on right now was little more than a hiss.

Blake crossed the room to take her by the upper arms, his hands gently massaging the tension gathered there. 'Hey.'

Tillie pressed her lips together, shooting him a look from below her half-lowered lashes. 'And don't even think about buying me jewellery or a holiday house in the Bahamas, okay? That's even more tacky.'

His eyes were impossibly dark as they held hers, his body so close she could feel the electric pulse of it calling out to hers like a sonar signal. 'Is there anything you do want?'

I want you. She unwound her arms from across her middle and slid them up around his neck. 'Let's test that mind-reading ability of yours, shall we?'

A slow smile tipped up the sides of his mouth. 'You know that saying about getting out of the kitchen if you can't stand the heat?'

Tillie felt something unspool in her belly. 'I know it.'

He scooped her up and placed her on the bench, parting her thighs so he could stand between them. 'I'm about to turn the heat up. Think you can take it?'

'Try me.'

He brought his mouth down on hers in a blisteringly hot kiss that sent liquid heat to the core of her body. His hands tugged at her top, hauling it over her head before unclipping her bra and sending that to the floor as well. The rough urgency of his action thrilled her far more than the slow and tender sensuality of his previous lovemaking. His hands palpated her breasts and then he put his mouth to them in turn. His lips and tongue working their magic on her senses until she was whimpering and tearing at his clothes. Need surged in her body, raw, rampant need that wanted— begged for—immediate gratification.

His mouth closed over her nipple and areola; drawing on her in a sucking motion that was part pleasure, part pain. He went to her other breast, subjecting it to the same delicious attention before he came back up to her mouth. His tongue met hers in a stabbing thrust, duelling with it, mating with it in a dance that had echoes of lust in every pulse-racing second.

Tillie got working on the fastener on his waistband, releasing the zip so she could take him in her hands. He lifted up her skirt and pushed her knickers aside to touch her intimately. She was so worked up she almost came on the spot, her body wet and hungry, empty and aching for the pressure and friction of his.

He pulled her down off the bench and turned her so she had her back to him. She braced herself by gripping the edge of the bench while he sourced a condom, every cell of her body throbbing with excitement in the countdown to intimate contact.

He drove in from behind, the slick force of him snatching her breath and sending a hot shiver coursing down the back of her legs in quicksilver streaks. His movements increased in urgency but she was with him all the way, the almost shockingly primitive rhythm speaking to her flesh in a way she hadn't thought possible. The orgasm came with such force it made her bite back a scream as the sensations catapulted her into a spinning vortex. The spasms went on and on, deeper, richer, spreading to every corner and crevice of her body in ever increasing waves like a large stone dropped in a pond. Even her skin felt as if it had been electrified with a thousand tiny electrodes, raising it in a shower of goose bumps.

Blake gave a deep, shuddering groan and emptied, his hands gripping her hips until she was sure she would find a full set of his fingerprints on her flesh. He relaxed his hold once the storm had passed, his hands turning her so she was facing him. He was still breathing heavily, his eyes sexily bright with the gleam of satisfaction. 'You never cease to excite me.'

Tillie toyed with one of his dark curls of hair at the back of his neck. 'You do a pretty good job of exciting me, too.'

He brushed her mouth with his. 'Are you ready for dinner or do you have something you have to do first?'

'Only this,' she said and brought his mouth back down to hers.

Blake wasn't sure what woke him later that night. He glanced at Tillie lying beside him but she was fast asleep, one of her hands resting on his chest, her head buried against his neck. He'd been dreaming and then he'd woken with a jolt but he couldn't remember what the dream contained. All he had was a vague feeling of unease, as if a centuries-old ghost had stepped out of the ancient woodwork and placed a cold hand on the back of his neck.

The old house creaked around him, the noises both familiar and strange.

Or maybe it was his lingering sense of frustration

Tillie hadn't accepted his offer of the B&B premises that was disturbing his sleep. He'd already spoken to Maude Rosethorne about buying it—thankfully he hadn't said who or what for. He'd simply made her an offer and left her to think about it. But it wouldn't take much for Maude to join the dots once the time came for his fling with Tillie to end.

What was Tillie's problem? It was a generous gesture on his part and there were no strings attached. It was a gift that would keep on giving. Why wouldn't she accept it and leave it at that?

He glanced at her again, his hand moving to brush a wisp of hair away from her mouth. She gave a soft murmur and brushed at her face with her hand as if shooing away whatever had tickled her face.

He'd spent the whole night with lovers before. Lots of times. He wasn't that cold and clinical about the boundaries of a fling that he couldn't bring himself to share a bed with a sexual partner. But no one he'd shared a bed with had made him want to hold them close all night and every night. Usually, the longer the affair continued, so the distance between them in the bed increased. It was the subtle way he sent the signal that their time was coming to a close.

But somehow with Tillie he was moving closer, not further apart. He would wake to find himself spooning with her, or with her legs entwined with his and her head resting on his chest, his arms wrapped around her. Whenever she moved away he felt a strange sense of disquiet…as if something was missing.

Tillie suddenly opened her eyes and shifted against him like a warm kitten wanting to be stroked. 'What time is it?' Her voice had a sleepy huskiness to it that sent his blood south of the border.

'Too early to get up.'

Her hand slipped down from his chest to his groin. 'Looks like you're already up,' she said with a little smile that curled the edges of her mouth.

'I've used my last condom,' he said. 'I meant to pick some up on my way home but forgot.' How had he got through so many in the last week? Normally he had plenty to spare at this stage of a fling.

'We could do it without,' she said. 'I'm on the pill and we're exclusive…aren't we? And we're both free of any nasty diseases.'

Blake had seen her packet of contraceptive pills in the bathroom cupboard. He'd felt a bit of a jerk checking each day to see if she'd taken it, but still. He had to be sure she was being honest with him over what she wanted. But a part of him was worried she was in denial. She'd been hurt by the jilting. Deeply hurt. Who wouldn't be? It was the ultimate in rejection to be dumped on the day of the wedding you had planned and looked forward to for months.

But what if she was only saying what she thought he wanted to hear? What if behind her I'm-cool-with-the-terms-of-our-fling attitude was a secret yearning for it to morph into something else?

Something more lasting…

A frown suddenly interrupted her features. 'Why are you looking at me like that?'

Blake toned down the frown he hadn't realised had formed on his forehead. 'How am I looking at you?'

'Like you're cross with me or something.'

He stretched his mouth into a smile and tucked a strand of hair behind her ear. 'I'm not cross with you. Far from it.'

She chewed her lower lip as if she was mulling over something. 'Have you ever done it without a condom?'

'No.'

'Not ever?'

'No,' he said. 'Too much of a control freak.'

She began to trace a pathway over his clavicle with her fingertip, her eyes watching the passage of her finger instead of meeting his. 'If you don't want to, then that's fine. We can wait until tomorrow.'

Blake did want to. He wanted to so badly it wouldn't have mattered if some of those little pills hadn't been taken. If *none* of those pills had been taken. Right now he needed her as he had needed no one before. It was a fire in his blood. A red-hot fever that could not be quelled. He rolled her so she was beneath him and she gave a little gasp of surprise when his erection bumped against her mound. 'Sorry. Am I rushing you?' he said, checking himself.

Her hands grabbed him by the buttocks, drawing him close to her damp heat. 'I want you.'

'I want you too, so much,' he said, sinking in between her silken wet folds with a groan.

I can't seem to stop wanting you.

Her legs wrapped around his and he rocked with

her in a frenzied quest for satiation. His skin was alive with nerve endings, his blood racing, pounding with the thrill of being as close as it was possible to be to another person. Not just skin on skin. Intimate skin on skin. His mouth fed off hers, his tongue tangling erotically with hers, escalating the pulse of lust driving through him. He reached between their striving bodies, his fingers finding her swollen flesh, and within seconds she erupted into a rippling orgasm that catapulted him into the abyss…

Blake lost track of time. It could have been seconds, minutes or even half an hour before either of them spoke. He stroked the back of her head where her hair was matted from rubbing against the pillow. He was still a little stunned by the sensations that powered through him. Making love with her seemed to get better and better. More satisfying. More exciting.

More…everything.

Her fingers did a soft tiptoeing thing against his sternum. 'Blake?'

'Mmm?'

'It was a nice thought about buying Maude's B&B,' she said. 'A really nice thought.'

'But you won't accept it from me.' He didn't frame it as a question but as a matter of fact.

She raised her gaze to his. 'I've already accepted way too much off you. The money you paid off my debts with. This ridiculously expensive ring I'm wearing.'

He stroked a fingertip over the small frown creasing her forehead. 'I don't want you to feel exploited when this is over.'

Her eyes slipped out of reach of his. 'What if Mr Pendleton takes longer than you expected to make up his mind about selling? What if *this*—' she emphasised the word slightly '—drags on for longer than you expected?'

Blake was well aware things weren't going strictly according to plan. The old man was proving tricky to win over. He'd been sure the announcement of his engagement to Tillie would be enough to seal the deal but, if anything, it had complicated things. Deeply complicated things. Close to two weeks had already gone by and the old codger hadn't budged. Another week or two might improve negotiations, but it would also further cement the bond that was developing between Blake and Tillie. A bond he normally didn't form with anyone during a fling. The sort of bond that would not be so easy to dismantle when it was time to move on. Not just a bond of friendship and mutual admiration, but an intimate connection he had never felt with anyone before now.

He felt her touch in places no one had ever reached. It was as if she reached right into his chest with her soft dainty hand, resting it against the membrane of his heart. He could feel it right now. A presence. A weight. A pressure. Every time he breathed it was like he was breathing with her.

'We'll see how the rest of the month pans out and

then we'll take stock,' he said. 'That is, unless you're getting bored already?'

She gave a soft laugh and snuggled closer. 'Not yet, but I'll let you know.'

CHAPTER NINE

TILLIE WAS SERVING one of her regular customers in the shop when Simon's mother, Marilyn, came in. She kept her professional and polite smile in place and made sure her engagement ring was clearly on show when she placed her hands on top of the counter.

'Hello, Marilyn, what can I do for you today?'

'I'm not here to buy anything,' Marilyn said. 'I just wanted to…to see how you are.'

'Well, as you can see, I'm just fine,' Tillie said. 'But it was nice of you to think of me and take time out of your busy day to drop by.'

When you haven't graced me with your obnoxious presence for nearly four months.

Marilyn gave a version of a smile—a movement of her lips that looked like a thin ribbon stretching. 'Have you been in contact with Simon? I mean, recently?'

'No. No contact. But it's better that way, especially now I'm engaged and—'

'It was wrong what he did to you, Tillie,' Marilyn said, her hands gripping her handbag against her stomach. 'Terribly, unforgivably wrong. I should have said something before now. But the thing is… I always felt he was wrong for you. That's why I didn't encourage the relationship. I must have hurt you by being so cold and distant, but I thought you would finally realise you could do much better than Simon.'

Much better than her precious perfect son?

Tillie wasn't sure she was hearing properly. Could this confession/apology be for real? 'Look, it's really nice of you to—'

'I'm glad you've found someone,' Marilyn said. 'From all I've heard so far, Blake McClelland seems perfect husband material and apparently madly in love with you. I'm pleased for you, dear. I was worried you'd end up alone and moping about Simon for the rest of your life.'

Not flipping likely.

Tillie hadn't thought about Simon in weeks. She could barely recall what he looked like. 'Blake is a wonderful man and I'm very lucky he came along when he did.'

And isn't that the truth?

Her life was completely different now Blake was a part of it. She smiled more, she laughed more. She felt more. Things she had never felt before. Not just sexual things but other things.

Things that could not be so easily described.

Marilyn's expression turned sour. 'When I think of how I could have had you as a daughter-in-law instead of…of that…that creature Simon met online.

And now he's gone and got her pregnant so there'll be no getting rid of her now. She'll want a ring on her finger and a big flashy wedding.'

Tillie expected to feel shocked, even a little sad at the news of Simon becoming a father, but instead she felt…nothing. It was as if Marilyn were talking about a stranger. Someone who had not been in her life at all. 'But it will be nice for you to have a grandchild, won't it?'

Marilyn's eyes looked suspiciously moist. 'Oh, Tillie, how can you be so…so nice about this? I know your dad and stepmother brought you up to be polite and gracious but surely it's not healthy to be so calm and accepting about this? If you weren't so happy with Blake I would beg you to come back and talk some sense into Simon. But I guess that's not possible, is it?'

Tillie's conscience gave her a tiny prod. She was far too happy with Blake. Dangerously happy. What-am-I-going-to-do-now? happy. 'No. It's not.'

Soon after Marilyn left, Tillie saw an email had finally come in from her father and stepmother. She opened the message to find their monthly newsletter they sent to all their friends with a short missive addressed to her at the bottom, briefly congratulating her on her engagement and expressing their pleasure in her ability to forgive and move on from Simon.

She stared at the message for a long moment. So the main issue for them was still her forgiving Simon. Didn't they want to know more about Blake? How happy he made her? How much he made her feel alive? Didn't they want to rush home to meet him? Wasn't her happiness more important to them than anything else? She knew the problems her father and stepmother dealt with in Uganda were not trivial. They were life and death issues and she had no business feeling piqued they hadn't shown more interest in what was happening in her life. But just like the time they had moved parishes, she was left standing on the station platform, feeling terribly alone.

Later that day, Tillie went with Truffles to see Mr Pendleton after work. Blake had texted her to tell her he had some business to see to and would see her at home later, promising to take her out to dinner to save her from cooking.

Mr Pendleton was sitting in a recliner chair in his room and looking listlessly out of the window, but immediately brightened when she came in with Truffles. 'Ah, my two favourite girls.' He fondled the dog's ears and then looked at Tillie. 'Well, well, well, you've certainly got a glow about you these days.'

The only glow Tillie was aware of was the one currently blazing from her cheeks. Could Mr Pendleton somehow see that only that morning she'd had smoking-hot sex with Blake in the shower and all these hours later her body was still tingling? 'Have I?'

'So the engagement is still going strong, then, is it?'

'Yes. We're very happy. He's fun to be around and he's wonderful with Truffles. He takes her for long walks and he clears away after dinner. And he's sorted out a few maintenance issues at the Park for you. What's not to love?'

His expression was suddenly like an inquisitive bird. 'So you actually...*love* him?'

'Of course I love him,' Tillie said.

Gosh, how easy is this lying caper getting? That didn't even feel like a lie.

It had felt so easy to say much the same to Simon's mother earlier that day. She hadn't felt as if she was lying at all. The words had tripped off her tongue with an authenticity she couldn't explain. Didn't want to explain.

'Maybe I was wrong about that man,' he said. 'It's not that I don't like him. I do. He's got backbone, drive, ambition.'

I like him, too. Maybe a little too much.

Tillie sat down on the visitor's chair next to his chair. 'Have you decided what you're going to do about McClelland Park?'

Mr Pendleton's eyes met hers in a searching manner. 'Is that what you want, Tillie? To live there with him and raise the family you've always wanted?'

Tillie's throat was suddenly blocked as if she had tried to swallow one of the pillows.

Oh, God. Oh, God. Oh, God.

Why hadn't she realised this until now? Or had she done her usual thing of ignoring the blatantly obvious? Living in a state of denial until it was too late. No wonder she hadn't been upset to hear about her ex becoming a father, because the only person she wanted to father her children was Blake. The man she had fallen hopelessly in love with in spite of every promise and assurance not to. How could she not fall in love with him? He was everything she longed for in a partner.

He wasn't just Mr Right.

He was Mr Perfect.

He was *her* person. The go-to person she could talk to about stuff she hadn't talked about with anyone else. The person who listened and felt things on her behalf and made her feel things she had never felt before.

'Yes,' she said. 'I want that more than anything.'

It wasn't a lie. It was true. In every way it could be it was true. She wanted to be with Blake. Not just in a short-term fling.

She wanted to stay with him for ever.

Who was she kidding? She wasn't a single-and-loving-it girl. She was a marriage-or-nothing girl. It wasn't something she could change on a whim like changing a pair of shoes.

It wasn't changeable.

It was indelibly printed on her soul—she was a girl who wanted the fairy tale because she knew she couldn't be happy with anyone other than Blake. She didn't have to have heaps of flings with a bunch of men to know he was the right man for her.

The *only* man for her.

As soon as he'd kissed her something had happened that had ruined her for anyone else. He had turned on her passion—passion that could only ever be triggered by him.

Mr Pendleton released a sigh. 'I might be an old man now but I still remember what it was like to be in love. I miss my Velma every day.'

'I know, it must be so lonely for you.'

He tapped his gnarled fingers on the arms of his chair, his caterpillar-like brows almost touching over his eyes. 'I'm going to have to do something about that dog. I can't take her where I'm going.'

Tillie swallowed again. 'Where do you plan to go?'

'Plan?' He made a scoffing noise. 'That's the damn trouble with getting old. You lose the ability to plan anything. Things happen and you have no control over them.'

'It must be very hard…'

He turned his head to look out of the window again, blinking a couple of times in rapid succession, and his dentures making a clicking noise as if he was swallowing against a tide of emotion. Truffles stopped chewing the rubber doorstop behind the door and came over and sat with her head on his knee and gave him a melting look. His hand absently stroked her head and he slowly turned to look at Tillie. 'I'm going to move into a care facility. I don't want to but I can't manage on my own. The Park's way too big for an old man like me. The place is meant to be for a family, not some old geezer with one and a half feet in the grave.'

Tillie grasped one of his hands, so close to tears she could feel them stinging her eyes. 'I'll still come and visit you every day. And I'll take care of Truffles and bring her in with me—that is, if they allow dogs to visit.'

His expression had a touch of wryness about it. 'Won't you be too busy making babies to be worrying about me?'

No, I won't. I'll be sitting on my own watching PG movies with a dog chewing anything that isn't nailed down.

Blake swung by the respite facility on his way home to see Mr Pendleton before he took Tillie out to dinner. The old man had left a message on his phone saying he wanted to speak to him. He tried not to get too excited. Mr Pendleton could be manipulating him for all he knew. The month was almost up. He would have to make a decision soon for he couldn't stay in respite indefinitely. He would have to be moved to somewhere where his needs could be taken care of going forward. Blake wasn't going to get his hopes too high until he had seen the old man's signature on the documents.

He had a special evening planned for Tillie. Dinner in a small but excellent restaurant he'd got to hear of via a business client. After dinner there was a wine bar with live music for dancing, and after that home to bed.

Home.

It was funny how he was starting to think of McClelland Park and Tillie as if they were inextricably linked. But in a way they were. She was the reason he was this close to getting his ancestral home back. If he pulled this off, he would always be grateful for her role in that.

But it was more than that. Tillie made the big old house feel like a home. All the little touches she gave that reminded him of his mother. The vases of fragrant flowers, the home-baked goodies stacked in tins in the pantry, the freshly aired rooms and crisp clean linen on the bed. The house had a vibrant, almost palpable energy in it when she was there. On the days he'd got home first, the house had seemed cavernous, cold, creaky. But Tillie's bright presence shone light into every dark corner of that house.

Mr Pendleton was sitting by the window in a recliner chair and for a moment Blake stood watching from the doorway. The old man looked sad and weary, his thin frame seeming shrunken, as if the bones of his skeleton were too tired to hold him upright.

'Jim?'

The old man turned his head to look at him. 'McClelland.'

Blake brought another chair closer, his nostrils picking up a faint trace of Tillie's perfume in the air. 'Has Tillie just been in?'

'Half an hour ago,' Mr Pendleton said. 'She brought the dog. She's going to keep her for me. I can't take her into the care facility with me.'

'That's a shame,' Blake said. 'But Tillie will do an awesome job of looking after Truffles.'

Mr Pendleton's birdlike gaze pecked at his. 'She tells me she's in love with you. I didn't believe it the first time she told me. But I do now.'

Blake ignored the faint prickle on his scalp. Tillie was a fine actor. She knew how much he wanted to buy the Park back. She was pulling all the stops out to help him. Of course she was acting like a woman in love because that was their agreement. He was doing a damn fine impression of a man in love, too. Damn fine.

'I'm a lucky man,' he said, throwing in a smile for good measure.

Mr Pendleton's expression looked like a scrunched-up paper bag. 'You don't fool me for a second, Mc-Clelland. You're not in love with her.'

Maybe his acting could do with a little work after all.

'What makes you think that?'

'How far will you go to get back McClelland Park?'

Blake resisted the urge to shift his weight under the piercing scrutiny of the old man's gaze. He'd tussled and won with much tougher old men than Jim Pendleton. Much tougher. 'I'm prepared to pay you more than the market price. Double, even.'

Mr Pendleton gave a breath of a laugh. 'Money. You think I want money at this time of life? What I need is…never mind what I need.' His brows drew together again. 'I'll sell you the place. I was always going to, you know.'

You were?

Blake was proud of his poker face. So why the run around? What had the old man hoped to achieve? A last ditch at power games? He didn't know whether to be relieved his goal was finally nailed or angry he'd been made to jump through hoops like a circus dog.

'I loved living there all these years but it's never been the same without Velma and my daughter, Alice,' Mr Pendleton said. 'That's what makes a place a home—the people who live in it with you. But you don't need me to tell you that. I'm sure you remember all too well how empty a place can be once you lose someone you love.'

That was why Blake didn't love anyone *that* much. Not enough to be devastated when they were no longer there. Not enough to wrench his heart out of his chest and leave a giant bleeding, gaping hole.

'When do you want me to draw up the paperwork?' he said.

'As soon as you like,' Mr Pendleton said.

Blake wondered why he wasn't feeling the sense of satisfaction he'd thought he'd be feeling right now. He'd done it. He'd got the old man to agree to sell him back his home. 'Would you like me to take you to the Park so Tillie and I can help you sort through your things?'

Mr Pendleton shook his head. 'I couldn't bear it. I hate goodbyes.'

Yes, well, I'm not so fond of them, either.

Tillie was in the sitting room pacing the floor when Blake came in and dropped a kiss on her mouth before she could even say hello. 'Hey, guess what?' he said. 'Jim's agreed to sell me the Park.'

She knew she should be feeling happy for him but instead she felt sad. This was it. The end of the affair. 'You must be thrilled.'

He frowned at her listless tone. 'What's wrong? We did it. You did it, actually.' He gave a light chuckle. 'You totally convinced the old man you were in love with me.'

There was a beat of silence.

'That's because I am in love with you.'

His expression flinched as if she'd slapped him. He stepped further away as if distancing himself from such raw emotion. 'You don't mean that.' His voice had a rough edge to it. Harsh almost.

Tillie had been expecting exactly this reaction but, even so, a frail hope had still managed to rise in her chest that he might feel the same way about her. 'I do mean it, Blake. I know it's not what you want to hear but I can't help it. I had to tell you.'

'Don't do this, Tillie.'

'What am I doing?' she said. 'You said I could call it off when it was time. Well, it's time. You've got what you wanted. You've got back McClelland Park.'

His jaw worked for a moment as if he were trying to avoid swallowing a marble. 'Yes, but that doesn't mean we have to end things right here and now.'

'Then when will we end it? A week from now? A month? Two months?'

'As long as we're happy with how things are going—'

'But I'm not happy,' Tillie said. 'I'm playing a role I wasn't cut out for. I might be good at it but it's not true to who I am. I want more than great sex. I want marriage and commitment and kids and—'

'Hold on a minute.' He held up a hand. 'You told

me you weren't interested in any of that stuff any more. You said you were against marriage. You said no man would ever get you to wear a white dress and show up at church. Those were your exact words or close to them.'

Tillie let out a shaky breath. 'I know I said that. And I meant it at the time but—'

'Yeah, well, I meant what I said back then and I still mean it,' he said. 'I'm not interested in marrying you or anyone. I was completely honest with you on that and now you tell me you want me to change? Well, guess what, sweetheart. Not going to happen.' He strode to the other side of the room, standing in front of the fireplace with his hands gripping the mantelpiece so tightly as if he was going to tear it from its moorings.

Tillie had thought reading that text from Simon was bad but this was something else again. Her heart felt as if it were being crushed until she could barely draw in a breath. Her throat was knotted with emotion. 'Did these last weeks mean anything to you? Anything at all?'

He swung back around to glare at her. 'What's happened from this morning in the shower to now? I seem to remember you were pretty happy about the terms of our fling then.'

Tillie momentarily closed her eyes so she didn't have to see the acrid bitterness of his gaze. But when she opened them he had turned his back on her and was leaning against the mantelpiece again.

'Three things,' she said. 'I got a visit from Simon's mother this morning.' She saw the muscles of his back and shoulders stiffen. 'He and his partner are having a baby.'

Blake turned back to face her, his expression guarded. 'Were you upset?'

'No, not as much as I thought I would be, or should be,' Tillie said. 'But it made me realise I do want a family. Not just a kid with some random guy but with—'

'No. No. No.' His words were like a nail gun firing into a slab of timber.

'Blake, at least hear me out,' she said. 'I haven't told you about the second and third things.'

'Go on.' His lips barely moved as he spoke and he had his granite face back on.

She took another breath. 'My parents finally emailed me. They congratulated me on my engagement but I couldn't help feeling it was my being able to forgive Simon that was their main concern. Not whether I was happy and fulfilled but as long as I had done the right thing by Simon.'

'You can't change people so don't bother—'

'I'm not interested in changing my parents,' Tillie said. 'Anyway, I'm the one who's changed. I know what I want now and I'm not afraid of asking for it. You're the one who taught me that, Blake.'

His expression was still so stony it could have doubled for a retaining wall. 'You mentioned a third thing.'

'The third thing is I went to see Mr Pendleton after work. He asked me what I wanted. Whether I wanted to live here with you and make babies and I realised that's exactly what I want. I want that more than anything.'

He closed his eyes, as if hoping she wouldn't be standing there saying such things when he opened them again. 'I'm sorry, Tillie. But I can't give you the fairy tale. I told you that right from the start. I'm not—'

'I know, I know, I know,' she said. 'You're not the settling-down type. Well, here's the thing. I am. Which means we are at an impasse.'

He rubbed at his face as if he could erase the last few minutes. 'So you're ending our fling.'

'That was the plan, wasn't it? That I would be the one to call time?'

He gave a laugh that was a long way from amusement. 'Your timing sure could do with some work.'

So could your attitude.

'What? You wanted me to go out and celebrate with you on successfully achieving your goal?' Tillie asked. 'I can't do that, Blake. I won't do it. I've felt compromised the whole time we've run with this charade. I never wanted it in the first place. You forced it on me with your…your damned generosity, which isn't really generosity because you're so rich you probably don't even notice the dip in your bank account.'

'I'm not going to stand here and apologise for being successful.'

'You might be successful in terms of money and business but you're not successful where it counts,' she said. 'You've got this house back. Well done. But

what about when you're Mr Pendlet[...]
then? Who is going to be there for y[...]
have to pay someone or blackmail so[...]

A muscle beat a pulse in his face[...]
punching its way through his cheek.[...]
so smoky and grey they looked like brooding storm
clouds. 'I think you've made your position clear. Do
you want me to help you pack or have you already
done so?'

How could he be so cruel? So cold and unfeeling?
As if she were a guest who had outstayed her welcome. But maybe that was exactly what she was. A
visitor in his life. A passing fancy he had indulged in
to achieve a goal but now he was done with her. He
didn't need her. He didn't want her.

He didn't love her.

'I'll go and do it now,' Tillie said without showing
any of the emotion that was climbing up her throat.
Pride had got her into this mess and pride would get
her out of it. 'But you'll have to mind Truffles because I can't take her to a hotel. Once I sort out some
accommodation I'll make arrangements to come and
get her.'

'Fine.'

Blake took the dog for a walk so he didn't have to see
Tillie leaving. Why did she have to choose today to
end their fling? He was supposed to be celebrating
the successful buy-back of his home and now she'd
ruined it by insisting they end their affair. That it was
almost time on the month they'd agreed on wasn't the

...ue. It was the fact she'd dropped that I-love-you-and-want-to-have-babies-with-you bomb. He couldn't have made it clearer to her he wasn't the poster boy for marriage. He had made no promises, given her no false leads, told no lies. He'd been brutally honest and now she was telling him she wanted him to be the prince in her fairy tale.

But the main thing was he had McClelland Park back. That was what he should be focussing on, not the fact Tillie had called time.

Truffles pricked up her ears at the sound of Tillie's car moving down the ribbon of the driveway and she whined and cocked her head from side to side as if in confusion. Blake reached down and held her collar just in case she took chase. 'She'll be back for you, Truffles.'

The dog strained against his hold and whined again, every muscle in her body poised to spring off in pursuit.

'Yeah, I know the feeling,' Blake said. 'But believe me, you'll get over it.'

CHAPTER TEN

TILLIE HAD THOUGHT facing everybody after she'd been jilted had been tough, but when news got out her engagement to Blake was over she was besieged by disappointment from everyone in the village. It was brilliant for business as people came into the shop on the pretext of buying cakes, and, once they had their goodies bought and packaged, they would offer a word or two—or a few lengthy paragraphs—on why they were so devastated on her behalf as they thought Blake was perfect for her. Her profits shot up and she had to do extra time in the kitchen to keep up. She had even managed to attract a growing celebrate-a-break-up clientele. Tragic that somehow she was the poster girl for broken relationships, but she embraced it and added a new page to her website.

Tillie had managed to secure a pet-friendly rental property in the village and Blake had dropped the dog off while Tillie was at work. The fact he hadn't waited till she got home was both a relief and a bitter disappointment. So he didn't want to see her? Fine. She didn't want to see him, either.

The house she was renting was more of a housesitting arrangement but that suited her, as she wanted some time to think about what she would do next. She didn't want to pack up and leave the village, but if this intense focus on her love life, or lack thereof, continued she would go send-for-a-straitjacket mad.

Mr Pendleton had moved into the care facility, and, while it was a nice place with lovely staff—most of whom he knew in one way or the other—Tillie was conscious it was not home for him. How could it be? He couldn't have Truffles there and he seemed a little more dejected each day she visited.

McClelland Park had been signed over to Blake but that was all she'd heard or seen of him since he'd texted to say he'd dropped off Truffles.

Joanne was the only one who didn't commiserate with her. 'I think you should have stuck with him until he realised he was in love with you,' she said.

'But he's not in love with me,' Tillie said, putting the last touches on a divorce party cake.

Never was.

Never will be.

'Then why has he not been seen out with anyone else since your break-up?' Joanne pointed at the effigy of the ex on the top of the cake they were decorating. 'This guy's been seen out with four women since he separated from Gina. Bastard.'

Tillie drove a metal skewer through the groin of the marzipan figure. 'There. That should slow him down at bit.'

'Why haven't you made a break-up cake for yourself?' Joanne asked after a moment. 'We could have a party. I'll help you with the catering. You don't have to pay me. I'll do it for free.'

Tillie stood back from her handiwork. 'I don't need to get Blake McClelland out of my system. I'm over him.'

Not quite true. She spent most nights tossing in bed feeling empty and hollow. Her body missed him in every cell and pore. She sometimes felt she could still feel him moving inside her but then she would wake from that dream and realise with a sinking feeling he wasn't in the bed beside her. His arms weren't wrapped around her; his chin wasn't resting on the top of her head.

She was alone.

'Then why are you still wearing his ring?'

Tillie looked down at the diamond on her hand. For some reason, in spite of the weight she'd lost over the last two weeks, it was still firmly lodged on her finger. 'I haven't had time to have it cut off, that's why. But as soon as I get it off I'm going to give it back to him.'

Blake called on his father the day McClelland Park was officially signed over to him. He figured the last two weeks of misery he'd gone through would be worth it to see his dad's face when he presented the deeds to the house to him. Misery he hadn't expected to feel—misery that had eaten at his guts until he could barely take in food or water.

He didn't understand what was wrong with him.

He'd been the one to draw up the month-long plan with Tillie. Surely by now he should be feeling it was worth it.

'Dad, I want you to come with me for the weekend. I have a surprise for you.'

Andrew McClelland looked faintly sheepish. 'Now's not a good time for me. I have…something on this weekend.'

Blake frowned. 'Since when have you had something on a weekend? Every time I come here you're sitting staring blankly at the walls.'

His dad kept holding the front door of his town house in London only slightly ajar as if he was hiding something. 'Can we make it another time?'

Maybe his dad was doing his sad recluse thing, where he would lock the doors and close the blinds and not see or speak to anyone for days. Blake glanced at the window where his father's bedroom was situated. Yep, blinds down. 'Come on, Dad. I've been planning this for weeks. Surely nothing you're doing is that important. Some fresh air and sunshine will do you good.'

'I have someone with me just now.'

Someone? What someone? Blake frowned so hard he could have cracked a walnut between his brows. 'What's going on?'

His dad's cheeks had more colour in them than Blake had seen in years. 'I'm entertaining a guest.'

His dad was entertaining a guest? The man who had lived alone and refused to even go out shopping was *entertaining* someone? The man who consistently refused to come to any of the dinners and bridge parties and gatherings Blake organised for him in order to get him socialising a bit more actually had someone over? 'Who?'

'A lady I met at the heart rehab centre,' his father said. 'A widow. She lost her husband when she was in her thirties and hasn't been out with anyone since. We've struck up a friendship, well, more than a friendship. Can you come back some other time?'

Great. His dad was now officially having more sex than he was. Not that Blake wanted to have sex with anyone. Not since Tillie had ended their fling. Sex with someone else was the last thing on his mind. He got sick to the stomach thinking about getting it on with someone else. He couldn't imagine kissing or touching them the way he longed to be touching Tillie.

'I was going to tell you but you've been so preoccupied lately,' his dad said.

Preoccupied? I guess you could call it that.

'Dad, I bought back McClelland Park,' Blake said. 'I've been working on it for the last month. You have your home back. You can go back and live there any time you like. It's yours. I have the deeds here and—'

'Oh, Blake, I don't know what to say...' His dad's expression clouded. 'It's a wonderful gesture. Truly wonderful and typical of you to always think of me. But I can't go back.'

Can't go back?

What did he mean, he couldn't go back? Blake had turned inside out and back to front to get that damn property back. How could his dad not want to live there? 'But you love that place,' Blake said. 'It's your home. The place where you were the happiest and where—'

'It ceased to be home once your mum died,' his dad said. 'That part of my life is over. I'm finally moving on. If I were to go and live there now it would be like going backwards. I loved everything about that place, but without your mother it's nothing to me. It's just a big old empty house.'

'But it wouldn't be empty if you lived there with your new lady friend,' Blake said. 'You could set up a nice home together and—'

'I could, but that would be doing what you think is best for me instead of what *I* think is best for me,' his dad said. 'I know it's been tough on you these last twenty-four years. I've been a terrible burden on you and I want that to stop. Right here. Right now.'

Blake swallowed back his disappointment but it stuck in his throat like a tyre jack. His father didn't want McClelland Park? He had worked so hard to get that place back…for…for *nothing*? He had compromised himself. Stepped over personal boundaries, got caught up in a relationship with Tillie that he should be well and truly over by now.

'Blake, please,' his dad said. 'Will you just go? I'm okay. You don't have to babysit me any more. I'll call you in a day or two and Susie and I will have you over to dinner. You can bring someone if you like. Are you seeing anyone at the moment?'

So now his dad was organising Blake's social life for him? Weird. Just so damn weird. 'No one special.'

'Oh, well, just come on your own, then,' his dad said. 'We won't mind.'

No. But I will.

Tillie could see storm clouds brewing all Friday afternoon when she was working on the last touches of a cake for a client for a wedding on the Saturday. The power had threatened to go off a couple of times and she couldn't stop thinking about Truffles back at the cottage she was housesitting. Truffles hated storms. She hid under furniture or cowered in corners and whimpered as if the end of the world were at hand. It was distressing enough to watch, but not being there to make sure the poor dog was all right was a different type of torture altogether.

Tillie rushed back to the cottage early, leaving Joanne to close up the shop. The wind was howling and whipping the branches of the trees along the street as she approached. But when she arrived outside the cottage her heart came to a juddering halt. The gate leading to the front path was not just open but hanging off its hinges and a limb of one of the ornamental trees was lying across the pathway. Doing her best to shelter from the wind-driven pellets of rain and hail, Tillie dashed around to the back garden but there was no sign of the dog.

Panic beat a tattoo in her chest that was even louder than the hail falling on the cobblestone path. The one thing Mr Pendleton looked forward to each day was seeing Truffles. How could Tillie tell him she had lost her? What if Truffles was hit by a car and lying bleeding and broken in some rain-soaked and debris-ridden gutter? What if the dog was critically injured and had gone out of sight to die in one of the nearby hedgerows or fields or woods? It would break Mr Pendleton's heart if he lost Truffles. It would make him ever more despondent and depressed, and no amount of Tillie's marshmallow slice would cheer him up.

Tillie ran up and down the street calling for the dog but all she got for her effort was sodden with rain and splashed with mud. Her stomach was churning with dread—a cold fist that clutched at her insides until she had to stop and bend over with her hands resting on her knees to draw breath.

How could this be happening?

Where would Truffles have gone?

Think. Think. Think.

Could Truffles have headed to McClelland Park? It was her home after all, the place where she had spent the first two years of her life. The cottage here was not as familiar to her and perhaps she got spooked while out in the garden and took off.

Tillie didn't stop to consider the possibility of running into Blake. As far as she knew he hadn't been back to the Park since the sale was finalised. It wouldn't take her long to have a quick look around and see if Truffles had headed there. It was a few kilometres away, but she knew dogs could travel much further than that when distressed.

Please be there. Please be there. Please be there.
But Tillie wasn't sure if she was praying about the
dog or Blake or both.

Blake decided to go down to McClelland Park for the
weekend in any case. So what if his father was too
busy with his new love-nest buddy to celebrate the
return of their ancestral home with him? So what if
the weather turned foul as if to add a further insult?
It could rain and hail on his parade for all it liked. He
did not give a damn. He would drink the champagne
and eat the caviar by himself. He had a right to celebrate, didn't he? He had achieved what he'd set out
to achieve. So what if his father didn't want to live
there now? It didn't matter. The place was back in
McClelland hands and that was where it would stay.
    Living there himself hadn't really crossed Blake's
mind…well, maybe that wasn't strictly true. It had
crossed his mind. Heaps of times. He just hadn't allowed it any space to plant itself down and mess with
his head.
    The house seemed cavernously cold and empty
when he unlocked the front door. Like some abandoned Gothic mansion with clanging shutters and
creaking floorboards, especially with the storm raging like a howling beast.
    Blake closed the door against the wind and rain
and bullets of hail but there were no wonderful cooking smells wafting through the air to greet him, no
vases of fresh-smelling flowers on the hall table. The
furniture he had bought with the house was just fur-

niture. For all the comfort and welcome it gave, he could have been standing in an antiques warehouse. There were no excited barks from a mad dog with its paws scrabbling on the floorboards as it rushed at him in unmitigated joy at his arrival.

And worst of all…no Tillie.

Blake stood surrounded by the furniture and walls and roof of the house that was no longer a home. This was his prize. His Holy Grail. The mission he had spent years of his life dreaming of, planning, and working towards.

He had finally nailed it.

Why then did it feel so…pointless?

Blake walked into the sitting room, pulling back the curtains to look at the view over the lake and the old elm tree. The wind was thrashing the ancient limbs, shaking off leaves and twigs as if it cared nothing for the promise he had made all those years ago. But then he was almost blinded by an almighty flash of lightning, and then there was an ear-splitting crack of thunder followed by a splintering crash. He blinked to clear his gaze to see the ancient elm tree coming down like a felled giant.

Seeing that old tree lying there in such disarray forced him to take a good hard look at himself. The tree, once proud and strong and confident, was broken, battered, shattered. That tree had symbolised so much of his journey since childhood, but now it was worth little more than firewood and kindling.

How could Blake have got it so wrong? About this house? About his father?

About himself?

This property wasn't enough. This grand old house and all its memories were not enough. It wasn't making him feel satisfied. It wasn't making him feel anything but miserable. Lonely and miserable like an old house with furniture but no family.

His father was right, so too, wise old Mr Pendleton. What was a house without the one you loved sharing it with you?

Blake loved Tillie.

How could he have not realised that until now? Or maybe he had realised it. Maybe he had realised it from the moment he walked into that shop and encountered those sparkling nutmeg-brown eyes. But he had shied away from those feelings because it was too threatening to love someone who might not always be there.

But he'd lost her anyway.

Was it too late?

His heart felt as if it were crushed beneath the fallen ancient trunk of the elm tree. What if he'd blown his only chance with Tillie? He had let her walk away without telling her he loved her. He'd told her he didn't want a future with her, marriage and a family—all the things that had made this house the home it was meant to be.

But he did want those things.

He wanted them but only if he could have them with her.

Blake snatched up the keys, but on his way out to his car he saw a bedraggled Truffles bolting up the

driveway towards him. She shot through the front
door and disappeared into the house leaving a trail
of muddy footprints along the way.

He closed the front door and followed the dog to
her hiding place behind the sofa in the sitting room.
'What are you doing here, girl?' he said, crouch-
ing down to soothe her. She shivered and shook and
looked at him with the whites of her terrified eyes
showing.

He took a throw rug off the nearest sofa and gently
covered her with it to make her feel secure. He stood
to close the curtains to keep the storm from frighten-
ing her, but then, over the sound of the storm outside,
he heard the sound of a car coming up the driveway
and his heart leapt.

'Stay,' he said to the dog.

Tillie saw Blake's car parked in front of the house
and pulled up behind it, barely waiting long enough
to turn off the engine. The first thing she'd noticed
coming up the driveway was the elm tree was down.
Please God, don't let Truffles be under it.

Would the terrified dog have taken shelter under
its over-arching limbs? She sprang out of the car and
rushed through the pelting rain just as Blake opened
the front door.

'Is Truffles here?' she asked. 'The elm tree is
down. Please tell me she's here with you and not
under it crushed to death. I can't find her anywhere
and I can't bear telling Mr Pendleton she's—'

'She's here with me,' Blake said, taking her by the

hands and bringing her inside the house and closing the door.

'Is she all right? Is she hurt? Is she—?'

'She's safe.' He took her by the upper arms. 'She's cowering behind the sofa in the sitting room but she's fine. Are you okay?'

Am I okay? Of course I'm flipping not okay.

Tillie closed her eyes to get control of her emotions. She should be feeling relieved about finding the dog safe but seeing Blake again was messing with her head and with her heart.

How long had Truffles been here? Why hadn't he called or texted to tell her the dog was okay? Surely it wouldn't have hurt him to do that?

But no, he didn't want anything to do with her now.

'I was so worried,' she said. 'She hates storms. I should have realised and gone back earlier to check on her and lock her in the cottage or something but the wind ripped the gate off the hinges and she must have escaped and the least you could have done is sent me a text to tell me she was all right.'

Blake's hands slid down to hers, giving them a reassuring squeeze. 'I was about to call you. Actually, I was on my way to see you.'

Tillie could feel his thumb moving over the diamond on her left hand. 'Oh, right, about the ring? I'm sorry I haven't got it back to you yet. I've tried heaps of times but it still won't budge. I'm going to get it cut off. I would have done it before this but it's been flat out crazy at the shop and—'

'I don't want you to give it back,' Blake said. 'I want it to stay right where it is.'

Tillie's heart was beating its way out of her ribcage like a pigeon fighting its way out of a paper bag. 'You don't mean that. You told me you didn't—'

'Don't remind me what a fool I've been, my darling,' he said. 'I love you. I want to marry you. I want to live with you and make babies with you. Please will you say yes?'

Tillie gazed up at him in stupefaction. 'Is…is this a joke?'

He gave a self-effacing chuckle. 'I suppose I deserve that. Of course it's not a joke. It's the truth. I love you and can't bear the thought of spending another day, another minute, another second without you. Marry me, darling. Let's fill this sad old house with love and laughter again.'

'But what about your father?' Tillie asked. 'Isn't he going to live here?'

'That was another thing I got totally wrong,' Blake said. 'He has other plans. He's finally moving on with his life and I couldn't be happier for him. He's met someone. Someone who means more to him, much more than this house and all the memories it contains.' He brought his hands up to cup her face, holding her gaze with his. 'You are my special someone, darling. The perfect someone I want to spend the rest of my life with.'

Tillie moistened her lips; still not certain she was actually hearing what he'd been saying. Surely she was dreaming. Surely this couldn't be real. He loved her? He really loved her? 'You keep calling me darling.'

His grey-blue eyes twinkled. 'I do, don't I? That's because that's what I am going to call you from now on. You are the love of my life. I think I realised it the first time I met you when I made you blush. But I was afraid of loving you. Scared of being vulnerable because I'd seen what loving someone so much had done to my father when my mum was taken away.'

Tillie put her hands against his chest; she could feel his heart beating against her palm almost as fast as hers. 'I love you so much. I've missed you so much.'

'I've missed you, too,' he said. 'You have no idea how much. It's been like an ache deep inside. I haven't slept properly since you left. I keep reaching for you in the bed to find you gone.'

Tillie pressed closer to wind her arms around his neck. 'Do you really mean it? You really truly want to marry me?'

'Yes. As soon as it can be arranged,' he said. 'But if you can't bring yourself to get married in a church we could do it here. Down by the lake…although I think we might have to plant a new elm tree first.'

'That sounds like a great idea,' Tillie said, 'to symbolise a new beginning for McClelland Park.'

'So I take it that's a yes to my proposal?'

She gave him a teasing smile. 'Is this one for real or just pretend?'

He brought his mouth down to within reach of hers. 'This one's for real and it's for ever.'

EPILOGUE

One year later...

BLAKE CARRIED THE tea tray out to the garden of Mc-Clelland Park where Tillie was resting in the shade with Mr Pendleton. The new elm tree down by the lake wasn't quite big enough for shade yet, but every time he looked at it there in the distance, he thought of the future he was building with Tillie.

Blake's dad and Susie visited frequently and always enjoyed being there, but Jim Pendleton had been joining them just about every weekend ever since Blake and Tillie got back from their honeymoon. Jim loved seeing Truffles and he loved being around Tillie, but then, Blake had no argument with that. He loved being around her, too. More than words could ever say. More than he had thought it possible to love someone. His life was so full and enriched by her. There was nothing he didn't enjoy about being married to her.

But in a few months' time he would have someone else to love. Tillie was just over twelve weeks pregnant and he couldn't believe how excited he was about becoming a father. She was glowing with good health, hardly any morning sickness so far and the only cravings she'd had were for him.

Tillie's Tearoom in the village in Maude Rosethorne's newly renovated cottage was doing brilliantly. Joanne and another assistant were doing a magnificent job of running things so Tillie could start to pull back a bit to prepare for motherhood. He was so thrilled she'd made the tearoom such a success because he liked to think it made up for all the disappointments she'd had before. Sure, he had helped her achieve it, but in so many countless ways she had helped and healed him.

Truffles was chasing a butterfly but came bounding over with her ears flapping when she smelt the scones and jam and cream Blake had set down. Some things never changed, but, hey, that was part of the joy of living with a nutty dog. Of being a family.

Blake sat down next to Tillie and placed his arm around her waist, smiling down at her radiant face. 'Time to tell Jim our news, darling?' he said.

Tillie took Blake's hand and placed it on her abdomen. 'I have a feeling he's already guessed, right, Mr Pendleton?'

Jim Pendleton's face was wreathed in smiles. 'Congratulations. I couldn't be happier for you both and for McClelland Park.'

Blake looked at the new elm tree where it was anchoring its roots in the past and stretching its limbs into the future. He couldn't help feeling his mother would be happy the home she loved so much was going to be filled with joy and laughter once more.

He brought Tillie's hand up to his mouth and kissed the tips of her fingers, his heart swelling at the love reflected in her gaze. 'I think we should plant a new elm tree for each child we have. What do you think, darling?'

Tillie smiled. 'I think that sounds like a perfect plan.'

And it was.

* * * * *

LEGACY OF HIS REVENGE

CATHY WILLIAMS

CHAPTER ONE

'THERE'S A DAUGHTER.'

In receipt of this revelation, Matias Rivero looked at his friend and trusted associate, Art Delgado. Like Matias, Art was thirty-two. They had gone to school together and had formed an unlikely friendship with Matias the protector, the one who always had his friend's back. Small, asthmatic and bespectacled, Art had always been an easy target for bullies until Matias had joined his class and, like a dangerous, cruising shark, had ensured that no one came near the boy who had spent the past two years dreading the daily onslaught of beatings.

Now, all these years later, Matias was Art's boss and in return Art was his most loyal employee. There was no one Matias trusted more. He motioned for Art to sit and leaned forward to take the mobile phone handed to him.

He scrolled down the three pictures capturing a small, homely, plump little creature leaving Carney's mansion in an old car that looked as though its only wish was to breathe its last breath and depart for the great automobile parking lot in the sky.

Matias vaguely wondered why she wasn't in a car befitting a man who had always made social climbing his priority.

But more than that he wondered who the hell the woman was and why he hadn't heard of her before.

'How is it that I am only now finding out that the man has a child?' Matias murmured, returning the mobile phone to his friend and relaxing back in the chair. 'In fact, how do you know for sure that the woman is his daughter?'

At a little after seven, his office was empty. It was still summertime hot, it was Friday and everyone else had better things to do than work. There was nothing pressing to hold his attention. His last lover had been dispatched a few weeks ago. Right now, Matias had all the time in the world to think about this development in his campaign.

'She said so,' Art told him, pushing his wire-rimmed spectacles up his nose and looking at his friend with some concern. 'But I don't suppose,' he added uneasily, 'it makes any difference, Matias. Does it?'

Matias pushed his chair back and stood up. Seated, he was formidable. Standing, he towered. He was six feet three of solid, packed muscle. Black-haired and black-eyed, the product of an Argentinian father and a dainty Irish mother, Matias had resoundingly come up trumps in the genetic lottery. He was sinfully beautiful, the hard lines of his lean face wonderfully chiselled into absolute perfection. Right at this moment, he was frowning thoughtfully as he strolled towards the floor-to-ceiling bank of glass that overlooked the busy London streets in the heart of the city.

From this high up, the figures down below were matchstick small and the cars and taxis resembled kids' toys.

He ignored the latter part of his friend's remark and

instead asked, 'What do you mean "she said so"? Surely I would have known if the man had offspring. He was married and it was a childless union.' But in truth, Matias had been uninterested in the personal details of James Carney's life.

Why would he care one way or another if the man had kids or not?

For years, indeed for as long as he could remember, he had been focused on bringing the man to his knees through his company. The company that should never have been Carney's in the first place. The company that had been founded on lies, deceit and Carney's outright theft of Matias's father's invention.

Making money and having the power associated with it within his grasp was so entwined with his driving need to place himself in a position to reach out and wrench Carney's company from under his feet, that it would have been impossible to separate the two. Matias's march towards wealth had also been his march towards satisfying his thirst for revenge. He had gained his first-class degree, had bided his time in an investment bank for two years, making the money he needed to propel himself forward, and then he had quit with money under his belt and a black book stuffed with valuable connections. And he had begun his remorseless rise to the top via mergers and acquisitions of ailing companies, getting richer and richer and more and more powerful in the process.

Throughout it all, he had watched patiently for Carney's company to ail and so it had.

For the past few years, Matias had been circling the company, a predator waiting for exactly the right time. Should he begin the process of buying shares, then flooding the market with them so that he could plunge the company into a premature meltdown? Should he wait until the company's health deteriorated beyond repair so that he could instigate his hostile takeover? Choices, choices.

He had thought about revenge for so long that there was almost no hurry but the time had finally come. The letters he had recovered from his mother's possessions, before she had been admitted to hospital three weeks previously, had propelled him towards the inevitable.

'Well?' he prompted, returning to his chair although he was suddenly restless, itching now to start the process of retribution. 'You had a convivial conversation with the woman? Tell me how you came to your conclusion. I'm curious.'

Matias looked at Art, waiting for clarification.

'Pure coincidence,' Art admitted. 'I was about to turn into Carney's drive when she came speeding out, swerved round the corner, and banged into the car.'

'The woman crashed into my car? Which one?'

'The Maserati,' Art admitted. 'Nasty dent but her car, sadly, was more or less a write-off. No worries. It'll be sorted.'

'So she banged into my Maserati,' Matias hurried the story along, planning on returning to this little episode later down the line, 'told you who she was and then…what?'

'You sound suspicious, Matias, but that's exactly what happened. I asked her if that was the Carney residence and she said yes, that her dad lived there and she had just seen him. She was in a bit of a state because of the accident. She mentioned that he was in a foul mood and that it might be a good idea to rearrange whatever plans I had with him.'

'So there's a daughter,' Matias said thoughtfully. 'Interesting.'

'A nice girl, Matias, or so it would seem.'

'Impossible.' That single word was a flat denial. 'Carney is a nasty piece of work. It would be downright impossible for him to have sired anything remotely *nice*.' The harsh lines of his face softened. For all his friend's days of being bullied, Art had an instinctive trust in the goodness of human nature that he, Matias, lacked.

Matias had no idea why that was because they were both mixed race, in Art's case of Spanish descent on his mother's side. They had both started at the bottom of the pecking order and had had to toughen up to defend themselves against casual racism and snobbery.

But then, Matias mused not for the first time, he and he alone had witnessed first-hand the way criminal behaviour could affect the direction of someone's life. His father had met James Carney at university. Tomas Rivero had been an extraordinarily clever man with a gift for all things mathematical. He had also been so lacking in business acumen that when, at the age of twenty-four, he invented a computer program that facilitated the analysis of experimental drugs, he was a sitting duck for a man who had very quickly seen where the program could be taken and the money that could be made out of it.

James Carney had been a rich, young thing with a tribe of followers and an eye to the main chance. He had befriended Tomas, persuaded him into a position of absolute trust and, when the time was right, had accumulated all the right signatures in all the right places that ensured that the royalties and dividends from the software went to him.

In return, Tomas had been sidelined with a third-rate job in a managerial position in the already ailing family business Carney had inherited from his father. He had never recovered mentally.

This was a story that had unfolded over the years, although, in fairness to both his parents, nothing had ever been said with spite and certainly there had never been any talk of revenge on the part of either of them.

Matias's father had died over a decade previously and Rose Rivero, from the very start, had not countenanced thoughts of those wheels turning full circle.

What was done, was done, as far as she was concerned. The past was something to be relinquished.

Not so for Matias, who had seen his father in those quieter moments, seen the sadness that had become a humiliating burden. You didn't have to be a genius to work out that being shoved in some dingy back office while you saw money and glory heaped on undeserving shoulders had damaged his father irreparably.

As far as Matias was concerned, his father had never fully recovered from Carney's theft. He had worked at the company in the pitiful job condescendingly given to him for a couple of years and then moved on to another company, but by then his health was failing and Rose Rivero had had to go out to work to help make ends meet.

If his mother had cautioned against revenge, then he had had enough of a taste for it for the both of them.

But he knew that over the years the fires had burned a little less brightly because he had become so intensely consumed in his own meteoric rise to the top. It had been propelled by his desire for revenge but along the way had gathered a momentum of its own, taken on its own vibrant life force…distracted him from the goal he had long ago set himself.

Until he had come upon those letters.

'She must have produced her insurance certificate,' Matias mused, eyes narrowing. 'What's the woman's name?'

'I'll email you the details.' Art sighed, knowing without having to be told the direction of his friend's thoughts. 'I haven't had a chance to look at it but I took a picture of the document.'

'Good,' Matias said with some satisfaction. 'Do that immediately, Art. And there will be no need for you to deal with this matter. I will handle it myself.'

'Why?' Art was the only person who would ever have dared ask such a forthright question. Especially when the question was framed in a tone of voice that carried a warning.

'Let's just say that I might want to get to know her better. Knowledge is power, Art, and I now regret that I didn't dig a little deeper into Carney's private life. But don't look so worried! I'm not the big bad wolf. I don't make a habit of eating innocent young girls. So if she's as *nice* as you imply, then she should be as safe as houses.'

'Your mother wouldn't like this,' Art warned bluntly.

'My mother is far too kind for her own good.' For a few seconds, Matias thought of Rose Rivero, who was recuperating from a near fatal stroke at one of the top hospitals in London. If his father had never recovered from Carney's treachery, then his mother had never recovered from his father's premature death. When you looked at it, Carney had not only been responsible for his family's unjust state of penury, but beyond that for the stress that had killed his father and for the ill health and unhappiness that had dogged his mother's life. Revenge had been a long time coming but, if only James Carney knew it, it was now a juggernaut rolling with unstoppable speed towards him...

Sophie Watts stared up at the soaring glass tower in front of her and visibly quailed.

The lovely man whose car she had accidentally *bruised* three days previously had been very accommodating when she had phoned the number he had given her when they had exchanged details. She had explained the situation with her insurance policy and he had been sympathetic. He had told her in a friendly enough voice that she would have to come and discuss the matter personally but he was sure that something could be sorted out.

Unfortunately, the building in front of her did not look like the sort of user-friendly place in which cheerful and accommodating people worked, sorting out thorny situations in a cordial and sympathetic manner.

She clutched her capacious bag tightly and continued staring. Her head told her that she had no option but to move forward with the crowd while her feet begged to be allowed to turn tail and flee back to her low-key corner of East London and her little house in which she did her small-scale catering and baking for anyone who needed her services.

She didn't belong here and the clothes she had carefully chosen to meet Art Delgado now felt ridiculous and out of place.

The young women sweeping past her with their leather computer bags and clicking high heels were all dressed in sharp black suits. They weren't dithering. They were striding with purpose into the aggressive glass tower.

A small, plump girl with flyaway hair wearing a summery flowered dress and sandals didn't belong here.

Sophie propelled herself forward, eyes firmly ahead. It had been a mistake to come here *first thing* so that she could *get it over with*. That idea had been great in theory but she hadn't banked on the early rush-hour stampede of city workers. However, it was too late now to start chastising herself.

Inside, the foyer was a wondrous and cruel blend of marble, glass and metal.

Arrangements of sofas were scattered here and there in circular formations. The sofas were all very attractive and looked enormously uncomfortable. Clearly management didn't want to encourage too much lounging around. Ahead of her, a bank of receptionists was busily directing people while streams of smartly dressed worker bees headed for the gleaming lifts opening and closing just beyond an array of stunted palm trees in huge ceramic pots.

Sophie felt a pang of physical longing for her kitchen, where she and Julie, her co-worker, chatted and baked and cooked and made big plans for the upmarket bakery they would jointly open one day. She craved the feel of her apron, the smell of freshly baked cake and the pleasant playing around of ideas for meals they had booked in for catering jobs. Even though she was now talking to one of the receptionists, explaining who she wanted to see, confirming that an appointment had been made and stuttering over her own name, she was unhappily longing to be somewhere else.

Frayed nerves made her miss what the snappily dressed girl in front of her had just said but then she blinked and registered that a mistake had been made.

'I don't know a Mr... River,' she said politely.

'Rivero.' Eyebrows arched up, lips tightened, eyes cooled.

'I'm here to see a Mr Delgado.'

'Your meeting is with Mr Rivero.' The receptionist swivelled the computer towards her. 'You are to sign in. Anywhere on the screen will do and just use your finger. Mr Rivero's secretary will be waiting for you on the tenth floor. Here's a clip-on pass. Make sure you don't remove it because if you do you'll be immediately escorted out of the building.'

In a fluster, Sophie did as she was told but her heart was hammering inside her as she obeyed instructions, allowing herself to be swept along in a group towards the nearest lift and then staring fixedly at nothing in particular as she was whooshed up to the tenth floor, as directed.

Who was Mr Rivero? She had banked on the comfort of explaining her awkward situation to the very nice Mr Delgado. What sort of hearing was she going to get from a complete stranger? She was as tense as a bow string when, disgorged into the plushest surroundings she had ever seen, she was taken in hand by a very tall, middle-aged woman whose expression of sympathy did nothing to quell her escalating nerves.

And then she was being shown into an office, faced

with a closed door, ushered through it and deposited like an unwanted parcel in a room that was simply breath-taking.

For a few seconds, eyes as round as saucers, Sophie looked around her. She hadn't budged from where she had been placed just inside the door of a gigantic office. She cravenly recoiled from actually being bold enough to walk forward. Bag clutched tightly in front of her, she gradually became aware of the man sitting behind the desk. It was as if, suddenly, she focused, and on focus-ing felt the thudding impact of shock because the guy she was staring at was the most stunningly drop-dead gorgeous specimen she had ever seen in her entire life.

Her breathing slowed and even though she knew she was staring, she couldn't help herself. His hair was raven black, his eyes the colour of the darkest, richest chocolate, his features lovingly and perfectly chiselled. He oozed the sort of stupendous sex appeal that made heads swing round for a second and third look.

The silence stretched and stretched between them and then it dawned on her that she was making an ab-solute fool of herself.

'Miss Watts.' Matias was the first to speak. 'Do you intend to hover by the door for the duration of this meet-ing?' He didn't get up to shake her hand. He didn't smile. He did nothing to put her at ease. Instead he nod-ded at the chair in front of his desk. 'Sit down.'

Sophie shuffled forward, not knowing whether she was expected to shake his hand as a formality, but his expression was so forbidding that she decided against it and instead sank into the leather chair. She almost immediately leaned forward and rushed headlong into the little speech she had earlier rehearsed.

'I'm really sorry about the car, Mr...er... Rivero. I honestly had no idea that your friend was turning into the drive. It's so difficult to see round that bend, especially in summer. I admit I may have been driving a little faster than usual but I want to impress upon you that it was *unintentional*.' What she could have added but didn't was that her vision had been blurred because she had been doing her utmost not to cry after a stormy and upsetting meeting with James Carney.

Matias was watching her intently, his dark eyes narrowed on her flushed and surprisingly pretty face. He was a man who went for catwalk models, with long, angular bodies and striking, photogenic faces, yet there was something alluring about the woman sitting in front of him. Something about the softness of her face, the pale, vanilla shade of her unruly hair, the perfect clarity of her aquamarine eyes, held his attention and he could only assume that it was because of her connection to James Carney.

He hadn't known the woman existed but the minute he had found out he had recognised the gift that had landed in his lap for what it was.

He thought back to those letters he had unearthed, and his jaw tightened. That soft, wide-eyed, innocent look wasn't going to fool him. He didn't know the full story of the woman's relationship to Carney but he certainly intended to find out, just as he intended to exploit the situation he had been handed to discover if there were any other secrets the man might have been hiding. The broader the net was cast, the wider the catch.

'Employee,' Matias replied. This just in case she got

it into her head that special favours were going to be granted because of Art's personal connection with him.

'I beg your pardon?'

'Art Delgado is my employee. He was driving my Maserati. Miss Watts, do you have any idea how much one costs?'

'No, I don't,' Sophie said faintly. He was having the most peculiar effect on her. It was as though the power of his presence had sucked the oxygen out of the air, making it difficult to breathe.

'In that case, allow me to enlighten you.' He named a sum that was sufficiently staggering to make her gasp. 'And I have been told that your insurance policy is invalid.'

'I didn't know,' Sophie whispered. 'I'm usually so good at dealing with all that stuff but things have been a bit hectic recently. I know I cancelled my old policy and I had planned on renewing with somewhere cheaper but...'

Matias held up one imperious hand to stop her in mid flow. 'I'm not interested in the back story,' he informed her coolly. 'To cut to the chase, the damage you have done to my car will run to many, many thousands.'

Sophie's mouth dropped open. 'Thousands?' she parroted.

'Literally. I'm afraid it won't be a simple case of sorting out the dent. The entire left wing of the car will have to be replaced. High-performance cars charge high-performance prices.'

'I... I had no idea. I haven't got that sort of money. I...when I spoke to your friend...sorry, your employee Mr Delgado on the phone, he said that we would be able to work something out.'

'Sadly working something out really isn't in his remit.' Matias thought that his old friend would raise a sardonic eyebrow at that sweeping statement.

'I could pay you back over time.' Sophie wondered what sort of time line would be acceptable to the unforgiving man staring coldly at her as though she were an undesirable alien that had suddenly invaded his personal space. She somehow didn't imagine that his time line was going to coincide with hers. 'I run a little catering business with a friend,' she hurtled on, desperate to bring this uncomfortable meeting to an end and even more desperate to find some sort of solution that wouldn't involve bankruptcy for her and Julie's fledgling start-up company. 'We only opened up a year and a half ago. Before that we were both primary school teachers. It's taken an awful lot of borrowing to get everything in order and to get my kitchen up to the required standard for producing food commercially, and right at this moment, well…there isn't a great deal of spare change flying about.'

'In other words you're broke.'

'We're really making a go of things, Mr Rivero!' Heat flared in her cheeks. 'And I'm sure we can work something out when it comes to a repayment schedule for your car…'

'I gather you're James Carney's daughter.' Matias lowered his eyes, then he pushed back his chair and stood up to stroll across to the impressive bank of windows, in front of which was a tidy sitting area complete with a low table fashioned in chrome and glass.

Sophie was riveted at the sight of him. The way he moved, the unconscious flex of muscle under the expensive suit, the lean length of his body, the casual strength he exuded that was frankly spellbinding. He turned to look at her and it took a big effort not to look away.

His throwaway remark had frozen her to the spot.

'Well?' Matias prodded. 'Art was on his way to pay a little visit to James Carney on business,' he expanded, 'when you came speeding out of his drive like a bat out of hell and crashed into my car. I had no idea that the man even had a family.' He was watching her very carefully as he spoke and was mildly surprised that she didn't see to ask him a very fundamental question, which was why the heck should Carney's private life have anything to do with him?

Whatever she was, she clearly didn't have a suspicious nature.

Sophie was lost for words. She had been shaken by the accident, upset after the visit to her father, and Art Delgado, so different from this flint-eyed guy assessing her, had encouraged her into a confidence she rarely shared with anyone.

'Of course...' Matias shrugged, curiosity spiking at her continued silence '... I am not primarily concerned with the man's private life but my understanding was that he was a widower.'

'He is,' Sophie whispered, ashamed all over again at a birthright she hadn't asked for, the consequences of which she had been forced, however, to live with.

'So tell me where you fit in,' Matias encouraged. 'Unless, of course, that was a little white lie you told my employee on the spur of the moment.' He appeared to give this a little thought. 'Maybe you were embarrassed to tell the truth...?'

'Sorry?' That garnered her attention and she looked at him with a puzzled frown.

'Young girl having an affair with an old man? I can see that you might have been embarrassed enough to have said the first thing that came to your head, anything that sounded a little less unsavoury than what you really are to Carney.'

'How dare you?' Sophie gasped, half standing. 'That's disgusting!'

'I'm just trying to do the maths.' Matias frowned and tilted his head to one side. 'If you're not his lover, the man must have had a mistress while he was married. Am I right? Are you Carney's love child?'

Sophie laughed bitterly because nothing could have been further from the truth. Love had never come into the equation. Before her untimely death, her mother, Angela Watts, had been an aspiring actress whose great misfortune had been her Marilyn Monroe blonde-bombshell looks. Prey to men's flattery and pursued for her body, she had made the fatal error of throwing her net too wide. James Carney, young, rich and arrogant, had met her at a club and, like all the others, had pursued her, but he had had no intention of ever settling down with someone he considered a two-bit tart with a pretty face. Those details had been drummed into Sophie from as soon as she was old enough to understand. He had had fun with Angela and she had foolishly thought that the fun would actually go somewhere, but even when she had contrived to trap him with a pregnancy he had stood firm, only later marrying a woman he considered of the right class and social position.

'He met my mother before he was married,' Sophie confessed, belatedly adding, 'not that it has anything to do with…well, *anything*. Mr Rivero, I would be more than happy for you to draw up a schedule for repayment.

I will sign it right here and right now and you have my word that you will have every penny I owe you back. With interest if that's what you want.'

Matias burst out laughing. 'That's very obliging of you,' he drawled lazily. 'Believe it or not, I haven't become a successful businessman by putting my faith in the impossible. I have no idea what you owe the bank but I suspect you're probably barely making ends meet. Am I right?'

He tilted his head to one side and Sophie looked at him with loathing. He might be sinfully handsome but she had never met anyone she hated more on the spot. She wasn't stupid. He had all the money in the world, from the looks of it, but he wasn't going to be lenient when it came to getting back every penny she owed him and she knew that he wouldn't give a hoot if he drove her little company into the ground to do it.

Right now, he was toying with her like a cat playing with a mouse.

'We could work out a schedule,' he mused, 'but I would be on my walking frame before you made the final payment.' She really had the most wonderfully transparent face, he thought. Impossible though it was, she looked as pure as the driven snow.

But perhaps she wasn't fashioned in the same mould as the father. Certainly, she wouldn't have had the example set by him on a daily basis if she was the product of a youthful affair. He was surprised, in fact, that she had any contact with the man at all and he wondered how that had worked when Carney's socially acceptable wife had been alive.

Matias wasn't going to waste time pondering stuff like that, however. Right now, he was working out how best to use her to his advantage. When he pulled the plug on Carney, he intended to hit him on all fronts and he wondered whether she could be of use to him in that.

What other secrets was the man hiding? Matias knew that the company was beset with financial problems but, in the ether, there had been rumours of foul play... Sometimes skeletons were hard to find, however hard you dug, and Carney was a man who was sly and smart enough to cover his tracks. Wouldn't it be satisfying if all his dark secrets were to be exposed to the cruel glare of light...?

Could this fresh-faced girl be the key to unlock more doors? And what if there were personal skeletons? An attack on all fronts was certainly worth considering. He was honest enough to acknowledge that this level of revenge was probably beneath him, but those letters he'd found...they had made this personal...

'You could always ask Daddy for the money,' he ventured smoothly, knowing what the answer would be.

'No!' This time she did stand up. Her full mouth was drawn into a thin, obstinate line. 'I won't have... my father involved in this. Bankrupt me if you want.' She reached into her bag, pulled out one of the business cards, remembering how filled with optimism she and Julie had been when they had had them printed. 'Here's my business card. You can come and see the premises. It's just in my kitchen but the equipment must be worth something. I have a number of big jobs lined up, so if you're patient I can do those and you can have the money. As for the rest... I will sell my house and I should be able to sort out the rest of the debt with money left over after the mortgage has been covered.'

Matias looked at her, every line of his powerful body

indicating a man totally relaxed, totally unfazed by her emotional outburst.

Dark eyes roamed over her. She had tried to do something businesslike with her hair but somewhere along the line it had rebelled and tangled, white-blonde strands already curling around her cheeks. Her eyes were wide and a curious shade of turquoise and fringed, he noted, with thick dark lashes, which was at odds with the colour of her hair. And her body...

He shifted in his chair, astonished that he was even bothering to notice that she had curves in all the right places and luscious breasts that were prominent against the truly appalling flowered dress she was wearing.

She lacked sophistication and clearly had no style gene whatsoever, so what, he wondered, with a certain amount of irritation, was it about her that captured his attention so completely?

'You're overreacting,' he told her as she remained standing, her blue eyes dark with worry, anger and distress.

'You've just told me that you're not willing to come to any kind of arrangement with me about the money I owe you for your stupid car!' Easy-tempered by nature, Sophie was shocked at the stridency of her voice and the fact that she *was yelling at him*! 'I can't go to my bank and draw out the kind of money I would need to make good the damage. So, *of course I'm going to be upset.*'

'Sit down.'

'No. I'm going. You can get in touch with me on the number on the card! I'm going to have to talk this through with Julie. I don't know what she's going to say. She's put in most of her savings to try and get this business of ours going, as have I, so I'm going to have to find the money to pay her back too and make sure she doesn't have to pay for my mistake.' Her voice was wobbling and she stared off into the distance in an attempt to stop herself from crying.

Matias squashed all feelings of guilt. Why should he feel guilty? He was staring at a woman whose father had destroyed his family. In that scenario, guilt didn't exist. After all, all was fair in love and war, wasn't it?

'You could do that,' he murmured, 'or you could sit back down and listen to the proposition I have for you.'

CHAPTER TWO

'GO EASY ON THE GIRL,' Art had urged his friend the previous day. 'Because Carney's her father, doesn't mean that she has been cut from the same cloth.'

Matias hadn't argued the point with his friend, but he had privately held the view that the apple never fell far from the tree and an innocent smile and fluttering eyelashes, which he was guessing had been the stunt the woman had pulled on Art, didn't mean she had a pure soul.

Now, however, he was questioning the judgement call he had made before he had even met her. He was seldom, if ever, wrong when it came to summing people up, but in this instance his friend might have had a point. Matias wasn't going to concede that the woman spent all her spare time helping the poor and unfortunate or that she was the sort who wouldn't have recognised an uncharitable thought if it did a salsa in front of her. What he *did* recognise was that he would be better served in his quest for revenge by getting to know her.

She was an unexpected piece of a puzzle he had thought was already complete and he would have to check her out.

He had waited years for retribution. Waiting a couple

of weeks longer wasn't going to kill him and it might put him in an even stronger position than he already was.

He looked at her anxious face and smiled slowly. 'There's no need to look so worried,' he soothed. 'I'm not a man who beats about the bush, Miss…it *is* Miss, isn't it?'

Sophie nodded and automatically touched her ring-free finger. Once upon a time, she had had a boyfriend. Once upon a time, she had had dreams of marriage and kids and a happy-ever-after life, but reality had had something different to say about that.

'Boyfriend?' Matias hadn't missed that unconscious gesture. No ring on her finger. Had there been one? Once? Was she divorced? She looked far too young, but who knew? It wasn't his business but it paid to know your quarry.

Sophie sat on her hands. 'I don't see what that has to do with…your car, Mr… Rivers…'

'*Rivero.*' Matias frowned because it wasn't often that anyone forgot his name. In fact, never. 'And in point of fact, it has. You owe me money but if you're telling the truth, then it would seem that you have little to no hope of repaying me.'

'Why wouldn't I be telling the truth?'

Matias debated whether he should point out that her father would surely not be keen to see his child slaving in front of a hot oven cooking food for other people, so how likely was it that catering was her full-time occupation? Or maybe she was the sort who rebelled against their parents by pretending to reject money and everything it stood for? When you came from money and had comfort and security as a blanket to fall back on, it was easy to play at enjoying poverty. From what he knew of the man, keeping up appearances ran to a full-time occupation and surely his offspring would have been dragged into that little game too?

However, he had no intention of laying any of his cards on any tables any time soon. At any rate, it would be a matter of seconds to check her story and he was pretty sure she was telling the truth. Her car, for one thing, did not suggest someone with an enviable bank balance and the oversight with the insurance added to the impression.

He shrugged. 'Maybe you imagine that pleading poverty will touch some kind of chord in me.'

'That never crossed my mind,' Sophie said honestly. 'I can't think that anyone would be mad enough to try and appeal to your better nature.'

'Come again?' Momentarily distracted, Matias stared at her with outright incredulity.

The woman was here on the back foot, staring bankruptcy in the face if he decided to go after her, and yet she had the cheek to *criticise him*? He almost couldn't believe his ears.

Sophie didn't back down. She loathed arguments and avoided confrontation like the plague, but she was honest and forthright and could be as stubborn as a mule. She had had to be because she had had to take up where her mother had left off when it came to breathing in deep and pursuing what she felt James Carney owed her.

Right now, she had no idea where Matias was going with some of his remarks. He had mentioned a solution to the problem staring her in the face, but she couldn't help noticing that he hadn't actually said what that solution might be.

If he was stringing her along only to pull the rug

from under her feet, then she wasn't going to sit back and allow him to bully her in the process.

'If you had a better nature,' she pointed out, 'then you would try and understand what it's like for me. You probably don't have a clue about what it's like to struggle, because if you did then you would be able to put yourself in my shoes, and if you did that you might try and find a solution to the problem instead. If you give me a chance, then I will pay you back, but first you have to give me a chance.'

'Is this your idea of buttering me up?' Matias said coldly. 'Because if it is, then you're heading in the wrong direction. Let's not forget that you're here with a begging bowl.' He would come back to her father and exactly how hard he'd made Matias's family *struggle* in due course.

Sophie's soft mouth tightened. She had a lot of experience when it came to begging bowls and she had learned the hard way that buckling under threat never got anyone anywhere.

'You said that you had a proposition for me,' she reminded him, clinging to that lifebelt and already willing to snatch at it whatever the cost. Perhaps if she had had only herself to think about, she might have backed off, but there were more people at stake here than just her.

Matias was already pleased that he had decided to go with the flow and exploit the opportunity presented to him. Soft and yielding she might look, but it had quickly become apparent that she was anything but.

He felt the kick of an unexpected challenge. So much of his life was predictable. He had reached the pinnacle of his success and he was still in his early thirties. People kowtowed to him, sought his advice, hung onto his every word, did their utmost to please him. Bearing in mind that financial security and the power that came with it had been his ambition for as long as he could remember, he was now disappointed to acknowledge that there was something missing from his life, something that not even the glowing fires of revenge had been able to fulfil.

He had become jaded over time. When he thought back to the hungry young man he had once been, his whole body alive for the task he had set himself, he felt as if he were staring backwards at a stranger. Certainly, on a personal level, the fact that he could have any woman he wanted was something that had long lost its novelty value. Now, for the first time in ages, he was facing a challenge he could sink his teeth into and he liked the feeling.

'In two weeks' time…' Matias had returned to his desk and now he pushed back his leather chair and relaxed with his hands folded behind his head '… I am due to host a long weekend party at one of my houses. Around eighty people will be descending and they will be expecting the highest standard of catering. I will provide the food. You will handle everything else. Naturally, you won't be paid. Succeed and we can carry on from there. I have no intention of exercising my right to frankly bankrupt you because, for a start, driving without being insured is illegal. If I went the whole way, you'd be in prison by dusk. Instead, I will play it by ear.'

'In other words,' Sophie said stiffly, 'you'll own me until you consider the debt to be paid off.'

Matias tilted his head to one side and smiled coolly. 'That's one way of putting it…' Okay, so it was the only way of putting it. He would be able to take his time finding out about her and thereby finding other ways back to her father. Were those rumours of foul play in the company vaults true? Was that something the man had confessed to his offspring? If so, if that level of information could somehow be accessed, then he would have the most powerful weapon for revenge within his grasp. He couldn't care less about the damage to his car. He could take it to the nearest scrapyard and buy a replacement without even noticing any dent in his limitless income.

'And when you think about the alternatives,' he mused, 'you'll conclude, pretty fast, that it's a sweet deal for you.' He gave a gesture that was as exotically foreign as he was. 'You might even be able to...' he flicked out the business card she had earlier given him '...distribute these discreetly during the weekend.'

'And will I be able to bring my business partner?'

'I don't think so. Too many cooks and all that. I will ensure that you have sufficient staff to help but essentially this will be your baby.' He glanced at his watch but didn't stand, leaving it to Sophie to deduce that he was done with her. She stood up awkwardly and looked at him.

How could someone so effortlessly beautiful be so utterly cold-hearted?

Although, she had to acknowledge, at least he hadn't done what he had every right to do and contacted the police. She could have kicked herself for that little window during which she had forgotten to renew her insurance with a different company. So unlike her but then she had had so much on her mind.

'Will there be something...er...in writing?'

'Something in writing?'

'Just so that I know how much of the debt will be covered when I handle the catering for you that weekend...'

'You don't trust me?'

Sophie gazed off and thought of her father. She'd had to learn fast how to manage him. Trust had never been in plentiful supply in their relationship and she thought that it would be prudent not to rely on it in this situation either.

'I don't trust many people,' she said quietly and Matias's ears pricked up.

He looked at her carefully. 'No?' he murmured. 'I don't trust many people either but then, as you've pointed out, I don't have a better nature whereas I expect you probably do. Am I right?'

'I've found that people inevitably let you down,' Sophie told him painfully, then she blinked and wondered what on earth had induced her to say that. 'So it would work if I could have something in writing as I go along...'

'I'll get my secretary to draw something up.' All business now, Matias stood up, signalling that her time was up. 'Rest assured, you won't be required to become my personal slave in return for a debt.'

His dark eyes flicked to her as she shuffled to her feet. She gave the impression of someone whose eyes were always downcast and he could see how Art had been knocked sideways by her meek persona, but he wasn't so easily fooled. He had seen the fire burning just below the surface. She blushed like a virgin but those aquamarine eyes flashed like a siren call and he couldn't wait to get to the bottom of her...and discover in the process what she could contribute to the picture he had already compiled of her father.

* * *

'But I just think that there must have been *some other way* of sorting this situation out! I'm going to be left here for *several days* on my own and I just don't know whether I can manage the Rosses' cocktail party on my own!'

Sophie's heart went out to Julie and she looked at her friend sympathetically. Sympathy was about all she could offer. She had signed up to a deal with the devil and it was a better deal than she might have hoped for. Even though she hated it.

She had been over all the pros and cons of the situation, and had apologised profusely to her friend, who was not as confident in the kitchen as she was.

'But on the bright side,' she said in an upbeat voice, 'think of all the possible connections we could make! And,' she felt compelled to repeat because fair was fair, 'he could have just taken everything from us to sort out the damage to his car. I honestly had no idea *that a car* could cost that much to repair! It's mad.'

He was sending a car for her and Sophie looked at her watch with a sense of impending doom. A fortnight ago, his secretary had emailed her with an extensive list of things she 'should bring, should know and should be prepared to undertake'.

There was to be no veering off from the menu and she would have to ensure that every single dish for every single day was prepared to the highest possible specification.

She was told how many helpers she would have and how they should behave. Reading between the lines, that meant *no fraternising with the guests*.

She was informed of the dress code for all members of staff, including herself. The dress code did not include jeans or anything that might be interpreted as casual.

She gathered that she was being thrown in at the deep end and this detailed information was his way of being kind to her. She assumed that he had diverted his original catering firm to some other do specifically so that he could put her through her paces and she had spent the past two nights worrying about what would happen if she failed. Matias Rivero wasn't, she thought, callous enough to take the shirt off her back, but he intended to get his money's worth by hook or by crook. He might be unwilling to throw her to the sharks, but he wasn't going to let her get off lightly by agreeing to monthly payments that would take her decades to deliver what was owed.

This was the biggest and most high-profile job she had ever got close to doing and the fact that he would be looking at her efforts with a view to criticism filled her with terror. She wondered whether he hadn't set her an impossible task just so he could do his worst with a clear conscience when she failed. He struck her as the sort of man who saw ruthlessness as a virtue.

His car arrived just as she was giving some final tips to Julie about the catering job she would be handling on her own, and Sophie took a deep breath and reached for her pull-along case.

There would be a uniform waiting for her at his country house, which was in the Lake District. However, his instructions had been so detailed that she had decided against wearing her usual garb of jeans and a tee shirt to travel there and, instead, was in an uncomfortable grey skirt and a white blouse with a short linen jacket. At a little after ten in the morning, with the sun climbing in the sky, the outfit was already making her perspire.

She hung onto the hopeful thought that she would probably find herself stuck in the kitchen for the entire time. With any luck, she wouldn't glimpse Matias or any of his guests and she knew that, if that were the case, then she would be all right because she was an excellent chef and more than capable of producing the menu that had been emailed to her.

She wouldn't even have to bother about sourcing the ingredients, because all of that would already have been taken care of.

Her high hopes lasted for as long as the very smooth car journey took. Then nerves kicked in with a vengeance as the car turned between imposing wrought-iron gates to glide soundlessly up a tree-lined avenue on either side of which perfectly manicured lawns stretched towards distant horizons of open fields, shaded with copses. It was a lush landscape and very secluded.

The house that eventually climbed into view was perched atop a hill. She had expected something traditional, perhaps a Victorian manor house with faded red brick and chimneys.

She gasped at the modern marvel that greeted her. The architect had designed the house to be an organic extension of the hill and it appeared to be embedded into the side so that glass and lead projected as naturally from rock and foliage as a tree might grow upwards from the ground.

The drive curved around the back, skirting a small lake, and then they were approaching the house from the side where a sprawling courtyard was large enough to house all those important guests she had been expecting to find. Except the courtyard was empty aside from three high-performance cars parked haphazardly.

All at once, a quiver of nervous tension rippled through her. She could have become lost in a crowd of people. In an empty mansion, and it certainly looked empty, getting lost wasn't going to be that easy.

And for reasons she couldn't quite understand, reasons that extended well beyond the uncomfortable circumstances that surrounded her presence here, Matias made her feel…awkward. Too *aware of herself*, uncomfortable in her own skin and on edge in a way she had never felt before.

Her bag was whipped away from her before she had time to offer to take it herself and then she was being led through a most marvellous building towards the kitchen by a soft-spoken middle-aged woman who introduced herself as Debbie.

It was a cavernous space of pale marble and pale walls on which were hung vast abstract canvasses. She could have been walking through the centre of a fabulous ice castle and she actually shivered because never had she felt so removed from her comfort zone.

It had been hot outside but in here it was cool and quite silent. When she finally turned her attention away from her impressive surroundings, it was to find that Debbie had disappeared and instead Matias was lounging in the doorway of the kitchen.

'You're here,' he commented, taking in the prissy outfit and the flat black pumps and the neat handbag, which had apparently replaced the Santa's sack she had been carrying the last time he had seen her. He straightened and headed straight back in the direction of the kitchen, expecting her to follow him, which she did.

Sophie was tempted to retort where else would she be when she'd had no choice, but instead, she said politely to his back, 'I expected it to have been a bit busier.'

'The first of the guests don't arrive until tomorrow.' Matias didn't bother to turn around. 'I thought you might find it helpful to acquaint yourself with the kitchen, get to know where everything is.'

They had ended up in a kitchen that was the size of a football field and equipped to the highest possible standard. Sophie felt her fingers itch as she stared around her, dumbstruck.

'Wow.' She turned a full circle, eyes as wide as saucers, then when she was once again looking at him, she asked, 'So are you going to show me where everything is?'

Matias looked blankly around him and Sophie's eyebrows shot up.

'You don't know your way around this kitchen at all, do you?'

'I'm not a cook so it's true to say that I've never had much time for kitchens. I'm seldom in one place for very long and I tend to eat out a great deal. I'm a great believer in the theory that if someone else can do something better than you, then it would be cruel to deny them the opportunity.'

Sophie laughed and was surprised that he had managed to make her laugh at all. Her cheeks warmed and she looked away from those piercing dark eyes. Her heart was beating fast and she was confused because once again she could feel the pull of an attraction that went totally against the grain.

For starters, he had proven himself to have all the characteristics she despised in a man. He was arrogant, he was ruthless and he had the sort of self-assurance that came from knowing that he could do what he wanted and no one would object. He had power, he had money and he had looks and those added up to a killer combination that might have been a turn-on for other women but was a complete turn-off for her.

She knew that because he was just an extreme version of the type of men her mother had always been attracted to. Like a moth to an open flame, Angela Watts had been drawn to rich, good-looking men who had always been very, very bad for her. She had had the misfortune to have collided with the pinnacle of unsuitable men in James Carney, but even when that relationship had died a death she had still continued to be pointlessly drawn to self-serving, vain and inappropriate guys who had been happy to take her for a ride and then ditch her when she started to bore them.

Sophie had loved her mother but she had recognised her failings long before she had hit her formative teens. She had sworn to herself that, when it came to men, she would make informed choices and not be guided into falling for the wrong type. She would not be like her mother.

It helped that, as far as Sophie was concerned, she lacked her mother's dramatic bleached-blonde sex appeal.

And if she had made a mistake with Alan, then it hadn't been because she had chosen someone out of her league. It had just been…one of those things, a learning curve.

So why was she finding it so hard to tear her eyes away from Matias? Why was she so aware of him here in the kitchen with her, lean, indolent and darkly, dangerously sexy?

'Why don't you look around?' he encouraged, sitting at the kitchen table, content to watch her while he worked out how he was going to engineer the conversation into waters he wanted to explore.

She was very watchable. Even in clothes that were better suited to a shop assistant in a cheap retail outlet.

He was struck again by how little sense that made considering who her father was, but he would find out in due course and in the meanwhile...

He looked at her with lazy male appreciation. She had curves in all the right places. The hazy picture he had seen on Art's phone had not done justice to her at all. His eyes drifted a little south of her face to her breasts pushing against the buttons of the prissy, short-sleeved shirt. At least the jacket had come off. She was reaching up to one of the cupboards, checking the supply of dishes, he presumed, and the shirt ruched up to reveal a sliver of pale, smooth skin at her waist, and a dormant libido that should have had better things to do than start wanting to play with a woman who was firmly off the cards kicked into gear.

'Everything looks brand new.' Sophie turned to him, still on tiptoes, and he could see that indeed the crockery and the glasses in the cupboards could have come straight out of their expensive packaging. 'How often has this kitchen been used?'

'Not often,' Matias admitted, adjusting position to control his insurgent body. He glanced away for a few moments and was more in charge of his responses when he looked at her once more. Her hair was extraordinarily fair and he could tell it was naturally so. Fine and flyaway—with her heart-shaped face it gave her the look of an angel. A sexy little angel.

'In summer, I try and get up here for a weekend or so, but it's not often possible. Taking time out isn't always a viable option for me.'

'Because you're a workaholic?' Not looking at him, Sophie stooped down to expertly assess what the situation was with pots and pans and, as expected, there was no lack of every possible cooking utensil she might need. Next, she would examine the contents of the fridge.

With her catering hat firmly in place, it was easy to forget Matias's presence on the kitchen chair and the dark eyes lazily following her as she moved about the kitchen.

'I've discovered that work is the one thing in life on which you can depend,' Matias said, somewhat to his astonishment. 'Which, incidentally, is how I know your father.'

Sophie stilled and turned slowly round to look at him. 'You know my father? You actually *know* him?'

'I know *of* him,' Matias admitted, his dark eyes veiled. 'I can't say I've ever met the man personally. In fact, I was contemplating a business venture with him, which accounts for Art heading towards the house when you came racing out of the drive and crashed into my Maserati.' The delicate bones of her face were taut with tension and his curiosity spiked a little more.

'You had an appointment with my father?'

'Not as such,' Matias told her smoothly. 'Art was going to…let's just say…lay the groundwork for future trade…' In other words, he had sent Art to do the preliminary work of letting Carney know that his time was drawing to a close. He, Matias, would step in only when the net was ready to be tightened.

'Poor Art,' Sophie sighed, and Matias looked at her with a frown.

'Why do you say that?'

'I don't think he would have got very far with James even if he'd managed to gain entry to the house.'

'*James?* You call your father *James*?'

'He prefers that to being called Dad.' Sophie blushed. 'I think he thinks that the word *dad* is a little ageing. Also…'

'Also,' Matias intuited, 'you were an illegitimate child, weren't you? I expect he was not in the sort of zone where he would have been comfortable playing happy families with you and your mother. Not with a legitimate wife on the scene.'

Sophie went redder. What to say and how much? He was being perfectly polite. He wasn't to know the sort of man her father was and, more importantly, the reasons that had driven her mother to maintain contact with him, a legacy she had passed on to her daughter. Nor was she going to fill him in on her private business.

But the lengthening silence stretched her nerves to breaking point, and eventually she offered, reluctantly, 'No. My mother was a youthful indiscretion and he didn't like to be reminded of it.'

'He got your mother pregnant and he refused to marry her…' Matias encouraged.

Sophie stiffened because she could see the man in front of her was busy building a picture in his head, a picture that was spot on, but should she allow him to complete that picture?

The conversation she had had with her father just before she had blindly ended up crashing into Matias's car had been a disturbing one. He was broke, he had told her.

'And don't stand there with your hand stretched out staring gormlessly at me!' he had roared, pacing the magnificent but dated living room that was dark and claustrophobic and never failed to make Sophie shudder. 'You can take some of the blame for that! Showing up here month in month out with bills to settle! Now, there's *nothing left*. Do you understand me? *Nothing!*'

Cringing back against the stone mantelpiece, truly fearful that he would physically lash out at her, Sophie had said nothing. Instead, she had listened to him rant and rave and threaten and had finally left the house with far less than she had needed.

What if he was telling the truth? What if he *was* going broke? Where would that leave her…? *And more importantly, where would that leave Eric?*

As always, thinking of her brother made her heart constrict. For all her faults and her foolish misjudgements, her mother had been fiercely protective of her damaged son and had determined from early on that she wasn't going to be fobbed off by a man who had been happy enough to sleep with her for four years before abandoning her as soon as the right woman had finally appeared on the scene. She had used the only tool in her armoury to get the money she had needed for Eric to be looked after in the very expensive home where his needs were catered for.

Blackmail.

How would those fancy people James mixed with like him if they knew that he refused to support his disabled son and the family he had carelessly conceived, thinking that they would all do him a favour and vanish when it suited him?

James had paid up and he had continued paying up

because he valued the opinion of other people more than anything else in the world, not because he felt any affection for either the son he had never seen or the daughter he loathed because she was just an extension of the woman who, as far as he was concerned, had helped send him to the poorhouse.

If there was no money left, Eric would be the one to pay the ultimate price and Sophie refused to let that happen.

If Matias was interested in doing a deal with her father, a deal that might actually get him solvent once again, then how could it be in her interests to scupper that by letting him know just how awful James was? If her father had money then Eric would be safe.

'That's life.' She shrugged, masking her expression. 'There aren't many men who would have found it easy to introduce an outside family to their current one.' She took a deep breath and said, playing with the truth like modelling clay, 'But he's always been there for my mother... And now...er...for me...financially...'

Matias wondered whether they were talking about the same person. 'So you would recommend him as someone I should have dealings with?'

Fingers crossed behind her back, Sophie thought of her brother, lost in his world in the home where she visited him at least once a week, her brother who would certainly find life very, very different without all that care provided, care that only money could buy. 'Yes. Of course. Of course, I would.' She forced a smile. 'I'm sure he would love to have you contact him...'

CHAPTER THREE

MATIAS LOWERED HIS stunning dark eyes. So she either had no idea what kind of man her father was or she knew perfectly well enough and was tainted with the very same streak of greed, hence her enthusiasm for him to plough money into the man.

He wondered whether, over time and with her father's finances going down the drain faster than water running down a plughole, she had found herself an accidental victim of his limited resources. She had just declared that her father had supported her and her mother and Matias had struggled to contain a roar of derisive laughter at that. But she could have been telling the truth. Perhaps the dilapidated car and the debt owed to the bank were the result of diminishing handouts. She might have been an illegitimate child but it was possible that Carney had privately doted on her, bearing in mind that his own marriage had failed to yield any issue. Advertising a child outside marriage might have been no big deal for many men, but a man like Carney would have been too conscious of his social standing to have been comfortable acknowledging her publicly.

For a moment and just a moment, he wondered whether he could notch up some extra retribution and

publicly shame the man by exposing a hidden illegitimate child, but he almost immediately dismissed it
because it was…somehow unsavoury. Especially, he
thought, shielding the expression in his dark eyes, when
the woman sitting in front of him emanated innocence
in waves. There was such a thing as a plan backfiring
and, were a picture of her to be printed in any halfway
decent rag, a sympathetic public would surely take one
look at that disingenuous, sensationally sincere face
and cast *him* in the role of the bad guy. Besides, Carney's close friends doubtless knew of the woman's existence already.

'I will certainly think about contacting your father,'
Matias intoned smoothly, watching her like a hawk. He
became more and more convinced that she was playing him for a sap because she was suddenly finding it
seemingly impossible to meet his eyes. 'Now, you've
looked at the menu. Tell me whether you think you're
up to handling it.'

Sophie breathed a sigh of relief at the change of subject. She hated the little white lie she had told, even
though she was surely justified in telling it. Matias
might be disgustingly rich and arrogant but he still
didn't deserve to be deceived into believing her father
was an honourable guy. On the other hand, if the choice
was between her brother's future safety and well-being and Matias investing some money he wouldn't ever
miss, then her brother was going to win hands down
every time.

But that didn't mean that she'd liked telling Matias
that fib.

She jumped onto the change of topic with alacrity.
'Absolutely.' She looked around her at the expensive

gadgets, the speckled white counters, the vast cooking range. 'And it helps that your kitchen is so well equipped. Did you plan on doing lots of entertaining here when you bought the house?'

'Actually, I didn't buy the house. I had it built for me.' He went to the fridge, extracted a bottle of chilled white wine and poured her a glass. It seemed wildly extravagant to be consuming alcohol at this hour of the afternoon but she needed to steady her nerves, which were all over the place. 'And I had no particular plans to use the space for entertaining. I simply happen to enjoy having a lot of open space around me.'

'Lucky you,' Sophie sighed. After two sips of wine, she was already feeling a little less strung out. 'Julie and I would have a field day if we had this sort of kitchen. I've done the best with what I've got, but getting all the right equipment to fit into my kitchen has been a squeeze and if the business really takes off, then we're definitely going to have to move to bigger premises.'

Matias wondered whether that was why she had encouraged him to contact her father and put some work his way. Was it because she would be the happy beneficiary of such an arrangement?

Suspicious by nature and always alert to the threat of someone trying it on, he found it very easy to assume the worst of her, in defiance of the disingenuous manner she had. Judge a book by its cover and you almost always ended up being taken for a ride.

Not only did he have the example of his father to go on, who had paid the ultimate price for judging a book by its cover, but he, Matias, had made one and only one catastrophic misjudgement in his heady youth. On the road to the vast riches that would later be his and caught

up in the novel situation of being sought after by men
far older than himself who wanted to tap his financial
acumen, he had fallen for a girl who had seemed to be
grounded in the sort of normality he had fast been leaving behind. Next to the savvy beauties who had begun
forming a queue for him, she had seemed the epitome
of innocence. She had turned down presents, encouraged him to sideline the sort of fancy venues that were
opening up on his horizon and professed a burning desire to go to the movies and share a bag of popcorn. No
boring Michelin restaurants for her!

She had played the long game and he had been thoroughly taken in until she had sprung a pregnancy scare
on him. Talk had turned to marriage pretty quickly after
that and God knew he might just have ended up making
the biggest mistake of his life and tying the knot had
he not discovered the half-used packet of contraceptive
pills in her handbag. Quite by accident. Only then, when
he had confronted her, had her true colours emerged.

That narrow escape had been a turning point for him.
A momentary lapse, he had discovered, was all it took
for your life to derail. Momentary lapses would never
again occur and they hadn't. Matias ruled his own life
with a rod of steel and emotions were never allowed free
rein. He took what he needed out of life and discarded
what ceased to be of use to him.

Art was the only person on earth who knew about
that brief but shameful episode and so it would remain.
Matias had had little time for the perils of emotional
roller-coaster rides, having grown up as witness to the
way his father's emotional and trusting nature had led
him down a blind alley, and his disastrous love affair
had been the final nail in the coffin, after which he

had entombed his heart in ice and that was exactly the way he liked it.

'You said you've only been in the catering business for a year and a half. What prompted the change of career?'

'We both enjoyed cooking.' Sophie realised that her glass of wine was empty and he appeared to have topped it up. She moved to sit at the wonderful kitchen table fashioned from black granite and metal. 'We became accustomed to friends asking us to cater for them and bit by bit we came to the conclusion that, in the long run, we might very well be better off doing something we both loved and were good at. Julie was fed up with her teaching job and I guess I just wanted a change of career.'

'It must have been a leap of faith for you. Changing career that dramatically takes guts.' Had she embarked on that career change with the mistaken impression that her father was still wealthy enough to fund her? Had she had to resort to borrowing from the bank when she found herself out of a job and unable to turn to her parent for a handout? Was that why she was struggling financially?

Lucas knew that James Carney's financial position had been poor for a few years.

'Maybe. Haven't *you* ever had to change career or were you born with a silver spoon in your mouth?' she asked.

'You say that as though you're not familiar with that situation yourself.'

'I'm not,' Sophie said flatly and Matias looked at her through narrowed eyes.

'I confess I find that hard to believe, given your father's elevated lifestyle.'

'I'd really rather not talk about him,' Sophie hedged warily.

'You don't like talking about your father? Why is that? I grant you, it must have been a nuisance living in the shadows, if indeed that was the case, but surely if, as you say, he helped you and your mother through the years…well, he must be quite a character because many men in a similar situation would have walked away from their responsibility.'

Sophie muttered something inaudible that might have been agreement or dissent.

'Of course, life must be altogether easier for you now,' Matias continued conversationally. 'I gather his wife died some years ago, so presumably he has taken you under his wing…'

'We don't have that sort of relationship,' Sophie admitted stiffly and Matias's ears pricked up.

'No?' he encouraged. 'Tell me about him. The reason I ask is simple. If I'm to have any financial dealings with him, it would be useful to try and understand the sort of person he is.'

'Do you take this close an interest in *all* your…er… clients?' This more to divert the conversation than anything else. Sophie had no real idea how people in the business world operated.

'I have slightly more elaborate plans for your father's company,' which wasn't exactly a lie, then he shrugged.

'Is that what you do?'

Matias frowned. 'Explain.'

'Well, do you…er…invest in companies? The truth is I honestly don't know the ins and outs of how companies operate. I've never had much interest in that sort of thing.'

'I see...so you don't care about money...'

'Not enough to have gone into a career where I might have made a fortune. Life would have been a lot easier if I had.' For starters, she thought, she wouldn't have had to endure the monthly humiliation of picking up where her mother had left off, and going to her father with cap in hand because Eric's home was costly and there was no other choice. 'I don't suppose I'm ruthless enough.'

'Is that a criticism of me?' Matias asked wryly, amused because it was rare for anyone to venture any opinion in his presence that might have been interpreted as critical. But then, as she had pointed out, whatever better nature he had was seldom in evidence and things weren't going to change on that front any time soon.

Sophie was caught between being truthful and toeing the diplomatic line. Talking about her father was out of bounds because sooner or later she would trip up and reveal exactly the sort of man he was. Telling Matias Rivero what she thought of him was also pretty questionable because he had thrown her a lifeline and he could whip it back whenever it suited him. If she succeeded in this task, a good proportion of her debt to him would be wiped out. As agreed, she had received a detailed financial breakdown of what she could expect from her weekend's work.

Getting on the wrong side of him wasn't a good idea. But he *had* asked...

And something about the man seemed to get her firing on cylinders she didn't know she possessed.

'Well, I *am* here,' she pointed out and Matias frowned.

'Where are you going with that?'

'You intend to get your pound of flesh from me by

whatever means necessary and if that's not ruthless, then I don't know what is.'

'It's not ruthless,' Matias informed her, without a hint of an apology. 'It's good, old-fashioned business sense.' On more levels than she could ever begin to suspect, he thought, dispelling a fleeting twinge of guilt because all that mattered was getting her despicable father to pay for what he had done all those years ago.

Matias thought back to the slim stash of letters he had found shoved at the back of his mother's chest of drawers. He would never have come across those letters if she hadn't been rushed to hospital, because he had had to pack a bag without warning for her. Her housekeeper had had the day off and Matias had had no idea what sort of things his mother might need. He had opened drawers and scooped out what seemed to be appropriate clothing and in doing so had scooped out those unopened letters bound with an elastic band.

His mother's writing. He had recognised that instantly just as he had noted the date on the stamps. They had all been sent over a period of a few weeks at a time when his father had been taking what were to be his last breaths before the cancer that had attacked him two years previously had resurfaced to finish what it had begun.

Curiosity had got the better of him because all those letters had been addressed to the same man. James Carney.

In actual fact, he need only have opened one of the letters because they had all contained the same message.

A plea for help. A request for money for an experimental treatment being carried out in America for precisely the sort of rare cancer his father had contracted.

None of the letters had been opened—they had just been returned to sender. It was plain to see that the man who had defrauded Matias's family and reaped the financial rewards that should have, at the very least, been shared with his father, had not had the slightest interest in what his mother had wanted to say to him.

Carney had been too busy living it up on his ill-gotten gains to give a damn about the fate of the family who had paid the price at his hands.

There and then, Matias had realised that retribution was no longer going to be on the back burner. It was going to happen hard and fast. The time for dragging his feet was over.

If Carney's illegitimate daughter now found herself caught in the crossfire then so be it. He wasn't going to lose his focus and the woman sitting opposite him was all part of his bigger plan. He could bring the man down the routine way, by bankrupting him, but he was getting a feeling…that there was more to the saga of his hidden daughter than met the eye. What could she tell him? Any whiff of a financial scandal, any hint that the health of his ailing company was tied up with fraud, would be the icing on the cake. Not only would such public revelations hit Carney where it hurt most, but a long prison sentence would loom on the horizon for him. All in all, a thoroughly satisfying outcome.

'Julie, my partner, wouldn't agree with you.' Sophie stuck her chin out at a mutinous angle. 'I've left her barely coping with one of the biggest contracts we've managed to secure since we started our catering company. We could really harm our business if she doesn't succeed because one poor job has a knock-on effect in the catering world.'

'You don't have my sympathy on that score,' Matias told her bluntly. He was unwillingly fascinated by the way she coloured up when she spoke and the way her aquamarine eyes, fringed by the lushest lashes possible, glittered and sparkled like precious gems.

Her skin was as smooth as satin and she didn't appear to be wearing a speck of make-up. She oozed *natural* and if he wasn't the cynical guy that he was, he would be sorely tempted to take her at face value because that face appeared so very, very open and honest.

Step up the memory of the ex who had almost got his ring on her finger on the back of appearing open and honest! Good job he wasn't the sort of idiot who ignored valuable learning curves.

'Here's a free piece of advice...never go into business with anyone. However, considering you've passed that point, you should have made sure that you weren't going into business with dead wood. Have you got anything signed allowing you to disentangle yourself from a ruinous partnership without feeling the backlash?'

Two bright patches of colour stained her cheeks and she glared at Matias without bothering to conceal a temper that was rarely in evidence. She looked at him, furiously frowning, all the more irate because he returned her glare with a lazy, amused smile. Her skin tingled as he held her gaze and kept on holding it, sucking the breath out of her and making her agonisingly aware of her body in ways that were confusing and incomprehensible.

Her breasts felt heavy and *full*, her nipples were suddenly sensitised, their tips pebble hard and scratchy against her bra, and there was a tingling between her legs that made her want to touch herself.

Sophie was so shocked that she looked away, heart hammering hard, barely able to breathe normally.

What on earth was going on with her? It was true that she hadn't had any interest in men since she had broken up with Alan, but surely that wouldn't make her susceptible to a man like Matias Rivero? He epitomised everything she disliked and if he was, physically, an attractive guy then surely she was sensible enough to be able to get past outward appearances?

'Julie is *not* dead wood,' she denied in a voice she barely recognised.

'If she's panicking because you're not there to hold her hand, then she's incompetent.'

'Thank you for your advice,' she said with sugary sarcasm, 'although I won't be paying much attention to it because I actually haven't asked for it in the first place.'

Matias burst out laughing. Against all odds, he was enjoying himself with the one person on the planet he should have wanted to have as little to do with as possible. Yes, he was on a fact-finding mission but he hadn't anticipated having fun as he tried to plumb her depths for some useful information on her father.

'Would it shock you to know that I can't think of anyone who would dare say something like that to me?'

'No,' Sophie told him with complete honesty and Matias laughed again.

'No?'

'Men with money always surround themselves with people who suck up to them and, even if they don't, people are so awed by money that they change when they're around rich people. They behave differently.'

'But you're different from them?' Matias inserted

silkily. 'Or are you just someone who can afford to make penury their career choice because there has always been a comfort blanket on which to rely should push actually come to shove?'

'I don't expect you to believe me,' Sophie muttered. 'James supported us because he had to. I was grateful for that, but there was never any question about there being any comfort blanket for the…for us…'

Matias looked at her narrowly, picking up *something* although he couldn't quite be sure what.

'Because he had to…' he murmured. 'You're not exactly singing his praises with that statement.'

'But like you said,' Sophie pointed out quickly, 'he could have just walked away from his responsibility.'

'Unless…' Matias let that single word hang tantalisingly in the air between them.

'Unless?' Sophie gazed at him helplessly and thought that this was what it must feel like to be a rabbit caught in the headlights. There was something powerful and *inexorable* about him. His head was tilted to one side and his midnight-dark eyes were resting lazily on her, sending little arrows of apprehension racing through her body like tiny electrical charges.

'Unless he felt he had no choice…'

Sophie stilled. She was caught between the devil and the deep blue sea. Tell him everything and he would have nothing to do with her father, who would probably have to declare bankruptcy if everything he said was true, and where would that leave Eric? Yet say nothing and who knew where this conversation would end up?

She remained resolutely silent and thought frantically about a suitable change of subject. Something innocuous. Perhaps the weather, although that alert expression in Matias's dark, brooding eyes didn't augur well for some inconsequential chit-chat at this juncture.

He looked very much like a dog in possession of a large, juicy bone, keen to take the first bite.

'Is that it?' he pressed softly. 'Did your mother apply a little undue pressure to make sure she was taken care of? Is that the relationship you have with your father now? I expect a man like him, in a reasonably prominent position, might have found it awkward to have had the mother of his illegitimate child making a nuisance of herself.'

Lost for words, Sophie could only stare at him in absolute silence.

How on earth had he managed to arrive at this extremely accurate conclusion? And more to the point, how had the conversation meandered to this point in the first place?

'I thought you might have been the secret child he spoiled, bearing in mind his marriage failed to produce a suitable heir.' Matias was shamelessly fishing and not at all bothered at Sophie's obvious discomfort.

'I really don't want to talk about James,' Sophie eventually said, when the silence had become too much to bear. 'I know you're interested in finding out what you can before you sink money into…er…his company, but you're really asking the wrong person when it comes to business details and I don't feel comfortable discussing him behind his back.' Something her father had said, in the rush of anger, rose to the surface of her addled brain…something about *where* all the money he had given them over the years had come from, a paper trail that should have been brushed under the carpet but was threatening to re-emerge under the eagle eyes of independent auditors. She shivered.

Matias debated whether to press the issue or fall back on this occasion and he decided that, with time on his hands, there was no point trying to force her into revealing secrets that might be lurking just below the surface.

For sure, something wasn't quite right but he'd discover what that was sooner or later.

In the meanwhile…

'Is there anything you need to know about the job?' he asked briskly, finally changing the subject to her obvious relief. The details could very well be left to his head housekeeper, who was busy with preparations in the vast house somewhere, but Matias was drawn to continuing the conversation with her.

His life had become very predictable when it came to women. He had made one youthful mistake, had learnt from it and ever since his relationships had all had two things in common. One was that they followed exactly the same pattern and the second was that they were all short-lived.

The pattern involved mutual attraction with the expected lavishing of expensive presents, in something of a brief courtship ritual, followed by a few weeks of satisfying sex before he began getting bored and restless.

It didn't matter who he dated or what sort of woman happened to catch his eye. From barrister to catwalk model, his interest never seemed to stay the course.

Was Sophie right? People behaved differently in the presence of the powerful, influential and wealthy. Were the women he dated so awed by what he brought to the table that they were unable to relate to him with any kind of honesty?

Unaccustomed to introspection, Matias, for once, found himself querying how it was that he was still so resolutely single at his age and so jaded with the re-volving door of relationships he enjoyed. When had no-strings-attached fun turned into liaisons that seemed to get shorter and shorter and become less and less satisfying?

He frowned, disconcerted by this *breach of protocol* and refocused on the woman in front of him.

'Would you be able to help me if I had any ques-tions?' Sophie quipped and he dealt her a smile that was so sudden and so devastating that she had a mo-ment of sheer giddiness.

She blinked, owl-like, mouth parted, her cheeks tinged with delightful colour.

She wasn't angry…she wasn't defensive…she wasn't on the attack…

She was *aware*.

Matias felt that kick of his libido again, forbidden, dangerous but, oh, so pleasurable.

It had been a little while since he had had a woman. His most recent girlfriend had lasted a mere two months, at the end of which he had been mightily re-lieved to see the back of her because she had gone from compliant to demanding in record time.

Was his brief sexual drought generating a reaction that was as thrilling as it was unexpected?

There was certainly something undeniably sexy about Sophie and he couldn't put his finger on it. Maybe it was because he knew that he shouldn't go anywhere near her.

A thought entered his head like quicksilver. Why not? She was attractive. Indeed, it was a while since he had had his interest sparked by a woman who appeared to be uninterested in the usual game playing. There had been no coy looks, fluttering lashes or suggestive remarks. Admittedly, she was here under duress because he had placed her in an impossible situation, but even so she was doing a good job of keeping him at arm's length.

Matias watched her with brooding interest. If he wanted information on the Carney man, then surely pillow talk would yield everything he wanted to know?

Just like that, his imagination took flight and he pictured her in his super-king-sized bed, her tangle of long white-blonde hair spread across his pillow, her voluptuous pale nakedness there for his enjoyment. He wondered what her abundant breasts might look like and he imagined suckling at them.

An erection as solid as steel made him twinge in discomfort and he did his utmost to drag his mind away from imagining salacious, tawdry details about her.

'You're right,' he drawled, settling further into the chair, his big body relaxed, his hands loosely linked on his lap, his long legs extended to one side. 'If you want help, you're going to have to talk to my housekeeper. I have next to no interest in the workings of a kitchen, as I've already mentioned.'

'How lovely for you to be in a position like that,' Sophie said politely, still reeling from the way he *got to her* and made her whole body vibrate and rev up and behave almost as though it didn't belong to her at all.

'In case you're thinking that I was born with a silver spoon in my mouth, you're wrong.' He frowned because it wasn't in his nature to tell anyone anything about him that wasn't strictly essential. He didn't do confiding, especially not in women who could take one small slip-up and celebrate it as a signpost to the nearest bridal shop.

'I never said that,' but Sophie had the grace to blush because she'd certainly been thinking it. Rich, arrogant and privileged from birth had been her assumption.

'You have a very transparent face,' Matias told her wryly. 'You don't have to spell it out. It's there in your expression of disapproval. You think I'm an arrogant, ruthless tycoon who has it all and has never suffered a day's hardship in his entire life.'

Sophie didn't say anything. She was busy trying to get her body to behave and to look past Matias's devastating and unwelcome sex appeal. However, no matter how hard she tried to tell herself that she was only responding the way any normal, healthy young female would respond to a guy who would have been able to turn the head of a ninety-year-old woman with failing eyesight, she still could scarcely believe that he was capable of having that huge an impact on her.

To combat the drag of her disobedient senses, she even did the unthinkable and disinterred the mental image of her ex, Alan Pace. On paper, he had been the perfect life partner. Sandy-haired, blue-eyed and with just the sort of even, friendly disposition that had made her feel safe and comfortable. Sophie had really begun to nurture high hopes that they were destined for the long run.

She was always careful to vet the people she introduced to her brother; when, after three months, she'd filled Alan in on Eric, he had been surprised that she hadn't said anything sooner and had been happy to meet him.

Unfortunately, meeting Eric had marked the beginning of the end for them. Alan had not been prepared for the extent of her brother's disabilities and he had been quietly horrified at the thought that taking Eric out was a very regular activity and one which Sophie enjoyed and did without complaint. He had envisaged the possibility of him having to become a joint carer at some indeterminate point in the future, and although Sophie had squashed that suggestion because Eric was very, very happy where he was, she had not been able, in all good conscience, to rule it out altogether. After that, it had just been a matter of time before Alan had begun heading for the nearest exit.

Yet harking back to Alan, she had to admit to herself that not even *he* had affected her the way Matias seemed capable of doing. And before it all went belly up, Alan had been the perfect boyfriend! So what the heck was going on with her?

Not only was the man gazing at her with dark-eyed intensity very much *not* the perfect *anything*, but the last thing she felt in his presence was *safe and comfortable*.

Privately Sophie was appalled that she might bear any resemblance to her wayward mother, who had spent a lifetime making all the wrong choices and going for men just like the one sitting opposite Sophie, men who had *Danger, health hazard* stamped all over their foreheads in bright neon lettering.

'It doesn't matter what I think of you,' she said quickly, because this was the only way she could think of to bring their interaction to an end and she desperately wanted to do just that. 'I'm here to do my duty and now, if you'll excuse me, might I go and freshen up? And then perhaps I could talk to the person I will be working alongside? Also someone who can show me how everything works here?'

He was being dismissed! Matias didn't know whether to be amused or outraged.

He stood up, as sleek and graceful as a panther, and shoved his hands in the pockets of his trousers.

Sophie looked away. She knew that her face was bright red and that she was perched on the edge of her chair, rigid with tension and so aware of him that she could hardly breathe. He was just so staggeringly good-looking that she had to consciously *not* look at him and even *not* looking at him was making her go all hot and cold.

'Excellent idea,' Matias drawled, his keen eyes taking in every sign of her discomfort and also the way she was pointedly avoiding his eyes. He felt the thrill of a challenge and was already circling it, playing with thoughts of what happened next in this little scenario. 'Wait here. I will ensure that you are shown the workings of the kitchen and then to your quarters, which I trust you will find satisfactory.'

And then he smiled, slowly and lazily, and Sophie gave a jerky nod of her head, but he was already turning and striding out of the kitchen.

CHAPTER FOUR

SOPHIE HAD ONLY dimly speculated on what a long weekend party might be like. She had mostly thought along the lines of one of those upper-class country affairs where a dozen people wafted around in flowing robes, smoking cigarettes in long cigarette holders and talking in low, restrained, cut-glass accents. She had seen stuff like that in period dramas on television. Generally speaking, there was always an unfortunate death at some point.

Matias's party, she could tell as soon as guest number one had arrived, was not going to be quite like that.

Through the kitchen windows, which overlooked the spread of lawns at the back of the house and the long avenue and courtyard where the cars would be parked, the first guests arrived in a roaring vintage car, which disgorged a couple who could have stepped straight out of a celebrity magazine.

Debbie, the lovely housekeeper in her fifties who had, the day before, showed Sophie the ropes, had been standing next to her and she had said, without batting an eyelid, that everyone in the village had been waiting for this party with bated breath because the guest list was stuffed full of celebrities.

And so Sophie had discovered as the day had continued and the guests had begun piling up. All told, there would have been getting on for eighty people. Many would be staying in three sumptuous hotels in the vicinity, where chauffeurs were on standby to take them there at the end of the evening and return them to the house in time for breakfast and whatever activities had been laid on.

Through a process of clever guesswork, Sophie deduced that this wasn't so much a weekend of fun and frolic with Matias's nearest and dearest, but something of a business arrangement. The scattering of A-list celebrities from the world of media and sport was interspersed with a healthy assortment of very rich, middle-aged men who oozed wealth and power.

Sophie guessed that this was how the fabulously wealthy did their networking.

The supply of food was constant, as was the champagne. Having had a brief respite the day before, when Matias had done as asked and introduced Sophie to the people she would be working with, Sophie had been hard at it since six that morning.

Brunch was the first thing on the menu. An elaborate buffet spread, then tea before supper made an appearance at seven-thirty in the evening.

Sophie had no idea what these people did when they weren't eating and she didn't have time to think about it because she was rushed off her feet cooking and giving orders and hoping and praying that nothing went wrong.

She didn't glimpse Matias, even in passing. Why would he venture into the bowels of the kitchen where the lowly staff were taking care of his needs when he had the movers and shakers there to occupy him?

Strangely Art, Matias's employee, *had* put in an appearance in the kitchen and he had been as lovely as she recalled. Kind, gentle, almost making her think that there might be a purpose to his surprise visit, even though he had just briefly passed the time of day with her. And she wasn't quite sure why Matias had made sure to make the distinction that Art was only his *employee*, because it was clear, reading between the lines, that the two had a close bond, which, in turn, made her feel, stupidly and disturbingly, that Matias couldn't possibly be the cruel ogre she thought him to be. Didn't people's choice of friends often tell a story about *themselves*? Crazy.

Nose to the grindstone, she nevertheless still found herself keeping an eye out for Matias just in case he put in an appearance and when, at a little after eleven that evening, she made her way up to her quarters, she was foolishly disappointed not to have seen him at all.

Because she needed to make sure that everything was on target for her repaying some of the stupid debt she owed him, she reasoned sensibly. She had worked her butt off and she wanted to know that it hadn't been in vain, that day one had definitely wiped out the amount that had been agreed on paper.

The last thing she needed was to be told, when it was all over and done with and she'd shed a couple of stone through sheer stress, that he wasn't satisfied or that he'd had complaints about her or that the food had given his guests food poisoning and so she would have to cough up the money she owed him even if it meant her going bust.

She, herself, had no idea what the reaction to all her hard work was because she didn't emerge from the bowels of the wonderfully well-equipped kitchen for the entire day and night.

Waiters and waitresses came and went and an assortment of hired help made sure that dirty crockery was washed and returned for immediate use.

In addition to that plethora of staff on tap, Sophie also had a dedicated sous chef who was invaluable and did all the running around at her command.

But it was still exhausting and she had two more days of this before the first of the guests would start departing!

Surely, she thought, she would see Matias *at some point*! Surely he wouldn't just leave her to get on with it without poking his nose into the kitchen to see whether he was getting his pound of flesh!

It was simply her anxiety given the circumstances that resulted in Matias being on her mind so much.

She was cross with herself for letting him get under her skin. She recalled the way her body had reacted to his with a shudder of impatience. He'd given her the full brunt of his personality in all its overpowering glory when there had been no one else around, but now that he was surrounded by his cronies he couldn't even be bothered to check up on her and make sure he was getting value for money.

It infuriated her that, instead of being relieved that he wasn't hovering over her shoulder or popping up unexpectedly like a bad penny, she was disappointed.

By the time the festivities were coming to an end and the end of the long menu was in sight, she had reconciled herself to the fact that she would leave without seeing Matias at all and would probably find out the outcome of this exercise in repaying the money she owed him via his secretary.

He'd made his appearance and he wasn't going to be making another one.

She hadn't even had a chance, with everything happening, to have a look around the house! Not that she'd wanted to mingle with the guests. She knew her place, after all, but she'd hoped that she might have had a chance, last thing at night, to peep into some of the splendid rooms. No such luck because there had always been someone around or else the sound of voices from one of the rooms had alerted her to the presence of people who seemed to think nothing of staying up until the early hours of the morning.

The guests finally departed during the course of Monday in a convoy of expensive cars. The sound of laughter and chatter filtered down to the kitchen where most of the hired help had tidied, cleaned and left to go back to the village, where they would no doubt regale their family and friends with excited tales about what and who they'd seen.

Had Matias gone? By five-thirty, with just Sophie and Debbie left on the premises doing the final bits of tidying, she knew that he had. Without telling her how she had performed.

For some reason, she was booked to remain in the sprawling mansion until the following morning, and she had naturally assumed that there would be guests to cook breakfast for on that morning, but now she realised that she had been kept on to do cleaning duties after the guests had left.

He'd bought her lock, stock and barrel. She hadn't been asked to simply prepare meals, which was her speciality, but he had also kept her on to do basic skivvy work and he knew that she had no choice but to comply.

'You take the left wing of the house,' Debbie told her kindly. 'I've checked and all the guests have gone. There shouldn't be anything much to do at all because the rooms have all been cleaned on a daily basis. This is just a last-minute check to make sure nothing's been forgotten…and you've been saying that you wanted to have a peep at some of the rooms. It's worth a look. Mr Rivero doesn't come here very often but it's always a treat for us when he does because it's such a grand house.'

Finally back in her comfortable jeans and tee shirt, Sophie decided to do just that. Having not stuck her head over the parapet for the past three days, she took her time exploring the various rooms she had been allocated.

Debbie had been right: there was hardly any tidying to be done at all. Rooms had already been cleared of debris and vacuumed. She wound her way up the marble and glass staircase, admiring the canvasses on the walls as she began checking the bedrooms on the first floor.

The house looked untouched, having been completely tidied by a small army of staff.

Her mind was a complete blank as she pushed open the final door at the end of a long corridor that offered spectacular views of the lake from behind vast floor-to-ceiling panes of reinforced glass.

The first thing she noticed was the feel of pale, thick carpet under her feet as most of the house was a mixture of marble, wood and pale, endless silk rugs. Automatically, she kicked off her sandals and then stepped forwards.

Her eyes travelled to the huge bed…the white walls… the chrome and glass built-in wardrobes…the window that was just one massive pane of glass, uninterrupted by curtains or even shutters, through which Nature in all its lush green glory stretched towards the still black waters of the lake.

Then, to the left, a door she hadn't even noticed because it so cleverly blended into the pale paint opened and she was staring at Matias.

In pure shock, she took a few seconds to appreciate that he was semi naked. Obviously, he had just had a shower. His dark hair was still damp and a white towel was loosely draped around his lean hips. Apart from that scant covering…nothing. Bare chest, bare legs, bare *everything else*.

Sophie wanted to look away but she couldn't. Her mouth fell open and her eyes widened as she took in the broad muscularity of his shoulders, the width of his hard chest, the arrowing of dark hair down towards that low-slung towel. He was so absurdly, intensely *masculine* that all the breath left her in a whoosh.

She knew that she was staring and she couldn't do a thing about it. When she finally looked him in the face, it was to find him staring back at her, eyebrows raised. 'Inspection over?'

Matias had made a point of steering clear of her for the past few days. He'd regrouped and realised that what he had viewed as an interesting challenge that could lead to a number of pleasurable destinations with Sophie was in fact a poorly thought-out plan generated by a temporary lapse in his self-control.

She might be intensely attractive and he might very well be able to rationalise his visceral response to her, but taking her to his bed could only be a bad idea. Yes, pillow talk might result in him hitting the jackpot when it came to finding out more about Carney but there had been no point kidding himself that that had been the overriding reason for his sudden desire to act like a caveman and get her between the sheets. She'd done something to him, cast some spell over him that had made him lose his formidable self-control and that wasn't going to justify whatever jackpot it might or might not lead to.

So he'd kept away. He'd even considered sleeping with one of the single women who had been at the party, a model he had known briefly several months previously, but in the end had ditched the idea.

Because having entered his head, Sophie had stubbornly lodged there like an irritating burr and he'd found he didn't want anyone else.

And now here she was. His dark eyes roved over her flushed face and then did a quick tour of her body. These were obviously the clothes she was most comfortable in and she looked sexy as hell in them. The faded jeans clung to her curves like a second skin and the tee shirt revealed breasts that were gloriously abundant.

The kick of his libido demolished every single shred of common sense. Matias had no idea what it felt like to operate without self-imposed boundaries. He was finding out now as he looked at her and surrendered to a surge of lust that could not be forced into abeyance.

The thrill of a challenge waiting to be met was one that wasn't going to go away until it was dealt with.

He padded across to the bedroom door and quietly shut it and Sophie's head swung round in alarm.

'What are you d-doing?' she stammered, frozen to the spot.

'I'm closing the door,' Matias told her gently. 'In case you hadn't noticed, I'm not exactly dressed for visitors.'

'I was going to leave…' Sophie shuffled a couple of paces back but it was laborious, like swimming against a strong current. 'I had no idea that you were still here.'

'Where else would I have been?'

'I thought you'd left with all the other guests.'

'And not had a talk to you about your performance?'

'Have I done something wrong?' Sophie asked in a rush, red as a beetroot, torn between wanting to flee and needing to stay to hear whatever criticisms of her work that he had.

Matias didn't answer. He turned around and headed towards his wardrobe and Sophie broke out in a film of nervous perspiration.

'I'd rather talk to you…s-somewhere else,' she stuttered. 'If I'd known you were in here, I would never have entered.'

'I make you uncomfortable,' Matias said flatly, spinning round to look at her and at the same time throwing on a snowy white shirt without yet removing the towel. He didn't button it up but left it hanging open over his fabulous chest and Sophie's mouth went dry.

'You're barely clothed,' she pointed out breathlessly. 'Of course I feel *uncomfortable* and I certainly don't imagine I'll be able to have a conversation about my duties in your bedroom!' She went a shade redder. 'What I *mean*…is that this is…*isn't* the place for a serious conversation. If I've failed in the task you set me, then… then…' She looked in horror as he hooked one finger over his towel.

She turned away and Matias laughed softly. Okay, so the woman had somehow reduced him to a level of dithering unheard of. Normally, he approached women and relationships with just exactly the same assured directness with which he approached work. Both were a known quantity and neither induced anything in him other than complete certainty of the outcome.

But with *her*...his taste for revenge had been diluted by desire. What should have been clear-cut had become cloudy. He had vacillated like a hapless teenager between pursuit and withdrawal and had tried to reclaim the loss of his prized self-control only to find it now slipping out of his grasp.

He'd acted out of character and that disturbed him because it never happened.

'You haven't failed,' he said quietly. 'If you give me five minutes, I'll meet you downstairs in the kitchen and we can debrief.'

He headed towards the en-suite bathroom and Sophie fled back down the stairs to the kitchen where she had to take a few seconds to regain her self-control. She was sipping a glass of water when the kitchen door slid open and there he was, drop-dead gorgeous in a white shirt cuffed to the elbows and a pair of black jeans that showed his powerful body off to perfection.

'Have something a bit more exciting than water.' He headed straight for the oversized wine cooler and extracted a bottle of wine and then two glasses. 'You must feel as though you need it. I've thrown you in at the deep end and you've risen to the occasion.' He poured them both a glass of wine, sipped his and then, eyes on her face, tilted his head in a salute.

Sophie cleared her throat. 'Were you expecting me to fail?'

'I thought you would pull through. I didn't think that you would handle the situation with such efficiency. Everyone raved about the food and I was impressed with the way the timetable was adhered to.'

'Thank you.' She blushed and drank some of the wine.

'Naturally, the past few days only cover a proportion of the debt but you've made a start.'

'Will you be in touch about…er…another arrangement so that I can try and schedule my jobs accordingly? Julie did very well handling the cocktail party on her own but she was very nervous and I would rather not put her through that. If I know when you need me, then I can make sure I'm only missing food preparation on the premises rather than in situ at a client's house.'

'No. I can't tailor my timetable to suit your partner, I'm afraid.' He paused, gazed at her, again felt the fierce kick of desire and wondered how he could have been sufficiently short-sighted to have imagined that he could make it disappear on command. It would disappear but only after he'd had her, only when he'd sated a craving that made no sense and had sprung from nowhere. 'Did you enjoy the long weekend?'

'I was under a great deal of pressure,' Sophie confessed stiffly. 'But it was challenging catering for that amount of people. It was the largest party I've ever done.'

'I didn't see you put in an appearance.'

'I was busy overseeing the food. Besides…'

'Besides?'

'What would I have done out there? Asked everyone if they were enjoying the food?'

'You could have circulated, handed out your business cards.'

'I would have felt awkward,' Sophie admitted truthfully. 'Those sort of big bashes aren't my thing. I wouldn't have fitted in.'

'You underestimate your...charms,' Matias said softly. 'I imagine you would have fitted in a great deal better than you think.'

Sophie looked at him and wondered whether she was imagining *something* in his voice, something low and speculative that was sending a shiver down her spine and ratcheting up her painful awareness of him and her heightened reaction to his proximity. Was he actually *flirting* with her? Surely not.

Confused, she stared at him in silence and he stared right back at her, holding her gaze and making no effort to look away. He sipped his wine, gazed at her over the rim of the glass and the effect was devastating.

She was utterly defenceless. She didn't know what he was playing at. This made no sense at all. She was lower than the hired help! She was the hired help plus some!

'I sh-should head upstairs,' she stuttered, half standing on wobbly legs. 'If it's all the same to you, there's nothing left here for me to do. Er...and...if you're satisfied with...with my efforts...then maybe your secretary...can contact me...'

She ran her fingers through her tangled hair and licked her lips because *he was still looking at her with that brooding, veiled expression and it was doing crazy things to her nervous system*.

'And if...if it's okay with you, then I shall get a cab to

the station tonight. I was under the impression that there would be some guests here until tomorrow morning, which is why I was…ah…booked to stay for one final night…' She took a deep breath and exhaled slowly. 'I wish you wouldn't stare at me like that,' she said, licking dry lips.

'Why?'

'Because it makes me feel uncomfortable.'

'Funny, I've never had any complaints from a woman because I haven't been able to keep my eyes off her. On the contrary, they're usually at great pains to make sure that they position themselves directly in my line of vision in the hope that I'll notice them. This is the first time I can genuinely say that I've found myself in the presence of a woman I can't seem to stop looking at.'

Shocked, Sophie literally could find nothing to say. Her vocal cords had dried up. All she could do was stare. He was so ridiculously beautiful that it seemed utterly mad for him to be saying this sort of stuff to her. Even more crazy was the fact that her whole body was surging into overdrive and melting like wax before an open flame.

She wasn't this person! She was level-headed and practical and she knew when and where to draw lines. Not that she had had to draw any since her break-up with Alan. Since then, and that had been over three years ago, men had been put firmly on the back burner and she hadn't once been tempted to dip her toes back into the dating pool. Not once. So why was her body on fire now? Because a guy with too much money, too much charm and too much in the looks department was coming on to her?

'Don't you feel the chemistry between us as well?'

'I don't know what you're talking about,' Sophie whispered and Matias raised his eyebrows in an expression of frank incredulity.

'Of course you do,' he corrected her casually. 'Although,' he continued, 'I understand that you might want to deny it. After all, it's not exactly something either of us bargained on, is it?' No truer words spoken, Matias thought wryly. All things considered, he would have placed greater odds on him catching a rocket to the red planet.

He shrugged eloquently. 'But there you are. These things happen.'

So he fancied her and wanted to have sex with her. Sophie's brain finally cranked into gear and anger began building inside her with the force of suppressed molten lava. He was a rich, powerful man who had her on the run and, because of that, he figured he could come onto her because he happened to find her attractive.

And the worst thing was that he had picked up vibes from her, vibes that had informed him that the pull was mutual. But if he thought that she was now going to fall into bed with him then he had another think coming!

'I'm sorry,' she said coldly, 'but I'm not interested.'

Matias laughed as though she'd cracked a hilarious joke. 'Telling me that you don't feel that electric charge between us?' He noted the blush that crept into her cheeks. 'Ah, yes. Of course you do. You're feeling it now. Why deny it?'

'I won't be...doing anything with you.' She wanted to walk through that door, head held high with contempt and hauteur, because he could buy her services but he *couldn't buy her*, but her feet were nailed to the ground and she found herself standing up but going nowhere.

'You're mistaking me for one of those women who *plant themselves in your line of vision*,' she continued, voice shaking with anger and mortification, 'but I'm not. Yes, I'm here because there's no other way I can pay off the money I owe you, and I can't let my colleague down because she would stand to lose out financially, just as I would if you called the debt in, but that doesn't give you the right to sit there and make a pass at me!'

Her feet finally remembered what they were there for and she stalked towards the door.

The sound of his voice saying her name brought her to an immediate stop. As noiseless as a predator stalking prey, he was right behind her when she spun round and she stumbled backwards a couple of steps, heart beating wildly behind her ribcage, her every sense alert to his commanding presence.

Her nostrils flared, an automatic reaction to the clean, woody scent of whatever aftershave he was wearing.

'Do you honestly think,' Matias asked in a voice that managed to be measured and yet icily condemnatory at the same time, 'that I might actually believe your body comes as part of the repayment schedule for the damage you did to my car?'

Sophie went bright red. Put like that, she could see what an idiot she'd been because when it came to women he certainly didn't need to use any unnecessary leverage. The guy could have whomever he wanted, whenever he wanted.

And he'd wanted her.

That treacherous thought slithered into her head, firing her up against her will.

'I suppose not,' she grudgingly conceded, 'but I

feel vulnerable being here, singing for my supper.' She looked away and then raised her bright blue eyes to his. 'I'm not anything like those women who were here this weekend...'

Matias's eyebrows shot up. 'I didn't think you'd noticed who was here and who wasn't.'

'I saw them coming and going through the kitchen window and some of the guests came on kitchen inspection a few times over the weekend.'

'And?'

'And what? They were all clones of one another. Tall and skinny and glamorous. I assumed that one of them might have been your...er...girlfriend.'

'If I had a girlfriend, we wouldn't be having this conversation.'

'We don't even like one another,' Sophie breathed, 'and *that's* why we shouldn't be having this conversation!'

'Do you have a boyfriend?'

'What if I had? Would it make a difference?'

'Possibly.' He tilted his head to one side. 'Possibly not. Why do you compare yourself to other women?'

'I'm just saying that I'd imagine those women you asked to your house here were exactly the sort of women you normally dated...and so what would you see in someone like me except *easy availability*?' She was playing with fire but the sizzling danger of this treading-on-thin-ice conversation was weirdly and intensely seductive. It was the sort of conversation she had never in her life had before with any man.

'Want me to spell it out for you?' Matias husked. 'Because I will, although I'd rather do that when you're lying naked in my bed.' He vaguely recalled when he

had originally played with the notion of getting her between the sheets because pillow talk might reveal secrets he could use to his advantage. Standing here now,
with a fierce erection that was demanding release, the
only talking he wanted to do in bed was of the dirty
variety. In fact, just thinking about it was driving him
completely nuts.

He didn't know what it was about this woman but
she made him lose his cool.

'And that won't be happening,' Sophie informed him
prissily, edging back, away from the suffocating radius
of his powerful personality. 'Ever!'

'Sure about that?' Matias laughed softly, fired up
on every possible cylinder. 'Because that's not a concept I recognise.'

'Too bad,' Sophie muttered, and then she turned tail
and fled before she could get even more sucked into a
conversation that was dangerously explosive and *dangerously, dangerously exciting.*

Not even the luxury of her accommodation, which
still made her gasp after four nights, or the calming,
long bath she had could clear her head.

Matias's dark, brooding, insanely sexy face swam
in her head, stirring her up and making it impossible
for her to fall asleep and when, finally, she did, it was
a restless, broken sleep until eventually, lying in the
darkened room at nearly two in the morning, she decided that counting sheep wasn't getting her anywhere.

She made her way as quietly as she could towards
the kitchen. Aside from the security lights outside, the
house was shrouded in darkness, which should have
been spooky but was strangely reassuring.

She already knew her way round the kitchen like the

back of her hand and there was no need for her to switch
on any lights as she padded unhesitatingly towards the
fridge to get some milk so that she could make herself
a mug of hot chocolate. Time to find out whether it was
true that hot chocolate encouraged sleep.

Stooping and reaching to the back of the shelf for
the milk, Sophie was unaware of footsteps behind her
and certainly, with only the light from the fridge, there
were no helpful warning shadows cast so the sound of
Matias's voice behind her came as a shock.

She straightened, slammed her head against the
fridge shelf, sent various jars and bottles flying and
stood up as red as a beetroot to confront a highly amused
Matias staring down at her with his arms folded.

CHAPTER FIVE

BROKEN GLASS LAY around her. One of the jars had contained home-made raspberry jam. Sophie had remarked on how delicious it was when she had first had it on a slice of toast a few mornings ago and had been told that Mrs Porter, who lived in the village, made it and sold it in one of the local shops.

Sophie didn't think that Mrs Porter would have been impressed to see her hard work spilled all over the tiled kitchen floor like blobs of gelatinous blood. It joined several gherkins and streaks of expensive balsamic vinegar.

'Don't move,' Matias commanded.

'What are you doing here?' Sophie said accusingly, remaining stock-still because she was barefoot, but horribly aware of her state of undress. She hadn't dressed for company. It was a mild night and she had forsaken her towelling dressing gown and tiptoed downstairs in the little skimpy vest she wore on warm nights and the tiny pair of soft cotton pyjama shorts that left an indecent amount of thigh and leg on display.

Indecent, that was, if you happened to be in a kitchen with the man who had been haunting your dreams kneeling at your feet carefully picking up bits of glass.

He didn't look up at her. He seemed to be one hundred per cent focused on the spray of broken glass around her. Looks, however, could be deceiving for Matias was acutely aware of her standing there in a lack of clothing that was sending his blood pressure through the roof.

'I own the house,' he pointed out with infuriating, irrefutable logic as he continued with his glass retrieval while trying to divert his avid gaze from her fabulously sexy legs, pale and shapely in the shadowy darkness of the kitchen. 'I find that seems to give me the right to come and go as I please.'

'Very funny,' Sophie said tightly.

'I'm here for the same reason you are.' He sat back on his haunches to cast a satisfied look at his cleaning efforts, then he raised his eyes to hers and took his time looking at her. 'I couldn't sleep.'

'Actually, I was sleeping just fine.'

'Which is why you're here at a little after two in the morning?'

'I was thirsty.'

'Stay put. There are probably fine shards of glass on the ground still and I suppose I should clear up all this mess.' He seemed to give that a little thought. 'No. Scratch that. I'll leave the mess but I meant what I said about staying put and the shards of glass. Get a sliver of glass in your foot and you'll probably end up having to be taken to hospital.'

'Don't be ridiculous!' But she daren't move. Bleeding in his kitchen wasn't going to do. Coping with her embarrassing state of semi-nudity was definitely the better option. She would just have to stand here while he took his time removing every piece of glass from the floor.

She could have kicked herself for being so stupid but bumping into him was the last thing she had expected.

Meanwhile, she could barely look down at herself because all she could see was her pale skin, her braless breasts, which were unfashionably big, and her nipples poking against the fine ribbing of her vest.

And all she could do was to make unhelpful comparisons in her head. Comparisons between herself and the women who had been at his party. Next to most of the women there, she was the equivalent of a walking, talking dumpling, and while none of them had been his girlfriend Sophie had no doubt that those were exactly the sort of women he went for. Long and thin with poker-straight hair and faces that seemed to resent the business of occasionally having to smile.

'This could take for ever,' Matias gritted, standing up and peering down at the floor. 'I don't have for ever.' He stepped forward and before she had time to even open her mouth in protest he was scooping her up as though she weighed nothing.

'Good job I was sensible enough to come down here wearing shoes,' he murmured, grinning as he looked down at her.

'Put me down!'

'Not until you're safe and sound and not until I make sure that those very pretty feet of yours are free from any slivers of glass...'

'I'd know if I'd stepped on glass,' Sophie all but sobbed, acutely aware of the way her scraps of clothing were rucking up everywhere. One of her breasts was practically popping out of her vest. She couldn't bear to look. She wasn't wearing underwear and she could feel the petal softness of her womanhood scraping against the side of the pyjama shorts.

And worst of all was what her disobedient body was doing. Turned on by the strength of his arms and the iron-hard broadness of his muscular chest, her nipples were tight and pinched, the rosebud tips straining against the vest, and she was so wet between her legs.

She could only hope that he didn't notice any of that on the way to her room.

She squeezed her eyes shut and didn't open them when she felt him push open a bedroom door.

'Ostrich.' Matias was fully aware of her body, every succulent inch of it, soft and warm in his arms. He could just about see the rosy blush of a nipple peeping out. 'Why have you got your eyes shut?'

Sophie duly opened her eyes, glared at him and then, slowly but surely, it dawned on her that they weren't in her bedroom. He had taken her to a bedroom that was unapologetically male, from the chrome and glass of the fitted wardrobes to the walnut and steel of the bed, over which hung an abstract painting that was instantly recognisable, the bedroom she had frantically backed out of a few hours ago.

'Your bedroom.' She gulped, when her vocal cords finally decided to play ball.

'Let me check your feet.'

'Please, Matias…'

'Please, Matias…*what*?' He deposited her very gently on his bed, as though she were as fragile as a piece of porcelain, but he wasn't looking at her. Instead, he was once again kneeling in front of her and he then proceeded to take one foot in his big hand, to inspect it closely for wayward glass.

It was ludicrous!

But the feel of his hands on her…wreaked havoc with her senses and also felt just so…*sexy*.

Something that sounded very much like a whimper emerged from her throat and their eyes met.

Understanding passed between them, as loud and clear as the clanging of church bells on a still Sunday morning.

Desire. Loud and thick and electric and definitely mutual.

'We can't,' was what Sophie heard herself whimper, breaking the silence between them. She didn't even bother to pretend that she didn't know what was going on any more than he pretended not to recognise the capitulation behind that ragged, half-hearted protest.

'Why not?' Matias had thought about sleeping with her for his own purposes but now he couldn't remember what those purposes were because cold self-control had been replaced with a raging urgency to take her to bed whatever the cost.

'Because this isn't a normal situation.'

'Define normal.'

'Two people who want to have a relationship.'

'I won't deny that I don't do relationships, but sex doesn't always have to lead to a once-in-a-lifetime relationship.'

'Not for you,' Sophie whispered as her resolve seeped away the longer he looked at her with those dark, sinfully sexy eyes. 'But for me…' She turned away and swallowed painfully.

Matias joined her on the bed and gently tilted her head back to his. 'For you?'

'My mother wasn't careful when it came to men,' she

told him bluntly. 'She was very attractive…she had that *something* that men seem to find irresistible…'

'You talk as though that *something* is something you don't possess.'

'I don't,' she said simply, raising her eyes to his and holding his gaze with unwavering sincerity. 'Men have never walked into lampposts when I sauntered past, they've never begged or pleaded or shown up with armfuls of roses in the hope that I might climb into bed with them.'

'And they did all those things for your mother?'

'She had that effect on them.'

'If that were the case, why didn't she and your father marry…considering he fathered a child with her?'

Sophie opened her mouth to tell him that James Carney had fathered more than one child but something held her back. What? Was it her fierce protectiveness over Eric? A need, born of habit, to save him from the curiosity of other people, even though he wouldn't have cared less?

Or was it a hangover from the way Alan had ended up reacting to her disabled brother?

Sophie told herself that she didn't care one way or another what a perfect stranger thought of her situation, least of all someone like Matias. She told herself that if he planned on doing business with her father, then the presence of her disabled brother wouldn't matter a jot, and yet she pulled back from the brink and swallowed down the brief temptation to spill her guts. She was a little startled that she had even been tempted to tell him at all.

'James always thought that he was too good for my mother.' Sophie hid the hurt behind that crisply delivered statement of fact. 'He was rich and he was posh and he didn't think that my mother was the right sort of woman for him.'

Matias's jaw clenched because this came as no surprise at all to him, and Sophie saw his instinctive reaction with a trace of alarm as she remembered how important it was for him to inject money into her father's nearly bankrupt company.

'It happens.' She shrugged and moved on quickly. 'You might fancy me, but you can't pretend that you don't feel the same way about me as he did about my mother. You're rich and powerful and it doesn't matter who my father is or isn't—the fact is that I have never grown up in the sort of circles you would have moved in.'

'You don't know what sort of circles I moved in as a child,' Matias heard himself say. He was uneasily aware that this was a deviation from his normal handling of any sort of *situation* with a woman. Since when had he turned into the sort of touchy-feely person who wanted to waste time talking when a perfectly good bed beckoned?

'I can guess. I'm not stupid.'

'You're anything but stupid. Although it *was* fairly stupid of you to be driving without insurance.'

'Please don't remind me.'

'My parents had no money,' Matias said abruptly. 'They should have but they didn't. I grew up as the kid on the wrong side of the tracks. I went to a tough comprehensive where I learned that the only way to get out in one piece was to be tougher than everyone else, so I was.'

Sophie's mouth fell open, partly because this was so

unexpected but mostly because he was confiding in her and everything was telling her that this was a proud, arrogant man who never confided in anyone.

She felt a little thrill and her heart turned over because the unexpected confidence marked something more between them than *lust*. You didn't confide like that in someone you just wanted to take to bed and throw away afterwards.

Sophie didn't work that out in any way that was coherent or analytical. It was more of a *feeling* that swept through her and in the wake of that *feeling* she softened. *This was how barriers got broken down; this was how defences were surmounted.*

Except she wasn't thinking any of that right now, she was just ensnared by a desire to know more about him.

'Enough talking,' Matias said gruffly, meaning it. 'Because I'm rich and powerful now doesn't mean that I don't fancy you for all the right reasons.'

'Which are what?' Sophie whispered, and Matias dealt her a slow, slashing smile that sent every nerve in her body quivering in high excitement.

'You have a body I would walk over broken glass to touch,' he expanded, not touching her but wanting to with every pore in his body.

'Don't be silly.' She laughed shakily, driven to bring this whole crazy situation down to a prosaic, pedestrian place because she just couldn't quite believe that she was impressionable enough to be swept off her feet by a man like him. 'I'm short and I'm...well covered. The world is full of short, plump women like me. We're a dime a dozen.'

'You're doing it again, running yourself down. You shouldn't, because what you have is more than just a body I could find anywhere.' He laughed. 'You might think that your dear mama failed to pass on that special *something* but you'd be wrong because you definitely have it in bucketloads.'

Don't say that, something in Sophie wanted to yell, but over and above that was a hot yearning at the soft, lazy timbre of his voice and a melting feeling at the way he was looking at her. This was the sort of textbook situation she had always cautioned herself against and yet here she was, blossoming like a flower in the sunshine and wanting this inappropriate man more than she could have ever believed possible.

Belatedly, she realised that her clothes were still askew, her vest tugged down, her shorts scrunched up at the crotch. She shifted and just like that words melted away, replaced by the delicious frisson of burning desire.

Matias straightened. A full moon streamed through the floor-to-ceiling panes of glass, casting a silvery glow through the room. She was so beautiful that he could barely contain himself. And *still* he wasn't sure what she would do if he touched her.

Or what *he* would do if he touched her and she turned away. A cold bath wouldn't begin to sort it out.

He didn't have long to ponder the problem because she took the decision right out of his hands. She reached up and stroked the side of his face, her huge eyes wide, her full mouth softly parted.

Matias caught her hand and drew her finger into his mouth. His gaze didn't leave hers as he sucked it, sucked it so that she knew that that was just how he was going to suck her nipple and, without even realising it, she responded by pushing her breasts out. Her nipples were tingling. Eyes half closed, she gasped when he slid his hand under the vest and cupped her breast.

He still had her finger in his mouth and was still sucking it, and still holding her gaze, his dark eyes lazy and hypnotic as he rolled his finger over the stiffened bud of her nipple. That was all he did and it was enough for her body to shriek into a response that was a hair's breadth away from orgasmic.

It was electrifying.

Sophie moaned. 'I want you.'

Matias held her hand, playing with the wet tip of her finger. 'Your wish is my command. You want me? Rest assured that you will have me, as hard and as often as you want.'

She'd expected him to drive into her without further ado. She could see the hunger in his dark eyes and it matched hers. He didn't. Instead, he arranged her on the bed, straddled her for a few seconds and then slowly pulled down her shorts.

She was so soft, so silky smooth, her skin so pale in the moonlight. He had to stare and even as he stared he did his damnedest to control his breathing, but he was so turned on that he had to make an effort to remember that breathing involved sucking air in and releasing it out.

In one swift movement, he stood up, holding her riveted attention, and stripped off.

Sophie had never seen anything so magnificent in her entire life. No artist would have been able to do justice to the sheer perfection of his body. A broad chest tapered down to a washboard-flat stomach and then lower, to an erection that was impressively huge, a thick, long shaft of steel that made her want to pass out because she was so turned on.

She'd had one serious boyfriend. Her level of experience was very definitely on the lower end of the spectrum and nothing had prepared her for the impact of being in the grip of true, shameless, wanton desire. Desire shorn of everything but a need to live for the moment and take what was on offer. Desire that was looking for nothing beyond the next sixty seconds and the sixty seconds after that.

Sophie would never have believed herself capable of actually *being here and being this person* because it contravened all her principles. But now that she *was* here, she felt wildly, wickedly decadent.

Naked, Matias spread apart her legs and then lowered himself to do something that felt so intimate that she froze for a few seconds.

'Problem?' he purred and she blushed madly.

'I've never had anyone do…that…'

'Then relax and enjoy. Trust me, you'll be begging for more.' With which, he flattened her thighs wide open, hands placed squarely on them, and he lowered his dark head between her legs. His tongue was delicate between her wet folds and then, delving deeper, he found and teased her clitoris until he could feel it throbbing. Her whimpers became cries mixed with moans. Her fingers dived into his dark hair. One minute, she was pushing him down to suck her harder, the next she was tugging him up and squirming in a futile attempt to control her reaction.

Sophie had never, ever felt anything like this before. She hadn't known that this level of pleasure even existed. She half opened her eyes and his dark head moving between her legs made her shudder and gasp. She bucked against his mouth as the rush of building pleasure began to consume her, began to take over her body, then she was coming and she could no more stop the crescendo of her orgasm than she could have stopped a runaway train with the palm of her outstretched hand.

She cried out and then panted and arched and cried out again as she spasmed against his mouth.

It seemed to last for ever.

'Matias…' this when she was finally back down on planet earth '…you shouldn't have…'

'Shouldn't have what?' He had moved up to lie alongside her and he tugged her so that their bodies were pressed so closely against one another that they could have been joined. 'Pleasured you? I wanted to. I wanted to taste you in my mouth when you came.'

'It's not just about me.'

'Kiss me and hold me. You're so beautiful. I want to feel your mouth on me…but first I need to taste your breasts. I've been fantasising about them for so long. I want to see if they taste the way I imagined they do.'

'You've been fantasising about my breasts?'

'It's hardly my fault that they're so damned gloriously big.'

'Too big.'

Matias propped himself up on one elbow to examine them. He circled one nipple with his finger, watched it pinch and stiffen. She had generous full breasts and her nipples were boldly defined circular discs. He leant down and delicately darted his tongue over one and then he suckled on it. It tasted better than his wildest imaginings. Sweet as nectar, yet with the tang of salt.

It throbbed in his mouth as he drew it in and the touch of her hand at the nape of his neck and then curled into his hair was the most powerful aphrodisiac imaginable.

She was so headily responsive and yet she wasn't doing the usual gymnastics that so many of the women he bedded performed, gymnastics they always hoped would impress him enough to cement their staying power in his life.

Sophie was honest in all her responses and her little whimpers of pleasure carried a note that was almost of surprise, as if every touch was new and pretty sensational.

Good God, he thought, hanging on to restraint by a thread, a man could get addicted to this sort of thing. It was just as well that he was cool-headed enough to recognise this for what it was and to recognise himself for what *he* was. He was immune to being snared even by a woman who was driving him crazy.

He guided her mouth to his erection and knew, in the way she hesitated at first, that this was probably new to her as well, and that gave him a kick as powerful as a rocket launcher.

Sophie licked his shaft and enjoyed the way he shuddered. It made her feel more comfortable about coming into his mouth the way she had, with such wild abandon. Then she took him in her mouth and built up a rhythm of sucking that had him groaning out loud as his fingers tangled in her silver-blonde hair.

Her experience ran to the very basic when it came to sex. Her innocent fumblings with Alan, the guy she had thought she might end up marrying, were a thousand light years away from…*this*.

Her body was aching and yearning and tingling all

over again. She released him and lay down again, her back arched, her hair fanning out on the pillow, her eyes closed. He was watching her. She could feel it and it thrilled her.

When she sneaked a peek, she blushed shyly and was tempted to cover her breasts with her hands but she didn't.

'I want you,' Matias groaned heavily and she sighed and smiled at the same time, not quite believing what they were doing but wanting more of it and wanting it *now*.

'Then take me,' she whispered.

The seconds it took for him to fetch a condom and put it on felt like hours because she was so hot for him.

She parted her legs and then the joy and pleasure of him entering her made her heart swell and turned her on in every corner of her body. He thrust long and deep and hard and built a rhythm that started slow, getting firmer and stronger until their bodies were moving as one.

She was so tuned into him…it felt as though they had been lovers for ever. She knew when he was going to come as surely as she knew when *she* was, and when he groaned and arched back, his big, powerful body shuddering, she, too, felt her own body ascending to a climax, coming along with him, moving to the same primitive beat.

Spent, Sophie lay in his arms. His breathing was still a shallow rasp and she could feel the perspiration binding their bodies, making them hot and slippery. It felt so good and she wriggled and nestled into him, enjoying the way his arms clasped around her.

Did she fall asleep? She must have done although when she drowsily opened her eyes she was still wrapped in his arms, his thigh between her legs, her breasts squashed against his chest.

Half asleep, she reached down to touch him and felt the immediate stir of his body as he came to life in her hands. He was no more awake than she was. He was warm and half asleep and so was she, and the merging of their bodies was as natural and instinctive as the rising and setting of the sun or the changing of the tides.

When she woke the following morning, the sun was creeping into the room, weak and grey. There was a fine drizzle of rain. Where was Matias? Not lying next to her. Sophie yawned and shifted, turning onto her side to find him working at the desk by the window.

Matias heard the sound of her stirring and immediately stiffened because this whole situation had unnerved him. The sex had been amazing but afterwards…

Hell, they had fallen asleep together, wrapped around one another like clambering vines. Sleeping was something he did on his own. Women lay in his bed for sex but retreated to another bed for sleep or, better still, cleared off. Yet he had thought nothing of falling asleep with her in his arms, and then, in the middle of the night, they had made love again, and without protection. He'd barely been awake and it had been the most mind-blowing experience of his life, almost dreamlike and yet at the same time so exquisitely *real*. Their bodies had joined together and fused and he'd come explosively.

And now…

'We didn't use contraception.' He swivelled to face her, his body already responding to her warm, flushed face and the peep of her soft, generous breasts. He wanted to have her again immediately and that unnerved him as well.

'Huh?'

'Last night. You woke me up and we made love without protection.'

Sophie shot up into a sitting position, pulling her knees towards her. 'I—I didn't think…' she stammered. She wouldn't be pregnant. She *couldn't* be pregnant. Alarm and dismay flooded her face. 'There's no way there could be an accident,' she shot back, eyes huge. 'It's the wrong time of the month for me…'

Was it? She was too fraught to do the maths.

'And I couldn't be *that* unlucky.'

Disconcerted, Matias frowned. 'Unlucky?'

Sophie leapt out of the bed, belatedly remembered that she was buck naked and dragged the duvet out to cover her. Having sex with no protection had catapulted him right back to the conniving girlfriend who had almost booked herself a trip down the aisle on the back of a fake pregnancy scare, but the horror writ large on Sophie's expressive face was telling a different story and as she scuttled away from him his instinct wasn't to pursue his accusations. His instinct was to chase her right back into his bed.

'Do you honestly think I would *want* to find myself pregnant by *you*?' Her voice was high and unsteady.

Matias stood up, as sleek and graceful as a panther, and as dangerous to her state of mind. 'Why are you bothering to try and cover yourself? I've seen you in your birthday suit and, besides, your left breast is out.'

Sophie looked down and was confronted by the sight of her pink nipple perkily defying her attempts at concealment. When she raised her eyes again it was to find Matias standing right in front of her. He had slipped on his boxers to work but aside from that he was gloriously naked and she almost fainted at the surge of desire that swept through her like a tidal wave.

'You don't mean it when you say that you'd be unlucky if you discovered you were pregnant by me,' he grated and Sophie glared at him.

'You're *so* arrogant.'

'You like it.'

'You're *so* not my type.'

'You like that too. It's boring when you're with someone who's just like you. Where's the excitement in that?'

'I don't want exciting. I've *never* wanted exciting. My mother wasted most of her life *wanting exciting*.'

'You're not your mother,' Matias returned without skipping a beat, settling his hands on her soft shoulders and gently massaging them. 'And you may not want *exciting* but that doesn't mean that your goal in life should be to settle for *deadly dull*. I'm taking it,' he continued, the low, lazy drawl of his voice sending shivers up and down her spine, 'that you're putting me in the *exciting* category.'

'This isn't funny, Matias!'

'It's anything but,' he agreed. 'Especially,' he surprised himself by adding, 'considering I had a narrow escape with a woman who claimed to be pregnant so that she could get me to put a wedding band on her finger.'

'What?' Sophie tried to recapture some of the anger she had felt but his fingers were doing things to her body and she was relaxing and unbending and turning into a rag doll at his touch.

She was also, she discovered, heading back to the bed, a fact she only realised when she toppled back onto the mattress, with the duvet flying off her, leaving him in no doubt that, for all her protests, she was most definitely turned on by him. The tips of her nipples were stiff peaks and the rub of wetness between her legs was practically audible.

Matias didn't give her time to think. He'd never considered himself the sort of guy who could fall prey to the mindless demands of his body, but he was discovering that that was just the sort of guy she turned him into. It wasn't going to last longer than a heartbeat so why, he thought, shouldn't he just yield and enjoy the once-in-a-lifetime experience?

He shoved her over so that he could take up position lying next to her and before she could start protesting he slipped his hands between her legs and edged his finger into her, feeling her wetness with a soft moan of satisfaction.

'Stop doing that,' Sophie protested, squirming half-heartedly to distance herself from his exploring fingers. 'I can't think when you do that. You're arrogant and you have a nerve implying that I would be the sort of girl who would engineer a pregnancy to try and get you up the aisle!'

'Did I imply that?'

'Yes, you did! What girlfriend?'

Matias lay back and stared up at the ceiling. 'I was young and cocky and on my way up. I thought I knew it all and could take on anything. Turned out I was no match for a woman who wanted to start at ground zero with me. She'd spotted my potential. I was already a massive earner by then and driving around like a strutting bull in a red Ferrari.'

'Obnoxious, in other words,' Sophie muttered darkly, but she was secretly won over by the way he could mock himself.

'Very,' Matias confirmed drily. 'She told me she was pregnant. Turned out she wasn't but that was something I only discovered by accident.'

'You told me I'm not my mother,' Sophie ventured, still on the defence and still smarting but wanting him so badly it hurt, 'and I'm not your ex-girlfriend.' She wasn't going to curl into him, which was what she wanted to do, but she wasn't turning away either. She couldn't.

'And now that we've established that…' he moved his hand away from the dampness between her legs to her breast and the teasing pink nipple begging to be licked '…why don't we skip breakfast and carry on with our magical mystery tour of one another?'

'I have to get back to London,' Sophie said raggedly, her body already quivering in acquiescence.

'No, you don't. Have you forgotten that you have a debt to settle?'

'Not like this!'

'No,' Matias agreed seriously, 'not like this, but I *would* like to commission you to cook me breakfast and I'm not hungry yet, at least not for food.'

'Matias…'

'I want you in my bed, Sophie, and then, when we've made love and I've pleasured you in every way I know how, I would like to employ you to prepare breakfast for me because there's still the matter of that pesky debt to be paid off. Will you do that?'

'I'll do that.' Sophie frowned. 'But when we leave here…'

Matias raised his eyebrows and teased the fluff between her legs until he could see her thoughts getting all tangled up in her head. 'Hmm…?'

'When we leave here,' she panted, giving in as he

knew she would, 'none of this happened. Okay? I go back to being the caterer you employ so that I can pay off the money I owe you. It's back to business.'

'Sure,' he agreed smoothly, wanting her even more now that she was setting just the sort of rules and regulations that should, in theory, appeal to him, because they were exactly the ones he would set himself. 'But enough talking...'

CHAPTER SIX

FOR THE FIRST time since she had arrived, Sophie was able to appreciate Matias's sprawling mansion at leisure because she stayed to cook him breakfast the following morning and the morning after that.

'But I thought all the guests had gone,' Julie had proffered in a puzzled voice, when Sophie had phoned and told her the situation.

Sophie had muttered something and nothing about not all the guests having gone just yet, and what choice did she have considering she was indebted to the man and so had to do as he commanded or else face having their business dismantled like a house of Lego bricks in the hands of a hyperactive toddler.

She could just about extrapolate sufficient truth from what she had said to paper over her guilt at playing truant, because that was what it felt like.

She was preparing breakfast for Matias but that was just a nonsense excuse for what she was really doing. She was his lover and she was enjoying every second of it. Having curled up into herself after her experience with Alan, she was feeling liberated in a way she had never hoped to be. She was, she felt, on a journey of self-discovery and she had stopped asking herself how that was possible when Matias was so unsuitable. She just knew that he gave something to her, added some crazy dimension to her life that made her forget all the principles she had spent her life nurturing.

She was being reckless for the first time in her life and she was liking it.

You're not your mother, Matias had told her and she had actually listened and allowed herself to unbend and live a little without beating herself up about it. Okay, so Matias wasn't going to be around for ever but that didn't mean that she was going to suddenly develop a taste for inappropriate men. No, Matias was her walk on the wild side and why shouldn't she enjoy him while she had the chance?

He was rich, he was powerful, he was arrogant and he was self-assured to the point of ridiculous, but he was also, she had discovered, an extremely thoughtful lover, a good laugh, was weirdly tuned into her thoughts and just so, so unbelievably clever.

Hovering on the fringes of her enjoyment, however, was the looming certainty that he wouldn't be around for much longer, although when she thought about that a guilty little voice whispered in her head, *But won't he be...? After all, you'll still have to pay off the rest of your debt...maybe there'll be more breakfasts to be prepared...*

Breakfast this morning had been an elaborate con-coction of eggs, spinach, ham and a hollandaise sauce on freshly baked bread.

The smell of the bread still lingered in the kitchen as Sophie tidied away the dishes while Matias reclined at the kitchen table like a lord and master, replete after having his appetite sated.

She turned around and he beckoned her across and patted his lap.

'Sit,' he commanded with a grin, watching as she sashayed towards him, fresh as a flower without make-up and sexy as hell in some cut-off faded jeans and a baggy tee shirt.

She wasn't wearing a bra. He liked her without one. He liked being able to reach out and touch her without having to go through the bother of unclasping boring fastenings.

They'd been larking around for two days like teen-agers and Matias still couldn't get enough of her. He hadn't steered the conversation towards her father again. Hadn't even thought about it. The only thing on his mind had been her fabulous body and what it did to him.

'Nice breakfast,' he murmured as she settled obedi-ently on his lap. He slipped his hand under the tee shirt, found the generous swell of her breast and the tight bud of her nipple, then he lifted the shirt and angled her so that she was straddling him and began suckling at her breast.

He had no idea what she possessed that could make him act like a horny teenager but she had it. In his saner moments, he remembered who she was and what his original plan had been in getting her to repay her debt by working for him. Unfortunately, those saner mo-ments had been rarer than hen's teeth.

Watching her bustle about his kitchen, in a parody of domesticity that should have sent him running for the hills, had kick-started a nice little erection and suck-ing her nipple now was intensifying it to the point of painful.

He shifted under her and felt her smile as she reached

down and found his hard shaft, holding it firmly but getting little traction because of his jeans.

Too little traction. He adjusted his big body and, reading him and responding instinctively, Sophie slid off his lap, discarding her tee shirt along the way, and then she eased off his trousers with a little help from him.

He was so beautiful he took her breath away. She couldn't believe that in a space of just a few days she had moved from novice to wanton, had blossomed under his touch like a plant given life-saving nutrients. He'd encouraged her to touch, to experiment, to wallow in his open adoration of her body. He'd been a masterful teacher. He'd lavished attention on every inch of her body and taught her just how to touch him and where to make him feel good.

Now, with his trousers and boxers in a heap on the ground, she took his thick shaft between her hands and played with him, absolutely enjoying the way he slid a little further down the chair and loving the guttural moan that escaped his lips. His hand cupped the crown of her head as she took him into her mouth and his fingers curled into her hair as she began to suck.

They were in their private paradise, a delicious bubble where they had been able to indulge their appetite for one another without interruption, a bubble in which thoughts and conjectures and *reality*, at least *for her*, had not been allowed to intrude.

She stood up, noting that his eyes were closed, those thick, lush lashes casting shadows on his razor-sharp cheekbones. His nostrils were flared. He knew what she was going to do and was lazily waiting to be pleasured.

Sophie couldn't get her jeans and underwear off fast

enough. He did that to her, made her whole body agitate with an urgency to be satisfied. She was wet between her legs, dripping, aching to have him inside her.

She knew where he kept his condoms and quickly fetched one from the wallet in his trousers on the ground. They had made love without protection that one single time and never again. Now, she slipped a condom out of its foil and took him between her hands so that she could put it on him.

His eyes were slumberous on her, hotly working her up to a peak of excitement, and she groaned out loud as she lowered herself onto him, her every nerve ending tingling as he circled her waist with his big hands, then she was moving on him, pressing down to feel him deep inside her, letting him take her to places only he could.

He levered her head towards him and kissed her as she moved on him, a deep, hungry, urgent kiss that made her moan and then she was coming, hurtling towards that peak of satisfaction, her body moving in perfect rhythm with his until the world exploded and all she could feel was the intense pleasure of her climax that went on and on, subsiding eventually in little, erotic waves that left her shaking and trembling.

She sagged against him, head against his chest, listening to his slow, ragged breathing that very gradually returned to normal. They were both practically slipping off the chair and she reluctantly climbed off him and began sticking back on her clothes.

He looked so peaceful there, his big body relaxed, his eyes half closed as he watched her scramble to put on her tee shirt and then hop into her underwear.

He wasn't at all self-conscious about his body. Where, even now that they had made love what felt like a thousand times, she still needed to put on her clothes rather than parade her nudity, he couldn't care less.

He stood up, flexed his muscles and looked at her sideways with a satisfied smile.

'Work is beginning to call,' he drawled, eyeing the puddle of clothes on the ground and deigning to put on his jeans but nothing else. 'She's an extremely demanding mistress.'

'Yes, I have to get back as well.' Sophie's heart sank but she smiled brightly at him. 'Julie's beginning to tear her hair out because we've just landed a pretty big order and it's hard planning a menu together over text or on the phone.'

'You still owe me for my car...' He swerved round her and, standing behind, wrapped his arms around her waist and leant down so that he was talking into her hair, his voice a little muffled.

Sophie literally thrilled. She couldn't help grinning from ear to ear. She knew that this situation wasn't going to last and was probably the least sensible thing she could be doing but the pull of having fun was irresistible. She couldn't think beyond it.

'But,' Matias continued gravely, 'you're paying off the debt quickly. That said... I might still need you to do some catering for me and I rather enjoy the private catering you've been providing, by which I mean those excellent breakfast options you've presented to me.'

Sophie swivelled round so that they were facing one another and she looked up at him. 'I like cooking you breakfast,' she told him. 'Do we...er...put a date in the diary? How does this work?' She sighed and reached up to link her fingers behind his neck. 'I mean, Matias, how does this *really* work? Is there a time frame? And if I choose to stop…*this*…then what happens? I feel vulnerable thinking that we've entered new territory.'

'Do you think I'm going to penalise you if you decide you want to stop being my lover? I won't. I'm not that kind of guy. You're free to make your choice. I still want you, Sophie, but there's no way I want you to feel that you're somehow committed to pleasing me for fear of what I might do if you change your mind.'

The bubble was beginning to burst. They weren't going to be in one another's company twenty-four-seven, making love, talking, making love again. True, Matias had taken himself off for brief periods to work, during which time she had video called Julie so that she, too, could remember that real life was going on outside his glasshouse mansion, but most of their time had been spent in one another's company.

Living in the moment had been easy. She had been able to turn a blind eye to real life because real life was located somewhere outside the glass and concrete of his house. Real life was back in London. Well, they were returning to London soon and although she had told him that, once they left, what they had would come to an end, she didn't want it to end and that frightened her.

They hadn't mentioned actual numbers at all in terms of the money she still owed him for the damage to his car. She didn't care about that because she had discovered that, despite the fact that he could be stunningly arrogant, he was also incredibly fair and incredibly honourable.

What did concern her was the deal he was considering making with her father. That, too, was a subject that hadn't been raised, but it would be just as soon as they drove away from their little bubble and the real world started to intrude. She had promoted James Carney as someone he *should* deal with, had sidestepped most of the truth about her father because what was at stake was the fate of her beloved brother.

Suddenly it was vitally important that she tell him about Eric. She didn't have to compromise any deal Matias wanted to do with her father, but at least when the deal was done and should her father show his true colours, *which wasn't inevitable because he would be on the back foot*, Matias would put two and two together and understand why she had done what she had, why she hadn't warned him off.

Not that, Sophie feverishly told herself, there would be any problems. Her father was broke. He needed Matias. He would be on best behaviour.

'Good,' she said vaguely, wondering how to send the conversation in the direction in which she wanted it to go and finally deciding to just say what she had to say. 'And about my father…'

'Yes?' Matias's ears pricked up. He marvelled that this was the first time Carney had been mentioned in their couple of days alone together when the original purpose of her being here was to provide information that he could use. It irked him that he had been so sidetracked by her that he had taken his eye off the ball.

'Will you still…er…be interested in investing money in his company?' Sophie had the whole back story about Eric prepared for Matias and was a little taken aback at the sudden deathly silence that greeted her question.

'Ah. We haven't discussed that, have we?'

'I guess there have been a few distractions.' She laughed nervously.

'So there have.' Matias looked at her coolly, his quick

brain putting two and two together and not liking what he was coming up with.

'What's wrong?'

'What makes you think that something's wrong, Sophie?'

'I don't know. What have I said? I just thought that… we're going to be leaving here and I wanted to talk about what happens next.'

'Why would that lead to a discussion of my plans for your father? But now that we're on the subject…you've, apparently, no idea about the ugly business of making money, but did you know your father is…shall we say… battling one or two financial problems…?' Matias was watching her intently and he was as still as a statue.

She knew. It was there, written plainly on her face. She'd played the clueless card, but she'd known all along that her old man was broke. She wasn't even trying to deny it.

'And,' Matias continued, testing the ground as the steady burn of rage began to build inside him, 'of course, if any deal is to go through, then there will have to be certain background checks…'

'Background checks?' she squeaked.

Matias shrugged but he was picking up everything he wanted to know and more from her reaction. 'The business community is a small world. There have been certain rumours of shady dealings…'

Sophie's face drained of colour. Her legs felt shaky. Her brain was in meltdown as she thought of what would be revealed in *background checks*. She knew nothing for sure, but she suspected…

'Surely that wouldn't be necessary,' she whispered.

'Oh, dear.' Used. He'd been used. She'd slept with

him to facilitate a deal with her father whom she knew to be penniless and crooked. She was clearly running scared from background checks that she must know could open up a can of worms. He'd got the information he'd wanted after all, but the fury of finding himself played once again was volcanic in its intensity. 'You seem apprehensive. Did you think that you could *distract* me into putting money into your bank account without doing my homework thoroughly?'

Sophie's face drained of colour as she tried to make sense of what he was saying but the dots weren't joining up. What was he implying?

Some part of her was desperate to give him the benefit of the doubt and to find a reasonable explanation for the cold, veiled expression on his handsome face but a chill was growing inside her and it make her feel sick and giddy.

'I d-don't know what you're talking about,' she stammered.

'Don't you?' Not even his duplicitous ex-girlfriend from long ago had managed to produce a rage like this. He'd learned *nothing* because he'd been conned again. If he'd smashed his fist against the wall, he would have driven it right through the brickwork, so powerful was the torrent of emotion coursing through his body. 'I don't know why I didn't stop to question your sudden departure from shy and blushing to hot and ready for sex.'

'That's an awful thing to say!'

'If memory serves me right, you had your claws out when we first met…'

'Because you were horrible to me! Because you threatened to shut down my business to pay off a debt!'

'But then we came to a satisfactory conclusion, didn't we? But when did you decide to hop in the sack with me? Was it when you found out that I might decide to have business dealings with your father? Did you think that you were clever in trying to withhold the true state of your father's coffers and the fact that he's a crook? Did you think that your sexy body would seal the deal for me regardless of that?'

Sophie stared at him round-eyed. She was looking at a stranger. Gone was the teasing, seductive guy who could turn her off and on like a light switch.

'No! I would never do something like that! The only reason I mentioned my father and…well…is because I wanted to tell you something that…'

Matias held up one imperious hand. 'Not interested. The fact is there's something you should know.' He killed the tight knot in the pit of his stomach. Sex was sex but business was business and this was the business of retribution and he'd been a fool to have ever been distracted by her gorgeous body and beautiful, duplicitous face.

Sophie was spellbound, filled with creeping dread and apprehension. He was pacing the kitchen, restless and somehow vaguely menacing in the soft prowl of his movements.

'Regrettably, you've got hold of the wrong end of the stick. The fact is, the only interest I have in your father won't be leading to any lucrative deals that might result in more money lining your pockets.' He looked at her flushed face narrowly and it got on his nerves that he half wanted her to deny that she had any interest in any of her father's money that might come her way, but she remained silent and he could tell from the expression on her face that money trickling down into her grasping little hands had been exactly what she had hoped for.

She'd turned into his compliant lover because sex was a most persuasive tool. His mouth tightened and cold hostility settled like glacial ice in his veins.

'You don't understand,' Sophie protested weakly, but everything seemed to be moving at bewildering speed and her brain couldn't keep up.

'I think I understand very well indeed. But here's what *you* don't understand. Not only will I *not* be putting money into your father's business, but my intention couldn't be more different. I won't be the making of your bankrupt, disreputable scumbag of a father. I will be the ruination of him.' He clenched his jaw as her mouth fell open and the colour drained away from her face. 'You may not remember but I mentioned in passing to you that my parents should have had money and all the little luxuries that go with the sort of well-oiled lifestyle your daddy dearest enjoyed, but sadly they didn't.'

'I remember… I meant to ask you about that…but…'

'Distractions…ah, yes, they got in the way.' Matias smiled coldly. 'Let me fill in the gaps. Your father stole my father's invention and used it to prop up the sad sack company he had inherited that was already on its last legs, and in the process made himself rich beyond most people's wildest dreams. My father was naïve and trusting, a simple emigrant who believed the rubbish your father told him about them going in as partners, jointly reaping the financial rewards of something my father invented. I know, because I've seen the proof of those conversations with my own eyes in letters that were kept in a folder. It never occurred to my parents that they could have taken the man through the courts and got what they deserved.'

'No.' But she already believed every word that was being said because that was very much the sort of thing her father would have done.

'My father never recovered from the betrayal of his trust. What your father did infected every area of my family's life. My father died prematurely from a rare cancer and do you want to hear the worst of it? I recently found more letters, hidden away amongst my mother's things, begging letters from my mother to your father, pleading for some money to send my father to America where groundbreaking work was being done in that area, clinical trials that were beyond my parents' meagre means.'

'I'm so sorry,' Sophie whispered brokenly.

'So,' Matias rammed home, every syllable filled with icy condemnation made all the more biting because he knew that he had allowed himself to drift into territory he should never have occupied, 'my intention was always to make your father pay for what he did.'

'What are you saying?'

'I think you know. I knew about Carney's penury. I wanted more information and I got it. A stint in jail seems appropriate considering what he did, wouldn't you agree? So thank you for corroborating what I suspected. Now I know exactly which rocks to turn over when I have your daddy's company in my hands.'

A wave of sickness swept through her. She had accepted that they were ships passing in the night and had justified her extraordinary response to him on all sorts of grounds about lust and desire, but now that the extent of his deception was unravelling in front of her she knew that she had felt a great deal more for him than lust or desire.

He had managed in drawing out a side of her that she hadn't known existed. He had made her laugh and forget all the worries that plagued her. When she had been with him, she had stopped being the girl who had been let down by an ex, the girl who had to grovel for handouts, the girl with the disabled brother whom she fiercely protected, the girl whose career could crash and burn at any moment, leaving her nowhere. When she'd been with Matias, unlikely as it was, she had been carefree and sexy and *young*.

But that had been an illusion because he had used her to get information about her father out of her, and the depth of her hurt was suffocating.

'I played right into your hands with that accident, didn't I?' Her voice was stilted but despair, as toxic as acid, was filling every corner of her. 'You don't care a jot that *I* never hurt your family.' She wasn't going to try and explain anything about Eric to him now, nothing at all, and she hated herself for allowing him to get so close, close enough for her to have been tempted to open up about her beloved brother. This ruthless, unfeeling man in front of her wouldn't even care. 'Did you even fancy me?' Tears stung the backs of her eyes. She was asking questions and she didn't want to know the answers but she couldn't help herself.

Matias flushed darkly. It pained him to see the wounded hurt in her eyes but he wasn't going to be sidetracked by that. This time he was going to stick to the brief. No way was he going to let her swing the tables round and cast him in the role of the criminal.

She'd been after money and that was the long and short of it, end of story.

'I should have stopped to ask myself why a man like you would have looked twice at me,' Sophie continued bitterly.

'Can you deny,' Matias intoned coldly, 'that you wanted me to pour money into your father's company because you knew that, if I did, some of it would inevitably come your way?'

Sophie closed her eyes.

She had needed that money but she would die before she explained it to him now. Instead she had to accept that she had been a tool to be exploited by him in his search for revenge. They hadn't been getting closer. That had all been in her stupid mind because he hated her for a crime she hadn't committed.

Matias noted that she couldn't even meet his eyes and he bunched his fists, resisting the urge to punch something very, very hard. He was uncomfortable in his own skin and that enraged him. He moved to the door, remained there for a few seconds, his body deathly still and yet seeming to exude a savage, restless energy.

'Our return to London will mark the end of any relationship between us.'

'But what about the money I still owe you?' Panicked, she licked her lips nervously.

'Do you honestly think that I would want to set eyes on you ever again, Sophie?'

Tears gathered at the backs of her eyes and she swallowed painfully, not wanting to cry in front of him but fearing that she would. Her heart was thundering inside her and her head was beginning to hurt.

'You're going to take my company away from me,'

she said flatly. 'You don't care who you hurt in your desire for revenge. It doesn't matter that I had nothing to do with whatever my father did to your father.'

Matias's jaw clenched. His eyes drifted down from her defiant heart-shaped face to the body he had so recently taken and he was furious that, in defiance of the hostile atmosphere simmering between them, his body was still insisting on responding to hers with unbridled gusto.

He harshly reminded himself that whatever she trotted out, nothing could excuse the fact that she had tried to encourage him to open dealings with her father because she'd wanted his money. Whatever guise it took, the apple never fell far from the tree. Greed was in her blood and nothing else mattered.

'Consider the debt to me paid in full,' he gritted. 'I won't be going after your company so you can breathe a sigh of relief. I walk through this door and all dealings between us, as I've said, come to an end. I will instruct my secretary to email you confirming that you no longer owe me anything for the damage to my car and you should consider yourself fortunate, because there are no limits for me when it comes to getting justice for what your father did to mine. In life, there is always collateral damage.'

Being referred to as *collateral damage* just about said it all, Sophie thought, devastated. Thank goodness, she hadn't confided in him about Eric. Thank goodness she hadn't allowed him even further into her heart.

'I shall go and pack my stuff up and then I think I'll get a taxi to the station and take the first train back to London.'

'My driver will deliver you to your house. In the

meantime, I have ignored work demands because of certain *distractions*.' His mouth curled into a sardonic smile. 'It's time for me to return to normality and not a moment too soon.'

Every word that passed his beautiful mouth was a dagger deep into the core of her but, no, she wasn't going to break down in front of him. She wasn't going to let him see how far he had already burrowed into her.

She nodded curtly and remained where she was as he turned his back on her and walked out of the kitchen.

Then and only then did her whole body sag, like a puppet whose strings had been abruptly cut.

But only for a few minutes, a few minutes during which she breathed deeply and did her best to find the silver lining in the cloud. It was what she had spent a lifetime doing. She'd done it every time she visited her brother and reminded herself that life with him in it, however damaged he was, was so much better than life without him in it. She'd done it every time she'd gone to her father, cap in hand, to beg for the money needed to keep Eric safe and happy, and left with the cash.

She would do it again now, and she would thank her lucky stars that she hadn't had the opportunity to emotionally invest even further in a guy who'd used her. And she'd thank her lucky stars that her debt to him was repaid in full.

But, as she got ready to leave, flinging her possessions in the case she had brought with her, her heart was still telling her that life was never going to be the same again.

CHAPTER SEVEN

SOPHIE LOOKED AT the innocuous white stick with the two bright blue lines and felt a wave of nausea surge through her all over again.

This was the third pregnancy test she had done and still her mind refused to compute the enormity of what was staring her in the face. She was sorely tempted to use the last one in the box but she knew that she had to accept the horrible, terrifying truth that she was pregnant. One reckless mistake had resulted in the baby growing inside her. She could do a hundred more tests and nothing was going to change that inalterable fact.

She was having Matias's baby.

A guy who had played her, used her and then discarded her without a backward glance. It had been a little over five weeks since she had last seen him, disappearing through the kitchen door of his over-the-top hillside mansion. Since then she had received a formal email from his secretary informing her that all monies owing to him had been cancelled. Since then, her father's company had gone into liquidation and was now in the process of being eaten up by Matias's sprawling empire. Sophie knew that because it had been on the news. Her father, needless to say, wanted no more to do with her because of the situation he was in. He had no more money to give her and the last time she had seen him, he had angrily accused her of helping to send him to the poorhouse. He'd conveniently overlooked the fact that the failure of his company had been down to his own incompetence and she had not reminded him, choosing instead to walk away and deal with the problems the bankruptcy presented to her brother's future.

Had Matias put the final nail in the coffin and sent the police after her father as well? She didn't know. If so, that was a further public humiliation to come.

Released from having to maintain appearances for the sake of his peers, she and Eric had been cut loose and Sophie had spent every night for the past fortnight trying to find a solution to the problem of how to keep her brother in the safe home he had grown accustomed to.

She was stressed beyond belief and now this had happened.

'You'll have to tell him,' was the first thing Julie said to her later that morning when she showed up at the house.

Sophie looked at her friend, utterly defeated and without a silver lining in sight. 'How can I?' she asked, remembering how they had parted company and feeling the stamp of pride settle in her like a stone. 'You know what happened, you know...' her voice cracked and she took a deep breath and continued in a rush '... what his motives were for getting involved with me.'

'But this is no longer about your father, Soph, or whatever revenge Matias Rivero was after. This is about a new life growing inside you that can't be made to take the blame for a situation he or she had nothing to do with.'

Sophie knew that in her heart of hearts. How could she withhold the baby's existence from his own flesh and blood? Matias would have to know but only because she could see no other way around it. She would have to make sure he knew that she *wanted nothing from him*. She didn't care how much money he had. As far as she was concerned, she would do the right thing and tell him about the baby, but after that she would walk away.

And he would be able to breathe a sigh of relief because she knew that the last person he would want to see show up at his office, again, would be her.

First time, she had shown up having crashed into his car. Now, she would be showing up with a baby-shaped wrecking ball solidly aimed at his life.

She could remember just how she had felt that first time she had shown up at his impressively scary office headquarters and spoken to the receptionist. Sick with nerves at an uncertain outcome, and yet with just enough hope that everything would be okay because although she wasn't going to be seeing the very empathetic Art Delgado, deep down she had clung to the belief that the guy she *would* be seeing might be cut from the same cloth.

One day later, as Sophie yet again stood outside the impressive building that housed Matias's legendary empire headquarters, hope was nowhere in existence.

She had had several hours to get her head round her situation and yet she was no nearer to locating any silver linings.

She strode into the glass building with a great deal more confidence than she was feeling and asked for Matias with the sort of assurance that implied an audience would be granted without argument.

'It's a personal matter,' she added to a frowning young blonde girl, just in case. 'I think Matias... *Mr Rivero*...would be quite upset if you don't inform him that I'm here. Sophie Watts. He'll know who I am and it's urgent.'

Would he see her? Why should he? His parting shot had been that he never wanted to set eyes on her again, even if that involved kissing sweet goodbye to the thousands of pounds she still owed him.

About to go to the boardroom to close a multimillion-pound deal, Matias was interrupted by his secretary and told that Sophie was in the foyer several stories below.

For approximately two seconds, he debated delivering a message back that he was unavailable.

He didn't. He'd walked away from her weeks ago but hadn't managed to escape whatever malign influence she had over him. She'd lodged under his skin like a burr, appearing like a guilty conscience just when he least needed it and haunting his dreams with infuriating regularity.

Everything was going nicely when it came to dismantling her father's company, ensuring that the man was left standing out in the cold with no shelter in sight. Behind the scenes, further revelations would come when he moved to phase two, which would involve the long arm of the law. An eye for an eye.

It should have given him an additional sense of satisfaction that his daughter, whose greed had matched her father's, would also be standing in the same cold spot, without any shelter on the horizon. Unfortunately, every time he tried to muster the appropriate levels of satisfaction at a job well done, the image of her soft heart-shaped face popped into his head, giving him pause for thought.

Revenge had been served cold, but it was not as sweet as it should have been.

It didn't help that his mother had read all about the takeover in the newspapers and had summoned him to the hospital where she was recovering nicely. She'd never agreed with his thirst for retribution and nothing had changed on that front.

All in all, he was pleased that he had done what he had done, because as far as he was concerned those wheels of justice had to turn full circle, but he was surprised at how dissatisfied he remained at what should have been a stunning victory of the present over the past. And he knew it was all down to Sophie.

'Show her up,' he told his secretary in a clipped voice, instantly deciding to put his meeting on hold, regardless of the value of the deal. 'And tell Jefferies and his team that Bill Hodgson will be handling the initial closing stages.' He ignored the startled look on her face because such an about-face was unheard of.

His mind was already zooming ahead to what Sophie might want from him.

Money was the first and only thing that came to mind. She had encouraged a deal with her father so that she could benefit from the financial injection. No deal meant no financial injection, which meant that she still wanted money, except it wasn't going to come from her dear papa.

He was outraged that she would try her luck with him. He knew that he certainly shouldn't be allowing her any chink through which she might try and slip. But he couldn't resist the opportunity to see her and he was, he acknowledged, curious to see what approach she would take to try and wheedle cash out of him.

Would she shoot him one of those sweet, innocent, butter-wouldn't-melt-in-her-mouth smiles? The kind of smile that instantly went to his groin and induced all manner of erotic, dirty, sexy scenarios in his head? He got a kick imagining her sashaying into his office, hot for sex. He'd send her on her way, but he still experienced a massive surge of desire playing with the thought.

The single knock on his door found him relaxing in his chair, his hands loosely linked on his washboard-flat stomach, his expression one of mild curiosity.

'Yes.' The door opened, his secretary stood to one side and there she was, tentatively walking into his office, blushing in the way that would send any normal, red-blooded man's pulse through the roof. She was wearing a pair of grey trousers and a white blouse and his eyes immediately dropped to the soft swell of her breasts and, right on cue, his brain lurched off at a predictable tangent, remembering exactly what those luscious breasts had felt like, had tasted like. 'What have you come for?' he asked abruptly, putting paid to the raunchy turn of his thoughts. He pushed himself away from the desk but did nothing to make her feel comfortable. Why should he?

'Can I sit down?'

Matias nodded to the chair. 'I wouldn't make myself too comfortable if I were you,' he drawled. 'Time is money, after all. On the subject of which, I'm taking a stab in the dark here at the reason for your sudden, unexpected visit. Because this isn't a social call, is it?'

'No.' Her voice was steady and Sophie was proud of

that, although that, in fairness, was the only part of her that felt remotely controlled. She hadn't laid eyes on him for weeks but she hadn't stopped thinking about him, and, seeing him in the flesh now, she was shocked that she could have so massively underestimated the impact of his physical presence.

His lean, dark face was even more stunningly beautiful than she recalled, his mouth more cruel, more sensuous, his body...

Sophie didn't want to think about his body. She just wanted to say what she had come to say and leave before her steady voice went the way of the rest of her. She reminded herself of the man he had turned out to be, vengeful and ruthless, and a lump of ice settled inside her, the cold knot of hatred, which she welcomed.

'Didn't think so.' Matias's lips thinned. He was recalling in vivid detail the mind-blowing sex they had shared... He was also recalling the reason she had slept with him. 'I expect you read all about your father's downfall in the financial pages.'

'You must be pretty pleased with yourself.'

Matias flushed darkly, nettled by the cool disdain in her voice. 'Your father got what he deserved.' He shrugged. 'And yes, I'm quietly pleased with myself, although I have to say that had he not let his company run aground, my job would have been considerably less easy. He was a thief, a conman and eventually an idiot who let go of the reins and never thought that the horse might bolt. A great deal of highly suspect financial dealings is being uncovered, but that won't come as any surprise to you. In due course, your father and Her Majesty will be more than nodding acquaintances, but not in the way he would doubtless like. But you haven't come here for a chat. I'm a busy man so why don't we just cut to the chase, Sophie? No deal with your father means no rescue of his terminally ill company, which means no cash in hand for you. So I'm guessing that you're here to see whether there isn't another way to elicit money out of me.'

'I wouldn't accept a penny from you if my life depended on it,' she snapped. Every word that had passed his beautiful lips stung, every word was a reminder of exactly what he thought of her.

If she could have turned tail and run for the hills, she would have, but Julie had been right. A father deserved to know about the existence of his child, even if he chose to do nothing with the knowledge. However much she hated him for how he had treated her, she was fair enough to recognise that simple fact.

'We're going round the houses here, *querida*. In one sentence, why don't you just tell me what the hell you're doing in my office?'

'We had unprotected sex, Matias. Do you remember?'

Two sentences that dropped into the still silence between them with the power of an unexploded bomb.

Usually quick on the uptake, Matias could literally feel his brain slowing down, skidding to a halt in the face of what she had said and what she hadn't.

'I remember...' he said slowly. It was strange but that languorous bout of lovemaking, in that quiet surreal lull between sleeping and waking, had stayed right there, between the sheets, trapped in a moment in time. Had he subconsciously shoved it to the back of his mind rather than face the possibility that taking her without protection might have had consequences? Or had it just seemed unreal in the light of day and therefore easily forgotten?

He was remembering now, remembering the way their bodies had fused, warm and lazy and barely awake.

'I'm pregnant, Matias,' Sophie told him flatly.

She'd not envisaged what sort of reaction she would get from her announcement. In her head, she said what she had to and then walked away. Now, as she watched the vibrant bronze of his face slowly pale, she found herself riveted to the chair into which she had sunk.

'You can't be,' he denied hoarsely.

'I've done three tests. I didn't even think about it until I started feeling nauseous every morning and re-alised that my period hadn't come.'

'It's impossible.' Matias raked his fingers through his hair and realised that his hand was shaking. Pregnant. She was having his baby. Just like that, his eyes darted to her still-flat stomach, then to her breasts, which now, suddenly, seemed bigger and lusher than he remembered. 'And if this is your attempt to try and get money out of me, then you're barking up the wrong tree. You seem to forget that I've had ample experience of a woman who will use a so-called pregnancy to worm her way into my bank balance.'

Sophie rose on shaking legs. 'I'm going now, Matias. I know you had a poor experience in the past and I'm very sorry that I've had to come here and spring this on you, but I'm not your ex-girlfriend, I'm not lying and I certainly don't want a penny from you. After what you did to me, do you honestly think that I could ever want anything from you? *Ever?* I'm here because I felt you should know about your baby.'

Matias watched as she began walking towards his office door. Everything seemed to be happening in slow motion or maybe it was just that his brain had now totally seized up, unable to deal with a situation for which he had not, in any way, shape or form, prepared himself. He didn't move as she opened the office door but then he did, suddenly galvanised into action.

He caught her as she was barrelling along the corridor towards the bank of lifts and he placed his hand on her arm, forcing her to a stop.

Who cared whether his bizarre behaviour was being observed?

'Where do you think you're going?' he gritted.

Sophie's eyes flashed. 'Back home! Where do you think? I can't believe you would have the nerve to accuse me of faking a pregnancy to try and extort money out of you. What sort of person do you think I am? No. Don't bother answering that! I know already!' She yanked her arm out of his grasp and hit the button on one of the lifts, which obligingly opened at her command. She stepped in, eyes firmly averted from Matias, but she was all too aware of him stepping into the lift with her and slamming his fist on one of the buttons, which instantly brought it to a shuddering stop between floors.

'What are you doing?' Alarmed, Sophie finally looked him squarely in the eyes and then blinked and made a huge effort to drag her eyes away because, even when she was seething with hatred, she still couldn't help finding him so impossibly attractive. It wasn't fair!

'We need to talk about this and if this is the only way to get you to talk to me, then I'll take it.'

'You can't just *do that*.' Sophie was shocked because

wasn't that breaking the law? Normal people didn't just *stop a lift to have a conversation*! But then since when was Matias Rivero a *normal human being*?

'Why not?'

'Because…because…'

'Are you going to have a conversation with me about this or are you going to put on your running shoes the second we're out of this lift? Because you can't drop a bombshell like that in my lap and then try and dodge the bullet.'

'I don't want anything from you,' Sophie repeated fiercely. 'I hate you!'

'Message received loud and clear.'

'And I didn't engineer getting pregnant to try and get money out of you! That's a vile thing to say even from you, but why should I be surprised?'

'Let's not waste time going down that road. It's not going to solve anything.'

'And I have no intention of getting rid of this baby, if that's what you're thinking!'

'Did I insinuate that that was what I wanted?' Matias raked frustrated fingers through his hair. Her colour was high, her eyes were glittering like aquamarines, and she was the very essence of bristling feminine fury. He set the lift back on its way down. 'We're going to go to a small wine bar five minutes' walk from this office. I know the guy who owns it. I'll make sure we get a good seat at the back somewhere and we can have a civilised conversation about this problem. Agreed?'

Sophie scowled. 'You used me just to get dirt on my father.' She looked at him narrowly and with hostility. 'We can talk about this if you like but I don't want you to forget how much I detest you for doing what you did.'

Matias hung onto his temper. He had no doubt that she was telling the truth and, with the dust settling, the grim reality of what had happened was beginning to take shape. He was going to be a father. When it came to his bucket list, having a kid had never been on it and yet here he was, with only a few months left of sweet independent singledom because of one crazy mistake.

Life as he knew it was about to undergo a seismic change and getting wrapped up in blame and counter-blame wasn't going to alter that.

The wine bar was half empty and they were, indeed, afforded utter privacy at the very back, where they were tucked away from the other tables. Matias ordered a coffee for them both and then looked at her directly.

'When did you find out?' he asked quietly, shunning anything that might lead to another emotive outburst.

'Yesterday.' Sophie glared bitterly at him and fiddled with the handle of her cup before taking a sip and grimacing because her taste buds were no longer quite the same. 'And don't think that it wasn't as big a shock for me as well! Don't think that I haven't thought about how Fate could have been so cruel!'

'Whatever has happened in the past, we have to put behind us or else we'll be stuck on a treadmill of never moving forward and the only way we can deal with this problem is to move forward towards a mutually agree-able solution.'

Sophie stared coldly at him because every word he said, while making perfect sense, left her feeling angry and defensive. Problem? Mutually agreeable solution? She rested her hand protectively on her stomach, a gesture that Matias keenly noted, just as he understood that treading on eggshells about summed up where he was right at this moment. She had come to his office under duress and was not inclined to give him the benefit of any doubts, but she was hardly the saint she made herself out to be, he thought. She talked a lot about him using her but hadn't she been after his money? No, she wouldn't be in line for a halo any time soon, but, like it or not, he had to listen to his own words of advice and approach the situation dispassionately.

'That's easier said than done,' Sophie said tonelessly and Matias heaved an impatient sigh.

'You wanted me to engineer a deal with your father because you thought he might be able to help you financially if he wasn't in financial trouble himself. Am I right?' His voice was level and cool. 'So when you rant and rave about what a bastard I am, take a long look at yourself and try and put things into perspective.'

He hadn't wanted to raise this thorny issue because he didn't see what the point of raising it might be, considering it wouldn't advance any sort of solution to their problem, but raise it he had and he was disconcerted by the absolute lack of suitable apology on her face. Clearly a sense of guilt didn't feature in her repertoire.

And yet that seemed strangely at odds with the person she came across as being. Surely his judgement couldn't be that skewed?

'You *are* a bastard.' But she flushed because he'd never given her the chance to explain about Eric and it was understandable that he had somehow ended up with the wrong end of the stick. She looked at him, her bright eyes filled with unspoken challenge. 'And how very lucky you are that I won't be hanging around and making a nuisance of myself by demanding anything from you. I'm not the nasty gold-digger you seemed to think I am and I wouldn't touch a penny from you if my life depended on it!'

'You're telling me that you weren't after money from me by trying to encourage me to do a deal with your father? Even though you knew that his company was on the brink of collapse? Even though you knew that he was probably criminally involved in skimming cash from the till?' Matias laughed shortly. 'Let's have your definition of a gold-digger, then, Sophie…'

'I don't care what you think of me,' Sophie said tightly. She'd had her tale to tell, had been ready to spill the beans about Eric because she had been seduced by Matias on an emotional level, had taken him for being someone he had not been. She'd had a narrow escape— so should she spill the beans *now*?

No way, she decided grimly. He was still after her father and there was no way she would allow Eric's privacy to be invaded by the press, which was exactly what could happen should Matias choose to publicise her brother's existence. Her darling, fragile brother was not going to be part of Matias's retribution or even unintentional *collateral damage*.

Matias instantly realised that that simple statement held the distinct possibility of opening up another quagmire and so he opted for silence.

'So what is your explanation for your behaviour?' he eventually demanded, grudgingly curious to find out what she would be able to come up with that didn't begin and end with her need to have money injected into her company.

'I don't have to provide you with an explanation,' Sophie retorted quickly, cringing back from a vision of reporters banging on the window of her brother's bedroom, terrifying him because he would be hopelessly confused and panicked.

'I just need to take everything you say at face value and believe you. Is that it?'

'You don't have to do anything you don't want to do. I haven't come here because I want anything from you and there's no *we* in this situation. I came here because I felt it was the right thing to do but this isn't a problem that I'm forcing you to face. I don't trust you, Matias, but you deserved to know about the pregnancy so here I am.'

'We're back to this again. Let's move away from that and focus on the present and the future. And just for your reference, there very much *is* a *we* in this situation because half of my chromosomes, whether you like it or not, happen to be inside you right now in the form of a baby neither of us expected but which both of us have to deal with.' His instinct was to qualify what he had to say by telling her that everything depended on whether she was telling the truth, but he decided that silence on that subject was definitely going to be the diplomatic course. 'You're having my baby...' For a few seconds he was stunned again by the impact that had on him. Matias Rivero, a father. He still couldn't quite get his head round that. 'If you thought that you could just pass on that information and then walk away, job done, then you were sorely mistaken. I won't be walking away from my responsibility, Sophie.'

'I don't want to be your responsibility.'

'You're not but my unborn child is, whether you like it or not. I didn't sign up to this but it's happened and we have to deal with it. You have an unhappy family background so maybe that's led you to imagine that stability is overrated, but I haven't and I am a firm believer in the importance of having parents in a child's life. Both parents.'

'I happen to believe very strongly in stability,' Sophie corrected him tightly, '*because* I've had an unhappy family background. I didn't know how you would react when I came to see you, bearing in mind the way we parted company, but you can rest assured that I won't stand in the way of your seeing your child.' She hated the way he made her feel. She didn't want to be here, and yet, in his presence, she felt so *different*, as though she were living on a plane of heightened sensation. She felt *alive*. She wanted to walk out but felt compelled to stay. She wanted to ignore his staggering, unwelcome impact on her senses but was drawn to him by invisible strings that she couldn't seem to sever. She loathed him for what he had done and loathed herself almost as much for knowing that somewhere inside her he still stirred something…something only he could somehow manage to reach.

'That's not good enough, *querida*.' Matias had never contemplated marriage and now here he was, facing marriage as the final frontier, and not simply marriage, but marriage to the woman who was the daughter of his sworn enemy. And yet what other solution was there? He had no intention of being a bit player in his child's life, forking out maintenance payments while having his visiting rights restricted and curtailed by a vengeful mother. Sophie wouldn't forget the circumstances that had brought him into her life and she would have the perfect opportunity, should she so choose, to wreak a little healthy revenge of her own by dictating how much or how little influence he had over his own flesh and blood.

He thought of his mother, recovering in a private hospital in London. She would be so upset if she ended up as only a part-time grandparent, snatching moments here and there with a grandchild caught in a tug of war between two warring parents. Matias might have been put off emotional commitment thanks to a conniving ex and the lessons learnt from his own emotional father and where it had got him in the long run. That said, he hadn't been lying when he'd told Sophie that his childhood had consisted of a strong and supportive family unit and now, in the face of this unexpected development, that strong family bond locked into place to override everything else.

'Twenty minutes ago, you were telling me that time was money, so I'd better go now.'

'Things change. Twenty minutes ago I didn't realise that you were carrying my baby.' His sharp eyes were glued to her face while he programmed his brain to accept the news she had broken to him, to start thinking outside the box. 'You're now set to be a permanent feature in my life. I want to be there for my child twenty-four-seven and the only way that can be achieved is if we marry.'

Deathly silence greeted this extraordinary statement and Sophie's mouth inelegantly fell open in shock.

'You've got to be kidding.'

'You might have come here out of a sense of duty but I have no intention of going away like an unpleasant smell because you refuse to accept that the past is over and done with.'

'I will never forget how you used me in your quest for revenge. You used me once and who's to say that you won't use me again?' She thought of Eric, the secret that Matias could not be allowed to uncover because what if his desire for revenge hadn't been sated? She looked at him from under lowered lashes and shivered. So beautiful, so powerful and so incredibly ruthless.

'Sophie, that story has ended. We are travelling down a different road now.' But Matias was genuinely puzzled by her statement. What else could he possibly use her for? For better or for worse, he had uncovered everything there was to uncover about her father.

He continued to look at her and noted the way her cheeks slowly coloured, arrowed in on the soft tremble of her full lips. The air between them was suddenly filled with a charge he recognised all too well, a sexual charge that made him immediately harden for her. He vividly recalled the silky wetness that always greeted his exploring fingers, his questing mouth, and he clenched his jaw.

He motioned, without looking around, for the bill and wondered whether she was conscious of the signals she was sending out under all the hostility and mistrust, signals that were as powerful as a deep sea-depth charge, signals that advertised a connection between them that was founded on the oldest thing in the world...sexual attraction.

'Think about it, Sophie, and I will call you tomorrow so that we can pick up this conversation.' He smiled slowly and watched intently as a little shiver went through her. 'I think we both need to do a little private reflection, don't you?'

CHAPTER EIGHT

SHE'D TURNED DOWN his extraordinary marriage proposal and she'd done the right thing.

Of course there were pros and there were cons. Every decision was always laced with pros and cons! But she had done the right thing. She'd been to see Eric, sat in his soothing presence, watched his contentment in his peaceful surroundings. Somehow she'd find the money to pay for him carrying on living there, but she would never expose him to the cruel glare of a curious and judgemental public.

Was she being selfish? Was she failing to consider the reality, which was that a child would always be better off with two parents as opposed to one and that was something that should override every other concern?

No. How could you hitch your wagon to a man you didn't trust? A man you felt might betray you again? And anyway, trust issues aside, two parents only worked if the glue that bound them together wasn't a child, but love. Matias didn't love her and he had never pretended that he did. He felt responsible for her, responsible for the child he had sired, and was admirably willing to step up to the plate and do his duty, but duty was a far cry from love.

Duty would wear very thin at the edges as time marched on. Duty would be the very thing he would come to resent when he found himself harnessed to a woman he would never have voluntarily chosen to spend his life with.

But three weeks had gone by and Matias just seemed to *be around so much*.

He hadn't said it in so many words, but there had been no need because every look he gave her and every word that passed his lips said *don't fight me*.

She'd turned him down but, like a predator waiting for the right moment to strike, he was simply biding his time.

He didn't realise, she thought, that he would never wear away her defences because there was more than just her and their baby at stake. At stake was a brother he knew nothing about and never would and that bolstered all her resolve when his presence just felt *too overwhelming*.

Nothing he could say, no logic he could use, could ever make her do anything that might jeopardise her brother's privacy and happiness.

She was congratulating herself on being strong as she sat, the first to arrive, at the posh restaurant where Matias had arranged to meet her for lunch. He had been away for the past three days and her stomach was already tightening in nervous knots as she braced herself for that first glimpse of him. On the one hand, she had been relieved that, although he had been scrupulous about maintaining contact with her by phone, he hadn't imposed his presence on her on a daily basis. On the other hand, she wondered whether she might have become more blasé about his physical presence if he were around more, if she had a chance to get accustomed to him. She didn't like the way he still made her feel and she hated the memories of him touching her that refused to go away. They weren't on that page any longer! Things had changed and they were never going to be on that page together again.

Lost in thought, she looked up to find that he had arrived and he wasn't alone.

Art was with him. She hadn't seen him since the weekend party in the Lake District and she rose to her feet, already smiling as he walked towards her. Behind him, Matias towered, unbearably sexy in his work clothes, one hand in his trouser pocket, the other hooked to his jacket, which was slung over his shoulder.

Seeing that warm, genuine smile on her face as she looked at Art, Matias sourly thought that it was something *he* hadn't seen for a while. She'd repeatedly thrown his marriage proposals back in his face and he'd been sharp enough to realise that the harder he pushed, the faster she would back away.

There was no way he was going to let her run out of his life because it suited her. Pride refused to let him forget that she had slept with him as a ruse to get him to invest in her father's company, but common sense dictated that he get her onside because he was never going to be persuaded into the role of part-time father.

He watched, his expression shuttered, as she and Art chatted away like the old friends they weren't and something hit him hard, something so unexpected that it was like a punch to the gut.

He didn't like seeing her relaxed interaction with his friend. He didn't like the way she was so at ease in his company. He didn't care for the tinkling of her laughter as they found God only knew what to talk about, considering they'd known each other all of five seconds.

Jealousy and possessiveness rammed into him with the weight of a sledgehammer and he interrupted their conversation to coolly inform her that Art wasn't going to be joining them for lunch.

'That's a shame.' Sophie sighed with genuine disappointment, which got on Matias's nerves even more.

He scowled, met Art's curious eyes and scowled even more. 'Don't let us keep you,' he said abruptly, and Art grinned broadly but stood up, moving to drop a kiss on Sophie's cheek before heading out.

'That was *so* rude,' she said. 'It was lovely seeing Art again! I had no idea you two were so close. You never said! I can't believe you *grew up together*!' They were like brothers and it had brought her up short to acknowledge that Art adored Matias. Even in the space of half an hour, she had been able to glean that from their interaction and seeing them together had unwillingly reminded her of just why she had been seduced by him. There was a side to Matias that wasn't a bastard, a side that could elicit a depth of affection from a loyal friend who was clearly a wonderful human being. It was suddenly confusing to admit that he was also many other things, a complex guy with so many dimensions, it made her head swim.

Not that she was going to let that deflect her from the path she had decided to take.

'I had no idea I had a duty to tell you every detail of my life just because you're carrying my baby,' Matias drawled lazily, sitting back as menus were placed in front of them. Her cheeks were still flushed and she looked so damned sexy that the jealousy that had attacked him from nowhere five minutes ago staged another onslaught. He knew he was being irrational but he couldn't help it.

'You never said that you were going to visit your mother…'

'I could hardly let her find out about us via the grapevine.'

'She must have been disappointed,' Sophie said quietly. 'No mother likes to think that her child has… well…is going to have a family…you know…so unexpectedly…and without the usual build-up…'

Matias allowed her to run aground. Seeing his mother had reinforced his belief that the only solution was to marry the woman blushing opposite him. If she was going to dig her heels in, then he would have to work along the lines that there was more than one way to skin a cat. He'd seen the way she still looked at him. 'Naturally,' he murmured smoothly, 'she would have preferred the love and marriage scenario…'

'But you told her how it was? That this isn't that sort of situation?'

Matias didn't say anything because he had told his mother no such thing. 'Pregnancy becomes you, Sophie,' he said instead, relaxing into the chair and staring at her until the faint colour in her cheeks deepened and he saw the latent *awareness* of him that she was always so careful to try and conceal. 'Your body's changing. You're wearing looser clothes. Are your breasts getting bigger?'

'Matias!' Sophie was shocked because he hadn't been direct like this before.

Heat blossomed inside her. Her breasts ached and she felt the tingle of awareness stickily making its presence felt between her legs. *That* was what those casual words were doing to her!

'It doesn't get more intimate than having my baby…' he shrugged, his fabulous eyes not leaving her face '…so why are you so surprised that I am curious about the physical changes occurring to you? It's natural. I'm fifty per cent responsible for those physical changes.'

'This conversation is not appropriate! We no longer have that kind of relationship!'

'You think that we are more like…*what*?'

'Well, *friends*. At least, that's what we should be aspiring to become! We've talked about this and we both agree that it would be best for our child if we remain on good terms.' She cleared her throat and tried to ignore the suffocating effect his intense gaze was having on her nervous system. 'Remember we agreed that you would be able to see him or her any time you wanted?'

'So we did…'

'We may not have expected this…' she dug deep to repeat the mantra she had told herself '…but we're both adults and um…in this day and age, marriage isn't the inevitable solution to dealing with an unexpected pregnancy… We discussed this.'

'Indeed…'

'There's too much water under the bridge between us.'

'I won't deny that.' She had deferred, for once, and he had ordered for both of them, a sharing platter that was now placed between them. 'But I'm curious. What do you suggest we do with the mutual desire that's still putting in an unwelcome appearance?'

Sophie's mouth fell open. He had brought out into the open the one thing she had desperately tried to shove into a locked box. 'I don't know what you're talking about!'

'Liar,' Matias said softly. 'I could reach out and touch you right now and you'd go up in flames.'

'You couldn't be further from the truth,' Sophie denied weakly. 'I could never be attracted to someone who used me like you did. Never!'

'*Never* is a word that has no place in my vocabulary.'

'Matias…' She thought of Eric and the importance of hanging onto her resolve, but seeing Matias with Art had weakened that resolve, had reminded her of those sides to him that could be so wonderfully seductive, so thoughtful and unexpectedly kind.

'I'm listening.'

'I know you find it funny to make me uncomfortable.'

'I think about you all the time. I wonder what your changing body looks like under those clothes.'

'Don't say things like that! We don't have that kind of relationship! We talked about that.' She sought refuge in the platter in front of her but she could feel him staring lazily at her, sending her into heady meltdown. Her whole body was throbbing with the very awareness he was casually dragging out into the open and forcing her to acknowledge.

'I don't like to stick to the script. It makes for a boring life.' Matias sat back. He let his eyes drift at a leisurely pace down her curvaceous body and felt his mouth twitch because she was as rigid as a plank of wood, as if her posture were fooling him. 'In fact,' he drawled, 'I'm taking the afternoon off.'

'Why?'

'Do I have to provide a reason? And stop looking at

me like that. You should be thrilled at the prospect of spending time in my company. And do me a favour and refrain from telling me that we *don't have that kind of relationship.*'

'I can't leave Julie in the lurch.'

'She's going to have to get used to you no longer holding her hand when you finally decide to listen to me and quit working. She's a big girl. She'll cope.'

'I can't *quit working*, Matias.'

'Let's not go there. You don't need the money.'

Sophie thought of Eric and her mouth firmed. The irony was that Matias wanted to throw money at her. Once upon a time not all that long ago he had turned his back on her and tossed her to the kerb but now that she was pregnant, everything had changed. They had not discussed money in any great depth yet, but he had already made it clear that his child, and her by extension, would want for nothing.

And yet, how could she allow herself to ever become financially dependent on him? Her pride would never allow it and, more than that, what if she began to trust again only to find that she had once more made a mistake? What if, by then, she was totally reliant on the money he was so keen for her to have because she'd stopped working? No, there was no way she could give up her job. Maternity leave was one thing. Resignation was quite another.

Another roadblock, Matias thought with frustration. He impatiently wondered why she couldn't just recognise that his solution was the best and only way to move forward. What woman wouldn't want a life of luxury? What woman wouldn't want to be able to snap her fingers and get whatever she wanted? It wasn't as though they didn't have an electric connection still thrumming between them like a live charge. What more advantages did he have to bring to the table for her to accept his proposal? Why, he thought, did she have to be so *damned stubborn*?

'I've taken the afternoon off, *querida*, because I have a surprise for you.'

'I hate surprises,' Sophie confessed.

'I know. I'm not a big fan of them myself but I am hoping you'll like this one. It's a house.'

'A house?'

'For you,' he said bluntly and her eyes widened in surprise.

'You've gone and bought a house *for me*?' She bristled. 'Why would you do that?'

Matias sat back, taking his own sweet time, and looked at her evenly. 'Because,' he said calmly, 'you won't be bringing up our child in that tiny box of yours with its converted kitchen.'

'There's nothing wrong with *that box*,' Sophie cried hotly as pride kicked in and lodged inside her.

'Don't argue with me on this.' Matias's voice was forbidding. 'You've turned down my marriage proposal, in defiance of common sense. You've dug your heels in and dismissed all financial help I've offered as unnecessary handouts. You've insisted on working long hours even though you're unnecessarily putting our child at risk. You are *not* going to wage war with me on this.'

'How have I been putting the baby at risk?' Sophie asked furiously.

'You don't have to work until midnight baking cakes for anyone's anniversary party.'

'*Once*. I've done that *once*!'

'Or,' Matias ploughed on remorselessly, 'waste three hours in traffic delivering a four-course meal for a dinner party.'

'That's my job!'

'You're overexerting yourself. You need to take it easy.'

Sophie released a long sigh but… *Had anyone ever really looked out for her? Ever really cared whether she was taking on too much or not?* Of course, this wasn't about *her*, but about the precious cargo in her stomach, and it would be downright foolhardy to start thinking otherwise *but still…*

'I know you're not a gold-digger, Sophie. You don't have to keep trying to prove it to me over and over again.'

'That's not what I'm doing.'

'No? Then what is it?'

'I won't rely on you financially. I can't. I need to have my own financial independence.' Suddenly she felt small and helpless. She wished she were able to lean on him and just accept what was on offer. He made it sound so easy. Clean break from what had happened between them in the past and onward bound to the future he wanted her and his child to have, but there was so much more to the story than he knew.

'Well, you're going to have to compromise on this, whether you like it or not, *cara*.' His voice was cool and unyielding.

Their eyes tangled. He reached out and brushed a speck of something from the side of her mouth, then left his finger there for a few seconds to stroke it over her lips. 'A little bread,' he said roughly, his big body firing up immediately because it was the first time he'd touched her in weeks.

Sophie's eyes widened. For a minute there she had leaned towards him and her whole body had burned from the inside out, as though molten lava were running through her veins. *The way he was looking at her, with those deep, dark, sexy eyes...*

Yearning made her weak and it was a struggle to pull away from the magnetic drag on her senses.

'You have no idea what my taste is like. In houses.' Which was as good as accepting whatever over-the-top house he had flung money at, in defiance of the fact that he must have known that she would have kicked up a fuss about it. Her heart was still hammering and she lowered her eyes and took a few deep breaths before looking at him once again. She could still feel the burning of her skin where he had touched her. 'Don't get me wrong, Matias.' Her tone crisped up but her body, awakened by his touch, *wanted more*. 'You have a lovely place in the Lake District but I couldn't imagine living in a massive greenhouse like that. I don't know what your apartment's like but I'm guessing it's along the same lines...'

'Damned by faint praise,' Matias murmured, wanting her more than he had ever wanted anything or anyone in his life before and damn well determined to have her because he could *smell* the same want radiating from her in waves.

'What I'm saying is you and I obviously don't have the same taste in houses so it's unlikely I'm going to like whatever it is you've bought.'

'I haven't bought it yet,' he drawled. 'I may be arrogant but I thought you might actually like to have a say in the house you want to live in.' Eyes on her, he signalled for the bill and then stood up.

He dominated the space around him and she was helplessly drawn towards him, like a moth to a bright light. She couldn't quite understand how it was that he could continue to exercise this powerful effect on her after what he had done, or how common sense and logic hadn't prevailed when it came to stepping back from him. She wondered whether pregnancy hormones had taken over and were controlling all her responses, heightening her emotional state and making her vulnerable to him when she should have been as detached from him as he was from her and getting down to the business of building a friendship for the sake of the child she was carrying.

Outside, his chauffeur was waiting for them, but instead of accompanying them he drove them to his office where they switched cars, and Matias took the wheel.

'Where is this house?' Sophie asked because she had expected something in Chelsea or Mayfair or one of those frighteningly expensive postcodes close to where he had his own apartment.

'I'm going to disappoint you…' he slid his eyes sideways to glance at her and smiled '…by keeping it a surprise. Now, talk to me, *querida*. Don't argue with me. Tell me about that client of yours…'

'Which client?' Because stupidly, even though she had so many defences erected when it came to Matias you could construct a small town behind them, she *still* found it frighteningly easy to talk to him when he turned on that charm of his.

'The vegan with the wart on her face.'

'I didn't think I'd mentioned her to you.'

'When we're not fighting,' Matias murmured softly, 'we're getting along a hell of a lot better than you give us credit for. There's so much more we could be doing, *querida*, instead of making war...'

Sophie only realised that they had been driving for longer than she thought when the crowded streets and houses fell away to open space and parks and they pulled up outside a picture-perfect house shaped like a chocolate box with an extension to one side. Wisteria clambered over the front wall and, set right back from the lane, the front garden was dilapidated and overgrown.

'It needs work,' Matias told her, reaching into the pocket of his jacket, which he had flung in the back seat, and extracting some keys, which he jangled on one finger as he opened his car door. 'And it hasn't been lived in for several months, hence the exuberance of the weeds.'

'I hadn't expected anything like this.' Sophie followed him up to the front door, head swinging left to right as she looked around her. The house stood in its own small plot, which was hedged in on three sides. He opened the door, stood aside and she brushed past him and then stood and stared.

There were rooms to the right and left of the hallway. Lovely square rooms, all perfectly proportioned. A sitting room, a more formal living room, a study, a snug and then along to the kitchen and conservatory, which opened out at the back to a garden that was full of trees and shrubs and plants that had taken advantage of absentee owners and decided to run rampant.

The paint was faded. In the sitting room, the gently flowered wallpaper seemed to speak of a different era.

'The house was owned by an elderly lady who lived

here for most of her life, it would seem,' Matias was murmuring as he led her from room to room. 'She didn't have any children, or perhaps they might have persuaded her that the house was far too big as she got older, but it would seem that she was too attached to it to sell up and leave and as a consequence the latter part of her life was spent in only a handful of rooms. The rest were left in a state of gradual decline. When she died a little over a year ago, it was inherited by a distant relative abroad and the probate took some time, hence it's only just come onto the market.'

She walked from room to room. Her silence spoke volumes. She wasn't bristling; she wasn't complaining. In the matter of the house, he had clearly won hands down.

Matias intended to win hands down in every other area as well.

He was waiting for her in the hallway, leaning against the wall, when she completed her third tour of the house, and he didn't budge as she walked towards him, her eyes still wide as saucers.

'Okay.' Sophie smiled crookedly. 'You win.'

'I know.'

'Don't be arrogant, Matias,' but she was still smiling and she wasn't trying to shuffle more distance between them. The silence stretched until she licked her lips nervously.

But she hadn't taken flight.

'I don't just want to win when it comes to finding a house for…you,' he said gruffly.

'Matias, don't.' But her voice was high and unsteady, and against her will her body was straining with desperate longing towards him, liquid pooling between her legs, the swollen tips of her nipples tightening into sensitive buds.

'Why do you insist on fighting this thing that's still here between us?'

'Because we can't give in to…to lust…'

'So you finally admit it.'

'That doesn't mean anything. It doesn't mean I'm going to do anything about it.' She looked at him and couldn't look away. His dark eyes pinned her to the spot with ruthless efficiency. She couldn't move, couldn't think, could scarcely breathe.

Her head screamed that this was *just not going to do*. She couldn't afford to lose sight of what was sensible but her body was singing from a different song sheet and when he lowered his head to hers, her hands reached out. To push him away? Maybe. Yet they didn't. They curled into his shirt and she melted helplessly as he kissed her, softly and teasingly at first and then with a hunger that matched her own.

His tongue found hers. His hands, on her shoulders, moved to her arms then cupped the full weight of her breasts.

He played with her nipples through her top but then, frustrated, pushed open the buttons and groaned as he felt the naked skin of her chest and then, burrowing beneath the lacy bra, finally got to the silky fullness of her breasts and the ripe protrusion of a nipple.

'You're definitely bigger.' His voice was shaking.

'Matias…'

'Touch me.' He guided her hand to his erection, which was a hard, prominent bulge against the zipper of his trousers.

'We can't make love here!'

Wrenched back to the reality of what she was saying, Matias struggled not to explode in his trousers. He breathed deeply, cupped the nape of her neck and drew her to him so that their foreheads were touching.

Her breath was minty fresh, her skin as soft as satin and he ached for her. 'We talk, Sophie,' he breathed in a driven undertone. 'Don't tell me we're at one another's throats all of the time. And we want one another.'

Sophie knew what he was saying and she longed to capitulate but she was only in this place because she was pregnant. Had she not been, they would be enemies on opposite sides of the fence. Were it just a question of her, then would she think about his offer? Maybe. She could cope if it turned out that she couldn't trust him. Again. But she couldn't trust him with Eric. Could she?

Confusion tore through her.

'Come back to my place with me,' he urged.

'I won't marry you,' she said weakly.

Matias all but groaned in frustration but he didn't. Instead, he smoothed his hands over her shoulders and kissed her very gently, very persuasively on her mouth and felt her move from hesitation to abandon. He kept kissing her. He kissed her until she was breathless. He kissed her until he knew for certain that there was nothing and no one left in her head but him, then he broke apart and said, in a barely restrained voice,

'Let's go.'

CHAPTER NINE

HER HOUSE.

In her head, to go to Matias's house would have been a complete declaration of defeat. Within the confines of her own four walls, however, she could kid herself that she was still in control, even though she had lost it in his arms and even though *she wanted to carry on losing it.*

If I sleep with him, she thought, then it would be *a conscious decision.* It wouldn't mean that she had lost all control and it certainly didn't mean that she would marry him. She would never trust him again. How could she? She would never jeopardise Eric's privacy because she'd made another mistake, but…

She wanted Matias so badly. He was in her system like a virus and she wanted to be cleared of that virus because it was driving her round the bend.

He reached out to link his fingers lightly through hers in the car. They barely spoke but the electricity between them could have set a forest ablaze. His mobile phone rang several times. He ignored it. Looking at his strong, sharp profile, the lean contours of his beautiful face, Sophie wondered what was going through his head. He didn't love her but he still fancied her. He'd told her that there was no need for her to keep trying to prove to him that she was no gold-digger, but deep down she knew that he would always believe her culpable of trying to get him to sink money into her father's dying company and invest in a man who had turned out to be a thief. He had no idea that Eric existed and so would never understand why she had done what she had, and she could never tell him about her brother because family loyalty was more powerful than anything else.

But whatever the situation, he was right. A fire burned between them and what were they to do about it?

Having never invested in the crazy notion that lust was something that couldn't be tamed, Sophie was realising just how far off the mark she'd been with her orderly, smug little homilies.

It was after four-thirty by the time they made it to her house. Sophie thought it was serendipity that Julie was out on a job, setting up with an assistant they had hired, for a lavish dinner party in Dulwich.

Compared to the glorious setting of the house they had just seen, her two up, two down, squashed in the middle of an uninspiring row of terraced lookalikes, was a shock to the system. She'd vigorously defended her little place but now she felt that she could see it through Matias's eyes. Poky, cramped, unsatisfactory.

She turned to find him looking at her with a veiled expression as he quietly shut the door behind them. Shivers of anticipation raced up and down her spine.

'Empty house?' he asked, walking very slowly towards her, and Sophie nodded.

'Julie's on a job. She won't be back until tomorrow afternoon. Matias... I'm glad about the house... This place would really not have been suitable for a baby. I mean, of course, it would have worked if there were no other option but…'

'Shh.' He placed one finger over her lips and her heart sped up. 'Don't talk.' He was directly in front of her now and he bent his head and kissed her. A long, lingering, gentle kiss that made her weak at the knees. 'Much as I enjoy the sound of you telling me that I was right, there's more, a lot more, I want to enjoy right now.' He cupped the back of her neck and carried on kissing her, taking it long and slow and feeling a kick of satisfaction as her body yielded to his, moulding bit by bit to his hard length until they were pressed together, entwined.

Without warning, he lifted her off her feet and Sophie gasped and clung to him as he made his way up the narrow staircase.

He'd seen enough of her place to know that finding her bedroom wasn't going to require in-depth navigation skills. The place was tiny. He doubted there were more than two bedrooms and he was proved right, finding hers with no trouble at all as it was at the top of the stairs.

Cheerful colours tried to make the most of a space that could barely contain the bed, the chest of drawers and the wardrobe that were crammed into it. Two posters tried to attract the eye away from the view outside of other terraced houses and beyond that a railway line.

He set her down on the bed and she promptly pushed herself up onto her elbows to look at him as he drew the curtains together, shutting out the weak sunlight and plunging the room into subdued tones of grey and sepia.

'It's been too long,' he intoned with a slow, possessive smile that ratcheted up her spiralling excitement.

He was standing with his back to the window and he remained there for a few seconds, just staring at her, before walking towards the bed, ridding himself of clothes on the way.

He was sheer masculine, powerful beauty in motion and he took her breath away.

She was frankly amazed that she had been able to withstand his potent sex appeal for as long as she had, but then today was the first time he had yanked that monster out of the cupboard and forced her to confront it.

She half closed her eyes, watching as, down to his boxers, he stood by the side of the bed and gazed down at her.

Tentatively, she reached out and ran the tips of her fingers across the washboard hardness of his flat stomach.

He was wired for her. His erection was prominent under the boxers, which didn't remain on for longer than necessary.

'I don't have to tell you how much I want this,' Matias said gruffly. 'The evidence is right in front of you.'

Sophie gave a soft little whimper and sat up straighter, angling her body so that she could lick the shaft of his pulsing erection.

She tasted him like someone savouring an exquisite delicacy. Her tongue flicked and touched, her mouth closed over him and she sucked while, with her hand, she enjoyed the familiar feel of his hardness. His taste was an aphrodisiac.

She felt as if somewhere, in the back of her mind, she had stored the memory of the noises he made when she did this, his deep, guttural grunts. His fingers clasped in her hair were familiar. She wanted him so badly she was melting for him and wanted nothing more than to fling off all her clothes so that he could take her.

Reading her mind and knowing that if he didn't watch it, he would come right now, in her mouth, Matias reluctantly separated her from him. When he glanced down, his shaft was slick and wet and he had to clench his fists to control the urge to put her right back there, have her take him across the finishing line with her hands and her mouth.

No. He'd fantasised about this for far too long to blow it on a horny, teenage urge to grab and take.

But hell, he was on fire as he sank onto the mattress so that he could remove her clothes.

She was wearing far too much and he was way too fired up to do justice to the striptease scenario. He needed to get under the layers of fabric as quickly as possible so that he could feel her.

Her clothes hit the deck in record time and she helped, squirming out of her cumbersome bra and wriggling free of the lacy underwear, which, he noted in passing satisfaction, was of the sexy thong variety, a choice of lingerie he knew he had encouraged her to wear.

It was almost a shame that he was so hot and hard because he would have liked to have taken his time teasing her with his tongue through the lace of her underwear.

'Matias…' Sophie fell back against the pillow and arched a little so that her full breasts were pushed out invitingly to him.

He was kneeling over her and, on cue, he took her breasts in his big hands and massaged them gently until his thumbs were grazing her nipples and sending shivers of racing pleasure straight downwards.

She circled him with her hand and played with him, knowing just how fast and firm he liked the rhythmic motion of her hand.

'Matias…what?' he encouraged with a wicked smile and she looked back at him with wry understanding because she knew just what he wanted.

'You know…' she blushed furiously '…what I like…'

'Oh, I know…' He bent to suckle her nipple, drawing it into his mouth and taking his time to lave it with his tongue, circling the aching tip until she was writhing under him.

He knew her so well. It felt as though they had been making love for ever. Knew that she liked him to be just a little rough, to nip her big, pouting nipples until she became even wetter and more restless. He knew what else she loved, and he explored lower down her glorious body, taking time to appreciate all the small changes he had wondered about.

Her breasts were at least a cup size bigger and her nipples were more pronounced in colour, no longer a rosy blush but a deeper hue. Her belly was just a bit more rounded. Having never thought about babies or becoming a father, at least not since the hapless incident a thousand years ago with the ex-girlfriend who had tried it on, he had never looked twice at pregnant women, but this woman, with his baby inside her, was beyond sexy.

Her roundness thrilled him, made him even harder than he already was.

Working his way down her body, he slipped his hand between her legs and played with the soft down between them. Then he slipped his finger into her and she moaned softly and squirmed until his finger was deeper inside her, finding her softness and working a path to the tiny bud that was begging for attention.

He knew that if he dawdled too long there, she would come. She was the most responsive woman he had ever known. So he played with the tingling bud, then stopped, then played with it again, until she was begging him to take her.

'Not just yet,' he whispered. Hands on her waist, he dropped down between her legs and nuzzled, breathing in her honeyed sweetness.

He flicked his tongue along the slit of her womanhood, then began exploring her wetness.

His finger had already teased her and now his tongue did the teasing, until she was moaning and wriggling, pushing him down hard one minute, jerking him up the next, her fingers curled into his hair.

She bucked against his mouth, rising up with jerky movements, and he cupped her buttocks, holding her still and torturing her with the insistent push of his tongue inside her.

'I'm going to come,' she gasped as her body began moving quicker to capture every small sensation of him between her legs. 'I don't want to come like this, Matias… I want to *feel you inside me*.'

Matias rose up. He automatically reached down to find his wallet but then he remembered that there was no need for protection and he dealt her a slashing smile.

'The horse has already bolted…' he grinned '…so no need to do anything about locking the stable door.'

Sophie drowsily returned his smile. Her body was hot and flushed and the waves of pleasure that had almost but not quite taken her over the edge were still there, making her want to wriggle and touch herself.

'You're so hot for me, *querida*…'

'I can't help it,' Sophie half groaned. 'It's a physical thing.'

'Now, now, don't go spoiling the mood. I want to ride you and take you to the outer reaches of the universe.' He prodded her with the blunt head of his shaft and she parted her legs, unable to contain her eagerness to have him deep inside her.

He slid in and the sensation was beyond belief. She was slick and wet and tight and her softness welcomed him in ways that he couldn't define but just knew made him feel better than good.

He wanted her so badly. This was going to have to be fast and hard. He couldn't hang around any longer, he couldn't devote any more time to foreplay or else he risked the unthinkable.

He drove into her, thrusting long and deep, and she wrapped her legs around his waist and, yes, he rode her until she was bucking and crying out with pleasure, until the breathing hitched in her throat. Until, cresting a wave, she came just as he did, with a rush of sensation that flowed over her and around her like a tsunami.

She arched up and stiffened as his powerful body shuddered against her and she panted and rocked beneath him until at last…she was spent.

Matias levered himself off her. It was a downright miracle of circumstance that he now found himself here, with her. The number of *what ifs* between them could have stocked a library.

What if…she hadn't crashed into his car?

What if…he hadn't lived a life hell-bent on revenge?

What if…he hadn't seen fit to weave her into his revenge agenda?

What if…she hadn't spent time under his roof at his place in the Lake District?

What if, what if, what if…?

But here they were, having made the most satisfying love imaginable. In no way, shape or form was he tiring of her. On the contrary, he desired her with an urgency that none of his other relationships had ever had. He felt a possessiveness towards her that defied belief.

He had accepted the shock to his system that impending and unforeseen fatherhood would confer.

He had risen above the challenge of playing a blame game that would get neither of them anywhere.

But had he really believed that this unforeseeable passion and downright *insatiable craving* would form a part of the picture? Was it the evidence of his own virility and the fact that she was carrying his baby that made his feelings towards her so…*ferociously powerful*?

She had stuck to her guns about not marrying him, frustrating his natural urge to get what he wanted. His powerful need to *never* back down until he had what should be his within his grasp had hit a roadblock with her. He refused to contemplate any situation that involved him losing control over his child, and by extension, he told himself, *her.*

Seeing his mother as she recuperated in hospital, as he had now done several times, had only reinforced his determination to take her as his wife.

Thus far, the inevitable meeting between his mother and Sophie had been avoided, but sooner or later his mother would want to meet the woman who was carrying her grandchild and when that time arrived Matias was determined that marriage would be on the cards. There would be no difficult conversation in which his mother would be forced to concede that the grandchild she had always longed for would be a fleeting presence in her life.

'Was that as good for you as it was for me, *querida*?' He shifted onto his side and manoeuvred her so that they were facing one another. He brushed a strand of hair away from her face and then kissed her very gently on her mouth, tracing the outline of her lips with his tongue.

Sophie struggled to think straight. She had done what she had spent weeks resolving not to do. She had climbed back into bed with him and where did that leave the *friendship* angle she had been working so hard at since she had turned down his marriage proposal?

What disturbed and alarmed her was the fact that it had felt *right*.

Because…because…

Because she loved him. Because he'd swept into her life, inappropriate and infuriatingly arrogant, and stolen her heart, and even though he had used her and couldn't be trusted, because who knew whether he would use her again, she still couldn't help but love him. She'd made love to him and it had been as wonderful and as satisfying as walking through the front door of the house you adored and finding safety within its four walls. Which was a joke, of course, but then so were all the stupid assumptions she had made about love being something she would have been able to control. She could no more have controlled what she felt for Matias than she could have controlled the direction of a hurricane.

'Well?' Matias prompted, curving a hand possessively around her waist, challenging her to deny what was glaringly obvious.

'It was nice,' Sophie said faintly, still wrapped in the revelation that had been lurking there, just below the surface, for longer than she cared to think.

'Nice? *Nice?*' Matias was tempted to explode with outrage but ended up bursting out laughing. 'You certainly know how to shoot a man down in flames.'

'Okay.' She blushed. 'It was pretty good.'

'Getting better,' he mused, 'but I still prefer *amazing*.'

'It was amazing.'

'When you showed up at my office,' Matias said softly, 'it was a shock, but I really want this baby, *querida*. You tell me you don't want to marry me. You tell me the ingredients for a successful marriage aren't in place, but we talk. Yes, we fight as well, but *we talk*. And we still have this thing between us. We still want one another passionately. Isn't that glue enough? You say you're not prepared to make sacrifices yet *I* am, because I truly feel that any sacrifice I make for the sake of our child will, in the end, be worth it. Don't we both want what, ultimately, will be best for our baby? Can you deny that? We can't change the past but we can move on from it. We can stop it from altering the course of the future.'

Sophie could feel the pulse in her neck beating, matching the steady beat of her heart, the heart that belonged to him, to a man who would never, *could* never return the favour.

He talked about sacrifices, though, and surely, *surely* he would never use her again? Not when they shared a child? Could she trust him or had the past damaged that irreparably?

'Maybe you're right,' she said, meeting his eyes

steadily. 'Of course I want what's best for our baby. Of course I know that two parents are always going to be better than one.' And maybe, she dared to hope, in time she would trust him enough to confide in him about her brother, despite what had happened between them. Alan had turned away from what he had perceived as a challenge too far in Eric and she had locked herself away after that. Of course, she had never consciously decided that remaining on her own was the preferred option, but how could any relationship ever have blossomed in the bitterness that had grown over the hope and trust she had invested in her ex-boyfriend? Alan had not deserved the faith she had put in him. Compared to Matias, what she'd felt for Alan was a pale shadow of the real thing. But however strong her love, she still couldn't guarantee that Matias, a guy who had been motivated by revenge when he had decided to *cultivate her*, would live up to her expectations.

But they were having a baby together and she *wanted and needed him*.

In due course, he might even jump through all the hoops and prove to be worthy of her trust, but that was something she would never find out unless she gave him a fighting chance.

Matias looked at her and wished that he could see what she was thinking so seriously about. She was staring back at him but her thoughts were somewhere else. Where? Never had the urge been so strong to *know* someone, completely, utterly and inside out. He had never delved into what the women he dated thought about anything. He had wined and dined them and enjoyed them but digging deep hadn't been part of the equation. Sophie made him want to dig deep.

'So…?' he murmured, with a shuttered expression.

'So we don't have to get married…' Sophie breathed in deep and prayed that she was doing the right thing '…but we can live together…' That was called giving him a chance, giving him an opportunity to prove that he could once more be trusted before she opened up that part of her he knew nothing about.

Matias greeted this with a lot more equanimity than he felt. Live together? It wasn't the solution he was after, but it would have to do. For now…

Matias got the call as he was about to leave work.

'I'm sorry.' Sophie was obviously moving in a rush. Her voice was tight and panicked. 'I'm going to have to cancel our dinner date tonight. Something's come up, I'm afraid.'

'What's come up?' Already heading to his jacket, which was slung over the back of the cream sofa that occupied the adjoining mini suite in his glasshouse office, Matias paused, returned to the desk and grabbed the little box containing the diamond bracelet he had ordered three days previously and had collected that day as a surprise for her.

He had taken to surprising her every so often with something little, something he had seen somewhere that had reminded him of her.

Once, it had been an antique book on culinary art in Victorian times, which he had quite accidentally found while walking to his car after a meeting on the South Bank. The bookshop had been tucked away next to a small art gallery and he had paused to glance at the offerings in painted crates on trestle tables outside.

She had smiled when he'd given it to her and that

smile of genuine pleasure had been worth its weight in gold.

Then he had bought her a set of saucepans specially made for the stove in the new house, because he had found one of her house magazines lying on the sofa with the page creased with an advertisement on their lifetime guarantee and special heat-conducting values. Whatever that was supposed to mean.

And again, that had hit the spot.

The diamond bracelet was the most expensive item he had bought thus far and he sincerely hoped that she wouldn't refuse to accept it. She could dig her heels in and be mulishly stubborn about things that were beyond his comprehension and for reasons he found difficult to fathom.

Matias knew that he was shamelessly directing all his energies into getting what he wanted because the longer he was with her, the more unthinkable it was that she might eventually want to cut short their *living together to see how it goes* status and return to the freedom of singledom, free to find her soul mate.

He shoved the box into the inside pocket of his jacket, which he had stuck on without breaking the phone connection.

Her voice, the strained tenor of it, was sending alarm bells ringing in his head. She had been fine when he had seen her the day before. They had met for breakfast because she had gone to help Julie and he had wanted to see her before he headed off to Edinburgh, where he was taking a chance on a small pharmaceutical company that was up for grabs.

'Where are you, *querida*?' he asked, doing his utmost to keep his voice calm and composed.

'Matias, I really have to go. The taxi is going to be here any minute and I have to get a few things together before I leave. In fact…wait…the taxi's here.'

'Taxi? Don't you dare hang up on me in the middle of this conversation, Sophie! What taxi? Why are you taking a taxi somewhere? What's wrong with the car? Is it giving you trouble? And where are you going, anyway?'

'The car is fine. I just thought that, in this instance…'

Her voice faded, as though she had dumped the phone on a table because she needed to do something.

What?

Matias was finding it impossible to hang onto his self-control. She sounded as though she was on the verge of tears and Sophie never cried. She had once told him that when things got tough, and there had been plenty of times in her life when they had, then blubbing never solved anything.

It had been just one more thing he had lodged at the back of his mind, something else that slotted into the complex puzzle that comprised her personality.

And now she was on the verge of tears for reasons she would not identify and she didn't want to talk to him about it. He had done his damnedest to prove to her that she had been right to take a punt on him. He had not batted an eyelid at the very clear nesting instincts that had emerged when she had begun decorating the house. He had also gone light on her creep of a father in the wake of the company takeover, allowing him to salvage some measure of self-respect by not sending him to prison for being trigger-happy with the pension pot, although Carney was much diminished by the end of proceedings, which had afforded Matias a great deal of satisfaction.

He had even deflected an immediate visit to see his mother, because, while she was recovering nicely, much spurred on by news of a grandchild on the way, he had wanted to protect Sophie from the inevitable pressing questions about marriage. The last thing he'd wanted was to have her take fright at his very forthright mother's insistence on tradition and start backing away from the arrangement they had in place.

But even with all of this, it was now perfectly clear that there were parts of her that still bore a lasting resentment because of the way their relationship had originally started.

Why else would she be on the verge of tears and yet not want to tell him why?

'What do you mean by "in this instance"?' he demanded, striding towards the door and heading fast to the bank of lifts.

Most of his employees had already left. The hardcore workaholics barely glanced up as he headed down to the underground car park where his Ferrari was waiting.

'I have to go.'

'Tell me where. Unless it's some kind of big secret?'

'Goodness, Matias!' Hesitation on the other end of the phone. 'Okay, I'm heading to Charing Cross hospital.'

Matias froze by his car, sickened at the thought that something was wrong with her or the baby. 'I will meet you there.'

'No!'

He stilled, unwilling to deal with what her stricken response was saying to him. 'Okay…'

'Matias, I'll see you back at the house. Later. I don't know what time but I'll text or I'll try to. You know what they can be like at hospitals.'

'This is my baby as well, Sophie. I want to be by your side if there's any kind of problem.'

'There's no problem there. Don't worry.'

Naturally, Matias didn't believe her. Her voice was telling a different story. She was frantic with worry but when it came to the crunch, she didn't want him by her side to help her deal with it.

She would show up the following morning and would be bright and cheery and would downplay his concern and they would paper over the unsettling reality that in a time of crisis she would simply not allow him to be there for her.

There was no point driving to the hospital—the parking would be hellish—but Matias was going to be there. He was not going to let her endure anything she might find distressing on her own, and, he grimly acknowledged, it wasn't simply because it was a question of *their* child.

He didn't think twice. His driver was on standby. He would hit the hospital running before she even got there. Playing the long game was at an end. Like it or not, there was going to be a pivotal change in their relationship and if he had to force her hand, then so be it.

Rushing into the hospital after too many hold-ups and traffic jams to count, Sophie raced through the revolving doors and there he was, right in front of her.

He towered, a dark, brooding presence restlessly pacing, hand shoved deep in his trouser pocket. A billionaire out of his comfort zone and yet still managing to dominate his surroundings in a way that brought her to an immediate skidding halt. The cast of his beautiful face was forbidding. People were making sure not to get too close because he emanated all kinds of danger signals that made her tense up.

'Matias…'

Eyes off the entrance for five seconds, her voice brought him swinging round to look at her. 'I'm coming with you,' he said grimly. 'You're not going to push me out this time.'

'I haven't got time to do this right now,' but her heart was beating wildly as she began walking quickly towards the bank of lifts, weaving through the crowds.

'Sophie!' He stopped her, his hand on her arm, and she swung to face him. *'Talk to me.'*

Their eyes tangled and she sighed and said quietly, 'Okay. It's time we had a talk. It's time you knew…'

CHAPTER TEN

MATIAS EXPECTED HER to head straight to the maternity ward. However, she ignored the signs, moving fast towards the lift and punching a floor number while he kept damn close to her, willing her to talk and yet chilled by her remoteness. She barely seemed aware of his presence as she walked quickly up to one of the nurses at a desk and whispered something urgently to her, before, finally, turning around and registering that he was still there.

Matias looked at her carefully, eyes narrowed. They hadn't yet exchanged as much as a sentence. He was a guy who had always made it his duty to keep his finger on the pulse and know what was going on around him, because if you knew the lay of the land you were never in for unpleasant surprises, but right now he didn't have a clue what was going on and he hated that, just as he hated the distance between them.

Was this the point when everything began to fall apart? A sick chill filtered through his veins like poison.

'What's going on?' he asked tightly and Sophie sighed.

'You'll find out soon enough and then we'll need to talk.' She spun round and he followed as she walked straight towards one of the rooms to gently push open the door.

Matias had no idea what to expect and the last thing he was expecting to see was a young man on the bed, obviously sedated because his movements were sluggish as he turned in the direction of the door, but as soon as he saw Sophie he smiled with real love and tenderness.

Matias hovered in complete confusion. He felt like an intruder. He wasn't introduced. He was barely noticed by the man in the bed. He was there to watch, he realised, and so he did for the ten minutes she gently spoke to the boy, holding his hand, squeezing it and whispering in soft, soothing, barely audible tones.

She stroked his forehead and then kissed him before standing up and gazing down at the reclining figure. The boy had closed his eyes and was breathing evenly, already falling into sleep.

She glanced at Matias, nodded as she raised one finger to her lips, and only when they were outside the room did she turn to him.

'You're wondering,' she said without preamble. He was so shockingly beautiful and she loved him so much and yet Sophie felt as though they had now reached a turning point from which there would be no going back. She hadn't considered when the time would be *right* for him to meet Eric. Fear of an eventual negative outcome had held her back but Fate had taken matters into her own hand and now here they were.

'Can you blame me?' Matias responded tersely, raking his fingers through his hair, his whole body restless with unanswered questions.

'We need to talk but I don't think the hospital is quite the right place, Matias.'

Matias was gripped by that chill of apprehension again because there was something final in her voice. 'My place. It'll be quicker than trying to get back to the cottage.' On this one, single matter he could take charge and he did. Within ten minutes they were sitting in the back of his car, heading to his penthouse apartment, to which she had been only a handful of times.

The silence between them was killing him but he instinctively knew that the back seat of a car was not the place to start demanding answers any more than the environs of a hospital would have been.

He glanced at her a couple of times, at her averted profile, but she was mentally a million miles away and he found that incredibly frustrating. He wanted to reach out and yank her back to him. He found that he just couldn't bear the remoteness.

Caught up wondering how she was going to broach the taboo subject she had successfully managed to avoid so far, Sophie was barely aware of the car purring to a stop outside the magnificent Georgian building that housed his state-of-the-art modern penthouse apartment.

It was an eye-wateringly expensive place, now seldom used because he had become so accustomed to spending time at the cottage. They had fallen into a pattern of behaviour and it was only now, when the possibility of it disappearing was on the horizon, that she could really appreciate just how happy she had been.

Even though she knew that he didn't love her, he was perfect in so many ways. He just didn't feel about her the way she felt about him.

The cool, minimalist elegance of his apartment never failed to impress her, although, for her, it was a space she could never have happily lived in.

Now, though, with so much on her mind, she barely noticed the large abstract canvasses, the pale marble flooring, the pale furniture, the subtle, iconic sculptures dotted here and there.

She went directly to the cream leather sofa and sat down, immediately leaning forward in nervous silence and watching as he sat down opposite her, his body language mirroring hers.

'So?' Matias asked, his beautiful eyes shuttered and tension making his voice cooler than intended. 'Are you going to tell me who that guy was?' He saw the way she was struggling to find the right words and he added, tersely, 'An ex-boyfriend?'

'I beg your pardon?'

'Is he an ex-boyfriend, Sophie?' Matias demanded icily. 'The love of your life who may have been involved in an accident? I watched the interaction between the two of you. You love the guy.' Something inside him ripped. 'How long has he been disabled? Motorbike accident?' Every word was wrenched out of him but he had to know the truth.

'I do love him,' Sophie concurred truthfully. 'I've always loved him.'

Matias's jaw clenched as the knot in his stomach tightened. He wasn't going to lose it but he wanted to hit something hard.

'And he wasn't involved in an accident, at least not in the way you mean. Eric has been like that since he was born.'

Matias stilled, eyes keen, every pulse in his body frozen as he tried to grapple with what she was saying.

'Eric is my brother, Matias,' Sophie said quietly.

'Your brother...'

'He lives in a home just outside London, but something spooked him and he had a panic attack and went a little berserk. Hence why he's in hospital. He hurt himself while he was thrashing around. Nothing serious but they couldn't deal with it at the home.'

'You have a brother and you never told me...'

'I have no idea where to begin, Matias. If you just sit and listen, I'll try and make sense. My father only had contact with our family because he was left without a choice. When Eric was born, my mother knew that the only way she would ever be able to afford to take care of him would be with financial help from James. She had a lot of faults but a lack of devotion to Eric wasn't one of them. She made sure James paid for Eric's home, which is very expensive, and when she died it was up to me to make sure he carried on paying. It sounds callous, Matias, but it was the only way.'

'You wanted me to invest in your father's business because you wanted to make sure he could carry on paying for your brother's care.'

Sophie nodded, relieved but not terribly surprised that he had picked it up so quickly. For better or worse, it was a relief to be explaining this to him. If he chose to walk away, then so be it. She would be able to deal with the consequences, even though she knew that she would never be the same again without him in her life.

'I've always managed to put aside a nest egg and I've been dipping into it to cover the costs of Eric's home since James's business went to the wall, but, yes, I encouraged you to think that investing in James would be a good idea, not because I wanted the money for myself, but because I would have done anything, I'm afraid, to make sure my brother is safe and happy.'

'Why didn't you tell me?'

'How could I, Matias?' Sophie tilted her chin at a mutinous angle, defensive and challenging. 'You used me to confirm your suspicions about James and even when you came back into my life, it was because you felt you had no choice.'

'Sophie…'

'No, let me finish!' Her eyes glistened because if the end was coming then she would have to be strong and she didn't feel strong when she was here, looking at him and loving him with every bone in her body. 'I didn't tell you about Eric because there was no way I wanted you to think that you could exact more revenge by going public with what my father had done, shaming him by telling the world that he had fathered a disabled child he had never met and only supported because he had no choice.'

And just like that, Matias knew the depth of her distrust of him. Just like that he saw, in a blinding flash, how much he had hurt her. She had bowed her head and listened to him accuse her of things she had never been guilty of, and she had closed herself off to him. She clearly didn't trust him and she never would.

'I wish you had told me,' he said bleakly.

'How could I?' Sophie returned sadly. 'How could I take the risk that you might have been tempted to involve Eric in your revenge scheme, when the press would have turned it into a story that would have ended up hurting him, destroying both his privacy and his dignity? And also…'

Matias was processing everything she said, knowing that he had no one but himself and his blind drive for vengeance to blame for where he was right now. 'Also?' He looked at her.

'Eric is fragile. When Alan, my ex-boyfriend, walked out of my life, having met him just the once, Eric was heartbroken and felt responsible. I thought Alan was the one for me and I just didn't think that he would walk away because the duty of caretaking Eric was too much.'

'Any creep who would walk away from you because of that was never the one for you,' Matias grated harshly. 'You should count your lucky stars you didn't end up with him.'

'You're right. What I felt for Alan wasn't love. I liked him. I thought he was safe, and safe was good after my mother's experiences with men. But yes, I had a lucky escape. Don't think I don't know that.'

'I was driven by revenge.' Matias breathed in deeply and looked at her with utter gravity. 'It was always there, at the back of my mind. I was always going to be ambitious, I guess. I was always going to be fuelled to make money because I knew what it was like to have none, but I also knew what it was like to know that *I should have*. Your father was to blame and that became the mantra that energised a lot of my decisions. For a while, the chase for financial security became a goal in itself but then, like I told you, my mother fell ill and I discovered those letters. At the point when you entered my life, my desire to even the score with your father was at its height and…you became entangled in that desire. You didn't deserve it.'

Sophie looked at him questioningly, urging him to carry on and weak with relief that he seemed to have taken the situation with her brother in his stride.

'I thought you wanted to push me into investing into someone you knew was on the verge of bankruptcy and probably crooked as well because you wanted to carry on receiving an allowance from him.'

'I understand,' Sophie conceded, 'that you would have thought that because you knew nothing about Eric… You didn't know that there were other reasons for my doing what I did.'

'I saw red,' Matias admitted. 'I felt I'd been used and I reacted accordingly, but the truth was that deep down I knew you weren't that kind of person. *Querida*, you didn't trust me enough to tell me about your brother and I can't begin to tell you how gutted I am by that, even though I know that I have no one but myself to blame. I expected you to wipe away the past as though it had never existed, and I couldn't appreciate that I hurt you way too much for you to find that easy to do.'

This was the first time Matias had ever opened up and she knew from the halting progress of his words that it was something he found difficult, which made her love him even more. He was apologising and it took a big man to do that.

'I never want to hurt you again, my darling. And I will always make sure that your brother is protected and cared for in the way he deserves. Just give me the chance to prove to you how much I love you and how deeply sorry I am for putting you in the position of not thinking you could trust me with the most important secret in your life.'

Sophie's eyes widened and her heart stopped beating before speeding up until she felt it burst through her ribcage.

'Did I just hear you say…?'

'I love you,' Matias told her simply. 'I never thought that I would fall in love. I was never interested in falling in love, but you came along and you got under my skin and before I knew it you had become an indispensable part of my life. When we went our separate ways, it was weird but I felt as though part of me had been ripped away. I didn't understand what that was about, but now I realise you were already beginning to occupy an important position in my life.'

'You never said,' Sophie breathed. 'Why didn't you say?'

'How could I?' Matias smiled wryly at her. He stood up and went to sit on the sofa next to her but he didn't try and pull her towards him, instead choosing to reach out and link her slender fingers through his. He absently played with her ring finger, giving no thought to what that said about the road his subconscious mind was travelling down. 'I was barely aware of it myself. We never expect the things that take us by surprise. Love took me by surprise.'

'As it did me,' Sophie confessed, so happy that she wanted to laugh and cry at the same time. 'When I first met you, I hated you.'

Matias's eyebrows shot up and he shot her a wolfish smile. 'Yet you still managed to find me incredibly sexy...'

'Don't be so egotistical, Matias.' But Sophie couldn't resist smiling back at him because he could be incredibly endearing in his puffed-up self-assurance. 'I thought I was going to see Art and instead I was shown into the lion's den.'

'It's a good job you *didn't* see Art,' Matias said drily. 'You would have walked all over him. He would probably have ended up giving *you* a new car and forgetting all about the damage you did to mine. You charmed the socks off him.'

Sophie blushed. 'We would never have met, though...'

'We would have,' Matias asserted. 'Our paths were destined to cross, even if you *did* hate me on sight.'

'Well, you *were* threatening to pull the plug on my business because I'd bumped into your car...'

Matias acknowledged that with a rueful tilt of his head. 'And so the rest is history. But,' he mused thoughtfully, 'I *should* have suspected that the ease with which I became accustomed to the notion of being a father was a pointer as to how I felt about you. If I hadn't been so completely crazy about you, I would have never slipped into marriage proposal mode so seamlessly.'

'And then I turned you down...'

'You did. Repeatedly. You have no idea how much I've wanted to prove to you that you could take a chance on me.'

'And you have no idea how much I've wanted to take that chance, but I was just too scared. I think, to start with, it really was because I was suspicious and unsure as to what you might do if you found out about Eric. My gut told me that I could trust you, despite all the water under the bridge, but my gut had lied once and I dug my heels in and refused to listen to it a second time. And then, later, I was scared to think about how you might react to Eric. Alan had been a dreadful learning curve for me. I'd been hurt and bewildered at the man he turned out to be and Eric had been terribly upset. He doesn't have the wherewithal to cope with upsets like that. Whatever happened, it was very important to me that he not become collateral damage. I could cope with that but he would never be able to.'

'I'm glad I met him,' Matias said seriously. 'Now can we stop talking? Although, there *is* one thing I still have to say...'

'What's that?' Sophie whispered, on cloud nine.

'Will you stop sitting on the fence and marry me?'

'Hmm...' Sophie laughed and pulled him towards her and kissed him long and hard, and then she brushed his nose with hers and grinned. 'Okay. And by that I mean...yes, yes, yes!'

A handful of months later, another trip had been made to the hospital. Sophie's labour had started at three in the morning and had moved quickly so that by the time they made it to the maternity ward baby Luciana had been just about ready to say hello to her doting and very much loved-up parents.

She had been born without fuss at a little after nine the following morning.

'She has your hair.' Sophie had smiled drowsily at Matias, who had been sitting next to her, cradling his seven-pound-eight-ounce, chubby, dark-haired baby daughter.

'And my eyes.' He had grinned and looked lovingly at the woman without whom life meant nothing. His life had gone from grey to Technicolor. Once upon a time, he had seen the accumulation of wealth and power as an end unto itself. He had thought that lessons learnt about love and the vulnerable places it took you were enough to put any sensible guy off the whole Happy Ever After scenario for good. He had sworn that a life controlled was the only life worth living. He'd been wrong. The only life worth living was a life with the woman he adored at his side.

'And let's hope that's where the similarities end,' Sophie had teased, still smiling. 'I don't need someone else in my life who looks bewildered at the prospect of boiling an egg.'

And now, with their beloved baby daughter nearly six months old, they were finally getting married.

Sophie gazed at her reflection in the mirror of the country hotel where she and her various friends, along with Matias's mother, had opted to stay the night.

Rose Rivero was back on her feet and, as she had confided in her daughter-in-law-to-be some time previously, with so much to live for that there was no question of her being ill again any time soon.

'You look stunning,' Julie said and Matias's mother nodded. The three of them were putting the final touches to Sophie's outfit, making sure that every small rosebud on her hairpiece was just right. 'You're having the fairy-tale wedding you've always longed for.'

Sophie laughed and thought back to the journey that had brought her to this point. 'It's not exactly been straightforward,' she murmured truthfully.

'I could have told you that my son is anything but straightforward,' Rose quipped. 'But you've calmed him down and grounded him in ways I could never have imagined possible.'

'You wouldn't say that if you could see him storming through the house looking for his car keys, which he seems to misplace every other day.' Sophie laughed and walked to the door, while the other two followed, to be met by the rest of the bridal party in the reception downstairs, where cars were waiting to take them to the quaint church, perched on a hillside with a spectacular view of the sea beneath.

Never in her wildest dreams had she imagined a life as perfect as this.

She still had an interest in the catering firm and frequently went there to help out, but it was largely left to Julie and her three helpers, who now ran the profitable business with a tight rein. Their beautiful new premises had been up and running for some months and they were even thinking of expanding and opening a restaurant where they would be able to showcase their talent on a larger scale and to a wider audience.

James Carney had avoided the harsh punishment originally planned by a vengeful Matias, but life had changed considerably for him. With the company no longer in his hands, he had been paid off and dispatched down to Cornwall where he would be able to lead a relatively quiet life, without the trappings of glamour that had been gained from his underhand dealings with Tomas Rivero. Occasionally he dropped Sophie an email and occasionally she answered, but she had no affection for the man who had made her mother's life and her own a nightmare of having to beg for handouts and always with the threat that those handouts could stop at any given moment.

Matias was in possession of the company, which his father should have jointly owned, and it was now a thriving concern, another strand in his hugely successful empire.

But it was with Eric where Sophie felt the greatest flush of pleasure, for her brother could not have been made more welcome by Matias and he was developing skills that still continued to amaze her. He was no longer living in his own little world, really only able to communicate with her, his carers and a handful of other patients. Now, he was making strides in communicating with the outside world, without the fear and panic that had previously dogged him, and she could only think that Matias's patience and little innocent Luciana were partly responsible for that progress. And maybe, she occasionally thought, he was intuitive enough to realise that the sister who came to visit him was no longer stressed out. He was safe for ever. He had begun a specially adapted computer course and was showing all sorts of talents hitherto untapped.

Sophie thought of her daughter as she was driven to the church. Luciana would be there, with her nanny, and although the ceremony would mean nothing to her she would enjoy the photos when she got older.

Sophie breathed in deeply as she stepped out of the chauffeur-driven Bentley and then she was in the church, as nervous as a kitten to be marrying the man who meant everything to her.

Matias turned as everyone did, as the music began to play. This was the final piece of the jigsaw. He was marrying the woman he loved and he could not have been prouder.

The breath hitched in his throat as he looked at her walk slowly up the aisle towards him. The cream dress fitted her body like a glove. She had returned to her former weight and all those luscious curves were back, tempting him every single time he looked at her. She was holding a modest bouquet of pale pink flowers and her veil was secured by a tiara of rosebuds that mimicked the flowers in her hand.

She was radiant. She was his. Possessiveness flared inside him, warming him.

He'd never contemplated marriage but now he knew he wouldn't have been complete without it, without her having his ring on her finger. And the wedding could not have been more to his taste. He might be a billionaire, but this simple affair was perfect.

'You look stunning, *querida*,' he murmured, when she was finally standing beside him and before they both turned to the priest.

'So do you.' Sophie gazed up at Matias. He did this to her, even though she saw him daily, even though he was as much a part of her life as the air she breathed. He made her breathing ragged and he made her heart skip a beat.

The special girl in my life, Matias thought with a swell of pride. Well…one of them.

He looked to the back of the church and there was the other one, being cradled by the nanny, fast asleep.

Matias smiled and knew that this was exactly where he was meant to be, and much later, when all the revelry had died down and the last of the guests had departed, he felt it again, that flare of hot possession as he gazed at the woman who was now his wife.

The following morning, they would be off on their honeymoon. Luciana would be there, as would her nanny and his mother.

'Why are you grinning?' Sophie asked, reaching to undo the pearl buttons of the lavender dress she had slipped into after the wedding ceremony had finished.

Sprawled on the four-poster bed in the hotel where they would be spending the night before flying by private jet to one of Matias's villas in Italy, he was a vision of magnificent male splendour. He had undone the buttons of his white shirt and it hung open, exposing a sliver of bronzed, hard chest.

'I'm grinning,' he drawled, 'because not many newly-weds take the groom's mother with them on their honeymoon.' He beckoned her to him with a lazy curl of his finger and watched, incredibly turned on, as she sashayed towards him, ridding herself of her clothes as she got nearer to his prone figure.

By the time she was standing next to the bed, she was wearing only the lacy bra that worked hard to contain her generous breasts and the matching, peach-coloured lacy pants.

Whatever he had to say to her flew through the window because he couldn't resist rolling to his side and then sliding his finger under the lacy pants so that he could press his face against her musky, honeyed wetness, flicking an exploring tongue along the crease of her womanhood and settling to enjoy her for a few moments as she opened her legs a fraction to allow his tongue entry.

Then he lay back and sighed with pure pleasure when, naked, she lay next to him and slipped her hand under his shirt.

'You and Luciana mean the world to her,' Matias said softly, 'and I want to thank you for that, for taking the sadness out of my mother's life and...' he stroked her hair and kissed her gently on her full mouth '... I want to thank you for being my wife. You put the sound and colour into my world and I would be nothing without you.'

Sophie pushed aside his shirt and licked his flat brown nipple until he was groaning and urging her down as he unzipped his trousers.

'I love you so much,' she whispered. 'Now you're going to have to keep quiet, husband of mine, because it's our honeymoon and there are a lot of things I want to do with you before the night is over...'

* * * * *

LET'S TALK

Romance

For exclusive extracts, competitions and special offers, find us online:

 MillsandBoon

 @MillsandBoon

@MillsandBoonUK

 @MillsandBoonUK

Get in touch on 01413 063 232

For all the latest titles coming soon, visit
millsandboon.co.uk/nextmonth

MILLS & BOON

THE HEART OF ROMANCE

A ROMANCE FOR EVERY READER

MODERN — Prepare to be swept off your feet by sophisticated, sexy and seductive heroes, in some of the world's most glamourous and romantic locations, where power and passion collide.

HISTORICAL — Escape with historical heroes from time gone by. Whether your passion is for wicked Regency Rakes, muscled Vikings or rugged Highlanders, awaken the romance of the past.

MEDICAL — Set your pulse racing with dedicated, delectable doctors in the high-pressure world of medicine, where emotions run high and passion, comfort and love are the best medicine.

True Love — Celebrate true love with tender stories of heartfelt romance, from the rush of falling in love to the joy a new baby can bring, and a focus on the emotional heart of a relationship.

Desire — Indulge in secrets and scandal, intense drama and sizzling hot action with heroes who have it all: wealth, status, good looks…everything but the right woman.

HEROES — The excitement of a gripping thriller, with intense romance at its heart. Resourceful, true-to-life women and strong, fearless men face danger and desire - a killer combination!

To see which titles are coming soon, please visit

millsandboon.co.uk/nextmonth

MILLS & BOON
MODERN
Power and Passion

Prepare to be swept off your feet by sophisticated, sexy and seductive heroes, in some of the world's most glamourous and romantic locations, where power and passion collide.

MILLS & BOON
True Love
Romance from the Heart

Celebrate true love with tender stories of heartfelt romance, from the rush of falling in love to the joy a new baby can bring, and a focus on the emotional heart of a relationship.